The Radon Files

SUSAN RUTHERFORD
13439 N.E. 115th Ct.
Redmond, WA 98052

Dave Biebel, director of communications for the Christian Medical and Dental Society, is an ordained minister in the Evangelical Free Church of America. He has written several books. *The Radon Files* is his first novel.

The Radon Files

DAVE BIEBEL

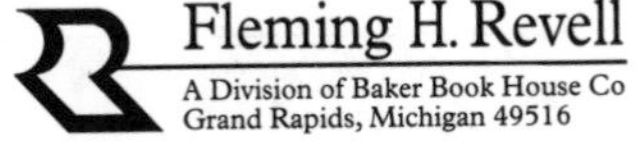
Fleming H. Revell
A Division of Baker Book House Co
Grand Rapids, Michigan 49516

Published by Fleming H. Revell
A Division of Baker Book House Company
P.O. Box 6287, Grand Rapids, Michigan 49516-6287

Second printing, April 1994

Printed in the United States of America

This story is fictitious. Any resemblance, whether in name, setting, or event, to organizations past or present, or persons living or dead, is not intentional.

Library of Congress Cataloging-in-Publication Data

Biebel, David B.
The radon files / Dave Biebel.
p. cm. — (The Rocky Mountain dossier)
ISBN 0-8007-5446-8
1. Government investigators—Rocky Mountains Region—Fiction. 2. Cults—Rocky Mountains Region—Fiction. I. Title. II. Series: Biebel, David B. Rocky Mountain dossier.
PS3552.I3436R34 1993
813'.54—dc20 93-20389

To

Hal

who believed in me

and rescued me

Twice

1

Wearing a baby blue suit to match his eyes, the Reverend Dr. J. R. Jenner strutted back and forth across the stage. "OURS IS THE KINGDOM," proclaimed a giant red-lettered backdrop as the orator built toward a crescendo, his deep voice echoing like thunder off the rafters.

"This is the terminal generation," the forty-five-year-old, golden-haired Jenner declared, "the end of the old and the beginning of the renewal of all things!" The crowd of twenty thousand loudly applauded the speaker, suspended above them in the spotlights like a supernatural being with a message straight from God.

From the press box high above the coliseum floor, FBI Bureau Chief Bruce Davidson scanned the audience, his 10x50 binoculars cutting through the semi-darkness. *What do they see in this guy?* he pondered, noting the same mix of people he'd observed elsewhere during this whirlwind tour—some internationals, especially students; many poor and destitute; a wide range of skin tones. *Prophets, prophets everywhere* . . . He checked the video to make sure it was working.

"Look at this world," Jenner shouted. "Instability, change, upheaval everywhere. Peace, peace, they say, but there is no peace, just a momentary lull before Armageddon, like the calm in the eye of a storm. But do not be deceived; this man-made peace is futile. Only the kingdom can bring peace. And the kingdom *is* coming! It is inevitable. It is written, in the stars and in this book."

The crowd clapped even more loudly as the founder of the End Times Renewal movement held aloft a scarlet-covered book, *The Master Plan of the Ages*, its gold-edged pages fluttering freely and majestically.

It was the same message leading to the same invitation Davidson had heard every night that week in a different northeastern city. *Hartford, New York, Rochester, Albany, Schenectady, Philadelphia. This is Philly; it must be Sunday.*

"Are you worried?" Jenner asked the crowd. "Are you afraid? Some so-called prophets say hide, build bomb shelters, hole up, and wait for the end. My friends, there is a better way, growing like a little seed until the whole world is filled and the rule of God is brought into the hearts of men."

Interesting visitors, again, Davidson noted as he panned the crowd, then turned the binoculars back to the speaker. *Petrolini. Strengster. Mosconasio. No kidding?*

"When the great war is over," Jenner's voice trembled, "when the final battle is done and the rich have killed each other off in their greed, who will bring unity from the chaos? The End Times Renewal movement! The movement of the common man!"

Actor? Charlatan? How can he work up a brow sweat night after night unless he believes it? Davidson mused, immediately chastising himself as he realized the repetition was weakening even his resistance. But at that instant he also thought of Clarice Conroy, the rookie agent he'd sent in to infiltrate ETR through the group's headquarters—the New World Institute in Walton's Creek, Colorado.

Hear anything enough times, it can start sounding true. Brainwashing 101. Clare's been there sixteen weeks. Wonder how many times she's heard this speech?

"When no manmade empire remains," Jenner continued, "tens of thousands, hundreds of thousands—the remnant—will arise right where they are, arise and build . . . arise and build a new world on the ashes of the old. A new world for *all the people.* This is not the death pangs of the human race, but the birth pangs of the kingdom."

Jenner paused, gazed out at the crowd, then swiftly stepped down off the platform and into the third row, where he leaned over and picked up a towheaded toddler offered by a mother. "This little child," he said through the wireless microphone as he held the boy in his arms, "this boy is what we all must become to enter the Way. Perhaps you, my son, will be one of the leaders of the kingdom. See how he trusts me! You, too, must trust," he added as he handed the child back and remounted the stage.

Again he tugs at the heart! Davidson thought. *And always a boy with Jenner's characteristics. Must be set up.* The bureau chief reached for the notepad inside his jacket.

"You must clear out the old if you would live in a new way," Jenner exhorted the crowd. "All around this auditorium tonight, hundreds are getting up from their seats to begin again . . . to start over, with us . . ."

Already people were flocking toward the front of the auditorium as if drawn by a magnet. Hundreds had gathered even before Jenner finished his invitation to come and receive materials, sign up for correspondence courses, or apply for the Institute's next session.

Lamb . . . Lambda . . . Lamboni . . . Langley. Clare Conroy's gloved fingers quickly flipped through the files in the personal safe of ETR's medical director, Florence Bradley.

LANDAU, LINDA K. was the name she was looking for. *No listing.* Conroy paused for a moment, focusing her mind on the brief, rather disjointed call from Landau that had launched this investigation. There had to be another way of finding her. The agent took a long, slow breath to stay calm. She had the tape memorized, locked in her mind, analyzed a hundred times in preparation for this moment. She reviewed it again.

"I want my baby back. . . . They've taken my baby boy and won't give him back. . . . I don't want to be part of the HANNAH project anymore. Please help me; somebody please help."

HANNAH. Bingo! Conroy's left hand reached for her compact, setting the controls of its miniature camera and adjusting the desk lamp for more light on the files in the otherwise dark office. Clicking as she scanned, Conroy tried to sort essentials from nonessentials.

> "So now I give him to the Lord. For his whole life he will be given over to the Lord" (1 Samuel 1:28).

Typical. Through four months of intense indoctrination, she'd seen Bible verses justifying everything, but never actually in a Bible. The only textbook allowed in the Institute was the one penned by Dr. Jenner. *Wish I'd brought along that little Bible from the InterVarsity group at Yale. Like to check this out. Guess I should have paid more attention.*

Conroy concentrated on the documents she'd infiltrated this organization to find. She browsed the pages, trying to find the missing link. *Landau, where are you?* But these files contained only case numbers, interspersed throughout in some kind of code.

Was that a noise in the hall? Conroy snapped off the light,

CONFIDENTIAL: AUTHORIZED ACCESS ONLY

PHASE ONE, latter-day eugenics program.

Voluntary participants, REGENCY level only.

Firstborn males, long-term loan to strategic international assets.

AN/PSQ-356 locators installed, all units.

Transmit codes classified: JACOB.

Recall, 2010.

Target: 120 Components.

82 Deliveries, Update 10/92.

Project Director: Florence Bradley, M.D.

quickly closed the safe behind its wall panel, and slid under the desk. Footsteps outside paused for a moment, as if the person were listening.

Great. Caught in the act. Good thing I have my own key as Bradley's assistant, but how do I explain working at two in the morning—or being under a desk in the dark? Should've been out of here by this security check. She tucked the papers still in her hand under the carpet protector and slipped off her lambskin gloves.

Through the door's semi-opaque window she recognized the profile of security guard Johnny Winston, handgun drawn and ready. The door strained against the bolt as Winston leaned hard on it with his left shoulder. The handle turned first one way then the other as he tested the lock.

Keys? Conroy lamented as she heard the telltale jangle. *He comes through that door and finds me under this desk!* Desperately she weighed alternatives, all of them unsatisfactory, chastising herself for not anticipating this possibility. But then the guard paused, turned, and continued down the hallway, evidently satisfied that the office was secure.

Conroy's adrenaline surge hit as the footfalls subsided. Surprised by the intensity and rapidity of her pulse beating in her ears, the agent tried to decide if any further risk was worth taking. *The HANNAH files are filmed. Still, no direct link to Landau. Need more.*

Quickly Conroy replaced the rest of the HANNAH documents, trying to recall their exact order. *How about REGENCY?* she wondered, paging through the other folders. *'Course not. It'll take more than a level-one clearance to get anything on ETR's core leadership group. Same for JACOB.*

But suddenly Conroy remembered that all personnel records for the Institute were kept by number in the computer data bank. She logged into the central computer and started with her own number: 007-92-4085. *That's me! Now to find Landau. She's been out at least one, maybe two, years.*

Finally, on the fifty-second entry for 1990: 106-90-4445, Conroy connected. The reason it took so long was that, upon her REGENCY initiation, Linda Landau had evidently become Martha Williams. *Is everybody in REGENCY sent out with an alias? Be nearly impossible to track. Have to check on it later.*

The agent examined the screen carefully:

WILLIAMS, MARTHA.
NEE: LANDAU, LINDA K.
BORN 10-12-66. BOSTON, MA
MOTHER: LANDAU, ANNA K.
FATHER: LANDAU, JOSEPH D.
NWI GRADUATE: ADVANCED.
ELECTED, REGENCY, 9-90.
MARRIED: JOHN WILLIAMS, REGENCY, 9-90.
HANNAH TRANSFER, 2-92. SITE: 2045.
WILLIAMS, MARTHA. DECEASED, 3/15/92.

Conroy sat there, stunned, staring at the last entry and remembering the date of Landau's call—15 March 1992. *Beware the Ides of March.* As far as she knew, this was the only clue to what had happened to Landau. The woman and her husband had simply disappeared without a trace before anyone could follow up the call. *Her husband. Have to get this to Bruce. Never find the guy, looking for "Landau."*

Snapping a quick picture of the computer screen before switching it off, Conroy tried to set the whole operation at a distance to view it as dispassionately as possible. *This is what you signed up for, kiddo. So what if it's more dangerous than anyone thought? Just be more careful, that's all.*

Obviously, someone was going to have to keep working this case from the inside. But the prospect of a long-term stay at NWI evoked the kinds of feelings Conroy preferred to keep locked away like the files in Bradley's safe. Not only might they influence her professional objectivity. They also vaguely represented an edge of instability beyond which she did not care, nor dare, to venture.

This place is starting to get to me, she thought. *But how can we keep an eye on this group if I don't stay inside? I bail out, we'd have to start from scratch.*

Conroy set her jaw, took a deep breath, turned the doorknob silently, and slipped out the back way, glad the long-term decisions were up to Davidson.

Stealing shadow to shadow across the quad, Clare paused to gaze at the fountain, its water jets sparkling in the colored spotlights. *Behold the charismatic, enigmatic J. R. Jenner!* she muttered, as she focused on the brightly lit life-sized bronze statue at the center of the fountain. It depicted ETR's leader holding the hand of a young boy and pointing—now ruby, now amber, now turquoise—into the heavens.

As Conroy instinctively followed the founder's finger into the black sky dotted with stars, a plaintive, familiar tune filled her mind, and the words drifted into consciousness: "*God is watching us . . . from a distance.*"

I hope you are watching us! she murmured—the first serious prayer she'd ventured since graduating from Yale to pursue a career in banking. Without the study group's support, it had been just too easy to let spiritual things slide.

Because I need all the help I can get. And while you're at it, help me figure out if our Dr. Jenner is just a charlatan or if he really knows a better way. It's getting harder to resist. Hour after hour, day after day . . . how can it be a lie when he seems so sincere . . . and so convinced?

The two-minute walk southeast from the fountain to her new apartment—one of the perks she enjoyed as Dr. Bradley's personal assistant—took a little longer tonight because Conroy stuck to the shadows. One close call was enough. She slipped through her own back door with a sagging sense of relief.

Curled up in her down comforter, the agent finally wound down to the sound of the kitten purring next to her ear. Just a week earlier she'd found the tiny animal abandoned in the horse barn. Ignoring the regulations against pets, she had taken in the forsaken fur ball—just until it was big enough to fend for itself. Clare's last coherent thought that night was wondering which of them was happier to see the other.

2

Bruce Davidson clicked the VCR to "Rewind" and stood up to stretch. "What do you think?" he asked Fred Billings, the younger agent who had become his friend as well as his right-hand man during the six years they had worked together.

"Don't know exactly, Chief," Billings replied as he stood up, too. "Came over to watch Monday night football, and you surprise me with home movies! You working for this guy," he chuckled, "or may I assume there's good reason to do this in your den instead of the office?"

"Private viewing," Davidson replied. "Not that the crusades of J. R. Jenner are very private, but for now, the fewer people know I'm interested, the better."

"But boss, you know I can't keep a secret!" Billings joked, laughing again.

"Well, this'll be your big chance," Davidson replied over his shoulder as he walked to the well-stocked walnut liquor cabinet to add some Irish Creme to his coffee. "Because I want you to start keeping regular tabs on this guy. Handled this myself so far—took in a few meetings, as you can see.

But now it's time to let somebody else in on the fun—somebody I can trust. You good with a camera?"

"Was that a question?" Billings asked. He had followed his boss into the office area of the den. As he poured Kahlua into his own coffee, he glanced at the framed degrees and certificates displayed on the wall behind Davidson's desk. The most prominent was a Ph.D. in psychology from New York University. Balancing the brimming cup, he returned to the leather-covered easy chair in front of the TV.

Davidson sat on the matching sofa and started the tape again. "By Sunday I could have given the message myself," he said. "Night after night, the same thing, almost word for word. And every time, identical response. Amazing!"

"Not just another blow-dried evangelist?" Billings asked.

"Maybe," Davidson said dryly. "Maybe not."

"Any theory about his popularity?" Billings probed.

"Everybody's looking for something," Davidson said, picking up his bent billiard dunhill pipe from its holder on the end table. "A little hope," he continued, pulling thoughtfully as he lit the #965 English Blend reserved for special moments—a habit picked up during a consulting stint in Scotland Yard. "Maybe something to identify with, like that guy Yahweh ben Yahweh in Miami. Make the right connections, and people follow guys like this off a cliff like a bunch of lemmings.

"Nothing illegal, on the surface," he continued as he ran the tape, mute. Suddenly he froze the frame, and Billings leaned forward to see more clearly.

"Strengster?" he gasped. "What's *he* doing there? I missed it the first time around," he scolded himself.

"Lighting's not that great," Davidson said. "Or maybe you dozed off. Done it myself in sermons many times, when Ellen used to drag me off to church. But Strengster's not the only dealer in attendance." Now the tape ran in slow motion.

"Notice the wad of bills he drops in the offering."

"Turning over a new leaf?" Billings laughed, as he leaned closer and his mouth dropped open. "Holy cow," he exclaimed. "Hundreds?"

Davidson propped his slippered feet on the glass-topped table between him and Billings and slapped his leg for Sandy, his English springer spaniel, to join him. The dog leaped onto the sofa, her nub of a tail quivering joyfully. She snuggled close to Davidson, chin on his thigh.

"Hundreds," he confirmed after a long pull on the pipe. "Maybe Strengster *has* turned over a new leaf, but he isn't known as the most generous businessman in the City of Brotherly Love. Burned a guy out once for less than he dropped in that plate!"

"Something funny's going on, that's for sure," Billings said.

"Exactly my impression, Mr. Watson!" Davidson laughed, stroking the dog's ears as he talked. "We became interested in this organization after a former group member filed a complaint, then disappeared. But when we started checking the group's finances, we discovered that large amounts have been transferred recently to Swiss accounts. If there's a connection between that and what you've just seen, I want to know about it."

He handed Billings a packet of airline tickets.

"Chicago. Milwaukee. Des Moines." Billings read the itinerary out loud. "Frequent flyer time."

"Didn't you tell me awhile back that you wanted to take Judy to Hawaii for your anniversary? Well, by the time this is over, you'll be able to get there free—that is, if she doesn't get too mad about your being on the road more than you're home over the next few months."

Davidson switched the TV to the football game, already

underway. "You still want Green Bay?" he asked, as the screen showed the Packers trailing.

"Why not?" Billings replied. "But from what you just said, maybe I better spend tonight at home. Hope you don't mind."

"No problem," Davidson replied with a little wink as he got up to walk Billings to the door. Sandy shadowed them, tail wagging all the way. "Just remember, this is our private party for now. It'll be better if even Judy doesn't know the details."

"Comes with the turf," Billings replied. "I don't offer; she doesn't ask."

Billings paused with one hand on the doorknob and reached down to scratch the dog's ears. "You still want us to watch Sandy the rest of the week so you can scout the mountains before opening day of elk season?" he asked.

"Course," Davidson replied. "I'll drop her by tomorrow morning. Eight o'clock too early?"

"Too late, far as the boys are concerned," Billings laughed. "They argued all day about who gets to feed her first and where they're going to take her and what kind of games they'll play with her while you're gone. She's a regular part of our family," he said. "How about I take her with me tonight and save you the time in the morning?"

"Thanks," Davidson paused, "but the house is empty enough as it is. We're best buddies, right, pup?" he said, kneeling down to pat the dog, too. Ecstatic, she rolled over and presented her belly to be scratched. "Who'll sleep with me tonight if she doesn't?"

Bruce Davidson watched his friend walk to his car and start it before he closed the door. Then he walked slowly back through the living room, pausing to look at the portrait on the mantle. "Pretty lonely here without you," he said to the photo, adding softly, "just like always." He could feel the tears forming in his eyes, the knot tightening his stomach—the same reactions he always had when he thought of the way Ellen had died.

Ten years hadn't done much to heal the hurt, although for Davidson the early "Whys?" that worsened the pain had long since given way to less agonized contemplations. For months he had worked hard to make sense of it. Why Ellen, so kind and good, so full of faith, should die so young, while the crooks he pursued day after day should live on—well, it just didn't compute if God really was in control.

It didn't help to know that, had the grief been hers instead of his, she would have only become more devout. But for Bruce, Rabbi Kushner's conclusion—that God is good, but not all-powerful—seemed the only sensible deduction. Faith in such a God might be an exercise in futility, but at least the explanation fit the pain.

I tried, he said to her photograph, for at least the thousandth time. *I thought there must be a reason, but I never could find it. I went to church. I read your Bible and that devotional booklet that kept coming in the mail for three years. I prayed. I even tried confession—me, a third-generation Baptist. But nothing worked, so now I just sort of ignore religion. At least I'm not reminded so often that saints and sinners have things pretty much the same, far as I can tell.*

"I'm sorry," he muttered, shaking his head sadly. Sandy, standing at his side, nuzzled his hand, whining softly.

When Davidson took his seat again in the den, his glass contained a triple shot of Old Grand-Dad, without much water. He set the bottle itself on the mantle, next to the life-sized mount of a red fox lunging for a ring-necked pheasant that had just taken flight.

The FBI man gazed sadly into his glass, then at Sandy, who had laid her head back on his lap. He stroked her ears fondly.

"Sometimes I think you and Old Grand-Dad are the only ones who really understand," he said, tossing down a large swallow. It burned a little, but not as much as it used to.

"You got a problem, kid?" Director of ETR security Milo Stanton asked as he opened his hotel room door to the young man's knock.

"No sir, Mr. Stanton," the late adolescent replied with a little grin. "Mr. Fazio regrets he can't attend the meeting tomorrow, but he would like to make a small contribution." He handed Stanton a black leather pouch filled with hundred-dollar bills.

Stanton looked in the bag, glanced down the hall both ways, then motioned for the courier to enter. Emptying the bills onto the table, Stanton counted. "Five thousand," he announced when he was finished. "Anything I need to know?"

"Word is, you need security people," the courier replied, grinning again, this time more relaxed. "Name's Ricardo, Freddy Ricardo."

Stanton pulled himself to his full six-foot-six, then looked down at Ricardo, nearly a foot shorter and at least a hundred pounds lighter. "We're very picky. What's your game?" he asked.

"Guns. Take 'em apart. Put 'em together. Make 'em from scratch if I have to. Pretty good with booby traps and other special effects, too."

"Trouble?"

"Might say that," Ricardo replied. "Mr. Fazio thought I should disappear for awhile."

"Catch a ride to the New World Institute, Walton's Creek, Colorado. Ask for Winston, Johnny Winston, my assistant. Here," Stanton said, scrawling out a note on a small piece of paper, "give him this. He'll be glad for the help. And . . . tell Fazio the *contribution* is appreciated."

Ricardo nodded respectfully, turned and left. After he was gone, Stanton stuffed the cash into a hidden compartment in the alligator-skin briefcase by the desk and reached for the phone.

"Hello, Worthy? Stanton here. Just wanted to let you know we got to Chicago okay."

"Glad to hear it," the ETR comptroller replied. "Sunday's receipts looked pretty good."

"Full house, as usual," Stanton said. "Local ads are paying off, and the *USA Today* feature helped. A hundred and ten thousand ain't bad, eh? Over fifty thou last week alone."

"Couple more weeks like that, and Jenner'll be able to pay the rent," Worthy snorted.

"Right. You want I should tell Dr. Jenner to cry and carry on like the rest? He's pretty happy with how this tour is going."

"Not necessary. He'll see the Central Committee report soon enough. Just keep him pumped up."

"Does that hisself. More famous he gets, louder he yells. Everywhere we go, people want his autograph, 'specially the ladies."

"You would notice that," James Worthy replied with a laugh. "But I suppose you do everything you can to put yourself between him and his admiring fans."

"Course. That's my job," Stanton replied with mock dignity.

"Well, just bring him back in one piece, please. We wouldn't want anything to happen to our favorite prophet, especially anything that might stop the cash flow."

"Do my best. Anything going on at the compound I need to know about before next week?"

"Pretty quiet here. No reports from Winston."

3

Bruce Davidson's pulse was racing, despite his confidence that the camouflage outfit and face paint rendered him virtually invisible against the mottled evergreen background. Inside the compound fence, the security guard, mounted on a horse, looked again directly at Davidson.

I can say I'm scouting for elk, since the season opens this weekend. But people go to the supermarket dressed like this, he joked to himself, trying to control his breathing. *Getting soft, old man. Hit forty, can't take the pressure anymore. Too much paper pushing.* He hoped his own horse, tied to a small pine two hundred yards downwind, would stay quiet.

Finally, the guard resumed his ride along the inside of the Institute fence—four strands of barbed wire marked only with a sign that warned sternly, "Private Property—No Trespassing."

For two days Davidson had been working his way around the thousand-acre compound, trying to get close enough to the Institute buildings to snap a few photos. Now that he was back where he had started, it was clear there were no good observation points on the ground. He had expected as much from the RF-4 aerial photographs.

Direct surveillance of the Institute grounds meant crossing that fence and a lot of open ground to get close enough. *Too risky.*

The only other direct access was through the main entrance to the northwest. Whoever had placed the Institute buildings in a canyon between two converging cliffs had been very interested in privacy. *For solitude or because they have something to hide?* he wondered.

Davidson took a circuitous route through the timber to the south, then back around and up the western side of Walton's Prairie to the rendezvous point he and Clare Conroy had selected on the topographical map before she went in. *Still have some time on my hands before Clare gets here.* Might as well relax. He made himself comfortable in the shade of a tall spruce nearby.

He didn't even know he had dozed off until he was startled awake by the loud thud of a spruce cone hitting the ground next to him. *Don't have a heart attack,* he laughed, *or she might have to give you CPR.* He looked up to see a blue grouse intently watching him from a perch about twenty feet overhead. *Probably been here the whole time. Bird's a sniper, I'm dead meat.*

He lay back on the springy needles and studied the bird, whose nervousness increased noticeably once it had been spotted. The encounter seemed to symbolize the reason he'd applied for the transfer to Boulder. Only a few hours into the mountains, by 4x4 and then on horseback, he could find places that seemed still untouched by the corruption and crime his position immersed him in most of the time.

These places also teemed with trophy mule deer and elk, not to mention some of the best trout fishing in the world. This particular expedition had been planned for months to correspond with the opening of elk season. He had scoped several good bulls on the way up. If things worked out, he might pay them a visit on his way down.

His favorite rifle was tucked away in the scabbard, just in case, a .270 Weatherby magnum with 3x9 Leupold scope. At four-hundred yards, with that beauty he could shoot a two-inch group. *Justifies the twelve hundred bucks,* he jested to himself. *A guy has to have some hobbies, after all. Some play golf, and when they can't play they dream about it. For me, it's mulies, elk, and rainbow trout.*

For now, though, we're after bigger game, he reminded himself, mentally reviewing his rapidly growing file on the career of the Reverend Dr. J. R. Jenner. Not that he had anything against Jenner, personally. But Landau's call, added to certain suspicions about ETR's finances, had launched an official inquiry into the various activities of ETR both inside and outside the Institute.

Early in his career, Jenner had focused his efforts mainly on establishing homes for orphans in places like Mexico, Jamaica, and the Philippines. He'd always been good at fund-raising, able to separate people from their very last penny with gripping tales of children who needed it more than they did.

But lately, especially since 1982, when he first began describing his "vision" for the Institute, a gradual shift had been occurring. Now, though he never totally ignored the children's homes, Jenner talked more and more about "end times," especially about a coming new world order with ETR at its center.

Davidson's reflections about Jenner were cut short by the sight of Conroy riding into the meadow, following the inside of the compound fence. He studied the twenty-six-year-old agent intently through his Zeiss 7x35 binoculars, looking for any visible signs of change from her four months of indoctrination. *You've been watching too many cult movies. What do you expect, a bald zombie in a toga?* She was riding easily, relaxed and confident, though her face showed some anxiety. That was natural enough, considering someone might be watching.

Conroy dismounted, tied the horse to a fence post, and slipped through the barbed wire strands into a ravine that crossed the prairie from inside the compound all the way into the timber where Davidson waited. The ravine was deep enough to crawl through without being observed from anywhere except directly overhead.

Davidson decided to impress Conroy with his ability to be invisible. He let her get within ten feet of his hiding place before he said, quietly, "Hello, Agent Conroy. How is the RADON detection business?"

Clare jumped, then they both laughed.

"You look well enough," he said.

"Thanks," she replied, eyeing him. "But you're certainly a sight."

"Trying to be invisible, see if I could get a peek inside," he said. "But now that you're here, I'll get it firsthand. Tell me, what's happening at the New World Institute?"

"You'll find this interesting," she said, handing him the microfilm. "The HANNAH project is confirmed."

Davidson nodded. "From our side, too—at least as far as we can tell. In the past two years alone, quite a few adoptions have been arranged through Jenner's orphanages."

"How many?"

"Sixty-two that we know of. And . . . at about the time of some of these adoptions, large amounts of cash were transferred to ETR accounts—sometimes in excess of ten thousand dollars."

"Any idea what's going on?"

"Well . . ." Davidson hesitated. FBI regulations required

him to withhold classified data sometimes, even when he might like to be more open with the facts. It was actually for Clare's protection. "Landau got us started," he said, "but not all the transfers have been infants. In fact, the larger sums are connected with older children, specifically adolescent females. We're not sure what that means, but there are some theories."

"Such as?"

"Such as forced child labor, for one thing, or maybe prostitution."

Conroy stepped back, her mouth open in surprise. Davidson wondered why she seemed so shocked. "A nickel for your thoughts," he ventured, studying her reaction.

"I was thinking," she started, hesitating, "how easy it is to be fooled. Day after day, night after night, all we hear is the voice of the prophet and the secrets of the kingdom. If you're not very careful, you start believing it, which I'm sure most of the rest of the students do. And even though I came in here to unravel the secret of Landau's missing child, for a moment there, when you mentioned prostitution, I felt defensive about ETR."

Davidson was relieved. Her personal identification with ETR was unsettling. But her ability to overcome it so quickly meant she hadn't really lost touch with herself, her mission, or her loyalty to him and the Bureau.

Yet if she were going to stay inside, he needed to be sure. "Identify your strongest reaction," he probed.

She thought for a moment, then responded, "*Outrage* is the best word I can think of to describe it," she said. "Outrage that a group like ETR may be abusing children, when on the outside the whole operation looks so . . . so wholesome."

"At this point, the pieces don't fit together very well," he said. "We need more information. You're in the best position to get it. But," he paused, "you're aware that whoever pursues this may be at risk. I cannot provide much support in an emergency. You can withdraw if you wish."

"I can take care of myself," she replied. "If I left ETR now, just disappeared, how long would it take to get someone else inside?"

When he didn't answer, she continued, "Besides, it's possible Landau is dead. You'll see for yourself," she nodded toward the microfilm. "On the other hand, the way this group operates, they might call someone 'dead' who has fallen away. It can't be coincidence that her listed date of death is the day she called us. If I opt out, we'll probably never know. We owe it to her, don't you think?"

"We can't afford to get emotionally involved," he said. "This is not a training exercise—remember that, whatever happens."

He knew she had decided already. "What's your plan?" he asked.

"Well, in relation to Landau, I could use an I.D. Her husband, too—a.k.a. John and Martha Williams. I've never seen her photo, though I'd know her voice anywhere. For all I know, I've met them both already."

"We're still working on it," Davidson said. "As you know, they vanished within hours of that call."

"I've been invited to join the REGENCY group," Conroy continued. "Many are called, but few are chosen," she added in a monotone, then glanced at Davidson with a twinkle in her eye. "Initiation is next week. Let me see how far I can get inside. I've been working for Dr. Bradley at the medical center, which is how I got into the HANNAH files. I don't know for sure what that's about. But there's another project, too—JACOB. And the whole thing is part of The Latter Day Eugenics Project."

"Sounds like there's something rotten in the state of Colorado," Davidson said with a laugh, "to use a Shakespearean phrase. I suppose you've been hearing a lot of sayings lately?"

"All day and sometimes all night, too. I was part of a religious study group at Yale, but we never got into stuff like this. We stuck to basics—you know, personal faith. But this prophecy angle is something else entirely. Fortunately, there's so much repetition you memorize it whether you want to or not.

"Might sound boring to an outsider," Conroy continued, "but when this guy talks about the future, it's like he's connected with something . . . something bigger. No kidding. I've never heard anyone speak with such authority. I wonder if anyone ever has."

Davidson was more than mildly dismayed at Conroy's positive regard toward their main subject, but he didn't let it show.

"He's going to attend the REGENCY initiation," she continued. "It'll be my first time to meet him face to face. He keeps a rather frenetic schedule. I'm anxious to know if he's as . . . interesting in person as he is on videotape."

"Is there a better word?"

"Charismatic, maybe. No . . . magnetic. That's probably more accurate."

4

Pretty long potty break, Johnny Winston muttered, tucking the binoculars inside his vest. *How'm I gonna keep a lid on this place with people wandering all over any time they feel like it? Have to have a serious talk with my Ivy League sweetheart.*

Winston arrived at the stables long before Conroy, who let her horse amble along as slowly as it wished. When Conroy rounded the corner to the barn, Winston was leaning back against the building in a straight-backed chair, chewing on a piece of grass, his hat pulled down a bit to shade his eyes. The wiry, bearded security guard had the rugged look of Charles Bronson, including the steely blue eyes. His silver security badge was highly visible, as was his revolver, when he tipped his hat and said, "Afternoon, Ms. Conroy. Have a nice ride?"

"Why yes, Winston," Conroy retorted coolly as she dismounted.

Winston reached back, grabbed a whip, and in one motion cracked it off the hindquarters of Conroy's horse. The animal raced to the other side of the corral, where it stood looking back at Conroy in confusion.

The security officer returned Conroy's glare with a grin. "Oh, did we hurt the little horsie? Nothing compared to what it would do to people skin, though. What do you think?"

"I'd never think of using such a weapon against another human being."

"'Course not, but no matter. My main concern is what you were doing out on Walton's Prairie today, and especially what you were doing in that ravine for such a long time." Again Winston grinned, this time even wider.

"You've been following *me* instead of fulfilling your security duties?" she replied.

"Well, yes . . . and no," Winston answered. "Following you around *is* fulfilling my security duties. Do you think we can let you go wandering off any time you want? How do we know you're not a spy or something!" He laughed derisively, as if this were the least likely possibility he could think of.

"Ms. Conroy," he continued seriously, "even though Dr. Bradley has arranged certain privileges for you, some of us aren't too happy about it, and we don't mind you knowing. So be careful, if you know what I mean."

"What I know is that you seem to enjoy intimidating a group of people who are here to study and build this organization. Shouldn't you be expending your energies keeping us safe?"

"Well," Winston replied, "you can count on that. But we have to keep the organization safe, too. And we're always suspicious when people disregard little rules, because sooner or later they find it that much easier to break the bigger ones."

"Whatever are you talking about?" Clare retorted.

"For example, wandering around in the middle of the night without any good reason." He watched her face carefully, but she did not react. "As in three A.M. a couple of nights ago . . . I'm sure you remember, unless you were sleep-walking!"

"I have a level-one clearance," Conroy replied. "Curfew doesn't apply to me. I just took a little walk because I couldn't sleep. My new position has my brain working overtime."

"And then there's that pet in your apartment—not that you deserve your own apartment, in my opinion. But to go and abuse that privilege by hiding an animal in there. Makes us wonder what you might abuse next."

"And how did you know about her?" she asked.

"We know everything that happens here."

"Is rescuing a kitten such a big deal?" Conroy responded. "I was only trying to help the little thing survive after it's mother abandoned her. I'll let her go when she's big enough to fend for herself."

"That'll be good," Winston guffawed loudly as he turned and started to walk away. "And while you're at it, teach her to run real fast, 'cause then she'll be an even better challenge for target practice than her mother was!"

Walton's Prairie meandered, like a giant horseshoe, west from the southeastern edge of the New World Institute compound, then south, before turning back east and down Miner's Pass. The pass nestled between two peaks that shot up dramatically to sixteen thousand feet, the summits already covered with snow. The only permanent building up here was Bruce Davidson's late afternoon objective after his meeting with Conroy. He wanted to discover what kind of mountaineer might choose such a rugged life, with all the comforts of civilization within easy reach. *Hermit? Malcontent? Fugitive?*

Approaching the cabin, Davidson's first impression was that this particular hermit cared a great deal about his home, as well as its setting. Several cords of wood were neatly stacked on one side of the building, a low cabin constructed of lodge-pole pine and carefully plastered with white chinking to protect against the blizzards soon to come. Each window was decorated with a neatly tied back New-England-style linen curtain.

The biggest surprise, however, was the reading material lying on a rocking chair on the cabin's front porch. *Our Daily Bread. That's the one Ellen used to read every morning—the one that kept coming even after she died. Well, at least this cabin's occupant probably hasn't been featured on "America's Most Wanted."*

Davidson's arrival was announced by barking. A golden retriever came bounding around the corner of the cabin, then stopped in confusion, evidently unsure what to do. Was this a serious threat that called him to guard duty or an opportunity to play with somebody new? After a few sniffs, which gave Davidson's horse the jitters, the dog dashed away to return with a stick in its mouth. "Time to play," Davidson muttered, as he dismounted to pat the dog.

He looked up at the sound of a footstep. A bearded, well-built, and very sweaty man of about forty-five stood at the corner, leaning a double-bladed axe against the cabin.

"Nice dog," Davidson commented, taking a step toward the mountaineer. "Bruce Davidson," he said, extending his hand.

"Glad t' know ya. Jeremiah Wilkes. Dog's Cyrus. Best friend I got." He smiled as the dog wagged his way over at the sound of his name and licked his master's hand.

"Nice place, too."

"Ayuh, thanks. Built it m'self. "Took a couple years, but time's one thing I got a lot of, so I just kept after it 'til 'twas done."

Interesting accent. New England somewhere—I'll bet Maine.

"Elk huntin'?" Wilkes continued, nodding toward the rifle and pack on the horse.

"Yeah. Trying to find the perfect head. You must see them quite often out here."

"So often I give 'em names, ya know, like they was my pets or somethin'."

"Oh, then I'll find another place to hunt," Davidson replied.

"Not necessary," Wilkes answered. "Take one 'bout once a year, m'self, usually just before the herd heads down fer winter. Dry some and smoke some, and about then my freezer starts workin'." He chuckled at his own joke. "Cuppa coffee?" He gestured for Davidson to follow him into the cabin.

"Sounds great!" As he stepped through the door, Davidson's olfactory senses were flooded with the aroma of venison stew. "Smells delicious." A couple of days eating MREs had ambushed his sense of propriety as he invited himself to supper. *Anything beats another helping of hot dogs and bean component.*

"Stew's done," Wilkes grinned. "Be pleased if ya'd join us—me and Cyrus, that is."

Davidson took one of the chairs. It was obviously handmade, as was the table. He was famished, but as he began to wolf down the bowl of stew, using the fresh-baked sourdough roll to sop up the juices, he noticed that Wilkes paused briefly and bowed his head slightly before beginning to eat.

"Didn't mean to embarrass ya," Wilkes said when their bowls were half empty. "Force'a habit I guess, since I was a kid."

"Me too," Davidson said, "but now I forget most of the time."

Sometimes I forget . . . sometimes I just don't feel like it. But I certainly can't put my real mission up here at risk by discussing it with somebody I just met. "Tonight, though, I'm thankful for such great food," he added with a smile.

"Lotsa good food up here, if you can find it and don't mind eatin' simple. But don't expect a Big Mac and fries! Good Lord provides all the meat or fish a fella could need, and I just forage around with the sheep for greens to keep me reg'lar. The rest—beans, coffee, sugar, and the like—I pick up when I go to town. Once in spring to bring up the flock and once in fall to take 'em down and once in the winter just to break the monotony. Take the sourdough with me, to keep it goin'."

Davidson had heard tales of Alaskan sourdough surviving from gold-rush days, personally prized by its current guardian to the point of sleeping with it on the coldest nights to make sure it didn't freeze. *The older the sourdough the better the taste,* he thought, enjoying another nutty mouthful.

"So . . . you're a shepherd?" Davidson asked, intrigued.

"Ayuh . . . work for Mr. Bryan, rancher who owns this land. Treats me pretty good, lettin' me build this cabin here and all. All he asks is fer me to keep an eye on the flock and the fences mended. Stuff like that."

"I'm an educator," Davidson said. *Wonder what he'd think if I said I was an FBI agent?* Teach psychology and a little anthropology at The University of Colorado, Boulder," he added.

"Ya'd find Mr. Bryan an interesting fella," Wilkes offered. "His grandfather was one of the first Mormons to move here. He tells some gruesome tales about their persecution in the beginnin'. Had to stick together just to survive. Wasn't so much they had more than one wife, but that they was differ'nt. People can be pretty mean."

"True," Davidson said. "I grew up in South Texas. Everybody down there was Southern Baptist, you know. We were, too. We had our particular way of doing things, that just seemed right. But then some other groups began to move in—Methodists, Presbyterians, and even some Moravians. Can't say we were very hospitable to any of them, until it was time to have another tent meeting. Everybody in town got invited to those."

"Been to a few tent meetings m'self," Wilkes said, in a voice that drifted off somewhere else. "Quite a few, in fact. But maybe tent meetin's in Texas are differ'nt from tent meetin's in Maine."

"I'll bet pretty much the same," Davidson said. "It was quite a while ago for me, but I remember a lot of emotion—repentance, rededication, commitment to missions . . . and a lot of passing the hat."

"Sounds 'bout the same, but in my case we never passed the hat . . . and," Wilkes hesitated, "it was a lot more recent. Fact, I was usually the one leadin' 'em ."

"Really," Davidson said, "were you a deacon or something?"

"Well, not quite. I was an evangelist to the loggers of northern Maine. Ever' year we'd make a tour up there in the summer and hold meetin's—me, my wife, and our little boy. We'd sing and give a testimony. Ya shoulda seen them loggers break down when little Bobby'd preach to 'em . It was truly amazin'."

Wilkes stopped. His voice had cracked, and he had turned away toward the window. Davidson had the distinct impression that Wilkes was crying. A full five minutes went by. Wilkes stroked Cyrus, who licked his hand, as his master tried to regain his composure.

What's he doing up here with a wife and son at home?

"Sorry," Wilkes finally said. "I never talk about this. Try not to think 'bout it much. Four years ago Bobby went out sleddin', and somehow he slid out in front of a car, and . . ."

Now he really broke down. He got up from the table, fists clenched, and paced around in front of the stove. “I came along just after it happened. I scooped Bobby up from that snow, prayin’ like mad, and wonderin’, How could this happen to such a beautiful, innocent kid who never hurt nobody? But there was nothin’ I could do. There was nothin’ anyone could do. I watched the color drain from his face, and somethin’ inside me died. I’ve never preached again. Don’t ’spect I ever will.”

Davidson just sat there quietly, nursing his coffee along and anticipating what would come next. Somewhere during his doctoral studies he had learned some statistics on the number of couples who end up divorced after the death of a child. *What was it—75, 80 percent?*

“We were okay—me and Marcy—for awhile,” Wilkes continued, after a long pause, “Ya know, sayin’ the right things. Doin’ the right things. Goin’ through the motions. But after ’bout a year, instead of holdin’ us together, the pain was driving us apart. She was goin’ her way; I was goin’ mine.

“Marcy wanted another baby, real bad, but I couldn’t stand the thought of losin’ someone else. Twice woulda killed me. We still loved each other—I love ’er now—but bein’ together was makin’ us more sad than happy. So one day I put the house in her name, left everythin’ she could use, and up and left. Took my guns and traps, snowshoes, and the dog. Just thought it would be better this way. Prob’ly nobody else understood. Only Cyrus here . . . and maybe God—I can’t say.”

Davidson felt himself becoming increasingly uncomfortable. *Who knows, man? Nobody!* he wanted to respond. *But Ellen knew. At least she knew enough to keep her satisfied. For her, faith was always so simple. Like a little child. Not so much facts, but trusting Somebody bigger and wiser than herself . . . who didn't care enough to keep her from dying a horrible death!*

He wanted to scream the last thought. But instead he said, quietly, "Who can say how somebody else should feel, or what somebody else should do in a situation like that? Twenty years ago, I might have given you advice. But the older I get, the more the questions seem to outnumber the answers."

He stopped, looked directly at Wilkes, and continued. "I'm not a theologian or a philosopher. But speaking as a psychologist, I think you acted rationally and responsibly toward your wife, and even toward yourself. Sometimes, in order to see things more clearly, people need a little space." He wanted to ask if Wilkes had ever thought about going back, but now was not the time.

"Space and time, lotsa both up here," Wilkes replied, rising from the table with several dirty dishes in hand. Turning toward the sink, he said, "But I'm 'fraid I've cut into yers with all my tales'a woe."

"Not at all, Jeremiah," Davidson said, carrying his own plates and utensils toward the sink. "When a guy's been through what you have, he's got to talk about it sometime, or he'll die inside." *Physician, heal thyself!* "I only wish I could help in some way."

"Ya already have, Dr. Davidson," Wilkes replied. "Just by listenin'. But hey, why don't ya call me Jerry."

"Okay, as long as you call me Bruce."

"Deal. Now, how 'bout another cuppa coffee 'fore ya go?" Wilkes said.

"Sounds great to me, Jerry. I'm in no particular rush."

Fred Billings checked the Handicam's hookup to the back of his motel room TV. *Got to get this.*

"And now we go to the steps of the Garden, for a special *Live On Five* interview. Here's WCVX's own Bethany Mathews with evangelist Dr. J. Reuben Jenner."

"Dr. Jenner," the reporter began, "you are in the middle of a nationwide speaking tour, at a time when many seem to have written off religion and most people have developed a rather deep distrust of media preachers. How do you explain your rather remarkable success?"

"Well," Jenner began, looking past Mathews and directly into the camera with a smile that radiated sincerity and warmth. "It's not for me to say we are *successful.* Too often humans take the short view of things. I've come to preach the kingdom and to prepare the hearts of men and women for the rule of God. In the long run, my success or failure depends entirely on how well I fulfill this calling."

"Dr. Jenner," Mathews continued, "historically, when people like you come along with such a clear vision for the future, they are called prophets. Would you call yourself a prophet?"

"Some people even go beyond that and call me God's anointed end-times prophet. I am willing to accept that designation because each part of it is true. I *have* been anointed—commissioned—to speak for God about the end times, that is, the period in which we are living."

Again Billings checked the connections. *Davidson'll love this. . . . Jenner is going over the edge just like all the rest. But why isn't this woman tearing him apart? Connie Chung would have had him for lunch.*

"But Dr. Jenner," the reporter continued, "in a rally like tonight's, some people will be hearing you for the very first time and will not be familiar with even your basic teachings. How do you get to the deeper things?"

The reporter extended the microphone toward Jenner, who replied, "As you know, Miss Mathews," Jenner replied, "several years ago we founded the New World Institute for lay leadership and mission training precisely to meet this need for enlightenment. Everyone can help complete the Master Plan of the Ages. Applications are available at all our crusades."

There was the beginning of a pink tinge to the small triangle of western sky visible from the front porch of Jeremiah Wilkes's cabin. Wilkes sat on the steps with Cyrus lying beside him. Behind him, Davidson creaked gently in the old rocker, a cup of coffee in one hand and his pipe in the other. Aromatic smoke from his pipe mingled in the calm air with the smell of pine smoke from the chimney.

It just doesn't get any better than this, Davidson thought, longing more than he liked to admit for the canteen of brandy stored inside his pack. *Wouldn't want to offend my new evangelist friend. Besides, may have to ride a bit yet before I set up camp.*

"Hear that?" Wilkes whispered, as the sound of an elk's

distant bugling drifted musically through the valley, hanging delicately in the air like the trill of a forlorn flutist. No matter how many times Davidson heard that unmistakable strain, it still filled him with wonder. It was more an event to be experienced than a sound to be heard—almost indescribable to someone who hadn't been there in person. Who would believe that a thousand-pound bull elk could create a song so light and airy, beautiful beyond any other sound in nature?

"That'd be Richard," Wilkes said quietly.

"Richard?" Davidson replied, mystified.

"Richard IV, t' be exact," Wilkes replied.

"You know him just by the sound?" Davidson asked.

"Course," Wilkes chuckled. "Don't take any special talent, just time enough to get acquainted, like anything else. Richard IV's king of the hill for this year. A real beaut, he is—six points, both sides, white as ivory on the tips. Watched him workin' off the velvet, seems like just a couple weeks ago. Tore up a stand'a pines pretty good doin' it, too!"

Again the sound echoed off the rock ledges, filling the valley where the little cabin nestled. But this time the bull's performance seemed somehow more personal. *Richard's song*, Davidson mused. He was surprised to find himself recoiling internally to think what some paunchy businessman might be delighted to do to Richard on opening day of the season. *What I might have done to Richard on opening day.*

"Richard sings mostly at night. Don't like much company," Wilkes commented.

"Probably enough of that with that Institute being built at the other end of the prairie," Davidson said.

"Ayuh. Lotta big trucks in and out all summer. Blastin' and buildin' all the time."

"Bryan ever mention why he sold prime grazing land to

them? Sure didn't do the elk any favors. And cut down your pasture considerably."

"Thousand acres ain't much to Bryan," Wilkes replied. "Maybe them people reminded him of his own ancestors. Y'know, differ'nt beliefs, and just lookin' for a peaceful place to escape the hassle."

"May be similar, may be different," Davidson said, after a moment's silence. "Nobody knows for sure. Pretty secretive group. Make an interesting research project, though. The scientist in me, I guess."

He paused, measuring his words carefully, "But from everything I've heard, you can't even get close enough to that compound for a photograph, much less interview the people inside."

"Well, there *is* a way to look inside," Wilkes said promptly. "Done it m'self, couple times. Curious, y' know. Good thing you ain't a cop, or I'm in trouble, right?" he chuckled.

Davidson didn't know whether he was more surprised or pleased, but he tried not to convey either as he encouraged Wilkes to continue. "Really? You have your own helicopter?" He laughed.

"No, but 'most as good," Wilkes said. "There's an old mine shaft into the mountain right behind the main buildings, starting from the east face. Don't go all the way through, but there's a natural crevice, prob'ly used fer air supply. Opens on the face of the cliff right behind the main buildings, maybe five hundred feet up. Must look like a crack in the rocks from below, but it's big enough in there to sit back in the dark and watch everything that's goin' on."

Davidson kept the rising excitement from his voice. "Sure like to take a peek myself sometime, maybe snap a picture or two."

"No problem. But no sense going in after dark if ya want pictures. I'm going in there, don't like to rush it, anyway.

Want to be sure nobody spots me. Mine opening is pretty much covered over from a rock slide, so ya hafta almost stumble on it if ya don't already know it's there. But somebody sees us disappear into the terrain and then looks real hard, they might be able to figure out where we went."

"Good reason to come back sometime," Wilkes continued, "after elk season. Which reminds me, you headin' fer that big outfitter's camp 'bout three miles up? Better be goin' or you'll be ridin' by moonlight."

"Actually, I'm hunting solo," Davidson said. "Pack a mountain tent and sleeping bag. Set up camp wherever I am when it gets dark."

"In that case," Wilkes smiled, "why not be our guest tonight. Maybe, we get up early enough, we'll pay that mine a visit and be back before breakfast."

"Thanks," Davidson replied. "Sounds great to me."

"Good. That'll be better in another way, too."

"Oh? How's that?"

"Well, a certain black bear thinks that cave's 'er bedroom. Last five winters she's been in there." He grinned at Davidson's rather obvious discomfort. "Don't worry. She'd be more nervous 'bout you than you are 'bout her. But we're better friends, her an' me, than she knows. I been in there when she was hibernatin' and seen two little baby cubs suckin' away fer all they was worth. Did you know black bears have their cubs while they're sleepin'? Never feel a thing. Course I wouldn't try it later on, even when she's half awake. Get between her and her young'ns, don't matter what kind of rifle you got!"

"What makes you think it will be safe tomorrow?"

"Ain't made 'er nest yet. But even if she has, all ya got to do is bring yer sneakers!"

"Sneakers?" Davidson asked, as Wilkes began to laugh.

"Ain't you heard 'bout the two guys out huntin' when a

big bear came chargin' after 'em ? First guy starts to run, but the other sits down and starts puttin' on 'is sneakers. 'Ya'll never outrun a bear,' the first one yells over his shoulder. The other guy yells back, 'I don't need to outrun the bear; I just need to outrun *you!*' Ha! Ha! Good one, eh?"

6

Wanda, Susan . . ." Clare Conroy called to the women who had been her quadmates before her promotion. "Wait a minute! Let me walk with you." She caught up to the others, who were just heading for the jogging path, a two-mile loop winding south through the timber behind the staff quarters and dining hall, up onto a small ridge, and back along the edge of Walton's Prairie before turning north and ending behind the medical center.

Every morning during recreation time, all the students jogged this trail. And every night after dinner and before group, everyone walked the same path. It wasn't required, but it was recommended—which was exactly the same if you wanted to advance in the movement. Dr. Jenner, the student handbook proclaimed, was very concerned with excellence, not only in mind and spirit, but in body. The true servants of the kingdom knew the meaning of discipline.

"I haven't seen you for so long," Clare commented. "Feels like years. What's happening?"

"Oh, Clare, it's only been a couple of weeks since you moved out," Susan Winters replied, eyeing the special staff housing they were just passing. "Not much has changed with us. You know, the same routine."

"What's the theme for group this week?" Clare asked, recalling the hours of interesting discussions in their quad, followed by even more intimate talks she and Susan had shared as roommates after the meetings. "I miss that more than anything."

"Connexion," Wanda Jackson replied. "Talk about a great theme to end Advanced! Summarizes everything that's always been missing from my life. I love what Dr. Jenner says about the vine and the branches! I mean, even though I'm going back to San Diego and you're going into REGENCY, these last few weeks has changed my life forever!

"Before, I was so lonely and afraid," she continued. "But now I know, wherever I go and whatever I do, I'm a part of something bigger. I've never wanted anything as much as this—just to contribute, just to think I can do something to help *him*, maybe even be able to talk to him sometime."

"We all want to help him, Wanda," Winters replied, "but do you really think Dr. Jenner has time for every person in ETR? If we're really committed, recognition isn't important. 'For me to live is the kingdom'; nothing else matters—"

"Maybe I'll stop by the quad tonight," Clare interrupted, "if that's all right. I've been feeling kind of disconnected, at least from you guys!"

"You can do anything you like, from what we hear," Winters replied.

"Don't know what to make of that."

"Your own apartment. Horses. No curfew. Who knows what else?" Winters said, an unmistakable coolness in her tone.

"Oh," Clare said. For the first time, she realized that her promotion, with all its added benefits, had effectively cut her off from the rest of the Institute community, especially the other three women with whom she'd shared more of her inner self than she had with anyone since that little study group at Yale.

"Guess I've gotten so involved in the research, I never even thought about your feelings," Conroy said apologetically.

"We're glad for you," Winters said quickly. "Rejoice with those who rejoice, weep with those who weep! We spend so much time trying to think and act as one, we don't know how to react when somebody is a little different. Come over anytime, of course."

When they finished the loop, Clare turned to enter her new apartment. At that moment, the agent experienced a sense of isolation she hadn't felt since sixth grade, when she'd told her friends her parents were getting a divorce.

"When I count to three, you will wake up. You will be refreshed and relaxed. You will remember everything you want to say, but you will not remember we had this conversation. One. Two. Three."

Linda Landau opened her eyes and looked at Dr. Bradley, who motioned with her right hand for Johnny Winston to start the camera rolling behind the two-way mirror.

"Dear friends," the disheveled young woman began, "friends of the kingdom, I speak to you out of great sadness, for I have betrayed the greatest trust ever placed in me. Once, I too was an advanced student at the New World Institute. It wasn't so long ago, though it seems like ages since . . ."

Her voice trailed off, and she seemed to be trying to recall what she had been saying. Her eyes were unfocused, and her pupils dilated as she continued, ". . . since two roads diverged in a mountain wood. And I, who could not travel both and be one traveler, chose . . . the way of Truth, as you have done. And as you will do, I hope, for your own good and the good of humanity.

"I was even part of REGENCY," Landau continued, "a privilege beyond my capacity, as it turned out. For even though the choice was freely made, and no one having put his hand to the plow and looking back is worthy of the kingdom, I made the greatest mistake of all, and questioned the way of life.

"When I left the kingdom way," the woman said, "I betrayed more than a sacred trust, my solemn vow. I violated my own inner self—and turning and turning in a widening gyre, the center cannot hold—I disconnected at the core of my being.

"My friends, you are the keepers of the keys, for you know the secrets of the ages. Do not cast these pearls before swine, for they will only trample them underfoot, and then turn and gore you, a horrible way to die.

"I myself deserved to die. I wanted to die. Yet I have been allowed to live, in hope that someday I, no longer worthy to tie even the thong of your sandals, may again contribute something . . . something . . . oh, God," she muttered, as her voice drifted away and she collapsed sideways on the couch where she was sitting. She was still mumbling, "What have I done? What have I done?" when Dr. Bradley reached out to break her fall and Winston turned off the camera.

If that doesn't warn'em what happens to traitors, don't know what will, Winston muttered as he rode out into the prairie. Brightly illuminated by the moon, the meadow stretched several miles ahead of him before it curved to the left. Here and there he could see dark spots—some small, some larger—moving slowly as the animals, mostly deer, fed peacefully.

But Johnny Winston was frustrated and very angry, especially at Landau. *Stupid b———, that's all she is. Couldn't control her emotions. Nearly ruined everything.* The more he thought about it, the worse it got. There would be no sleep tonight, unless he could release this rage. Killing something would certainly help.

Now as he walked the horse quietly along the southern edge of the timber, Winston finally spotted what he was looking for. He grabbed the Ruger M77 .270 from the horse and peered through the 3x9 Weaver scope, trying to tell if the bear feeding on a rotting deer carcass about three hundred yards ahead was big enough to bother with.

Crosshairs, he muttered, taking a prone position and preparing to fire. *Useless, black on black.*

The sound of the shot roared up the valley. By the time it rumbled back, all the animals except one had fled into the forest. Winston, blinded for a moment by the muzzle flash, began to walk toward the bear, now lying sprawled across the remains of its last meal.

Nice shot, Winston congratulated himself as he walked. But the closer he got, the smaller his trophy seemed to be. And by the time he had reached the dead animal, he was cursing himself for shooting a yearling, not much bigger than a cub, instead of waiting for a larger trophy to appear.

"Next time, your Daddy. Mommy will do. I'm not particular," he said as he skinned the animal, discarding its headless carcass next to the deer's. "Tender vittles for the next of kin!" he laughed.

Stretch the skin out on the barn; it'll look bigger. Impress the ladies, anyway, he assured himself. He rode back toward the compound, whistling a happy tune.

7

Jeremiah Wilkes chuckled as he knelt to tie his boot-lace, "Bring yer sneakers?"

Wilkes and Davidson were just outside the entrance to the mine shaft, cut into what was now a rockslide eight hundred yards wide on the east face of Promontory Point.

Davidson laughed to humor his guide, but his right hand instinctively fondled the .357 magnum revolver strapped to his leg. He gazed for a moment toward the eastern horizon, which showed just a hint of the coming sunrise. Wilkes had led him here in the dark. *Must know this mountain like the back of his hand.*

"I'll go in and check," Wilkes said as he began squeezing through a very small hole between two boulders. "Unless," he added, "you'd like to go first!"

Wilkes disappeared from view. Davidson noticed his heart was pounding as it hadn't done in ages—perhaps not since his first day out deer hunting at age ten when that big buck had crossed right in front of him. He just let it go, finger on the trigger, unable to fire. *Buck fever,* he muttered. *But is there such a thing as bear fever? And what will I do if there is one inside, and I have to go after Wilkes?*

To Davidson's immense relief, Wilkes emerged a few minutes later. "Nobody's been sleepin' in momma bear's bed . . . yet. Let's go. As Daddy used to say, 'It's 'most daylight in the swamp.'"

Davidson was only partly through the entry, his head in total darkness and his arms compressed against his body, when he began to scold himself for forgetting, in his excitement over finding an access to the compound, that he was more than mildly claustrophobic. *Spelunker, you're not, Davidson. Should've known better.*

But after six feet of closeness and wondering if he was going to black out, Davidson found himself standing in a much larger cavern, nearly twelve feet wide and seven feet to the roof. It was musty and cool, but at least it was space.

"C'm'ere," Wilkes said from the darkness to Davidson's right. "Here's 'er little cubbyhole. See the straw and twigs and stuff?"

Davidson turned his own flashlight into the den, a small hollowed-out area off the main shaft and just inside the opening they had crawled through. "You've been in *here* when she was in *there*!" he gulped.

"Ayuh. Ain't nearly as dangerous as it sounds. Come on back this winter; we'll pay a visit." Wilkes laughed, then aimed his flashlight down the mineshaft. It descended gradually into the mountainside as far as the beam could reach. "Care to explore?" Wilkes asked.

"No thanks," Davidson replied, hoping Wilkes couldn't hear the tremor in his voice. "But I *would* like to get a look at that Institute."

When they finally reached the open end of the fissure, after sometimes crawling on hands and knees in the damp darkness, Davidson was again near panic. His breaths came fast and shallow. His pulse raced.

But the agony seemed justified, when at last he peeked out into the daylight to find himself perched five hundred feet directly above and behind the New World Institute compound, looking southwest toward the main gate. For a moment he hid in the shadows, letting his eyes get accustomed to the light, memorizing every detail of the grounds.

When Davidson reached for his camera, Wilkes excused himself, saying he'd seen the buildings before and he preferred exploring in the mine. In the next twenty minutes, Davidson ran ten thirty-six exposure rolls of film through his motor-driven Canon EOS1. He was so close he had to switch lenses, just to get the whole compound into one frame.

There had certainly been a great deal of construction during the past few months, Davidson noted, comparing what he saw to his memory of the overhead recon taken that spring. At least one major building had gone up since then. Still under construction, it lay to his right and due north of the fountain, which centered the entire development like the hub of a wheel. Judging from the amount of electronics-related crates lying around outside, Davidson assumed it was a technical building of some kind.

There were many other buildings, too. Several long, low structures along the northwest ledge appeared to be dormitories. These flanked what most likely would be the dining room, where numerous people were heading. (The smell of frying bacon drifting past on the gentle northwest wind confirmed this hypothesis.) The more elaborately decorated buildings to the southeast, bordering the timber, seemed to offer more luxurious accommodations—perhaps apartments for the more permanent staff or special guests.

As he snapped away, Davidson thought he saw Clare Conroy walk down the steps of one of these buildings and toward the dining room. He would have to look at that frame more carefully later. Computer-aided enhancement would prove him right or wrong. Her movements more than any other characteristics clicked with Davidson. *Everybody's walk is unique . . . like a fingerprint. Course not too many people have such blonde hair, either.*

The medical center was easy to identify from the caduceus over the entryway. The main administration building was almost directly below him and to the right, with the rest of the Institute buildings up against the cliffs on the other side. Several rather nondescript buildings sat at a greater distance from his position, along the southwest perimeter, near the entry gate. From the equipment stored around them, these appeared to be grounds and maintenance buildings.

About a half-mile away, just beyond these buildings, another series of buildings appeared to be storage facilities, where workers were unloading fifty-five gallon drums from several eighteen-wheelers. He switched lenses again and continued snapping. Even at this distance, he could read the block letters stenciled on the drums: "DANGER. HYDROCHLORIC ACID. HANDLE WITH CARE." *Strange load for a religous organization.*

Wilkes returned holding two pieces of rock, one of which he handed to Davidson. "Topaz, imperial grade—a little pink," he said. "Not the best I seen, but not bad, either. Sorry 'bout the blood. Hit m' thumb knockin' it loose. Gold miners just ignored these. Take yers home and have it made into somethin' for yer wife," he said with a smile.

"Thanks," Davidson said, pocketing the crystals and wondering if he would tell Wilkes about Ellen. "I'll be through in a minute," he said, "soon as I finish this roll." He focused his lens on the single male walking just behind the administration building as he fired the last few frames through the

Canon. *Seen this one before somewhere, but not on a box of Wheaties.*

"Fool!" a woman in the front row shouted. "Judas!" another woman cried. Instead of a morning reading from *The Master Plan of the Ages*, the entire advanced studies group was watching a taped confession whose narrator seemed to be addressing them from her own personal twilight zone. Conroy fought to keep her composure as some in the group jeered mercilessly.

Leaning toward the screen, the agent tried to hear more clearly above the din. There was something about that voice. She'd heard it before, although to her knowledge she had never seen this person in her life. *Great actress—or psycho. Either way, nobody can possibly miss the point. Connected is for always.*

The fragmented woman's face was still in Conroy's mind a few minutes later, when she arrived for work at the medical center. But as soon as Clare sat down, it was replaced by the stern visage of her boss. Florence Bradley, M.D. strode over and dropped the HANNAH file on her desk.

Conroy recognized the folder immediately, and for a horrified split second wondered what was going on. But by the time she looked directly at Bradley, Conroy's expression was one of embarrassed apology. *Nice touch, babe. But be careful!*

"I'd like an explanation," Bradley said. "First the night watchman hears something in here at two in the morning. Then Putnam, our computer whiz, calls to ask who's working late. He knows every time someone uses the mainframe, even what they look at."

Conroy was instantly aware that her carelessness had jeopardized the entire operation. Based on the video she'd just seen, she also knew that if she wasn't very careful now, the personal consequences might be serious, too. Only once before in her life had she known the flush of fear that gripped her as she tried to formulate some kind of credible answer.

"It's a little embarrassing," she began, blushing. "I'm not sure how to put it, but I was worried, you know, about my initiation into REGENCY."

Conroy paused, translating the real fear she was feeling into the worried look of a bashful college girl as she looked into Bradley's eyes. "I mean, you hear rumors about how people are matched up—men and women, you know. And even though on my application I chose to renounce marriage for the sake of the kingdom, I guess my anxiety got the best of me. I'm truly sorry."

"We don't force marriage on anybody. *Nothing* is forced on anyone here. Why didn't you just ask? I thought we had a good relationship." The doctor's voice was that of a teacher chiding an errant child. "I don't have much interest in men, myself," she added, "but is there some special reason you want to stay single?"

"Well, I've never been much for romance," Conroy said, quietly. "I mean, with the intensity of my studies and all, I never had the time or energy either." *Sounds better than admitting that after Daddy left, no male I've ever met came close to measuring up.*

"But you're very attractive," Bradley said, putting her hand on Conroy's shoulder briefly. "From what I've heard about the Ivy League, you must have been fighting the boys off with a stick."

Pretty close, Conroy remembered, disgusted. "But somehow I managed to survive," she said. "From the way everyone talked, I must have been the only virgin left in New Haven by graduation. But with AIDS and all the rest, I can't say it was any sacrifice."

"That's why everyone gets such a thorough physical when

they come here," Bradley responded, "and the reason we have such strict rules about sexual expression. We're deeply concerned for the purity of the group. We match people as a service to them."

Dr. Bradley pulled her chair up next to Conroy's desk. "You know," she said, "I'm sorry to be losing you."

"What do you mean?" Conroy responded, shocked. "I know I've violated your trust, but I thought after initiation I could still work with you—that we might even be able to work more closely. I was hoping to learn more about genetics," Conroy added.

"Genetics *is* exciting," the doctor replied. "But eugenics is much more exciting. We've come a long way since Mendel, you know. There's a lot of research going on outside, but it's so hampered by regulations. Nobody can do anything creative without putting their government grant at risk. No room to blaze new trails, because every time we experiment with human beings, somebody squawks and the research stops again."

Conroy was doing her best to memorize every detail she could possibly glean, in case she never got further direct access to this information.

"If you're going to do any research worth doing," the doctor continued, "you have to do it scientifically, using control groups over long periods of time. That's what attracted me here. Our people are so willing to be part of studies that will benefit not just our movement, but ultimately all mankind.

"With any luck," she continued, "we should be able to complete some of the experiments interrupted by the collapse of the Third Reich. I'll bet you haven't heard about the genetic experiments that were underway. It's a shame, really, to have scientific knowledge withheld on purely emotional grounds.

"You seem shocked," the doctor said. "Nobody favors

another Holocaust; that's not the point. The real point was a superior-quality human race, and that's within our grasp without eradicating anybody. After all, once the real cream rises to the top, so to speak, there will still have to be others to do menial tasks."

Conroy suddenly felt cold and clammy just being in the presence of this person. It was the first time she had seen this side of her boss. And for the first time in her life, she had, for a fleeting moment, an almost overwhelming sense of evil. She wanted to protect herself, to hide somehow, but there wasn't anywhere to go. "But our goals are primarily spiritual, don't you think?" she blurted out, finally feeling like the schoolgirl she had been impersonating.

"Well, yes, so far. And even long-term, I suppose, although the specific agenda of REGENCY is to achieve whatever level of influence and prominence possible, worldwide. Instead of eradicating the opposition, we'll change things from the inside out."

"But we're striving for world peace, not world dominion," Conroy responded, startled that the party line was so ingrained.

"Is there really any difference? Either way, the critical long-range question is qualified and committed leadership. And REGENCY is the key," the doctor said. "At any rate, I've enjoyed preparing you for your next step during these past few weeks. But now I need to give you up so you can have a more important role."

Should I risk it? If I don't keep her talking, I may never know. "I wish I could stay," Conroy ventured. "I was looking forward to helping you complete the HANNAH project, whatever that is."

Bradley smiled, tightly. "Before long," she said, "you'll be very involved in *everything* that's going on, including the HANNAH project. The kingdom has need of you," Bradley continued, "as Dr. Jenner's personal assistant. He needs somebody to help with P.R. and especially to translate for him. He's never really sure the message is getting through now. With your background in languages, you're just what we need.

"Don't worry," Bradley added. "There will be a lot of travel, but you'll be treated royally. And . . . you have nothing to fear from Dr. Jenner. He is completely faithful to his wife."

Again Conroy was shocked. "I didn't know he was married." *Holy cow*, she thought, *how did we miss that, Bruce? What else will I be surprised with?*

"Very few people know that," Bradley said. "Years ago, Mrs. Jenner tried very hard—too hard—to be the perfect pastor's wife. That was before Jenner became a traveling evangelist. But the strain was evidently too much for her, and she had to be hospitalized. She hasn't been out in public in twenty years. Perhaps you've noticed the special wing of the medical center. Well, that was built primarily for Mrs. Jenner."

"Did they have any children?" Conroy asked as innocently as she could make it sound.

"No, and that is Dr. Jenner's greatest disappointment," Bradley answered. "There's a lot of nepotism in movements like this, and more than almost anything, he wanted to pass his work on to his own sons. But now that he has reached his mid-forties, he knows he will never have any sons by Mrs. Jenner to carry his legacy forward."

The doctor paused as if searching for words, then continued, "But we have a plan, even for that. Modern technology can work miracles, even when God lets a prophet down. One day Dr. Jenner confided to me that his greatest desire was to be like Jacob in the Old Testament—you know, the one with twelve sons.

"Well, I told him I could help, if he wanted, using modern technology. Not through his wife, of course, but through surrogate mothers. Many women in the movement would be glad to assist. They could become pregnant by artificial insemination, and we could also accomplish gender selection in advance.

"I guess my proposition surprised him, but a few months later he agreed. Then he hit me with the real kicker. If we went ahead, he said, all the eggs had to come from the same woman, a REGENCY level disciple—and she had to be a virgin."

Fat chance, Conroy thought. *How many women who find their way into the inner circle of ETR will also have that characteristic?* But as this thought fluttered off, Conroy suddenly realized she had been ambushed. She struggled, without success, to hide her reaction.

Many times in high school and college days, she'd wondered what rape might be like. Would it happen in a dark alley, or in the back seat of a car, or at gunpoint? She had prepared defenses for all the options her mind could create. But in her wildest dreams, she had never expected she could be raped by a technological procedure at the hands of a middle-aged female doctor.

"Hello, Florence. How are things tonight?" J. R. Jenner asked from his hotel room in Milwaukee.

"Mary's about the same," the doctor replied. "I wish I had a magic wand. I know every time you come home, you're hoping for improvement. But . . . the longer this goes, the more unlikely her recovery becomes."

"Will she understand how much I need her?" he asked.

"We try to manage her medication so she's at her best when you're here. But I don't want to get your hopes up too far."

"It's hard, you know, being gone so much," he replied sadly. "Just once it would be nice to return to someone. . . . Out here I'm surrounded by people, thousands of people. And everywhere I turn there's women. . . . Well, I won't go into it; we've talked about it enough already. Thanks for being a good listener. If I could only see some kind of progress, I might have a little more hope."

"Well, we *are* making progess, in another way," the doctor offered. "I was going to surprise you. I've finally found a suitable donor for the JACOB project. She's thinking it over, but I'm sure she'll cooperate when you decide it's time to go ahead. In the meantime, I'll line up twelve acceptable surrogates—nowhere near as difficult as fulfilling your criteria for RACHEL!"

8

After a sleepless night, Clare Conroy was back in the office, trying to talk her way out of Dr. Bradley's trap. "But don't you think it's playing God to just fool around with the human race in this way?" she protested.

"We are the masters of the master plan," Florence Bradley said flatly. "Technology is the mind of God breaking into human awareness. Of course," the doctor added, "you have the right to refuse—in which case I would have to bring your apparent disloyalty to Dr. Jenner's attention."

"I understand," Conroy said. "Maybe I should just go out and find a regular job."

"Anything's possible," Bradley said. "But some people here might want to know what you know about the contents of my safe before they're convinced it's prudent to let you leave. Beyond that, we wouldn't want you to experience the psychological fragmentation others have faced. For people who have committed heart and soul to the kingdom, it is usually unhealthy to dissociate from what has become the central integrating fact of their life."

Within her deepest self, Conroy felt a sense of righteous

indignation erupting. Not only for her own potential progeny, but now for herself, as well as for that woman on the video—who was, she suddenly realized, someone she did know. Even though slightly disguised, muffled, and very distraught, her voice was unmistakably that of Linda Landau.

Bradley was still talking. ". . . I'm willing to forget this whole incident if you should reaffirm your loyalty in some way. We must be certain you are a suitable candidate. Dr. Jenner will decide when it is time to proceed."

"If I am *suitable*?"

"People fool around sometimes, even people in the New World Institute. How can I advise Dr. Jenner that an appropriate provider has been found without confirming it?"

"But this whole idea is still so new to me. . . . I just don't know what to say."

"Well, then, why don't you go for a nice long ride and come back tomorrow morning—early enough so we can take care of it before anyone else is around, say six o'clock. I'm sure when you've thought it over, you'll see you've gotten yourself all worked up over nothing much at all."

Conroy's first impression upon hitting the open spaces was intense relief, as if she had just been released from prison. But as she rode toward Walton's Prairie, another image formed in her mind. *The inmate is released into a giant exercise yard surrounded by see-through walls, and unseen guards watch her every move. Now I'm into Landau's twilight zone!*

She rode along, reviewing Landau's confession and suddenly recalling what must have been the tapes' very last couple of inches—not more than a couple of seconds, where a hand reached in to cushion Landau's fall. *The bracelet! It was Bradley's. But those aren't Zs, like I always thought.*

They're broken crosses—swastikas. Landau is in the medical complex somewhere.

Conroy dismounted and headed for a rocky ledge where she liked to sit and think. She needed to sort out, as objectively as possible, the variety of issues that seemed to be converging in the RADON case.

Daddy would know what to do, she thought. But she hadn't seen him for fifteen years, since her parents' divorce. Her stepfather, Wilbur, had given her some good advice, however, when she began her studies at Yale. "Clare," he said, "you're going to face increasingly complex decisions in the next few years. And if there's anything you need to do first, it's to formulate an answer to this one question: 'On what basis do I make decisions?'"

To an eighteen-year-old, the advice had sounded archaic. Decisions, she had assumed, were just natural consequences of the situation at hand. Everybody does what they want to do, as long as no one is hurt, she had reasoned. Or if the decision affects others, you do what seems best for the greatest number.

But now, as she tried to resolve what to do about the JACOB project, and rescuing Linda Landau, and stopping Florence Bradley, and unraveling the whole ETR case, Clare Conroy suddenly realized that her guiding philosophy was impotent to help her decide. *What I would really like to do, what would feel right, would be to jump on my horse and get out of this place. Why allow myself to be violated? I'll take the information and run! But I really don't have enough hard evidence that will stand up in court. If I leave now, nobody will get this far inside again.*

Bruce had sent her in to carry out a task—one as yet uncompleted. Initiation into REGENCY might provide the missing pieces of the puzzle. *I'll jump through their hoops awhile longer,* she thought. *I'm a pretty good actress. I'll be the prophet's mouthpiece for a couple of months, without letting their propaganda affect me. And maybe, if I play it right, I can postpone the procedure long enough to take down this outfit.*

Conroy lay back on the moss-lined rocks and closed her eyes, pondering the possibilities. Before she knew it, she had fallen into a dream. She was a little white mouse in a maze, trying to find her way out. But each time she would near the exit, a hand would scoop her out of that maze and place her in another one, more complicated than the first. Finally, exhausted by her frantic but futile attempts to find a way through, she just lay down and went to sleep. Or died.

Conroy awoke with a start and sat up on the moss. She had risen to a kneeling position, preparing to stand, when an idea flashed through her mind: *Maybe I should ask God to help me.*

She paused, still on her knees, and looked up to the sky, which spread out above her like a distant turquoise canopy. Except for those last few months of her senior year at Yale, God had always seemed rather distant. Her friends in that study group had talked to God as if he had been right there in the room. And, as long as they were still around to support her, the whole thing had started to work for Clare. *I prayed that prayer. I asked you in . . . but are you still there? Are you right here, now?*

Suddenly the desire to communicate with Someone bigger than all of this had become an intense longing. Yet despite the loneliness of that moment, it seemed rather selfish to call out to a Being she had all but ignored these past few years. The only safe solution seemed to use an old standby:

"Our Father," she began, "who art in heaven. Hallowed be thy name. . . . Thy kingdom come—" Conroy almost choked on the word *kingdom.* She'd heard it so often in the past sixteen weeks, she no longer had any idea what it meant. Quickly she continued, "Thy will be done. . . ."

But who can really know what that means, either? she found herself asking. *How can anyone know it, for sure? But Dr. Jenner seems to.*

Finally, after what seemed like minutes but was really only seconds, she came to the end: "But deliver us from evil—" *Does Linda Landau pray this prayer every day? When are you going to answer? Am I your answer?* "For thine is the kingdom, and the power, and the glory, forever. Amen."

She paused, then added, *P.S. How about helping me find a way through this mess?*

As she stood up to return to her horse, Conroy looked out at Walton's Prairie, where a man and a dog were walking along the edge that led toward Miner's Pass. She'd seen them before, in the summer, as together they worked their flock away from the compound fence and back toward the higher meadows. Today, though, they seemed in no hurry—without a care in the world.

Watching them, Conroy felt a sudden impulse to cross the boundary and catch up with this shepherd, just for someone to talk to. Immediately she dismissed the thought. *Are you crazy? This whole op is classified. What could I tell him, anyway, that he would understand?* Instead, she turned, mounted her horse, and rode slowly back to the stables.

She arrived at the clinic at six the next morning.

"If my suitability is really an issue," she said to Bradley, "then I suppose there's no harm in resolving that."

"That's the spirit," Bradley affirmed. "Before long, you'll have so much on your mind that the JACOB project will be the least of your worries. No more than a minor inconvenience, when the time is right."

Conroy permitted herself an ironic chuckle. *Just think. I, the last virgin in New Haven, could become the mother of many nations if I'm not careful.*

Dr. J. Reuben Jenner watched his wife wipe the kitchen counter clean for the hundredth time that morning. Not that it needed it—their meals were specially prepared by the dining room chef, and the maid who brought the meal always cleaned up afterward.

It was part of Mary's sickness. He had learned in twenty years that there was little point in reminding her that these obsessive-compulsive actions were irrational.

Out, out damn spot, he murmured, as the anguish of Mary's unaltered debilitation sank into his sad heart again and he remembered, as he always did, the cheerful and bright college girl he had married. Together they had taken off to live in the backwoods of Michigan's Upper Peninsula, where he had accepted the call to pastor his first church. He still blamed himself for the transformation of his lovely bride, a change that had begun on their wedding night.

If only I had been more gentle . . . but how could I have been more patient? Less clumsy, maybe. But where could I have learned such things? Books? Maybe the back seat of a car. But I saved myself for marriage, and this is what I get for it!

Tears formed in his eyes as he watched Mary shuffle her way around the kitchen, wiping up nonexistent specks of dirt, rinsing the washcloth out at the sink, only to start over because she had missed a spot or, worse, because she had dirtied the counter by touching it.

Her hands were rough and red from washing and wringing, washing and wringing until she had no energy for anything else. Jenner could see it was an especially bad day for Mary, perhaps because the medication that normally kept her compulsions partly disengaged had been reduced by Dr. Bradley in view of his return home.

Jenner picked up the phone and dialed the clinic. "Dr. Bradley," he said, quietly, "I think Mary could use some *encouragement* today. . . . No," he paused, "I don't think you need to come personally. Yes, it will be fine to have Miss Conroy bring it over."

"Clare, take this to Dr. Jenner immediately. Mrs. Jenner is having a bad day. Here, use my keys," Dr. Bradley ordered.

Although Clare knew Jenner had returned, she had envisioned a different, more formal introduction to the prophet. She was rather taken aback, therefore, when an unshaven and somewhat disheveled Dr. Jenner opened the apartment's door. She tried unsuccessfully to conceal her surprise at his appearance, only to be almost as surprised by the immediate transformation in the man's expression. Clearly he recognized her, even before she could say a word.

"Why, good morning . . . Miss Conroy," Dr. Jenner said, brightly and rather warmly. "Please come in."

In the next moment, Clare noticed a woman behind Jenner, who turned to face them, as if startled but reacting in slow motion. She was dressed in a black, full-length robe and clutched in her hands a white dishrag. Except for the recent video of Landau, Conroy had never seen anyone more pathetic. There was something about her appearance—something eerie. She seemed distant—much farther away than the twelve feet that separated them.

Handing Jenner the packet, Clare looked at the woman for a moment. She could not imagine how her continuing presence in that place would serve any constructive purpose. It might even further upset Mrs. Jenner, who had locked her unblinking gaze on Clare's face.

Clare had no wish to intrude further in what was an obviously difficult situation. Beyond that, she felt a vague but compelling urge to flee this encounter. She turned to go, but Jenner said, "Miss Conroy, won't you stay for a moment? Let me introduce my wife, Mary."

"Mary, I'd like you to meet one of our recent students, Clare Conroy. In fact, dear, this is the very first time I have met her myself."

Mary Jenner wanted to believe her husband. As far as she knew, he had never lied to her. Yet later, even as the clouds of Anafranil carried her away from the anxiety of needing to perform for anyone, her suspicion returned. Clare Conroy was her enemy, masquerading as a friend; her husband's own greeting had betrayed her. Never, in their more than twenty years, had he used that tone of voice with anyone but her.

9

I'll be back in an hour—a few errands to run," Bruce Davidson said as he handed the film to chief lab technician Dana McPherson. "These are classified—my eyes only. Eight-by-tens of everything, please."

"Understood, sir," McPherson replied, slipping Conroy's microfilm into one container and Davidson's 35mm films into another and sealing both immediately. "They'll be ready."

Davidson's next stop was N. T. Michaud Jewelers, where his occasional consultant Norman Michaud expressed more than a passing interest in the topaz crystals the agent laid on the desk.

"Look here, Bruce," the appraiser said, handing Davidson the eyepiece. "See the pink? This one," he said pointing to one of the crystals, "is a particularly fine specimen. There are several superior gemstones here. Properly cut, they might be worth several thousand dollars."

"Really?" Davidson replied, examining the stones as he rotated them under the light. *Wilkes will be rich.* "What's the whole lot worth in the rough?" he inquired.

"A thousand, maybe more," Michaud replied, reaching

for the stone and eyepiece. "I'll give you that right now if it's for sale—but something tells me it's not."

"Just out prospecting," Davidson replied with a laugh, putting the stone back into his pocket. "But how about a trade? Make me a ring from the best gem, and you keep the rest."

"I'm sure we can work out something," Michaud said. "Meanwhile, should you happen to run across any more like this, I'd be happy to act as your broker."

"I'll keep it in mind, Norm, but for now . . . you never saw these, okay?"

"Of course." Michaud nodded, as Davidson got to his feet. They shook hands briefly. Then the bureau chief strode out through the shop and out to the curb, where he got back in the Bronco and headed to pick up his dog.

"Mr. Davidson! Mr. Davidson!" Jeffrey Billings ran across the front yard with Sandy right on his heels. "We taught Sandy to talk. Watch!"

"Sit," the five-year-old commanded, holding a dog biscuit as high as he could reach above the dog's head. The dog obeyed, her nub of a tail rapidly fanning the grass. "Say mama! Ma-ma. Come on, you can do it."

"Woof. Woof-woof," Sandy barked, springing high into the air as the boy tossed the biscuit up for her to catch. "Good girl," he said. "See, told you. She's a great dog, Mr. Davidson. Thanks for letting us play with her again."

"I should be thanking you," Davidson replied as he gave the boy a hug. "You take such good care of her," he said as the dog came bouncing to his side, sniffing his legs and whining happily.

"Want to go home?" he asked her, swinging open the Bronco's back door. She leaped into the back seat. But before Davidson had even closed the door, the dog was sitting in the front seat, behind the steering wheel, looking at him through the window.

"Mr. Davidson," the boy asked, "does she even know how to drive?"

"Probably thinks so," he laughed, hoisting the boy to his shoulders and heading for the front door. Fred Billings was now standing there, cup of coffee in his hand.

"Hi, boss," he said. "Good hunting?"

"Great trip," Davidson replied, setting the boy down. "Got some good snapshots. How about you?"

"The usual, but there's an interview you'll enjoy. Picked it off the TV."

"Well, bring it over."

"Tonight, before the ball game?"

"I was thinking this morning, actually. My place, soon as you can get there."

"Let's go check out the perimeter," Milo Stanton barked. "Need some action. Let's do some shooting, too. Have the boys meet us at the range at eleven. We'll have a contest. Have to think of a good prize. . . ."

"Sounds great to me, sir," Johnny Winston replied. "Just let me take a couple of calls. Chet'll have the horses ready, time we reach the stable."

"Any problems keeping a lid on things?" Stanton asked as they rode along the fence line.

"Nothing we can't handle," Winston replied.

As they rode southeast toward the prairie, they passed a number of Institute students, usually in groups of three or four, returning from their morning run. The one thing the students all had in common—besides fatigue—was their obvious respect for the security officers.

Suddenly Winston dismounted directly in the path of Christopher Townsend, a slight, pock-faced late adolescent whose main value to the Institute was his ability to fix anything electronic.

Townsend stopped running, obviously winded, and tried very hard to stand erect as Winston approached, grinning. "What's the matter, *Miss* Townsend? Can't keep up with the ladies today?"

"Why, yes, sir," Townsend replied, trying to catch his breath. "I mean, no, sir, not exactly. Some of them are in pretty good shape."

"They're *all* in better shape than you, Townsend," Winston laughed. "How can you stand to look at yourself in the mirror? Maybe you'd be in better condition if you quit playing with your gadgets for awhile."

Townsend protested, "But there are always more things to repair than I have time for . . . and the work is more important than anything else."

"Hear that, Mr. Stanton. Townsend here's always looking for ways to help. Isn't that right?" he asked Townsend.

"Yes, of course."

"Well, then, be at the shooting range at eleven, and you can help us with a little tournament. We'll let you retrieve the targets. That'll give you a little more exercise. Now get out of here and take a shower; you're stinking up the place."

"We'll have some fun with him later," Winston said to Stanton as he remounted. *That's the truth*, Stanton thought as he watched the runner disappear toward the compound buildings. *We'll have some real fun, but it won't be just at Townsend's expense. About time to see what my assistant's made of.*

As their horses ambled along the fence, Stanton congratulated Winston on the videotaped confession of Linda Landau. "Couldn't have done it better myself," Stanton said. "You write the script?"

"We made certain suggestions, and she added her own

ramblings here and there . . . actually helped us out, I thought. Bradley was involved, of course. She's been managing this case ever since we got back, you know." Stanton's nod was Winston's cue to keep going.

"Amazing what drugs and hypnotism can accomplish. She's so discombobulated, doesn't know where she is or even *who* she is. Doesn't know who I am, either, 'though I've made a few . . . *conjugal* visits. Dr. Bradley suggested it—to remind her she's good for something, even if it's only to keep me satisfied."

What kind of guy would turn in his own wife? Stanton mused, *and then use her like a prostitute?* Then he grinned. *This kid has real potential; reminds me of myself twenty years ago.*

"You mean, she doesn't even know you *then*?" he said.

"Not sure," Winston replied. "Nobody knows for sure what she's thinking, not even her. But she never says my name," he continued, "just seems like an actress going through the motions, like she's floating in outer space."

Sounds like some broads I've known, myself, Stanton thought, the most recent of which had been just a week earlier, in Chicago. One of the reasons he liked traveling with Dr. Jenner and company was his freedom. As director of security, he answered only to himself once the prophet was tucked in for the night. And this meant almost unlimited access to the things Stanton valued most in life, besides the money and power he took more or less for granted: good food, good beer, and good women.

Sometimes, though, with all the hoopla about AIDS, he wondered how wise it was to continue depending on prostitutes, escort services, and pickups. Lately, he'd been thinking of ways to convince some of the compound women that they could provide an important service to the organization by meeting the more urgent needs of one of its most valuable assets—himself.

Just then, as the two security men rounded a corner of the trail, they saw two women coming toward them on the path. Stanton quickly motioned for Winston to follow as he rode his horse back into the timber, then dismounted to wait.

"Know them?" Stanton whispered as the women approached, carrying on a spirited conversation about doings at the Institute and talking excitedly about their imminent graduation.

"Yup. Wanda Jackson, Susan Winters . . . Winters is a REGENCY candidate."

"Well, then, she's mine," Stanton replied, indicating for the first time what he had in mind just as he stood to his feet. "Hello, ladies, enjoying your little stroll?" Stanton asked.

"Why, yes, we were," Winters replied, as Jackson nodded.

"That's nice," Stanton commented, "but don't you think it's dangerous to be out here by yourselves, separated from the others like this?"

"We got a late start," Jackson answered, glancing around a little nervously.

"Maybe you'd appreciate a ride back, then?" Stanton offered. "I'm sure the horses wouldn't mind. Miss Winters, here, will ride with me," he said. "You can have the other one."

"Oh, God," Susan murmured quietly as she stood by the side of the horse, one hand on the heel of the saddlehorn. "Help me."

At that, Stanton effortlessly lifted her up onto the horse, and climbed quickly on behind her. The horse protested briefly, then settled down, as Stanton reined it around to face Winston and Jackson, who had mounted the other horse.

“You did ask for help, didn’t you?” he whispered quietly to Winters, nuzzling her neck a little with his cheek. “Well,” he said more loudly to the others, his arms around Winters, holding the reins from behind, “beautiful morning for a ride. You two go that way, and we’ll go the other. We’ll see who gets there first.”

10

Everything was ready for the shooting contest when Stanton finally arrived at the firing range. All twelve members of the security force were present, as was Christopher Townsend. Stanton shook hands with each guard, giving them all the quick check of a commander in chief and paying a little extra attention to Freddy Ricardo, the newest recruit.

Some motley crew, Stanton thought, *but better than nothing—for now. Have to get more of our people in here, though. Too much at risk. Need better equipment, too,* he thought as he looked over the small arsenal in the guardhouse. There were some AKs, a few Uzis, a couple of pounds of Semtex. *If these boys knew what that little package could do, they wouldn't come within a mile of this place.*

"Gentlemen, choose your weapons," Stanton called, choosing for himself a Remington .30-06 with a Redfield 3x9 scope and a .44 magnum handgun, equipped with an extra-long barrel, just to make a point once they got to the range.

"This competition will have three rounds," Winston announced. "First, bench-shot rifles, two hundred fifty yards.

Second, offhand rifles, a hundred yards. Third, handguns at twenty-five yards. Three shots each round. Winner totes this brand-new Smith & Wesson. Townsend here, is our volunteer gofer."

Stanton watched through the 20x spotting scope as one shooter after another grouped all three shots in the center at two hundred fifty yards. Except Ricardo, who couldn't seem to keep from flinching.

After each shooter finished, Stanton applauded, then it was his turn. *Been awhile since I shot a bolt-action,* he thought, as he waited for his heart to slow down a bit. Competition, no matter how insignificant, always got his adrenaline going.

First shot was an inch high, still in the black. Second shot hit dead center. Third . . . he stared through the rifle scope, as did Winston, watching through the more powerful spotting scope. The last shot had gone through exactly the same hole as the one just before it, a fact which even Stanton had trouble believing until he examined the target carefully himself, discovering a few telltale fibers where the third bullet had passed, a whisker higher than the previous one. *That should give 'em something to talk about!*

Winston and Stanton were dead even after round two, still perfect and each looking to prove something to the other with a handgun. At twenty-five yards they switched to silhouettes. Winston chose a .357 and shot first, aiming three shots into the heart of the man-sized target at twenty-five yards. After the third shot hit home, Winston grinned at Stanton, who was impressed, but not about to show it. He pulled out the long-barreled .44 magnum, the kind made famous by Clint Eastwood in the *Dirty Harry* movie series, and proceeded to match Winston's performance with the much more powerful weapon.

"Piece'a cake," he said with a laugh, eyeing the group to

make sure everyone noticed he wasn't shooting just an average weapon.

"Let's have a sudden-death shootoff," Stanton declared. "Townsend, here, is convinced we're both expert marksmen, isn't he?" Townsend nodded vigorously.

"So . . . Townsend will *hold* this twelve-inch target for us instead of pinning it on a backboard. If he can hold it steady enough, I'm sure there won't be any problem."

Now Stanton grinned, looking first at Winston, who seemed to turn a bit pale, and then to Townsend, who looked about to cry. "Townsend, we haven't even missed the bullseye yet today. You're not worried, are you?"

"No, sir. I mean, yes, sir. What I really mean is that I'm sure you could do it, but I wouldn't want to find out by personal experience."

Stanton looked at Winston, "Ready to concede?"

"Course not. You do it, I'll do it."

"Okay. Townsend. Grab a target and get out there. Try to hold still. They say you never hear the shot that kills you, anyway. And try not to pee your pants, huh?" Stanton laughed as the young man walked out to a distance of twenty-five yards, steadying himself against the upright of the backboard they had been using to hold the targets.

"Now, Townsend," Stanton chided, "if you want me to shoot and get this little game over with, you'll have to hold still for a couple of seconds." Townsend nodded, tears beginning to flow. Just as his arms tensed enough to hold the target steady for no more than a half-second, the .44 roared again. A hole appeared in the target, very close to its center.

Townsend started to cry in earnest now, dropping the target and covering his ears with his hands, his face on his knees as he slowly slid down the upright to the ground. Stanton was the only other person there who knew what the auditory trauma of a .44 was like at twenty-five yards. There was no way Townsend would be able to continue.

"Winston," he said, "the target seems to be beyond repair."

"Then we'll have a rematch some other time," Winston replied, relief showing in his voice and face.

"Agreed," Stanton said. "Look forward to it." The others cheered loudly. They headed into the security building for lunch.

"What do you think?" Davidson asked as Billings looked over his shoulder at the eight-by-tens spread out all over the floor of the den.

"How'd you get so close, and almost overhead?" Billings commented. "Thought their security was tight."

"Didn't get the nickname Ninja in Nam for nothing," Davidson replied. "But take a good look at this series here." He pointed to the photos of fifty-five-gallon drums being unloaded.

"Why would ETR be getting a major shipment of hydrochloric acid?" Billings asked.

"Drums mismarked, maybe. But for the moment, let's assume they're marked properly. Any theories?"

"Well," Billings mused, "I suppose this location could serve as a transfer station for cross-country hauling. But why would any company spend the extra bucks to haul their stuff up into the mountains and then back down again when there are plenty of stations down below?"

"What if they're hauling contraband? Would that justify the extra expense?"

"Perhaps," Billings answered. "But there are more clandestine warehouses along the front range than we can keep track of. Why bother?"

"Good question," Davidson said, "and the only good answer is that whatever's in there is extremely valuable."

"As in cocaine?"

Davidson nodded.

"As in Miami, couple of years ago?"

Again, Davidson nodded. "That was five-point-five tons," Davidson said. "And at twenty thousand bucks-plus per kilo, driving a few extra miles might be worth the effort, especially if you can store it in the relative safety of a secluded religious compound."

"Well, it would be easy enough to find out what's in there," Billings said. "There can't be too many roads to stake out. We could just wait until they try to ship the stuff and then nab the whole bunch."

"Not yet. We watch these guys awhile, we might catch some really big fish," Davidson said. "Let's be creative," he continued, "and use all the gadgets the boys can work into it. There's a small filling station at the bottom of the exit road that just might be for sale. *Anything's for sale at the right price.* Make a nice observation post.

"Code name is XRAY. I want to know about everything moving into and out of the New World Institute compound, including electronic data."

"I'll get right on it," Billings replied. "But we'll have to bring in a few more guys. Stevenson and a couple others okay with you?"

"Fine, but keep it as small as possible," Davidson replied, flipping open a file on the coffee table. He shoved the file toward Billings as he continued. "This guy here is Victor Francisco, forty-six. Former CPA. Charged with mail fraud but acquitted on lack of evidence in 1982, when the chief government witness died of an apparent heart attack. A year later Francisco dropped from view after making several trips to Colombia. Before today, it was suspected he was either deceased or possibly working with the Cartel. That's what I mean by big fish.

"But now we know where you've been," Davidson said, holding the photo at arm's length as he talked to it. "What we don't know yet is what you've been doing, Francisco, though we're pretty sure that whatever it is, it isn't good. Talk about a wolf in the sheep's pen!"

"My turn for show and tell?" Billings asked.

Davidson nodded, pouring himself a beer as Billings punched the remote to start the video from ETR's midwest tour. Running it mostly on high speed, Billings stopped the tape occasionally to show Davidson a particular face in the crowd or perhaps to highlight some portion of Jenner's presentation.

"What I really want you to see is this, though," he said when the TV interview segment finally appeared on the screen. "Just happened to be watching," he commented as the reporter's questions began.

"There . . . hear that?" Billings said, excitedly. "Jenner's going off the deep end."

"Give me that thing!" Davidson hissed, grabbing for the remote control as he stared at the screen.

"Sure, boss," Billings replied. "Don't you think he's . . ."

Davidson hit the stop button, ran the tape backward, and then froze the frame, checking to be sure his first impression had been accurate.

"Billings, what do you see?"

The agent leaned forward, "A beautiful TV reporter interviewing a self-declared prophet on what was originally a live news broadcast?" he offered.

"Look behind Jenner, in the shadows. See that face? Lock it in your 'most wanted' memory file."

"I think I've seen him before, but I'm sorry, Chief, I don't recall the name."

"George Perelli—hit man, explosives expert. Does that do anything to your insides?"

"Yes sir, but obviously not what it does to yours," Billings responded apologetically.

"I followed him once, for months, but I couldn't nail him," Davidson said flatly as he kept rerunning the short segment. Even without the seventies-style beard, Davidson would never forget this man's eyes—dark, penetrating, cold, murderous. *I'd give anything to see you fry.*

From his demeanor and his position in relation to Jenner, it was obvious that Perelli was serving as a bodyguard for the evangelist.

But why would Dr. J. Reuben Jenner, friend of the fatherless, need a bodyguard? *Why does the pope need a bodyguard?* Davidson reminded himself. But even if Jenner did need a bodyguard, how could it be Perelli, a regular employee of certain New York concerns specializing in *producing* orphans?

If Perelli was connected to ETR, the New World Institute was not a safe assignment for anyone, especially a novice like Clare. It would be nice to nab Perelli, but was that worth the risk of leaving her in there? *If anything ever happened to her . . .*

This was the kind of dilemma Davidson most disliked in espionage. To unravel larger cases, certain risks were necessary. And taking those risks could jeopardize a carefully constructed cover or even an agent's life.

The Israelis have it right. Swoop in, grab the bad guys, and get it over with, like a bird of prey grabbing its lunch.

Suddenly Davidson remembered a particular titanic battle he had witnessed between a bald eagle and a large muskellunge that had picked just the wrong place in North Fork Lake to surface that afternoon. Sitting on his cabin's porch, Davidson had watched the eagle dive, expecting it to rise from the water with a nice bass or something much smaller than a twenty-pound muskie. For what seemed like hours, but must have been minutes, the two had battled it out, the eagle just able to raise the fish out of the water a few feet before losing altitude again and splashing into the water. The eagle wouldn't let go. And the muskie, when it hit the water, would dive for the security of the weeds.

It had been a magnificent battle between the king of the sky and the king of the deep, but in the end they had both died. *That's the way such struggles usually finish. Nobody ever wins it clean.*

11

"Mr. Worthy, I fished all night, and look what I caught." Adam Putnam handed the comptroller a disk and a printout of file names. "You know, sir," Putnam added, "it's hard to believe you operated this mainframe without a secondary power supply all that time. Amazing you didn't lose more during that storm."

Worthy examined the printout carefully, then looked at the twenty-two-year-old computer expert. "You're a genius, kid. How'd we ever get along without you? Debugged almost the whole database in just four months. Remarkable."

"Will those numbers be helpful for the annual report?" Putnam queried. "Or should I keep looking?"

"Close enough for our purposes—that's for sure. Now, why don't you get a shower and some breakfast. You look awful."

Worthy took the papers into his office and closed the door. Quickly booting his workstation, the comptroller scrolled through the files on the disk supplied by Putnam.

Good, he muttered. *Very good.* Putnam had, indeed, found some irreplaceable data lost because of a power outage in July.

Retrieving the files one by one, Worthy renamed and then disguised them, incorporating portions into a draft of the annual financial report due on Dr. Jenner's desk in one hour.

At precisely 2:00 P.M., James Worthy handed the report to Dr. Jenner, then stepped back as the movement's leader scanned its pages.

"But, James," Jenner said finally, his distress obvious, "I don't understand. How can we be falling behind when every place we go, the halls are packed and the offerings are wonderful?"

"Dr. Jenner," Worthy replied, "the ministry *is* moving ahead, and it is remarkably healthy, in some ways. The orphanages are holding their own despite spiraling inflation in some of the countries involved. For the first time in the history of the movement, the orphanages are not draining the ministry."

"That's certainly good news," Jenner said. "Any explanation?"

"Cost-controlling measures, perhaps. But more important, these projects have attracted rather generous patronage in recent months. The ads in *Time* and *Newsweek* are helping, no doubt. If I had any advice about this aspect of the movement, I'd suggest we pursue our invitations to establish homes elsewhere—Peru, Brazil, Colombia, for instance.

"The Institute pays its own way," Worthy continued, "and the Media Center should be completed in another month or so. Also, there is a steady increase in inquiries and income from around the world. But . . . that's the end of the good news, I'm afraid. The cost of media time and space connected with the crusades is skyrocketing, and we have fallen behind in that area. And the biggest problem is our delinquency in repaying the original mortgage to Eagle Corporation. *Who can keep up with an annual 1 percent interest rate increase? Might as well hand over the checkbook.*

"So I've arranged a small bridge loan, and the company has agreed to continue furnishing my services to you at no cost until you no longer need me."

"You're a real godsend, that's for sure," Jenner said, "and I hope you can stay until we get this all sorted out. You know how I hate numbers and details. Any other suggestions?"

"Well, yes. Our main challenge is how to continue expanding the ministry's visibility without going broke buying media time. Production costs are high, too, when we have to work with outside firms. The media project is still the best long-range solution to the challenge of expanding our impact while containing costs.

"The first phase will give us the capability to mass-produce professional-quality videotapes at a rate of ten thousand per month. This is more than we need at present, but if we expand our program to include more instructional and inspirational programs, I'm confident the demand will eventually surpass the supply.

"As you know, Dr. Jenner, everywhere you go, even in the poorest Third-World areas, people have VCRs and TVs. This represents a vast new market, and would certainly take your message to people in the most remote places."

Worthy knew that Jenner could not resist the idea of his face, bigger than life, appearing on the TV screens of millions of unreached people.

"I like that," Jenner said. "It will mean more work for me, but I have been thinking about a series on prophecy."

Of course, Jenner, since I suggested it a year ago. "It can't happen too soon," Worthy said. "Meanwhile, with your permission, I'd like to subcontract the use of our new equipment—as soon as it's up and running and until we need the entire capacity ourselves. If we do that, phase one will soon be completely self-supporting. In fact, the revenues we receive will more than pay for our own production costs, so what was costing us before will now be profitable instead."

"Good planning, James."

"Thank you, sir, but let's not forget the biggest plan of all. . . ."

Worthy smiled at the responsive gleam in Jenner's eye as he continued: "Just imagine. To transmit our programs worldwide by satellite . . . perhaps even from here."

After his meeting with Worthy, J. R. Jenner returned to his apartment by way of the fountain. Today the bronze figures at its center seemed more real than ever before. He followed his own finger, pointing toward that universe of truth his work was bringing to the world. We can reach the whole world from this one mountaintop! The thought was exhilarating.

But then, as he gazed upon the young boy holding the statue's other hand, the hurt returned. *If only it were my own son,* he thought. *If only it were Mary's son, too.*

Opening the door of the apartment, Jenner was hoping against hope, but he knew what he would find: Mary straightening the furniture, exactly as she had been doing since breakfast.

"Mary," he said when his expectation was confirmed, "it doesn't matter if the corners aren't straight; you know that."

"I know. I know. But it feels better to get it right," Mary Jenner replied as she adjusted the coffee table in the living room again, then stepped back to see if it was lined up with the walls and the doorway at the other end of the room.

"Let me help you, then," he said. "Stand there and tell me where to put this one." He got down on his knees next to the table, waiting for her to tell him when to stop moving it.

"There? Is it perfect now?" he asked.

"Yes," she said. "It's perfect now. Of course it is; you put it there."

How can she stand it? All day she's been lining up the tables in the living room. It would drive me crazy! Turning away sadly, Jenner headed into the bathroom to ready himself for that evening's initiation. Even as he shaved, however, in the mirror he saw Mary move the same table a little bit more and then disappear around the corner into the kitchen. In a moment she returned, with a rag, and started to wipe everything down.

"Someday," he asked her as he tied his tie, "wouldn't you like to attend one of these ceremonies with me? Just once? These are our top people. It's exciting. I wish you could share it with me."

"I'm sorry," she replied without emotion. "I don't think I can help you. I never did help you. But I'm glad you're such a great success."

Clare Conroy was seated at one of six round tables that circled the oak-paneled hall, each lit by a crystal chandelier. Matching chandeliers sparkled over the head table, and a white floral centerpiece accented every sky-blue tablecloth. Susan Winters sat on Conroy's left; Adam Putnam on her right. Across the table, Christopher Townsend shifted nervously.

"My little children, ours is the kingdom," Dr. J. R. Jenner announced as he began the initiation address. "We are the chosen race, cornerstones of the new world order."

Immediately, the twenty-four REGENCY candidates applauded. They had worked and studied very hard to reach this level in ETR, and now their leader had come to supervise their initiation personally.

Conroy glanced at Winters as Dr. Jenner continued his speech. Normally a calm person, Susan was fidgeting nonstop with the napkin in her lap. Something was obviously very wrong. Reaching into her evening bag for a pencil, Conroy scribbled a note and handed it to Susan: "Can we talk later?" Susan nodded, her eyes welling with tears. *Maybe she's feeling overwhelmed with the significance of this weekend.*

A specially engraved ring in a gold-embroidered box had been placed on the banquet table before each candidate. Conroy focused on her ring, which had a simple design, much like a wedding band. Embedded in its center was a single opal surrounded by sapphires.

"Many are called, but few are chosen," Jenner proclaimed. The applause started up again, not loud and boisterous, but more than simply polite. Clare looked around the room at the other candidates. Each had entered ETR at the same time she had, as part of a much larger group. Each had evidently evidenced a special talent or perhaps a deeper loyalty than the rest—something to merit initiation into this select organization. *Or maybe they've all been snared like little rabbits, each one falling into a uniquely designed trap.*

She studied her comrades' faces as Jenner delivered his address. All seemed to be listening in rapt attention . . . except Winters and Townsend. And then Clare also noticed a certain tension in Adam Putnam, who sat with clenched fists and tight lips, staring intently at Jenner.

"We are the REGENTS. Organized religion has failed. The harlot is dying. The great renewal has begun. We will achieve what even Jesus could not—because he was frustrated by the limitations of his day, especially poor communications and transportation. He only reached a small group of people in a small region of the globe, but today we can reach millions at a time. In fact, the capabilities already exist to reach every person alive on the face of this planet at the very same instant. Technologies are the key. We thank God for technologies."

Adam Putnam put his hands on the table as if to push himself upright. Clare turned, surprised, at the movement. Quickly Putnam sat back down. He tried to make it seem that he was just shifting his position. But Clare had seen the panic in his eyes.

What gives with this guy? He's about to freak out.

"Down with organized religion," one of the women shouted. "Down with organized religion," the chorus of voices responded. "Up with REGENCY. REGENCY. REGENCY!"

Jenner seemed to enjoy the enthusiasm. He waved and smiled as the outburst dissolved into a standing ovation.

So, I suppose this particular version is dis-organized? Conroy thought as she stood, applauding with the others and looking around the room. As far as she could see, the only less than exuberant disciples were to be found at her table. *Must be contagious or something,* she thought, trying her best to make up for the others with her own display of devotion.

"For you, today marks an end to the old and a new beginning as you join the leadership core of this movement. You will take our word to the four corners of the globe. None of us knows in advance how this will work out. But in the past few years, some of our initiates have secured positions in business, education, media, politics, finance, publishing, law, medicine, religion, science and technology, even intelligence."

What? Conroy protested internally. Now she became more intensely focused on Jenner, intrigued with this strategy. In a way it was amusing to hear Jenner talk about wanting to penetrate the intelligence community, when she had already succeeded in infiltrating ETR. Maybe she should volunteer for that assignment, too, and become a double agent!

But her gloating was short-lived. *What if they already have people inside the Bureau?*

Again Conroy glanced around the room, this time a little more carefully. All eyes seemed focused on Jenner except for one person at the head table. Director of Security Milo Stanton was scrutinizing everyone present, one by one. For a moment their eyes met, and Clare had the impression of staring into the eyes of a timber wolf on the prowl.

"Some of you have requested marriage. And we have helped you in this regard because it is not good for a man or woman to be alone, except by choice. May you be fruitful and multiply and replenish the earth with children who are raised in the nurture and instruction of the truth. Perhaps, if it be the will of God, you may even be privileged to produce leaders for the days to come."

Why not tell them all they have to do is sacrifice their firstborn sons? Clare thought.

"Those who have chosen celibacy, as I have, can pursue the master plan more energetically than if we had the added cares of home and family."

Some celibate. What about Mrs. Jenner?

"Yet even we who remain single will also repeat the vows, for today we join our spirits in a mystical union that cannot be undone on this earth. All for one, and one for all, and everyone has everything in common.

"So, my friends, with these things in mind, we reaffirm our purpose and complete your initiation into REGENCY. Choose ye this day whom you will serve."

In one voice all in the room responded, "We will serve the King. We will build the kingdom." Everyone, that is, except for Adam Putnam, but there was so much noise, Clare couldn't be sure.

"Good. Now for the ceremony itself. The ring before you is a symbol of eternity, a symbol of unity and, in our case, *community.* As it never ends, the covenant we make this day before God and with ourselves as witnesses is unending. It is binding on earth, for it is made in heaven and sealed in blood.

"Do you now solemnly covenant before God, and with each other as witnesses, to faithfully serve the kingdom for better and for worse, in sickness and in health, to love and to cherish, 'till death us do part?"

"We do."

"Then repeat after me: Thy kingdom come, thy will be done on earth as it is in heaven."

"Thy kingdom come, thy will be done on earth as it is in heaven."

"As you place the ring on your finger, you will notice that inscribed inside the band is a name—a new name to symbolize your new beginning. For it is written, 'I will give him a white stone with a new name written on it.'"

Along with everyone in the room, Clare looked for the inscription. *Rachel. Interesting choice. I can live with that.*

"To establish this new covenant, we will take the cup, which is also on the table before you. It is a new covenant in our own blood, for it is wine mixed with one drop of blood from each person in this room, thanks to the blood bank at our medical center. It symbolizes the uniting of our lives forever."

He placed the cup to his lips and drank, as did all the others in the room, again with one exception. Adam Putnam just looked as if he were about to be sick.

But Clare didn't have much time to think about Putnam, because almost immediately Dr. Jenner was introducing two new appointees to the Central Committee. Clare, now named Rachel, Conroy, would begin serving immediately as administrative assistant to Dr. Jenner. Her fluency in Spanish, German, French, Russian and Japanese would make her an invaluable help in public relations. Adam, now Thomas Putnam, who had already proven invaluable in organizing the computer center, would now officially assume the role of director of data processing.

12

Bruce Davidson took the parabolic dish from Billings. "With this we can hear through windows?" he asked.

"Elementary, Chief," Billings laughed. "Picks up vibrations from the glass—even noises as small as keyboard clicks. Every key has a distinctive sound; did you know that? Runs into this recorder. Battery operated; the transmitter is encrypted."

"Nice unit," Davidson commented, folding the lightweight instrument back into its case. And the Christmas tree?"

"Look closer."

"Antenna? Perfect!" he said. "And was that little gas station for sale?"

"Had to go a little higher than expected. But like you said, anything's for sale," Billings replied. "Just don't go asking us to turn a profit. Fact, right now the place is closed for renovations. We'll pump gas again as soon as the phones are hooked up."

After the initiation reception, Clare found Susan Winters outside in the shadows.

"Does he treat you well, Clare?" Winters asked, getting right to the point.

"I'm not sure what you mean by *he*," Conroy replied. "But like you said the other day, I've gained certain privileges. . . ."

"I'm glad for you, personally," Winters said, hesitating, "but what I meant was—and I don't mean to pry, but after all we were good friends. . . ."

"*Are* good friends," Clare interrupted.

"Is he—I mean, is your new relationship with him . . . Dr. Jenner . . . more than purely professional?"

Interesting question, Clare thought as she tried to formulate a truthful response. *How shall I tell Susan I may become the mother of the prophet's children while technically still a virgin? Who'd believe that one? They probably all figure we've been melding much more than our minds.*

"You know me better than that, Sue," Conroy said, perhaps a little too defensively. "After all our intimate late night conversations you must know it would take a firing squad or worse to force me into bed—even the bed of someone like Dr. Jenner."

She paused, studying Sue's reaction closely. "Is that what you think . . . what everyone thinks? That I've slept my way up the ladder of success with the End Times Renewal movement? This isn't Hollywood, after all. It's a religious group, and Dr. Jenner is an honorable man." *Yes, Julius, they were all, all honorable men.*

"But he said that's the way things are in REGENCY, one of the unwritten rules, and he used you and Dr. Jenner as an example."

"Who would say such a crazy thing?" Clare snapped.

"Milo Stanton. The other day when Wanda and I were out walking, he and Johnny Winston met us out along the fence line and, well, they each took one of us off into the bushes and . . ."

Susan Winters started to cry as Conroy watched. At first mystified, then horrified, and finally infuriated, she held her friend until she had no more tears to cry.

God, I don't know what to do. I don't know what to say. Help! Clare prayed. But as soon as she had expressed her frustration in not knowing how to proceed, Conroy realized that perhaps crying until you are cried out might not be all that bad. *Maybe I should have done that, myself, after Daddy left*, she thought, as she waited for Winters to regain control.

"Can you tell me about it?" Clare asked gently.

"Yes, I suppose. I need to, actually . . . but I thought you already knew. In fact . . ." She looked at Clare for a long moment before risking her next words. ". . . I even thought you were part of it, somehow. I'm sorry. Can you forgive me?"

"Of course." . . . But what can you mean? How could *I* be a part of it?

"There are so many boundaries here, Clare. When you stepped over them, I didn't know how to relate to you anymore."

"When Stanton assaulted you, didn't you think he was abusing his boundaries, regardless of his position?"

"Well, yes . . . it did occur to me, in a way," Winters began, and then her voice trailed off to silence as she pondered how to describe what had happened. "I did object, at first. But he seemed so forceful, menacing even—like if I didn't give him what he wanted, something even worse might happen."

"Did he strike you or use force in any other way?"

"How can I answer that? There is something very scary about Stanton, a kind of power he had over me. Do you remember the power of Darth Vader in those Star Wars movies?" When Clare nodded, Winters continued, "Well, it was something like that—sinister and subtle, but very strong.

And for some strange reason, I really did not have the ability to resist him. When I reached for it, it . . . just wasn't there."

Even as she spoke, Clare could see a change in Susan, a withdrawal into herself. Conroy felt a wrenching sense of recognition. Many times, as an adolescent, she had retreated like that, trying desperately to find some safe place within herself, but never really quite succeeding. An odd thought ran through her mind: *Maybe the safest place isn't within me.*

But there was a major difference between herself and Susan. Naked terror had shown itself in Susan's eyes for a fleeting instant, only to be replaced by a distant tranquility.

Clare fought the urge to shout, "Come back, come back!" Instead, she asked quietly, "Susan . . . can I help you?"

"You always help me, Clare," Susan murmured tonelessly. "We are REGENCY. We are one."

Oh, God, Clare thought, *what has happened to this woman? This is not a Psych 501, but a real person—flesh and blood, Susan Winters, my friend who just fell off the deep end. . . .* And then, horrified, she observed, . . . *partly because she thought Jenner and I have been playing around. One thing's for sure. I'm going to give that animal Stanton a piece of my mind he won't easily forget.*

You are such a fool, Adam Putnam accused himself as he waited for the mainframe to boot. *How could you trade your heritage for a little recognition? For a cult. And you didn't even know it. So busy trying to be somebody. Just a stupid hacker, that's all. Just like always.*

Ever since he was a kid, Adam had loved computers—not just to play with, but to relate to. By sixth grade he had outgrown games. To him it wasn't enough to manipulate figures on the screen. He wanted to rewrite the files and redesign whatever life-and-death struggle was occurring on the monitor.

Putnam had also been a born-again, Bible-believing, baptized and confirmed, second-generation Pentecostal who'd been raised on Bible stories and Sunday school. Since infancy, he had sung the songs, talked the talk, and jumped through all the hoops required to demonstrate his faith.

But in late adolescence, his love for computers had overwhelmed every other concern—sports, girls, academics, even God. He lived and breathed data, programming, communications. And eventually he got into trouble for breaking into the files of the Mitre Corporation, a major Pentagon supplier. The orders he changed had only been worth a few million dollars, but the military took a much more serious view of the prank than he did. Given the choice between jail and working for the Pentagon, he'd gladly chosen the latter, serving there three years.

And after that he had just drifted, until the day he heard Dr. Jenner at a rally in Cleveland. He was accepted for the Institute almost as soon as he sent in the application. He didn't even have to pay the five-thousand-dollar fee like the rest. ETR was desperate for somebody who truly knew computers. Almost since his arrival, Putnam worked twelve hours a day trying to help the organization catch up to its own growth. And because of his work, he had been excused from the studies required of the others.

But now, as he began to follow some electronic rabbit trails, looking for clues to confirm his suspicions, Adam Putnam's mind also focused on certain debates of his youth, debates that had suddenly taken on a new significance as a result of his participation in the REGENCY initiation earlier that night. Specifically, he wondered if and how a person can lose his salvation.

Dear God, he prayed silently, *Can you forgive me? Have*

I committed the unpardonable sin? Is it too late? I hope not! Please don't let it be too late.

Tearfully, contritely, he continued the search throughout the night. When James Worthy arrived at the data center the next morning, Putnam handed him another stack of printouts.

"I think you'll find these interesting," the young man said.

"You look terrible," Worthy said, taking the papers rather perfunctorily from Putnam's hand. "Another all-nighter?"

Putnam nodded as Worthy poured himself a coffee, then motioned for the newly appointed director of data processing to follow him into the inner office.

"But I thought all the reports were in," Worthy continued. "The annual staff meeting is only three hours from now." Then the comptroller looked more closely at the printouts, which to most people might appear to be random data pulled from a variety of files.

From the change in Worthy's face, Putnam was sure he'd found what he wanted—the files Worthy had tried so hard to conceal, plus others even more incriminating.

"Need to study this material some other time," Worthy said, looking across the desk at Putnam. "Too pressed today, with the meeting and all, but maybe next week we could get back to it." He paused, then continued, "Is there any particular significance to these random numbers? Putnam, sometimes you seem to fixate on certain issues and end up sacrificing your effectiveness. Today, for instance, when we need you to be at your sharpest for the meeting, you've stayed up all night pursuing who knows what."

"But sir, shouldn't Dr. Jenner know about these figures? I mean . . . several large cash reserves not shown in our annual report, enough perhaps to offset our rather sizable deficit!" Putnam replied.

"The deficit isn't that substantial for an organization this size," Worthy mumbled, as if studying the numbers with renewed interest. "A few hundred thousand dollars is minimal at the rate we've been growing."

"True," Putnam parried, "especially if we have several million dollars stashed away somewhere that hasn't been showing on the books for awhile."

Quickly Worthy flipped through the pages. Then, looking directly at Putnam, he said in a most virtuous voice, "Millions? Now that would be quite a fortunate, but highly unlikely, discovery. I don't see anything here of that magnitude. Are you sure? We wouldn't want to give an unrealistically optimistic report, either."

Putnam smiled, "Just a rough estimate. Call it a subconscious computation of my internal calculator!"

"Putnam," Worthy replied, using his most official accountant's tone, "I'm not quite ready to risk my credibility as the chief financial officer of an international organization on mere conjecture—not when I have a professionally audited report already prepared." He paused, then added, "But let me thank you in advance, in case your persistence pays off. Why don't we return to this when the team is in the field again and we can really pursue it without distraction?"

He smiled benevolently, but tightly as he stood up, extending his hand to Putnam. "Now,.I suggest you get cleaned up before the staff meeting."

Putnam smiled, too, as he accepted the comptroller's compliment, and then turned to go. He was all but positive his strategy would work. It had to—not so much for spite as for the redemption of his eternal soul.

13

Milo Stanton finished bolting the door of the storage sheds, ignoring the voice of Clare Conroy behind him. He had just inspected the recent shipment, and he wanted to be sure no one paid any special attention to those barrels.

"I'm sorry," he said as he turned around, "I didn't quite hear what you said."

"I was just commenting on how hard it is to find you sometimes. What if we had a real emergency?"

Feigning a friendly smile, Stanton replied, "Why not use the radio?"

"What I want to discuss, you might want to keep private," she said, not bothering to dismount from her horse.

"Really?" Stanton said, only thinly disguising the mockery in his tone. "Then maybe I should thank you for keeping it our little secret! Can we get to the point?"

"The point is, several compound women were raped recently while on the jogging trail," Conroy began, watching his face intently.

"That's interesting," Stanton commented dryly without even a flinch. "We haven't heard about anything like that, though I suppose with all the hunters snooping around lately, something like that could easily happen. That's why we need to build a bigger fence. . . ."

"Some fences are built to keep people inside. Remember the Iron Curtain? Anyway, I don't know how many other Institute women you have brutalized, but your mistake this time was choosing victims who were my quadmates until very recently. In fact, Susan Winters was my roommate, and I care about her very much."

"She seemed to like it well enough," Stanton replied, now that he knew there was no evading Conroy. "Did she say she was raped?"

"Not exactly, but it was clear enough that she was raped."

"Now, Conroy," Stanton said, "Susan Winters is smart enough to know whether or not she was raped, don't you think?" Then with a sardonic smirk he added, "It's the old pot calling the kettle black routine, hearing this from you."

"Oh, really?" she responded. "What could you mean by that?"

"Well, if you think there are many secrets here, you got another think coming," Stanton replied with a loud guffaw. "We know everything you do and everywhere you go. We know you have visited the private quarters of Dr. Jenner. How else would you get to be his personal assistant? What do you take us for, anyway?"

Conroy was obviously uncomfortable, so Stanton pressed his advantage, just to be sure this woman half his size would think twice before tangling with him again. "Besides, Dr. Bradley tells me you and Dr. Jenner are involved with a reproductive project. Isn't it time to come down from your virtuous ivory tower and join the rest of us sinners?"

"I have never been to bed with Dr. Jenner, if it's any of your business," Clare declared. "And that particular project is confidential."

Conroy nudged the horse, gently tugging its reins to the left as she reponded carefully, "I suggest you leave my friend Susan alone, or this whole conversation, including your allegations about Dr. Jenner, will become an immediate matter of private conversation between him and me."

As Conroy turned and slowly rode away, Stanton fought to keep himself from ripping her off that horse to show her who was really in control of this compound. Not that this woman was much of a threat; she'd been stupid enough to fall into the trap set by Bradley and Jenner. And anyone who kept Jenner's attention diverted from the gold mine right under his nose was an ally, whether she knew it or not. *But when he's done with her, this little lady and me will have a one-night stand.*

James Worthy was waiting in Stanton's office when the security chief returned from checking on the shipment.

"We've had a little problem, something you should know about," Worthy said, handing Stanton the printouts. "Putnam—like a hound after a rabbit. Asked him to unscramble the data, and he hands me this."

Stanton took the papers, glanced at them briefly, then stated flatly, "Kid's a genius. Said so yourself, many times. Lots of numbers, but any real damage?" he asked, finally, placing the files on the desk.

"Not exactly," Worthy answered, dropping the papers into the shredder. "I've already renamed these and erased the originals. Best I can figure, the problem occurred during the power outage last summer. Computers can be temperamental when it comes to lightning. We're protected now with the backups we've installed, so it won't happen again."

"I hope not," Stanton said in a disapproving tone that Worthy clearly understood. "But just out of curiosity, what kind of money are we talking?"

"Well . . ." Worthy paused. "That depends . . . shall we say, on how you look at things."

"Well, the way I look at things," Stanton responded, "is that partners sometimes have to cover for one another. I mean, if we don't look out for one another, who will? It wouldn't be *healthy* to have our employers think their funds are being mismanaged."

"True," Worthy replied, "and we certainly wouldn't want them to think our security has been compromised."

"Agreed," Stanton said. "And the only way we can achieve both is to keep each other better informed."

Worthy hesitated, then nodded and said, "After what happened to Gonzales in 1989, losing fifty-four million in assets overnight to DEA, and then the BCCI fiasco, good laundries have become very valuable. This one's perfect—loan ETR a few million, collect it back with substantial interest. But the most creative idea was yours: Collect street money through rallies instead of taking it out and then back into the U.S. clean. . . ."

No lie, pal. Best idea I ever had. Nobody knows how much comes in, nobody knows how much is missing.

"So . . . how much are we talking?" Stanton pressed.

"Bottom line . . . after mortgage and interest to Eagle Corporation . . . in just the past twelve months we've put more than ten million in safe places through the local branch of Settler's Bank."

"And who would know," Stanton asked, leaning toward Worthy and lowering his voice, "if ten million came in but only nine made it to Switzerland, or wherever it's going?"

"People have been killed for a lot less than that," Worthy replied. "Our employers wouldn't like it if. . . ."

"*I've* killed for less than that," Stanton replied evenly. Worthy's mouth dropped open just a little. Stanton continued, "I'm sure we can be creative. But . . ." Stanton paused.

". . . if Putnam is in the way, maybe he should be planted somewhere."

"Birds like him are pretty rare. Losing him could set us back six months, maybe more, and that's if the mainframe didn't crash while we were looking."

"Well, then, suppose we make him *responsible* for safeguarding our records," Stanton said with a wink. "Tell him someone is trying to sabotage the movement and we're depending on him to keep our databank safe?"

"Perfect," Worthy said. "He already treats the computer like it's his girlfriend, so we'll let him defend its virtue. Then we could hold him responsible if anything goes wrong."

"Exactly my meaning," Stanton replied. "The kid is fishbait once he's dispensable. But I don't need to remind you who else will be held responsible if things go wrong." He paused, then added with a crooked little smile, "And if things go well, we'll get the credit . . . or even if things just *seem* to be going well."

Clare Conroy's brain had absorbed as many facts about the rapidly expanding ministries of ETR as her posterior would allow. All morning the Central Committee had been meeting. The executive conference room was comfortable enough and handsome as well—paneled in solid cherry, with a matching table three inches thick and a leather upholstered chair for each member of the committee. And the information she had gathered in that one session more than made up for the sacrifices required of her so far.

"Dr. Bradley will give us a medical update," J. R. Jenner was saying, "and then we'll break for lunch."

"With pleasure, sir," the doctor answered. "Since our last meeting, we've not had any major disease problems. Just the normal complaints of basically healthy people and a few minor injuries among the construction workers.

"In terms of special projects, after a brief suspension, the HANNAH program has resumed, but with increased selectivity in terms of participants. We will screen volunteers more carefully, to select out people who may not be able to handle the program's special stresses."

Stresses is something of an understatement, don't you think, Clare thought, *for giving up one's baby?*

"A second program aimed at producing leaders for the twenty-first century is ready to begin. This one, known as JACOB, is also highly confidential and has been on hold until only recently, while we searched for appropriate volunteers.

Conroy stared at Bradley, who simply smiled knowingly. Then she looked at Jenner. His blue eyes met hers only briefly, but long enough to see that he approved of Bradley's selection. *How long can I hold them off?*

Bradley continued, "In these leadership projects, we will utilize the latest technologies while anticipating future possibilities as well. Each HANNAH unit has been sent out with a special subcutaneous electronic device already operating. This device, located just behind the earlobe, will receive transmissions perceived as an internal voice. Dr. Jenner will be able to address them all, simultaneously, wherever they are.

The device's transmitter will allow us to locate any units at any time or place on the globe using highly sensitive satellites. By the time we need to do this, our people will have reached positions within NASA, the military, and various intelligence agencies, where they can easily access whatever systems are needed."

Conroy had by now forgotten both her fatigue and her hunger. *Some plan! Human robots, controlled and directed by a voice from the heavens. God . . . do you know you're about to be replaced? Have you ever dealt with wackos like this before? If so, I'm open to suggestions about how to shut down this plan before it's too late.*

It might be entertaining to find this plot in a novel or movie. But hearing it in person from the mouth of an apparently rational physician left Conroy with an unsettling mixture of indignation and horror. The agent already knew enough not to disregard this doctor's deleterious schemes or to doubt her ability to carry them out. Not only that, this plan meshed a little too perfectly with the doctrine of the "ingathering," a major focus of the Master Plan of the Ages.

For the first time since her father had walked out of her life, Clare Conroy experienced a crystal-clear sense of mission.

If I don't stop them, who will?

14

Seated at the large, solid rosewood desk in his spacious and richly appointed administrative office, Dr. J. R. Jenner was studying a two-by-three-foot, four-color, finely detailed historical chronology—the centerfold of his *Master Plan of the Ages.*

"Excuse me, sir."

Jenner jumped a little, surprised to see Milo Stanton already in the room. He had been so engrossed in plumbing the secrets of the universe that he hadn't heard Stanton's knock or the sound of the door opening.

"Yes," Jenner replied, "what is it?"

"Well, sir, I'm sorry to bother you. But I've been thinking about your safety and the safety of our people, and I have a suggestion for how everyone could be more secure. In the past few weeks a number of unauthorized persons have been snooping around the property—most of them armed. A simple barbed wire fence just is not adequate to protect Institute personnel from the kinds of loonies in our world today. If you would authorize a six-foot chain-link fence, I think we could install it by winter."

"Six feet? Wouldn't that make this place look more like a prison camp than a religious compound?"

"Not necessarily," Stanton replied. "But even if it did, I'm more concerned with our security than with what people think of our fence. And . . . since we're talking about security projects, we also need a secure facility where people who need it might be . . . restrained until they've seen the error of their ways."

"Really?" Jenner questioned, surprised. "Are there any problems I need to know about?"

"No, sir," Stanton answered. "Everything is under control. I'm just thinking ahead. At the moment, the only place to confine anyone is in the medical center, and we do occasionally need to admit someone there. But that isn't the best solution."

"I agree with that," Jenner agreed, remembering that Mary lived in a special section of that facility. Build whatever is needed," Jenner said, turning his attention again to the chart spread out before him.

There had obviously been a lot of equestrian traffic through Miner's Pass since Bruce Davidson's descent several weeks earlier. Now that elk season was over, even the outfitters had packed out their gear. As the horse slowly climbed the steep ascent, Davidson entertained himself by watching for fresh tracks in the overnight dusting of snow. Each set of prints bore silent witness to the never-ending conflict of predator and prey, locked in their life-and-death chase since long before the miners found ways to make these mountains passable.

Occasionally, Davidson dismounted to examine a particularly fresh imprint, imagining the scene he had missed, perhaps by minutes. Once he found where a hare had burst across the trail, its terror told by the distance between its leaps. The coyote in pursuit was hurrying, too, but its measured pace was that of a confident assassin. New snow never lies. And this particular rabbit's fate was more or less assured, unless it could somehow confuse its adversary by circling back on its own track. Even then, with its varying coat not yet fully turned to match the snow, it would have no place to hide.

As Davidson knelt in the snow, picturing this animal's apparent demise, he noticed a motion to his left. Turning to look, he reached for the revolver on his hip. The animal froze in its tracks—a medium-sized piebald snowshoe rabbit that now sensed danger from more directions than it could handle.

Davidson knew instinct would hold the animal motionless to the point that he could walk over and kill it with a stick, as he had done in similar situations as a youth. Visions of rabbit pie flashed briefly through the agent's mind as he slowly walked toward the animal, whose eyes were fixed elsewhere as if hoping it might still escape unseen.

"It's your lucky day, my little friend," Davidson muttered as he approached, slowly, until he was close enough to reach down and grab the animal. It did not struggle. Quickly, hoping the little creature would not die of fright in his hands, Davidson carried it a hundred yards down the trail and set it in the middle of a juniper, confident its pursuer would be none the wiser.

For a moment, Davidson considered waiting to see what the coyote would do when the scent of its quarry suddenly melded with that of human hands, then melted into thin air. He thought of dispatching the varmint with his sidearm when it arrived. But then decided he had interfered enough for today in the natural economy of Miner's Pass. Besides, he reminded himself as he remounted, it would be best to arrive at Walton's Prairie as quietly as possible, just in case anyone besides Jeremiah Wilkes might still be in the vicinity.

Cyrus, who had been sleeping on the porch, rushed out to greet Davidson, whining and wagging and searching around for a pinecone or a stick or something to present to his long-lost friend. The dog didn't have to find anything today, though, for Davidson had brought along a new toy, a bright yellow tennis ball, which he tossed as far as he could out into the prairie with Cyrus bounding ecstatically after it. Even before Davidson's feet were on the ground, the dog was back with the ball, begging yet another throw.

Wilkes opened the door, chuckling. "You got a friend fer life, no doubt about it," he said. "What a great surprise. Didn't think we'd see ya ag'in so soon."

"Didn't know it myself, when I left. But you said anytime, so here I am," Davidson replied, producing a bag full of dog biscuits, some rawhide chew-toys, and two more tennis balls. "Figured he'd like some treats, since you only shop a couple of times a year."

"Gee, thanks," Wilkes said. "Cyrus . . . cookies!" he called out, tossing high a large rawhide bone that the dog caught in midair before disappearing around the corner of the cabin with it in his mouth.

Walking over to the horse, Wilkes said, "Let me help with yer pack, there. Yer stayin' overnight ag'in, I hope." Grunting a bit, he swung the heavy pack onto his shoulder. "What's in here, bowlin' balls? Must be a hunert pounds."

"Oh, that . . ." Davidson hesitated. "Never know what cults are up to. Lot of 'em are pretty strange," he said. "Like to leave some recording equipment in that cave to keep an ear on things, so to speak."

"Hate to intrude, but ain't that illegal?" Wilkes asked, as he set the pack down inside the door.

"Well," Davidson paused again, "yes . . . and no. Yes, if just anybody tried it. No, if it's part of an FBI investigation . . . which it is."

For a moment Wilkes's mouth dropped open. Then he said, "But you said you're a professor."

"I am," Davidson replied, "part-time. But Dr. Davidson's real job is catching criminals and solving crimes. I'm taking a risk telling you this, but I need your help, and something tells me I can trust you."

Wilkes studied Davidson's face for a full thirty seconds before responding. "Okay," he said, finally, "but what kind'a crime kin a group like that be doin'?"

"Well . . ." Davidson hesitated again ". . . over the past few years a lot of kids in this country have come up missing—thousands, in fact. One theory is that some of them get involved in cults, either by choice or by force. But once they're in, they get *absorbed* so they can't get out or don't even want to. For a lot of them, the cult becomes the family they never had."

"But if they're that bad, why don't you guys just raid the place and shut it down?" Wilkes asked.

"Might work, but by the time we got there, the evidence would have been destroyed—or, the people might destroy *themselves,* instead. With groups like this, you never know. You remember Jonestown?"

"Ayuh," Wilkes replied. "Be glad to do what I kin, 'specially if they're hurting kids."

"Think of it this way, Susan. All your needs will be taken care of the rest of your life."

"But I don't want to become a mother," Susan Winters protested. "I thought Dr. Jenner said it is better to stay single, to have more energy for the work. Marriage scares me, actually. It just leads to conflict—at least, that's the way it always was with my parents."

"Who said anything about marriage?" Florence Bradley replied. "Truth is, I feel that way about it, myself. You can stay single if you want. Someone else will raise the child, anyway. I'm proposing something that will be the privilege of a select few. I'm just asking that you think about it. We won't be ready to begin this program until everything's in place, early next year."

In another part of the compound, Milo Stanton and James Worthy were touring the recently completed media center's mass-production studio. They were guided by master builder Paul Woodman.

"Nice work, as usual," Stanton commented. The room still smelled strongly of adhesive from the installation of the carpet, a custom-designed light gray with burgundy stripe, its pattern repeated in the cushions of the chairs at each of twenty workstations.

"Ten thousand tapes a month," Woodman announced as they walked through the room, which occupied the entire top floor of the building. "Double that, if we have to. All the best equipment, like the big companies."

"You're sure we'll be on line by the end of the month?" Worthy asked.

Woodman nodded, then led the way downstairs, past the unoccupied but completely finished reception room and main offices on the ground level and through what seemed a storage room in the back. Reaching behind a shelf piled high with blank videotapes, he pushed a concealed switch. Immediately a panel in the wall next to the shelf slid open to reveal a set of stairs leading down to another level.

"I like that," Stanton commented as they stepped through and the door slid silently shut behind them.

At the bottom of the stairs, a hallway opened into a fully functional, completely furnished production facility with two sets ready for immediate use. In the center, with doors leading to both sets, was a massive control panel—twenty-four monitors installed in three banks of eight in a board sixteen feet wide.

"Perfect, Woodman," Stanton said, impressed. "Everything wired as planned?"

Woodman nodded, "Miles of cable, seems like. But the cameras aren't in place yet. Need a few more weeks for that."

"Hard to believe you did all this since the last time we were here," Stanton said. "But, how'd you keep this floor a secret?"

"It wasn't that hard," Woodman replied with a smile, "considering all the crews for miles around crying for work these days. Just built each floor with a different crew. Nobody ever saw more than two floors of the building, just in case they should ever meet and compare notes. Installed the secret entrance myself.

"Keeping the tunnel a secret, though, I leave with you guys!"

With that comment, Woodman led them into yet another room, which was tastefully paneled in solid butternut with twelve small symbols of ETR decorating one wall—one-inch opals in four-inch sapphire circles.

When Woodman touched one of the opals, a hidden door slid open in the wall to reveal a tunnel, twelve feet in diameter and constructed from a galvanized steel culvert like those used under major highways.

The mile-long tunnel could be an escape route, if needed. But its most likely use, Stanton figured, was to provide secret access to this studio, the brainchild of the organized crime gang that had sent him to ETR in the first place. *Grab some runaway in Denver, and four hours later you're making a snuff video up here. Incinerate the remains and start over. Newest wrinkle in the video market. Maybe we'll use Linda Landau first.*

Stanton smiled, impressed with his own creativity in naming this project BAMBI. *That's what the tapes will say on the outside. But what it really means is* Bambi Meets Godzilla, *the best short movie ever made.*

Woodman continued his narration as the three men stood in the entrance of the tunnel. "Our friends with the heavy equipment did this in a few nights. Dug a new trench each day, then put the pipe in it that night and covered it over. Institute people thought it was new sewer lines. We even dumped a little sewage here and there to make it more convincing." He laughed.

Stanton pushed the opal again. The door slid sideways and then forward to fill the space perfectly, matching precisely the other vertical lines in the wall. He ran his hand along the seam, which had virtually disappeared. "Impressive! Anybody else know about this door?"

"Just us three," Woodman replied. "I'll let you surprise Dr. Jenner. He'll be thrilled to be able to tape his programs right here. Make a nice Christmas present, don't you think?"

"Not a bad idea," Stanton replied, turning to lead the others back toward the stairs. Once upstairs, he shook Woodman's hand, slapping him on the back with his left hand as he did so, before the builder returned to his supervision of the ongoing construction.

"Why not just stab him in the back, instead?" Worthy commented as the two men walked back toward the administration building.

"Wimping out on me?" Stanton replied. "It has to be done," he said, slapping Worthy lightly on the back in jest. "Trust me. If we do what we're planning, we have to get rid of the evidence. People know too much, *they* are the evidence."

"But Paul is such an asset. Knows the whole place backward and forward; built every inch of it," Worthy protested.

"All the more reason," Stanton replied.

"But he's as loyal as they come. He would never betray the movement, or Jenner."

"Ditto," Stanton added. "Which way would he choose, between us and Jenner?" When Worthy was silent, Stanton continued, "The loyalty we need is for sale, and we'll just buy a replacement. Quit worrying. Winston knows what to do, and when. We've already talked about it."

"But . . ." Worthy tried one last time. ". . . how do you know you can trust Winston?"

"How do I know I can trust you? Or vice versa, for that matter?" Stanton replied with a laugh. "You know your problem, Worthy? You're too squeamish. Me, I do what needs doing to cover my butt, which is one reason I been working on this great plan, just in case we ever need to destroy *all the evidence* at once. Too many loose ends—data building, storage sheds, and now the media center, not to mention the files in your office or even the medical center.

"I was sitting in Chicago, thinking about how to get rid of everything just by pushing one little button," Stanton continued, "and all of a sudden, I figured it out."

"How?" Worthy replied.

"All it takes is a few bucks, which is why you and I are partners, remember? You shop right, you can buy anything these days. The Ruskies got lotsa A-bombs, but no greenbacks. They'd much rather sell 'em than watch 'em turn to rust. Ever since I was a kid I been itching to get my hands on one of them babies."

He paused, looking at Worthy, who stood there with his mouth open. "Worthy, you worry too much. Did you forget the tunnel? We ever push that button, we're long gone before the thing blows. Just blame it on a bad military test or something. All we need's a little one. A perfect way to get rid of everything with one big bang instead of a bunch of little ones. Trust me!"

15

Bruce Davidson watched Jerry Wilkes disappear into the darkness between the rocks at the mine's entrance, wondering how he would control the panic already welling up from someplace deep within. *You can do this, Ninja,* he chided himself, calling on his Vietnam nickname for courage. *Have to do this, Ninja. Got to get this dish on line. Perelli's involved—need every advantage we can get.*

Wilkes was waiting just inside the cave entrance as Davidson squeezed through. "Quiet," Wilkes motioned, forefinger to his mouth as Davidson's flashlight illuminated his face. Then he pointed to the bear's den, shining his own light to the right very briefly, but long enough for Davidson to see the mound of black fur snuggled up against the far wall. A new smell now permeated the room—warmer, closer, more alive. *Like a 4-H stall at the fair,* Davidson thought.

The agent's first reaction was to reach for his revolver again. As he did so, he noticed he was pressing himself hard against the ledge at his back, trying to put as much distance as possible between himself and the animal.

"Hard to believe, ain't it?" Wilkes whispered in the dark.

"Certainly is," Davidson replied. *Harder to believe I'm standing here talking about it. This is no place for a rational human being.*

Davidson turned and started crawling through the passageway leading to the crevice. Twenty minutes later, he was showing Wilkes how to change the tapes and batteries of the voice-activated recording equipment they were setting up to spy on the New World Institute.

Davidson focused the parabolic dish on a window of what seemed to be the main office of the administration building. He listened for awhile with the earphones attached to the unit. Then he handed them to Wilkes, who listened for just a few seconds, then returned them, as if embarrassed to be eavesdropping on the argument the two secretaries were having at the moment. "Prob'bly hear all kinds of stuff with this thing," Wilkes said. "Little bit like God eavesdroppin' on us!"

This is impressive, to say the least, Clare Conroy thought as she studied the colorful chart laid out on the floor in front of her. Stroking her kitten with one hand and sipping jasmine tea from the fine china cup in the other, Conroy sat cross-legged on the plush baby-blue carpet in her apartment, studying the centerfold from the Master Plan of the Ages.

Never heard about this in that InterVarsity group, and some of those people really knew their stuff. Maybe nobody knew about it before J. R. Jenner came along. Is he in touch with some kind of higher knowledge? Hard to believe somebody could just make all this up.

The knock on the door startled Conroy, even though she had been expecting it for some time. "Clare, time to go. The van is waiting."

"Coming," Clare called as she downed the last half of a honey-glazed cinnamon roll. She shrugged on the jacket of her very stylish light-gray wool suit with its subtle burgundy stripes. The suit had arrived the night before. *Must have cost six hundred dollars!* she thought again as she picked up her purse. *And it fits perfectly. Wonder who knows my size that well?*

"You look marvelous," ETR Media Director Joyce Johnson commented, as Clare stepped into the hallway. "Perfect for this kind of P.R."

"Thanks, Joyce," Clare replied. "You look very nice yourself."

Their destination today was a midday dedication and open house at the recently completed elementary school in Walton's Creek, the town of about seven hundred that straddled the riverbed at the bottom of the valley where the access road to the compound originated. In a straight line, the town was only five miles northeast. But it was more like fifteen miles by the winding road that followed Crystal Creek's serpentine descent west, then north, then eastward down the ever-deepening canyon.

The town wasn't much to speak of. Founded a century earlier, it had only two streets, one on each side of the stream, with perhaps fifty frame houses. None of the homes were very ornate, and some were quite shabby. The one thing they all had in common was that they faced Crystal Creek in front and backed up against the rust-colored sandstone walls of the canyon.

The new school boasted eight little classrooms (one for each grade), a small gymnasium, offices, and a room with a fifty-person capacity for public meetings. The entire project had been completed in the year since a large anonymous donation had been made in honor of Dr. J. R. Jenner.

"The only expense left to the townspeople was the furnishings," James Worthy stated as he, Jenner, Johnson, and Conroy rode together toward town. "The donor thought it best to give the locals some sense of ownership of the project."

Jerry Wilkes got up from the table in midstory, to refill Davidson's bowl with venison stew. "Didn't really know much about sheep when I started," the shepherd said, returning to the table. "But I learnt fast enough, I reckon. First thing really stuck out was how all day them sheep stay in line with each other—like a peckin' order for chickens, I guess—but once a day, every one of them will wander on over and give me just a little nuzzle. 'Most like they was renewin' acquaintance with me. Then they go on back to grazin' until tomorrow."

"Never knew that," Davidson said. "Wonder if it's just this flock?"

"You can look it up at the library," Wilkes joked. Then, leaving the sentence hanging, he picked up his cup of steaming coffee and walked to the window, gazing out pensively for a moment before completing the thought. "Up here, I found a library of a different sort," he said. "And I ain't talkin' 'bout them books on the shelf, 'cept maybe the Bible.

"I'm talkin' 'bout my flock, for one thing, and the other critters, too. It was Job mentioned learnin' from the animals."

As he listened, Davidson was back in his own living room, listening to Ellen, who always seemed to find little lessons in everyday experiences. "Look at that little bird, Bruce," she would say. "Jesus said not one of them falls to the ground without God's permission." For the first time in years, thinking of her produced an inner warmth, at least for a fleeting moment, instead of its usual icy grip on his soul. Almost as quickly, the glacier took control again. *But what about you? Where was God when you needed protection?*

"Thought you gave up preaching," he asked Wilkes, more

gruffly than he intended. Once he opened his mouth, the irritation seemed impossible to suppress totally.

Wilkes studied Davidson silently for a moment, as if surprised. Then the mountain man smiled. "Ayuh," he said, "me too. Sorry. What I meant was, instead of me taking care of them sheep, I get the benefit of their company, y'know. Maybe that once-a-day nuzzle ain't just 'cause they need to know I'm there for them, but the other way 'round, too."

"Not sure I follow," Davidson said, relieved to focus again on sheep habits, but longing more than anything for a triple shot of *Old Grand-Dad*.

"Somehow it works both ways," Wilkes continued. "They know I care for 'em, and when they come over I check 'em and rub 'em and give 'em a hug. But when I do that, somethin' happens to me, too. Maybe it's that I can't be totally alone when they're with me. Sometimes I look up at the stars at night, and I think maybe that's what it's like between God and us, y' know. But I ain't got it figgered out yet. Don't know if I ever will."

"You sleep outside with them, right in the open?" Davidson asked, trying to turn the conversation in a different direction—any direction. Aren't you concerned about the wild animals—bears, cougars, coyotes?"

"Gets a mite excitin' sometimes," Wilkes laughed. "One night, there we was, way up in the high pasture—me, Cyrus, an injured ewe, and her little baby lamb that could hardly walk around. It was gettin' dark, and them coyotes was yappin' to beat the band. So I built us a fire and tucked that lamb inside my coat on one side, its mother on the other, with Cyrus at my feet. Spent that night starin' at coyote eyeballs, tryin' not to fall asleep."

"Think I'll keep my job," Davidson commented, standing up to stretch and to refill his coffee cup. "And my warm bed at night."

“Not me,” Wilkes replied. “Love to look up at the stars an’ think about David doin’ the same thing couple thousand years ago, then makin’ it into a psalm. ‘When I see the work of thy fingers. . . . What is man that thou art mindful of him?’”

“In witness to the indomitable pioneering spirit that has brought Walton’s Creek back from the edge of extinction,” Mayor Mindy Copperthwaite concluded, “and as a tribute to the individual who, perhaps more than any other, has been responsible for helping our town be born again, we hereby name this school the J. Reuben Jenner Elementary School.” With a flourish, the woman pulled away the scarlet satin covering to unveil an eighteen-by-thirty-six-inch black marble marker engraved in gold and set into a small cement slab near the school’s front door.

Dr. Jenner responded briefly, “It is certainly a great honor,” he said, “to be recognized in this way. In fact, it is one of the greatest honors of my life. . . .”

The crowd of perhaps two hundred townspeople, dressed today in their Sunday best, interrupted Jenner with applause. Before the school had opened in September, their children had been crowded into High Road Elementary, a drafty, deteriorating structure still standing from the gold-rush era. Now, thanks to this man, each child would have at least a chance at a quality education. The first new teachers in years had moved to town that summer, and everyone figured it was because of the new building.

“But I would like to redirect your attention from me, personally, to my work. For we are all just part of a larger plan, and the part we play, each of us, is relatively insignificant. What is far more significant is that each of us do what we can with whatever abilities and opportunities we have been given. And this is as true for all of you as it is for me. . . .”

He paused as the people applauded again, then concluded, "So, even though this school may bear my name, in my mind it will always be an honor shared with all my colleagues, both here at the Institute and around the world. We are part of each other.

"To represent that larger group, I have asked a recent Institute graduate, Miss Clare Conroy, who is now my personal assistant, to share a few thoughts today. . . ."

"On behalf of the worldwide ministries of the End Times Renewal," Conroy began after another delay of several minutes for applause, "we wish to thank you today for honoring our leader by naming this beautiful new facility after him. As you know, Dr. Jenner has always had an interest in the special needs of little ones. Lately he has had a similar concern for education. So it seems only natural that these two interests should be brought together in a project like this new school. Here, we hope, the foundations can be laid for future generations who will lead their world toward brotherhood and peace."

Bruce Davidson held the rather plain-looking transmitter as he instructed Jerry Wilkes about its operation. "Just pop the tape in here, and the rest is automatic. But avoid pushing this little red button by mistake. It's just for emergencies. Hit the switch, and it sends an S. O. S."

"But why would I send an S. O. S.?" Wilkes asked.

"You never know. Hope you never will. But if you get hurt or need help, it's built in, so you might as well know about it." What Davidson didn't say was that the same switch also activated an electronic self-destruct sequence within the transmitter, in the event it should fall into the wrong hands.

What seemed to impress Wilkes most was the antenna set outside in a small clearing, its cable covered with pine needles.

"Now, Cyrus," Davidson warned, "don't you take a liking to that tree, you hear!"

"Not a chance," Wilkes laughed as he watched Davidson pack to leave. "Be seein' ya 'gain soon?"

"Month from today okay?"

"Don't know, better check my social calenda'!" Wilkes chuckled. "And you better find yourself a good snowmobile. By then we'll have more than just this little bit."

"You've already done that room, Mary. You've done *all* the rooms. Everything is spotless, perfect. Come and sit on the couch next to me. I want to tell you about the ceremony at the school today. Better yet, let me show it to you."

J. R. Jenner clicked on the video player.

"I'll be there in a minute," Mary called from the bedroom. "Just a minute. I just want to check the windows. Make sure they're closed. Can't waste the heat, you know. It's getting colder outside. Every night it's colder."

Jenner paused the tape, walked into the bedroom, and led his wife back to the living room. "Watch this. I know it's just a little town, but it's the first thing that's ever been named after me," he said. "Mother would be proud."

"I'm proud, too," Mary said when the program ended. Then, looking at Jenner, she said, "She's beautiful."

"The school?"

"No, *she*. She's very pretty."

"Who?"

"Your new assistant."

"I . . . I . . . hadn't really noticed," he stammered. "She speaks five or six languages fluently, you know. We really need somebody like that to help us break through the barriers."

The six-foot TV screen displayed the most beautiful shots

of the earth, taken from space, that Clare had ever seen, as the voice of J. R. Jenner pronounced, "In the beginning, our universe and everything in it, including man, was good."

Somebody must have bribed NASA to get these.

Next the screen was filled with more earth-bound but no less impressive images of humankind: babies, children, couples, retirees, all looking extremely happy, well adjusted, and carefree. The strains of "I'd like to teach the world to sing in perfect harmony . . ." provided the background as Jenner continued his narration: "Now in those perfect early days, there was a sense of wholeness, a community of love. There was nothing negative—no pain, suffering, alienation, or deceit. And no death."

Instantly scenes of war, famine, pestilence, and an almost nauseating pulsation of evil reached out and enveloped Conroy. She could feel the tension in her gut, exacerbated by a painful dissonance of the background music.

"How far the race has fallen! We are beset by wars and rumors of wars, as nations and peoples strive for mastery over each other. See what greed has done to our beautiful world?" the words continued, now accompanied by a powerful documentary of ecological disaster—garbage barges, refuse-littered beaches, pipes discharging raw sewage and industrial waste into rivers coated with the rotting carcasses of a thousand fish. Conroy could almost smell the rot.

"Still, no one stops to consider where we're heading. But human history is not just a series of coincidences. No, my friends, it all is going somewhere."

A low rumbling sound began, then gradually increased until it actually shook the room. On the screen before Conroy, a volcano erupted with a mighty roar, rivers of fiery lava pouring out to inundate everything in their path.

"Human history is moving toward catastrophe. At least, that is how most will view the great war—everyone but the

Remnant. These faithful few understand that after the calamity, after the bombs and the bloodbath, will come renewal, rebirth—a new order."

The camera zoomed in on a single shoot, just a tiny sprig of grass, bravely poking through a still-smoldering field of cooling lava. In slow motion, the shoot became a flower, the flower a clump of flowers, and the clump a field of flowers feasting on the rich nutrients of the lava flow.

"It is up to us . . . to you and to me . . . to REGENCY, to prepare ourselves for the era that is coming, when from the chaos must arise a principle of unity more powerful than the world has ever known. A movement founded not on any single individual, but on bringing the rule of God into the lives of men."

Again faces of babies filled the screen—cooing, laughing, playing, sleeping peacefully.

"But to bring this mastery to others, we must first master ourselves. To master ourselves, we must become as little children who trust, who believe, who are willing to be trained and nurtured and disciplined by those who understand, until we know in the deepest part of ourselves that the only way to freedom is by surrender to the truth."

Conroy switched off the video and closed the book. *This guy is connected with something . . . something bigger. What if he's right?*

"Have you entered the way, my friend?" a voice said, the same voice she had been listening to, but without the electronic undertone.

Am I crazy? Some kind of hallucination?

She checked to be sure the video was turned off before realizing that the voice was coming from the real Dr. Jenner, standing in the dark behind her.

"Yes, of course, sir," she said, regaining her composure.

"In private," he said rather gently, "please call me Jacob.

And I will call you Rachel. You have much to learn, but there will be time. The fulfillment is not for many years."

When Jenner said that—or perhaps it was the *way* he said it—Conroy remembered that Rachel was the wife of the Old Testament patriarch, Jacob. Obviously, this Jacob was pleased with this Rachel, so far. But the real surprise was how satisfying it felt to be appreciated to this degree.

Is this how it starts? she wondered, reminding herself that she'd never really been romantically attracted to any man. *Holy cow. This guy's old enough to be my father. Careful, girl. You may have to play the game, but you also have to somehow keep the patriarch on hold.*

16

A pumpkin about the size of a human head, with a smiling face etched on it for effect, was mounted on the end of the six-foot-long pole at Freddy Ricardo's side. The young man seemed oblivious to how ludicrous he looked, standing there like a knight with a spear and dwarfed by the taller pumpkin-headed stick.

Stanton was almost doubled over in the effort to keep himself from laughing as Ricardo carefully stuck one end of the pole in the ground just outside the frame of the storage shed's open door.

"Party time," Ricardo said as he pushed the pumpkin into the darkness of the door. Instantly the smile face was skewered by eight evenly spaced stainless-steel spikes. They were mounted on a spring-loaded bar that slashed out of the shadows, slamming to a stop even with the doorjamb.

Sobered considerably, Stanton stared at the pins only three feet from his face, dripping with pumpkin juice. Then he grinned at Ricardo. "Love it. That'll keep the rats from the cheese. You're sure my key is the only one that unlocks this door without setting off the Punji stick?"

"Count on it, sir. But *don't forget it*, please. That's the problem with gadgets like this."

"Right. Now let's talk about the other hookups. Can you rig the data center before I get back from this trip? Work with Townsend; he's wiring the whole deal. But Winston's the only other person who knows what's up, understood?"

Bruce Davidson looked at the itinerary intercepted by XRAY. *Cali, Colombia?* The rest of the stops were typical for Jenner.

```
11/20/92 ARRIVE NEW YORK
12/06/92 DEPART NEW YORK
         ARRIVE MONTEGO BAY, JAMAICA
12/17/92 DEPART MONTEGO BAY, JAMAICA
         ARRIVE MIAMI (LAYOVER)
12/17/92 DEPART MIAMI
         ARRIVE CALI, COLUMBIA
12/22/92 DEPART CALI, COLUMBIA
         ARRIVE MEXICO CITY
```

New York . . . studio work. Montego Bay . . . wants to show off an orphanage. Miami . . . Layover on the way to South America. But Cali? ETR doesn't have anything in Colombia . . . yet. Whose idea is this? Mexico City . . . Their most developed children's home, a quick stop on the way back to Colorado.

Davidson scanned at the passenger list and compared it with the reservations made for November 20 through December 6 at the Waldorf-Astoria:

```
J. R. JENNER--SUITE 1201.
MILO STANTON--SUITE 1202.
CLARE R. CONROY AND JOYCE JOHNSON--
  SUITE 1203.
```

Must be a misprint. Clare's middle initial is G, *after her mother.*

On 6 December, Jonathan Dexter would join the group for the rest of the trip. Dexter was director of ETR children's homes. And the only reason he would need to go to South America would be to make a site inspection for another orphanage. *Street kids need all the help they can get, but this puzzle fits together a little too nicely. Wonder who they know in coca land?*

"Miss Peterson," Davidson said into his intercom, gazing out at the mountains to the west of his Boulder office as he spoke, "Is Agent Billings still on the premises?"

"Yes, sir," his secretary replied. "He said he was going downstairs to do some shooting."

"Think I'll join him there," Davidson said. "I'm a little rusty myself."

Fred Billings was on his third target in the underground one-hundred-foot range when Davidson took a position next to him. "Not bad," Davidson commented, looking at the first two targets, each of which had three kills out of five from the 9mm in Billings' hand.

"Not good enough," Billings replied. "The bad guys might have won."

As far as Davidson knew, Billings had never actually been in a shootout, and he hoped the assignment Davidson was about to give him wouldn't involve his first.

"Remember the minutemen?" Davidson asked, as he emptied a clip through his service revolver in about five seconds. "They picked off the British one by one from behind trees and stone walls as the soldiers paraded around in the open. Stealth beats almost everything else. And always cover your backside. Fair fights happen only in Peter Pan."

"What's up, boss?" Billings asked. "You never talked like this before."

"You're my main man in the RADON case," the Bureau chief replied, "and I want to keep the number small because one of our people is inside ETR, trying to collect as much data as possible before we close it down. As you know from the XRAY intercept, certain ETR personnel are about to travel internationally. But their itinerary takes them through New York first, and I would like you to be there, undercover, to get a message to her."

"Conroy, sir?" Billings asked, with a smile.

Davidson, startled, replied, "Why would you say that?"

"Just putting two and two together. Remember, about a year ago, when you were in a rather mellow mood, I asked if you'd had any romantic interests since Ellen's death?"

Davidson nodded. *Too much brandy.*

"Well," Billings continued, "you said there was somebody working out of San Francisco named Clare, but you weren't sure how she felt about you. Never said her last name, but from the XRAY intercept I assume it's *Conroy.*"

"Good detective work," Davidson replied. "But you and I are the only ones who know Clare is really working for us. "Here's an I.D.," Davidson added, pulling a file from the briefcase he'd brought along.

"Pretty," Billings said with a wink, "but a little young, don't you think?"

"Not at all," Davidson said, chuckling to conceal his anxiety that Clare might agree. "I keep myself in pretty good shape, the house is paid for, and there's even money in the bank. I can hold my own."

"No doubt," Billings agreed. "But have you made your interest known to the young lady?"

"Not exactly," Davidson replied, "at least not yet. Maybe when this case is closed. But let's get back to business. Think you can handle the assignment?"

"Piece of cake," Billings replied.

“Nothing is a piece of cake,” Davidson said, turning his service revolver on the targets again, “when Perelli is involved. Seems his ETR alias is Stanton. And New York is his old stomping ground. Whatever you do, don’t get in his way. He’d as soon kill you as step around you.”

“Understood, sir. I’ll be careful. Pack my bags today.”

“You like New York, don’t you, Rachel? Didn’t you grow up in New England?” J. R. Jenner asked.

“Yes to both questions,” Clare smiled. “Why would you ask?”

“Well, day after tomorrow we fly to New York for a couple of weeks, during which I’ll be working very hard on the new video project. Not that I like talking to a camera. For me, it’s easier to address fifty thousand people in the open air than to talk to one studio camera.

“But I think it’s time to get this series started, and Worthy is right. I’ve been all around the world, and it’s amazing. We’ll be out in the wilderness somewhere and find a ramshackle old hut with holes in the roof, but outside in the yard there’s a satellite dish and inside a video recorder and a very nice color TV. If we’re going to reach the masses, it will be through video, and for now this is the best plan.

“You can take in any session you like,” he continued, “but bring along some of your new study materials so you can use the time to master them.”

Probably never even get out of that hotel room, Conroy thought. *But it’ll be nice to get out of here.*

“You don’t mind staying at the Waldorf-Astoria, I trust,” Jenner said with a smile. “You’ll be sharing a suite with Miss Johnson, but she’ll be at the studio most of the time, so you’ll be able to concentrate during the day. Each evening we’ll have dinner out together at a different restaurant. Lady’s choice. No limits.”

Now you're talking. Never hit the right places on a Bureau expense account. But what will I wear? Top-drawer clothes didn't come with the assignment.

"Oh, were you thinking you don't have anything to wear?" Jenner asked with a little smile. "Well, now you represent the movement as my personal assistant. So you have your own expense account to cover whatever you need to make your service more, shall we say, professional, including clothes, jewelry, and so on."

He handed her a gold VISA card with her name already stamped on it: Clare Rachel Conroy.

"There is no credit limit with this card," Jenner said, "and the only person you answer to is me."

First stop, Saks Fifth Avenue, Conroy thought. *Then Tiffany's. Don't want to miss some of the smaller boutiques, either. Have to follow orders, after all.*

"And by the way," Jenner added, "we'll be in New York over Thanksgiving, so I've arranged VIP seats at the Macy's parade and after that a meager feast at Top of the Sixes. Otherwise, I'm open to suggestions."

Conroy tried without success to hide her surprise. *This guy is connected. VIP seats to that parade? You're lucky just to find a place to stand on the sidewalk.*

She and her parents had tried to see the Macy's Thanksgiving Day parade the year before their divorce. But they had found it such a hassle just to get close enough to see anything that they had vowed to enjoy it thereafter in the comfort of their own living room.

Not that that particular day with her parents had been wasted. The train ride into the city remained a highlight of her life.

Conroy still loved trains. While her friends were collecting dolls, she—with her father's encouragement—had collected trains. And not those puny little H-O setups, but Lionels—beautiful, powerful, accurate-in-all-detail Lionels.

When she was seven, they had started with just one little loop, a circle that grew over five years to fill their entire basement. They worked on it together—that was the best part—building tunnels and trestles, putting in landscape, wiring switches and all the other electronics until they had, without doubt, the best Lionel layout in New Haven. Five trains ran on it at the same time.

Clare remembered vividly the day they finished, put on their engineer caps together, and played until they were too tired to keep their eyes open. That had been the happiest day of her life.

But not long after that, everything had disconnected, it seemed. On the day that her father moved out, she had sadly closed the door to that room of her life. Until this very moment, she had never opened it again.

Interesting how things associate, she thought, as she snapped herself back to Colorado.

"Are you unhappy with my plans?" Jenner had just said.

"No," she replied, "just surprised. Forgive me, please. You've been too generous. What can I say but thank you? And . . . I do have an idea for Thanksgiving afternoon, which I'd like to keep a secret until then, if I may. It'll be fun, I promise."

"Did you know he gave her a VISA Gold with no limits?" Marsha Keating said to Jennifer Howard. Keating glanced around to be sure no one was listening. In the cave, the recorder clicked on.

"Really? Won't it be fun to see what she buys! Like shopping by proxy," Howard replied, locking her own file cabinet for the night.

"You can't mean it."

"Course I do. It's not my business how either one of them spends money. I just make sure the receipts get in the right file."

"But haven't you noticed the way he looks at her sometimes—you know, when they're just sitting in the office talking?"

"Dr. Jenner built this movement from nothing. Without him, we're looking for work. Think about that before you let your mind go wandering into the gutter."

"Come on, Jennifer, don't tell me you never thought about him yourself. This may be a religious movement, but it isn't exactly Sunday school."

"You have a one-track mind," Howard replied.

"Maybe, but at least I'm honest about it, which is more than I can say about you."

"Now you're not making any sense at all."

"You mean to tell me you don't find him attractive? Me—well, ever since I walked the aisle and started work here, I go to sleep every night thinking about Dr. Jenner, and hoping that someday . . . he might choose me."

"Cinderella is a fairy tale."

"Maybe, but I've done almost as well," Keating said.

"Oh, really, dear? Where's the glass slipper?"

"Mock me all you want, but I'll have the last laugh, 'cause I've been chosen. . . . I probably shouldn't be telling you."

"Come on. You can't stop now."

"I've been chosen for a new program. Dr. Bradley told me today. A special program. I'm going to bear a child. Dr. Jenner's son. Don't look at me like that. It's all high-tech stuff—in vitro fertilization. But if this is as close as I can come, I'm willing. I'd do anything to make him happy."

17

Clare Conroy settled into the DC-10's spacious and comfortable first-class seat next to Joyce Johnson. *Beam me up, Jacob*, she thought, as the aircraft cruised at thirty-four thousand feet and she drifted off to an uninterrupted, hour-long dream.

She was part of a train, the caboose, happily enjoying the scenery, when all of a sudden the train stopped with a jolt. They were in a dark tunnel, on an incline, and something must have happened to the engine because now she couldn't move. She tried—how she tried—only to realize she didn't have a motor. She might as well accept her fate, forsaken forever, without even the ability to disconnect herself from the car in front of her.

The dream ended abruptly when the airliner hit some minor turbulence. In a moment the steward, with only twelve people to attend to on this flight, noticed that Clare had awakened and asked if she would like her meal now. What she really wanted was to dive back into that dream, to find out how it really ended. But as soon as Joyce Johnson saw that Conroy was awake, she seemed to be full of questions and comments. In a moment the dream was gone, like a mist in the morning.

"I always wanted to go to an Ivy League school, but I didn't have the right connections, I guess," Johnson said.

"Doesn't hurt. But once you're in, you're on your own," Clare replied. "I had languages coming out my ears by the time I was through. Even dreamt in Japanese once," she laughed.

"Think we'll ever get there?" Johnson asked.

"New York?"

"Japan."

"Good question. I'm not the prophet that Dr. Jenner is. But judging by progress so far, I wouldn't be surprised."

Vincent Costellini refilled Stanton's glass with J & B Scotch and water. "Diversify, diversify—it's the name of the game," he said. "Creative idea, this BAMBI thing. Snuff's the rage right now. Pretty big bucks, and we been looking for a safe place—away from everything, you know. . . ."

"Ten thousand tapes a month for starters," Stanton replied. "Ready pretty soon, too. In a couple of weeks we can run the first batch. Even got a studio when we need it . . . and a couple of candidates in mind, too."

"Always candidates in mind," Costellini replied. "But we can't risk the best laundry we got at the moment, either."

Conroy was glad to get to New York. There was something about the Northeast, about the hosts of people. Looking down from the top floor of the Waldorf-Astoria, the very streets and sidewalks seemed alive.

Then there was the shopping! She had never "done" Saks Fifth Avenue or Bloomingdale's or Tiffany's. Not really. Window-shopping with twenty dollars in your pocket and your mother at your side is one thing. Having the ability to purchase whatever strikes your fancy—now, that's power. *This could be addictive,* she noted wryly, reminding herself she was an employee of the U. S. government. For the moment, she understood the plight of Imelda Marcos and Tammy Faye Bakker. Wasn't the twelve-hundred-dollar dress just a little nicer than that eight-hundred-dollar creation? And shoes. How could a person possibly get along with only fifty pairs of shoes? The jewelry had to match, too. Not too extravagant, but not cheap, either. Just something to accent the various outfits she would have to wear for the sake of the kingdom.

The salespeople were more than helpful, especially when they discovered the VISA had no limit. In no time, with their encouragement, Conroy had spent more than sixteen thousand dollars. And all just to look good next to J. R. Jenner.

Difficult job, but somebody has to do it, she told herself. *A person could get used to this.*

The bartender chuckled as he took Bruce Davidson's dollar. "You want the Cowboys by thirteen?" he asked.

Giants are hurting. Smith'll go 150 yards today—you watch. Anyway, gotta make it interesting," Davidson replied, taking a seat in the lounge of the Boulder Sportsman's Grill. The room was specially arranged and decorated in a holiday motif for the thirty or so men who spent Thanksgiving there each year. They all shared two things: they loved football and they had nowhere else to go.

Davidson was early, eager to catch the end of the parade on the six-foot screen. If he sat up close, it was almost like being there in person. But suddenly, there on the screen, were Clare Conroy and J. R. Jenner. They sat right in the front row, and he saw them every time the camera panned the crowd. *Certainly looks well cared-for,* he mused. *Fur jacket must have cost a bundle. Animated, happy, pretty good at taking care of herself. Too good?*

"Such a wonderful day," Conroy said, taking the arm of J. R. Jenner as they walked down Fifth Avenue. "And now it's time for my surprise. Ever been to FAO Schwarz?"

"No," J. R. Jenner replied, "but I think I'll like it."

"It's my favorite place in the whole world," she said, her excitement growing with each step as she told Jenner all about her love for trains. Her eyes shining, she described the layout she'd built with her father, the Lionels that ran on it, and—best of all—their Christmas trips to the city just to see the trains in the window of FAO Schwarz.

But the display was different now. No Lionels. In their place was something new, at least to Clare, who had paid little attention to the world of model railroading for at least ten years. They were Edlins, handcrafted, accurately detailed, bigger, and more beautiful and powerful than the Lionels.

Conroy stood transfixed, instantly ready to trade the old for the new. She didn't even hear Jenner say, "Let's go inside and get a closer look." She just stared in the window, hypnotized by circling cars, oblivious to the cold. She could have stayed forever.

She was so absorbed that she never noticed Jenner go in and talk to a salesman. And when he finally came back, she didn't realize he'd been gone.

Fred Billings watched Conroy from across the street, his own thoughts focused on how much his little boys would love to visit that wonderland and how he would like to take them there. It didn't help to see the constant procession of kids dragging their parents through the store's front entrance.

What are they doing right now? he wondered as his mind took him to Boulder and his eyes followed one particular couple with two little boys. *Bet they had the greatest pumpkin pie for dessert.* He could almost taste it as he turned back to find that Conroy and Jenner were no longer in sight. *I'll have to connect with her back at the hotel.*

Going out again, Conroy noted. She watched through the little eyehole in her door as Stanton walked by on his way to the elevator. Every night at about midnight since they had been in town, she'd heard his door close. But this was the first night she had the opportunity to tail him, since Johnson was visiting some friends on Long Island overnight. *Tomorrow we leave for Jamaica. It's now or never. Think I'll just tag along and find out what kind of business Stanton has going on the side.*

She watched as Stanton walked through the lobby and stepped into a dark blue stretch limo with blackened windows. Before the vehicle was out of sight, she was following at a discreet distance in a cab.

Billings had been sitting in the lobby of the Waldorf-Astoria since Conroy had returned after dinner. The numbness of boredom was just beginning to soak into his brain when he was jerked into alertness as George Perelli came striding through the lobby toward the front door. And not far behind him, following the man she knew as Milo Stanton, was Clare Conroy. Billings covered his face as she passed, just in case she had seen his I.D. somewhere.

They were both out the door by the time Billings made it across the lobby, and he emerged onto the front walk just in time to see Conroy's cab pull away.

He flagged the next cab, identically marked, handed the driver a hundred-dollar bill, and instructed, "Follow that vehicle, whatever it takes." He pointed to the limo and added, "But don't get too close, either."

"Yes, sir," and they were off to the races and into the Bronx. Occasionally Billings wondered if they were going to lose the others. At one point they did lose them. But amazingly, the driver caught up to the limo again by doing a quick zigzag through a couple of alleyways. *It's almost as if he knows where that limo is heading.*

The agent was so intent on trying to spot Clare's cab that he didn't notice his own cab had slowed down. Just ahead, the limo pulled to the curb in front of a nightclub. The Blue Flamingo—Billings knew the place by reputation. Owned by the Costellini family, it was the suspected headquarters for major underworld activities on the East Coast.

The doormen, obviously armed, stepped respectfully aside for Perelli, then restaked their claim to the pavement. Billings could see other men, possibly armed guards, stationed a block or so in either direction. *This is no place for Clare Conroy,* he muttered, relieved to see her cab pass the nightclub without even slowing down. "Let's go," he said to his driver, "I think we followed the wrong car."

Without revealing that he was now more interested in tailing the other cab, Billings gave his driver instructions that kept him within sight of Conroy, whom he thought was heading back to the hotel. *Good, now maybe we can find a quiet place to talk.*

But Conroy's cab, after traveling two blocks away from the scene, took a left, another left at the next corner, and then pulled over, Conroy got out. Billings couldn't believe his eyes. *Girl's got chutzpah: no wonder Davidson likes her. But then again, maybe she's crazy. Can't let her wander around this neighborhood alone.*

"This is far enough," Billings said, opening the door when

the vehicle came to a stop. "Keep the change." The cab sped away.

Conroy was obviously working her way back to the Blue Flamingo. Billings wondered, as he followed her in the shadows, if she might even be thinking of going into the place. *Hope to God she doesn't.* But when Conroy made the last left turn and crossed the street, it seemed to Billings that she might actually be planning to try to get past those sentinels.

Now, for the first time, he noticed that Conroy had adopted a suggestive swagger that could only mean one thing in this part of town. *That may get her inside,* Billings mused. *But how is she going to keep the scum off if she gets her wish?*

He was already too close for comfort. Remembering Davidson's advice, Billings glanced quickly over his shoulder. But when he turned back toward the nightclub, Conroy had vanished. *Must have stepped into an alley—or maybe one of the other clubs. Crap. Now I've lost her.*

In a moment, however, the problem of figuring out where Conroy had gone suddenly became insignificant compared to the question of where he himself was going to hide. Two men had just come out of the club and were now heading in his direction, one of them staggering drunkenly. The sober one was Perelli.

They were already too close. If he ran, Billings knew he would immediately alert all the sentries and he'd have no chance of escape. So he turned and started to walk away, casually, hoping that the other two would simply pass him by.

Instinctively he reached for his 9mm, hidden in the small of his back, trying to make it look like he was scratching an itch. For one agonizing moment it seemed like the others would actually pass him. But suddenly the drunk lurched into Billings. The force of the impact on his right shoulder spun the agent around just enough, and before he knew it, the cold barrel of a Glock 17 was pressing against his neck, just under his right ear. His right arm was being twisted so sharply behind his back he was sure the shoulder would separate. The pain screamed for expression, but Billings refused to give Perelli the satisfaction.

"What have we here, punk?" Perelli asked, retrieving Billings' gun from its holster. Standard government issue. Let's see the I.D.," he ordered, as the other thug rifled the agent's wallet.

"FBI. Caught ourselves a G-man. Cabbie was right; you did follow us. Let's take a little ride and find out why."

He shoved Billings into the limo, which had pulled up alongside, and they sped off. The whole interchange had taken only about thirty seconds. No one nearby even seemed to notice.

Clare Conroy had ducked into Half Moon Lounge to use the ladies' room as a place to reconsider the wisdom of pursuing Stanton any further tonight.

I know where he went, she thought as she locked herself in the only toilet in the place, *but I really want to know who he came here to see. The Costellinis run their empire from that club, so Stanton's certainly not on ETR business—or then again, maybe he is. Need to know what's going on in there. I could talk my way in, but what if Stanton saw me? Would it wash to say I followed him here because it's my business to know if somebody on the Central Committee isn't trustworthy?*

As Conroy weighed her options, she happened to look staight ahead at the crude drawing etched on the inside of the stall's door. It depicted a sexual act occurring on a pool table with numerous people watching. "You're next!" the words promised.

Conroy remembered the lowlifes she'd squeezed past on

the way to the bathroom, several of whom had squeezed her, in return. Suddenly she realized that these thugs wouldn't care diddly for the fact that she held an important position in an international ministry. *Tunnel vision*, she chided herself. *You're not in a compound in Colorado anymore. This is the real world.* As she began to sweat, the only thing that mattered now was how she was going to extract herself from this hole without being raped.

Luckily the Half Moon had a working phone. But Conroy had to plead almost to the point of tears to convince the dispatcher to send someone to this location at this hour. When the woman finally sensed the urgency in Conroy's voice, she reluctantly agreed. "Be on the street in exactly eight minutes," she said. "The driver will only make the run once, and he won't stop for more than ten seconds. Don't you know how many cabbies have been murdered down there this year just for the cash they were carrying?"

"Told you already," Billings mumbled, "routine . . . surveillance. That's all. Just doing my job."

"Yeah? What does that have to do with me?" Perelli asked, standing in front of Billings, who was tied hand and foot to a straight-backed chair.

"I don't even know . . . who . . . you . . . are," Billings said, fighting the pain of three newly broken ribs and struggling for enough breath to reply.

"I'll bet," Perelli said, "but you got one last chance to cooperate." With that he punched Billings directly in the face. The agent shook his head slowly, trying to think through the pain that now surged from more sources than he could count. He was bleeding profusely all over his gray suit and longing to wipe his face, but his hands wouldn't move. They were heavy, too heavy.

Tied down, he remembered as he blacked out, chin dropping to his chest accompanied by a strange and distant gurgling sound.

Billings drifted into the quiet but threatening oblivion of a crimson sunset. Suspended over a dark chasm, he was a bird trying to fly away. But he kept losing altitude, no matter how hard he flapped his wings. Now he was caught by an upward, foul-smelling draft and lifted higher, higher. It was the whirlwind of hell, suffused with the smell of torment. *Not sulfur though . . . garlic. . . .*

He opened his eyes to find himself face to face with Perelli.

"Wimp," he said, yanking even harder on the agent's hair, "wake up. You're not getting off that easy. We'll just have to break your fingers one by one 'till you tell me everything you know." Perelli laughed as he grabbed a vise and forced Billings' right trigger finger into it. "You were following me," Perelli said, grinning as the first finger broke and Billings stifled a scream. "Why?"

Unwilling to give in, and intent on protecting Clare, Billings slowly shook his head.

Perelli forced the agent's middle finger into the vise and twisted the handle, hard. "Not too bright, are you?" he jeered. "All you have to do is talk."

Billings barely maintained his composure as the second finger was crushed. Again he shook his head, fighting the pain, but just barely. He thought of Clare, wondering where she was, and whether either of them would escape this place alive.

"I should send you home in a body bag," Perelli warned. "But that would be more respect then you deserve." He forced Billings' ring finger into the vise.

Billings screamed. It started as a low moan from somewhere deep in his soul, then rose gradually, a wave of agony beyond articulation, to a crescendo of protest. Finally it faded back down the slope to emerge as a mere whimper.

"Ready to talk, pig?" Perelli said, grinning. "What do you know about me?"

Billings tried to focus his eyes, which the swelling in his face had almost closed. Three times he tried to speak. Then, finally, what started as a defiant shout in his mind emerged as a whisper: "Nothing . . . nothing."

Perelli leaned toward Billings. "But you will remember my face, won't you, Agent Billings. And I'll remember yours. It shows up again where it ain't welcome, I will rearrange it even more than it is already."

Perelli wrapped his fingers around a set of brass knuckles.

"And, just in case you feel like talking, this will help you keep your mouth shut," Perelli said, smashing Billings' jaw with such force that the chair tipped backward and broke. The impact of the agent's head on the cement floor would have knocked him unconscious, had he not been unconscious already.

18

The doctor handed Bruce Davidson a ragged piece of muddy notepaper, its message written in blood: "Curb dogs. Keep city streets clean."

"Keep the visit brief, please," the physician cautioned. We just gave him a painkiller. "It's been touch and go. Agent Billings owes his life to the bag lady who found him lying in a gutter near Central Park at four in the morning. He was unconscious, dressed in underwear, and tied hand and foot. His I. D. was stuffed in his mouth, and this message was pinned to his chest."

Perelli. Davidson growled internally. *Had to be Perelli. I'll get him for this, I swear.* Turning to the doctor, he spoke as cordially as he could manage. "Thank you for taking care of him. Do you think he will have any permanent . . . disabilities?"

"Ribs heal slowly," the physician replied. "Cracked mandible, maybe six weeks. Fingers the same, but he'll need a lot of physical therapy, especially if he shoots right-handed."

Davidson nodded, his rage increasing as the doctor commented, "Whoever did this means business, that's for sure."

“True,” Davidson responded. “So do we,” he said more quietly as he walked into the hospital room.

He set the small spray of daisies on the table as Billings opened his eyes—small holes in a maze of bandages.

“From Judy,” Davidson said. “She was pretty upset, but she took it very well. She’ll be here tonight. Our treat.”

“Thanks,” Billings murmured.

“Least we could do,” Davidson replied. “Sorry I got you into this mess.”

Billings shook his head slowly. “Own fault,” he grunted.

“Perelli?”

Billings nodded.

“Where?”

“Lew Lalino,” Billings said, shaking his head in frustration.

“Can you write it out?” Davidson asked, handing him a clipboard and pen.

Left-handed, Billings scrawled, “Blue Flamingo.”

“Costellinis?”

Billings nodded, writing on the pad, “Check drums.”

“Not yet,” Davidson said. “But now we’re sure.” He hesitated, then asked the question tearing at his gut since the phone call that had wakened him that morning at four o’clock Mountain Time. “Clare?” he asked softly.

“OK,” Billings wrote. “Chutzpah,” he muttered.

“Say again?” Davidson asked.

“Safe. No leaks,” Billings scrawled as the morphine took over. “But never told her . . .”

Sitting waist-deep in the gentle surf of Treasure Beach on the south shore of Jamaica, Clare Conroy was feeling slightly blitzed in mind and body. The change in climate was only part of it—going from JFK in flurries at eighteen degrees to Montego Bay with sunshine and eighty-six degrees was agreeable enough. *But going from the Waldorf-Astoria to just about anywhere is enough to give a person withdrawal.*

She filtered the smooth black sand through her fingers as the waves lapped gently against her lightly freckled skin. *Have to work on the tan. Looks like I've been living underground.*

Just offshore, a small boat moved past in the late afternoon sun. The sight of a vessel of any kind reminded her what was missing . . . recreational watersports. No sailboards, no sailboats. No speedboats or surfcasters or jet skis. *Thank God,* she thought, *no jet skis. If this were Ft. Lauderdale, I'd be at risk just sitting here like this.*

Then for the first time it hit her: *I'm the only person in the water.* The thought was unsettling enough to bring her to her feet. *Sharks? Barracuda? Pollution? Move this beach to Florida, and there'd be thousands of people trying to find twenty square feet to stick their umbrella.*

Behind her she heard the others from ETR splashing their way in her direction as they dove after a Frisbee they were tossing back and forth. "Clare, catch!" Joyce Johnson yelled as the disk hit the water in front of Conroy, who grabbed it and threw it back.

For twenty minutes they clowned around, splashing each other and having a great time. But as they played, Clare realized she was staring at Stanton and Jenner. *Quit ogling like a stupid adolescent,* she told herself as she dove into the water, swimming out deeper. *But they're really not in bad shape for a couple of middle-aged guys. Stanton's done some serious weight training, maybe football.*

But the real surprise was Jenner. For one thing, a minister in a bathing suit seemed like a non sequitur of some kind. *Bet he was a real hunk twenty years ago,* she thought. *Mary Jenner must have been proud to have him for a husband.*

Probably loved him to death. Wonder what put her over the brink, anyway? Too bad.

Dr. Florence Bradley stood in the bedroom doorway, watching Mary Jenner fluff the pillow and straighten the bedspread for the tenth time in as many minutes. "You're having an especially bad day today, Mary," she said. "Is something upsetting you?"

"Not really," Mary replied. "Nothing's wrong, exactly."

"Are you worried about something?" the doctor probed.

"Worried isn't the word I would choose, myself."

"Troubled?"

"That's closer. Did you see the parade?"

"Parade?"

"The Macy's Thanksgiving Day parade."

"No. What could there be in a parade that would trouble you like this?"

"He said he would be there. I knew it. So that was why I watched."

"Dr. Jenner, you mean. Was *he* in the parade?"

"Of course not. He was watching the parade . . . with *her.*"

Mary Jenner stopped pulling on the bedspread for a moment and looked at Dr. Bradley. "They looked so happy together!"

Dinner at the Treasure Beach Hyannis House was hosted by Martha White, whose REGENCY ring Conroy noticed during the meal of baked fish, curried goat, jerk chicken, and lots of fresh fruit, rice, and beans.

"What's this?" Conroy asked White as she sampled the creamy soup, which had a consistency of thick gravy and a texture of potato stew.

"Entrail soup," White replied. "A delicacy here."

"Oh," Conroy replied, putting down the spoon, "are there any other *delicacies* like this on the table?"

"Not exactly," White replied, "but if you'd like, I'll arrange some cow-foot soup for tomorrow. I'll be glad. . . ."

"Not necessary," Conroy laughed, "but I am looking forward to our tour of the high country. I'd like to sample some of the local food if we can."

"Of course," White replied, "but I'll pack a lunch, too, just to be safe."

"Make sure you take her by the market at Santa Cruz and the basket factory at Black River," Dr. Jenner, seated to Clare's right, interjected. "I want Miss Conroy to get a general exposure to this whole country, especially the way the people live and what their needs are. Perhaps after our visit she'll have some creative suggestions for the future.

"One reason our work is taking root here," Jenner commented quietly to Conroy, "is that we have linked our own vision to the Jamaican national motto, *Out of many, one people*. Until now, that has been more dream than reality for the masses. Our group is a unifying focus for this people's longing to emerge from a life of hard labor that gets them nowhere.

"Jamaica is our test case. We began with small groups, just as all other great movements in history have begun. These men here tonight are the group leaders.

"Gentlemen," Jenner said in a louder voice, as he stood to address the group, "this is my new assistant, Miss Conroy. Miss Conroy . . . our friends. Our hands to work for the cause. Our feet to carry the message of peace and harmony to the people. Our mouth to speak hope in a beautiful land where so many live in despair."

As he said this, obviously for the benefit of the Jamaicans, Jenner swept his hand around the small circle of adherents as if to present them to Conroy and she to them. Had she been watching this by videotape in a comparative religions class at Yale, Conroy might have laughed in derision. In person, she had an entirely different reaction that was hard to define, perhaps because it was so new—a mixture of satisfaction and pleasure that came partly from being the center of attention and partly from having so much power over people.

She smiled at the others and nodded—rather condescendingly, she noticed. *Have to work on that.*

The main order of business tonight was planning for the various public and private meetings scheduled for them to attend as they worked their way along the south shore toward Kingston. After a rally there, they would cross to the north coast, gradually proceeding westward and back to Montego Bay, with two days in Ocho Rios for R & R.

As the group's attention now turned to various small details, Clare tuned into the conversation taking place in the semi-darkness behind her on the veranda as the women cleaned up after dinner.

"Such a terrible thing," one woman was saying in the Creole patois. "She just sits and cries all day, and nobody there to help her."

"Sniffing glue and smoking gange (marijuana), he was, and he just grabs a machete and goes crazy—that's what I heard. And that poor little baby just too small to get away from that crazy man."

"Hang him pretty high, you betcha."

Conroy had heard this dialect before from Jamaicans around New York and Hartford, Connecticut. During her earlier days in linguistics, she liked to entertain herself by trying to decipher their comments whenever she heard them talking in public or over their radios near the airports. *Same here. They love to jabber away right in your face because they figure you can't understand. Have to feed their egos somehow.*

"Just turn this little key," Ricardo said. He handed the control box to Winston, who rotated the key clockwise one-half turn.

Immediately the homemade .30-caliber Gatling gun started firing. Ten seconds later the target, an eight-by-ten-foot sheet of plywood twenty-five yards away, had disintegrated. Winston flipped the mechanism off.

"Hate to get in the way of that bugger," he said. "Where's it going?"

"Right outside the data center, concealed in a box under the remote. Not too accurate, which is why they never worked out in the Wild West. Oughta make a thief think twice about stealing anything from that building, though."

"Stanton'll love it. Love it myself. It'd be great to put it on a tripod in the prairie and wait for a whole herd of deer to come walking by and turn them into Bambi burgers. That'd be a rush!"

19

For nearly two hours, Martha White had been maneuvering her Mercedes 300SL along a narrow dirt road in the mountains between Black River and Springfield, Jamaica. Clare Conroy, sitting to the driver's left, tried to concentrate on White's nonstop narration while at the same time hoping, each time they entered another sharp curve, that they wouldn't meet a bus coming from the other direction. The only place to swerve was the narrow verge between the road and the sudden dropoff down the mountain, and there were no guardrails. The road seemed narrower than it really was because lush tropical vegetation embraced it from both sides and sometimes formed a solid, leafy-green canopy overhead. Conroy tried to conceal her mounting anxiety, but her knuckles whitened with each new hairpin turn on the ever-steepening ascent. She braced herself between the dashboard and armrest, thinking, *Half my kingdom for a seatbelt!*

What finally convinced Conroy to relax, however, was not a change in White's driving, nor the fact that she sounded the horn each time they entered a turn, but an awakening interest in the countryside. About every half mile or so, especially as the road became steeper, they passed another rickety shack hanging out over the ravine, supported on the downhill side by alarmingly thin posts.

"Look at that one!" Clare exclaimed when they had nearly reached the top. "Must be sixteen feet off the ground in the back. Wouldn't pay to sleepwalk," she laughed. White laughed too.

"How do these people earn a living?" Conroy inquired.

"Agriculture, mostly. Used to be a lot of sugarcane and bananas. There's a banana tree now," she said, pointing. "Also tomatoes, carrots, sweet potatoes, melons, and crops like that. But when there is a good crop, they struggle to get it to market, and if they succeed, they may not get a good price.

"So it's mostly hand to mouth. They eat what vegetables they can grow. For meat it's goats, chickens, pigs, and a few cattle. When they do get some cash, most of them don't budget, so it's feast or famine. And a lot of it goes for Red Stripe beer."

As she said that, they passed a tavern, a small wood-frame building, maybe eight-by-twelve feet. It had once been painted, a long time ago, but now it settled for the reddish brown of Jamaican dirt. The only clean feature was the sign for Red Stripe beer. Sitting on the front steps were three young men, who stared at the two white women as they passed. "Reminds me of Milwaukee," Conroy said. "A tavern every couple of miles. Red Stripe any good?"

"Jamaicans love it," White replied, "but I wouldn't know by personal experience. You know the rules against beer and hard liquor."

Conroy noticed a youngish-looking girl carrying an infant on one hip and holding the hand of a toddler as the trio walked barefoot along the road. The toddler wore a little blue cap with a white baseball on its front. "Slugger," it proclaimed. *Do they play baseball here?* Conroy wondered.

"Stop, please," she said. "I want to talk to this girl."

Conroy got out and caught up to them as White followed at a distance in the Mercedes.

"Hello there," Clare began in as nonthreatening a voice as she could manage.

"Hello, ma'am," the girl replied, still walking. The toddler stared wide-eyed at Conroy. His mother seemed frightened.

"Your little brothers are really cute," Conroy offered.

"But these be my own babies, ma'am," the girl replied. "The big one be Eduroy Charles Daniels, and the baby be Maryellen Myersly."

Conroy was surprised. *She can't be more than sixteen years old.* "Very pretty names," she said, "but you don't seem old enough to be a mother, Miss . . ."

"Jackson, ma'am. Joanna Jackson", she replied. "I be fourteen already."

"Oh," Conroy said, flashing back for just a moment to her own adolescence. *Another world, that's for sure. And different names, too. Have to ask White about that.*

She decided to try a different tack. "Do you live in one of these houses here?"

"No, ma'am, about two miles from here. We be going to the store to buy some food for Eduroy."

"Couldn't your husband help?"

"Well, I don't know, ma'am. I mean, I don't have a husband, really. I live with my grandmother. When we have a little money, we buy the babies something."

"Is your mother . . ." *How could she say this?* ". . . passed away? I mean, has she died?"

"Oh, no, ma'am. She live in Kingston, where she work. And sometimes she send us some money, too."

"I'm sorry," Conroy said, "asking you all these questions. This is my first visit to Jamaica, and I want to learn as much as I can about the way you live." She paused, then continued. "Could we give you a ride home after you shop?"

"I don't know, ma'am," the young girl said, eyeing the vehicle. "I don't think so, thank you. I wouldn't want these babies to make dirty such a pretty car."

"Don't worry about that," Conroy said. "You can hold Eduroy, and I'll hold Maryellen. We should be able to manage for a couple of miles, don't you think?"

"Yes, ma'am. I mean, no thank you," Joanna said, looking as if she were about to cry.

"Tell you what, Joanna," Conroy said. "We'll wait while you shop, and if you change your mind, we'll be glad to take you home."

"Thank you, ma'am, but . . ."

"You can trust me; I work with the End Times Renewal ministry. We operate the children's home at Mandeville. Have you heard of us?"

"Oh, yes, ma'am," Joanna said, smiling for the first time and relaxing noticeably.

"We won't be long," the girl said quietly. "I be only buying some milk and a little biscuit."

Conroy briefly wondered how expensive food might be, then realized the problem was not price but resources. "Wait just a moment," she said, turning back toward the car. "I'll go in with you. Let me get my purse."

A half hour later, Conroy stood in the front door of one of the cliffside houses they had passed earlier with a bag of groceries in one arm and a baby in the other. She listened, amused, as Joanna told her grandmother in rather excited Creole how she happened to come home in a car that was cold inside, with two bags of groceries, when she had left with only enough money for a biscuit and a little milk.

The agent glanced around the little house as the grandmother scolded Joanna for making up such a tale. Conroy saw no refrigerator, no light fixtures, and nothing covering the bare walls, floors, or ceiling. There were only two rooms, neither of which was a bathroom. In fact, no plumbing of any kind was visible. The only furnishings seemed to be the table and chairs in the room where they were standing.

When Joanna finally mentioned ETR, her grandmother brightened and extended her hand in welcome to Conroy. "Hello, Miss Conroy," she said. "I am Winelda Storey. We are grateful for your generosity. I only wish I had something to offer you, but we are very poor. I cannot even give you a cup of tea."

"But, yes, Grandma, we have it now. Your favorite kind," Joanna interjected, reaching into one of the bags for the box of Twining tea bags.

"Then fetch the clean cups, child," the woman said, still holding Conroy's hand. "The water outside is hot. I am making some chicken soup. Perhaps our guest would like some soup, too?"

Behind the woman, Conroy could see the form of a recently plucked chicken hanging, headless. "Thank you, no," she said as politely as she could, "but a cup of tea would be nice." As she said that, she squeezed the old woman's gnarled and calloused hand just a little, only to have Winelda Storey visibly wince in pain.

"I'm sorry," Conroy said. "You are injured."

"No, ma'am. Just arthritis. I could not work today."

"But where would *you* work?" Conroy asked.

"In the fields, ma'am. But I can only work two or three days a week because I cannot hold the machete."

"But Mrs. Storey, why would you have to work in the field, especially with a machete?" Conroy said, using the same French pronunciation for the farm implement.

"Someone must work," the older lady answered, "or we

will not eat. My husband is gone many years. Joanna's mother is in Kingston, but she only sends money now and then. And Joanna cannot work, with the little ones. So I must go out. It is no bother, really. I have worked in the fields forty-nine years. It is our way; you must try to understand."

She paused, then continued, shaking her head sadly. "In Jamaica, a girl comes of age, and she naturally wants to prove she is a woman. Of course, the young men are only too happy to help. Then after the first child comes, the girl begins to wonder how she might find a husband, and when a fellow comes along with promises and dreams—or maybe with a gold chain—she ends up with another baby and still no one to take care of her. And later she will have to sell her gold chain to buy food for the babies. Sometimes she will even sell it back to the child's own father."

Joanna brought in the cups of tea, but then quickly excused herself to tend to the children, who Conroy noticed, were remarkably mild-mannered and obedient. *Haven't they heard of birth control?* Conroy wondered. But then she reminded herself that Joanna had become a mother by intention, at least the first time. And now, at the ripe old age of fourteen, this young mother's life story was already written.

But they don't seem very concerned. In fact, they seem rather well adjusted and content. Not like most of my classmates at Yale, whose greatest anxieties arise from the absolute necessity of acquiring things they don't really need.

"Mrs. Storey, thank you for helping me understand the way you live. If I hadn't met you both, I might have missed something very important. But if I may ask just one more question before I go, when you are well enough to work all day in the field, are the wages enough to meet your basic needs?"

"Yes, ma'am, I suppose so, although thirty dollars Jamaican does not buy as much today as it did last week."

Conroy quickly figured equivalencies at the exchange rate

she'd received in Montego Bay. *Less than three dollars a day for this lady's hard labor is hard to fathom*, she thought, *when a bellhop at the Waldorf might sneer at less just to carry two bags to your room. Why, the vehicle outside is worth twenty-thousand times that much!*

But just as Conroy began feeling rather self-righteous, she happened to glance down at her own shoes, for which she had spent the equivalent of three months' wages in the economy of Winelda Storey.

Suddenly feeling more like an intruder than a benefactor, Conroy was glad her empty teacup provided the opportunity to excuse herself.

She was still absorbed in thought when she opened the car door to Martha White's, "Something wrong in there? You seem upset."

"Oh, sorry," Conroy murmured. *Get a hold on yourself, Conroy,* she scolded herself. *Your mission is to uncover the cracks in ETR, not to become the personal savior of every orphan and widow in Jamaica.*

"Joanna introduced me to her grandmother," Conroy replied. "I couldn't just turn my back and walk out. Have to be sociable, after all."

"True enough," White agreed. "But if we're going to get to the basket factory, we can't make any more unscheduled stops."

"I understand," Conroy agreed, and she worked very hard to appear interested in the continuation of Martha White's guided tour. In her mind, however, she was still sipping tea with Winelda Storey and wondering how that woman could possibly experience peace of mind, much less contentment, in the midst of such poverty. Why, the low income housing in the Bronx was heaven by comparison!

20

C*yrus'll think I'm Nanook of the North. Probably attack and lick me to death,* Bruce Davidson chuckled. It was the first time he'd laughed since making the excruciating decision a week earlier not to terminate the RADON investigation—a decision based on Billings' word that the case was not compromised.

The new Arctic Cat EXT snowmobile sliced its way up Hunter's Creek Pass, with its ten miles of winding trail that ended at the southwest end of Walton's Prairie, about three miles from the compound. Obviously others knew about this access; the trail was well packed beneath the eighteen inches of fresh powder that kept blowing into Davidson's face like frigid confectioner's sugar. In the dry, subzero cold, the snow stung his face much like wind-driven sand at the beach. He was thankful for the heated handles, but the rest of his body was headed for a deep freeze.

Along the east side the prairie, a six-foot-high wall of drifted snow effectively blocked access to Miner's Pass and Jeremiah Wilkes's cabin. *Can't leave this baby out in the open,* Davidson thought. He gunned the engine, blasting through the drift at full speed, snow spraying in all directions. *Gotta try that again sometime just for fun,* he noted. He ran the machine as fast as possible afterward to avoid bogging down in the light snow. It was exhilarating to skim along the top of chest-deep powder. Considering his need for secrecy, however, Davidson would have preferred arriving on something much quieter, and without leaving such a clearly manmade track. *Good thing I got the EXT,* he mused, *but the stuff'll hit the fan when I put in for the fifty-eight hundred to pay for it.*

Cyrus was bouncing around on the cabin's front porch, a bright yellow tennis ball in his mouth, when Davidson arrived. The dog dropped the ball at the agent's feet the moment he climbed off the snowmobile. Davidson patted the dog, then tossed the ball just far enough out into the deep snow so that the dog would have to work to find it. Cyrus bounded after the toy, sprang into the snow, and disappeared in a cloud of white. Only his reddish-brown tail stuck out above the surface, waving like a flag on a bicycle in head-high fog.

Wilkes began laughing from the porch, "A dog's life," he exclaimed. "Never-ending game! Good to see ya," he added, stepping off the porch to greet Davidson and handing him a cup of steaming coffee. "You look like an Eskimo or somethin'. Come on in and unthaw yerself. I'll get the pack," he added, grunting a little less than the last time. Bowlin' candlepins today, 'eh?" he commented.

"Just more batteries." Davidson said, his face starting to unfreeze in the coffee's warmth. "What's candlepins?"

"You kiddin'? Little balls, hold 'em in your hand. Pins look like candles. Get three tries instead'a two, and use the deadwood. Can't believe you never heard of it. Have to take you bowling in Maine sometime."

"Lots of things I never heard of. But you got a deal. Next time you go to Maine, I'll come out just to bowl with you."

And to visit Marcy. Should I tell him the guys in Augusta found out she's still waiting, still hoping? After this is over, I will. For now, I need him up here.

"You ready to pay our furry friend another visit?" Wilkes chuckled as he put a bowl of stew on the table in front of Davidson. "Or you want me to change the batteries m'self?"

"I'd like to go along," Davidson said, smiling to mask his anxiety. "There was good information on the tapes you played us. Thanks. But it's time to maybe aim it at another building, see what else we can pick up."

"Anything strange, like you thought?" Wilkes asked.

"Ever read the novel *Brave New World*?"

"Nope, sorry. Never really had much time to read novels. Always out huntin', trappin', or diggin' potatoes, I guess. Or readin' the Bible."

"Well, in that story they were perfecting the human race by making babies in test tubes and cloning and a whole bunch of ideas that were very futuristic in the thirties. Those things are real possibilities now."

"Really? Here?"

"Not exactly sure yet, but something like that."

"And what happens to the babies? Must really screw them up. Don't they think about that?"

"Evidently not. Groups like this get so focused on their vision, they end up not caring what happens to the individuals involved."

"Miss Conroy. Excuse me, ma'am," the young, bronze-skinned girl said as she ran up to Conroy and Beatrice Moxley, matron of the Good Shepherd Children's Home in Mandeville, "but there is a girl outside asking for you. I tried to send her away, ma'am, but she insists you are her friend. She has a little baby. . . ."

"It is all right, Alicia," the matron said. "We will come soon, you may tell her."

"But who could it be?" Moxley asked. "Who could possibly know you in Mandeville?"

"Maybe she has me confused with someone else."

Conroy had been touring the home's facilities for the past couple of hours, and she welcomed the opportunity to sit down for a few minutes. The morning had been quite interesting; she had finally gotten a chance to see, in person, how an ETR orphanage was operated. Jenner had left her here in the care of Matron Moxley while he continued his whirlwind tour of the south-shore ETR study groups.

The Good Shepherd orphanage was home to 115 children ranging in age from newborns to age fourteen, with the older ones serving as helpers. Essentially, it was an extended boarding school that provided education comparable to, if not superior to, the Jamaican public system. Sometimes students went on from here to some form of higher education.

The Good Shepherd home tried to create as much of a homelike atmosphere as possible, Moxley explained. "We are the family these little ones never had."

"Does it give you a sense of satisfaction," Conroy asked as they walked back to the main office, "when a child leaves here for the university?"

"Yes, but I'm happy and sad at the same time. After all, these are all my children, and I miss them. Even though I never married, I've had thousands of children," she added, waving her hand toward the field where about thirty children were playing soccer.

Interesting how she said that, Conroy thought. *They're all her children . . . in the same way that REGENTS are all Jenner's people.*

"And is it any different when the children are adopted by benefactors in the U.S.?" Conroy asked.

"A little bit, perhaps. They are going to a land of opportunity, where they will have a chance to make more of themselves than they would ever have in Jamaica."

They had reached the main building, a tidy, freshly painted white-block building covered with a tin roof. Immediately as she walked through the door, Conroy was greeted by Joanna Jackson, who was holding little Maryellen Myersly, her infant daughter.

"It seems you two *do* know each other," Moxley commented.

"Yes," Conroy said. "We met the other day, but it was maybe forty miles from here—in Springfield. We had a nice talk, and Miss Jackson introduced me to her grandmother."

"Well, what is it, child?" Moxley asked impatiently.

"Well, ma'am. Miss Conroy has been so kind to us, and—I don't know how to say this—but Grandmother and I, we talked a long time, and we thought perhaps Miss Conroy might be able to take Maryellen back to the States with her."

It took Conroy a moment to comprehend what Joanna was saying. "But, Joanna, I couldn't—I mean, we couldn't. How could you even consider it? Maryellen is such a beautiful child, and it just wouldn't be right for her to be with anyone but her own mother. You do love her, I'm sure of it."

"Yes, of course, ma'am. We do love her, and that's the reason I have come to find you. How can I keep her when I know you could give her so much more in America? Even two bags of groceries will not last forever, and Grandmother will not be able to work much longer, and sometimes I wonder what is going to happen to us. But you came to us, like an angel sent from God. Won't you help my little baby not to make the same mistakes I have made?" She started to cry.

So much for the contentment theory, Conroy said to herself. *From a distance, resignation and contentment must look pretty much alike.* As she waited for Joanna to calm down, Conroy tried to form some kind of rational response.

The matron began to castigate the teenager, in Creole, obviously assuming Conroy would not understand. "Why have you come here to torment this lady?" she said gruffly. "You want to put all the problems on her you have created for yourself. Did someone force you to have this baby? Of course not! You are nothing but a village whore," she accused, using a word that made Conroy wince.

"Miss Moxley," Conroy said as calmly as she could manage, "do you think it might be possible for the baby to stay here at Good Shepherd? I've seen the conditions Joanna lives in, and I have no doubt Maryellen would do much better here."

"We have certain rules about who is eligible," Moxley replied as soon as she recovered her composure. "Otherwise, we would be overwhelmed with requests. We have developed these rules based on hard experience, especially with families who leave their baby as soon as it is weaned, only to come back when the child is strong enough to work in the fields."

Conroy saw Joanna's eyes fill with tears as she silently pleaded for her friend to intervene. "I'm sorry, Joanna. I think in helping you I may have only hurt you. If we had never met, you would not be hoping for something that is simply impossible. I myself could never give your baby what she needs. I travel for weeks at a time. I don't even have a home—just many places that I might stay for a little while. A baby needs more than that. She needs love and care, and cuddling and playing—things I could never give her. But you could."

Joanna was starting to understand.

"Perhaps I *could* help you, though," Conroy said. "I

wouldn't feel right just turning my back on you now that I know who you are, where you live . . . and how you live. Miss Moxley," she said, turning toward the matron, "isn't it true that sometimes specific children here are sponsored by outside benefactors?"

"Why, yes," the matron replied hesitantly.

Have to get a look at those records, Conroy thought.

"So, if you were to receive a guarantee that Maryellen's expenses would be paid, you might be able to make an exception?"

"I suppose so. Yes."

"But that wouldn't necessarily be the very best situation for Maryellen, who should stay with her own mother, and who would love her better than any other person could possibly love her?"

"True, but I'm becoming confused."

"To do both, Joanna would also have to stay here." When she said that, Conroy looked at the girl with as much compassion as she could communicate nonverbally. "But I don't think that would work out best for her, or especially for her grandmother. For who would take care of *her* then?"

Not to mention Eduroy. If Moxley knew about him, she'd blow her cork.

Joanna nodded, "Yes ma'am, I understand. Grandmother has been so kind to me, and now I must be kind to her."

"But what we could do, Joanna, is help you with Maryellen's expenses until you can work and provide for her yourself. Perhaps Miss Moxley and I can find a way to do that. How does that sound?"

Joanna smiled, grabbed Conroy's hand and kissed it. "Oh thank you, ma'am. I must go home and tell Grandmother. She will be so happy. But . . . will I ever see you again?"

"I don't know," Conroy replied, realizing that regardless of how this case resolved, she had just made a commitment she would have to keep. "We'll be leaving this part of Jamaica after the rally in Kingston tomorrow night, and I don't know when I may return. But you'll hear from me. You can be sure of that."

"Yes, ma'am. Thank you, ma'am," Joanna said as she turned to walk away.

"You are very generous," Moxley said after the girl had left. "But we must be careful, too, for the needs here are great. Before long, every young woman with a little mouth to feed will be pounding on our door, and none of them will understand why Joanna Jackson should be helped and not them."

Providence? Conroy wondered. *Or just plain old unadulterated fate? Was it just chance that I met Joanna Jackson on a little road in Springfield, Jamaica? Or did you have something to do with it*? she murmured, glancing upward for just a moment. *And what if we hadn't met*? she continued. *What difference would that make in the eternal scheme of things*?

21

Conroy pulled out the checkbook that accessed her discretionary funds. "I hope I haven't created too great a problem for you."

"It's all right," Moxley said, eyeing the checkbook. "It must be hard to come to our part of Jamaica and not be touched with the needs."

"I want to take care of little Maryellen's expenses for several years in one payment. Help me compute an appropriate amount to leave with you. I could leave it with you, couldn't I?" Conroy said. *Now I have her undivided attention; that's for sure.*

"Of course. Let me see. We figure a certain amount per year for education, clothes, food, medical and dental care, and so on."

"Let's not be skimpy," Conroy encouraged her. She was going to enjoy spending some of ETR's money on this little girl. "What figure do you use?"

"About a thousand dollars U.S. per student annually," Moxley replied.

"Here's three thousand to help Joanna Jackson feed her

little girl, herself, her grandmother, and . . . by the way, she has a little boy, too."

"Certainly," Moxley said. "And I will be discreet about it."

"Good," Conroy said. "In fact, this is our little secret." *If Jenner ever asks, I'll say I made a contribution to the Good Shepherd Children's Home. Better than another fur coat. He'll approve, no doubt, but Moxley will never tell, anyway.*

"By the way . . ." Conroy began as she followed Moxley back into the administrative offices, two small but very neat compartments off the main entryway. On a shelf behind the matron's mahogany desk, Conroy could see what appeared to be a ledger. With Moxley in her pocket, Conroy searched for a way into that book.

"We're impressed with your financial management," she said. "Would you show me how you transformed this orphanage into such a profitable endeavor?"

"Of course," Moxley replied, hesitating. "But didn't Mr. Worthy explain everything?"

"I'm so new in this position that Mr. Worthy and I haven't had much time to talk yet. Seeing things firsthand, I'm sure I'll understand better."

A little reluctantly, Moxley took down the ledger and spread it on her desk, opening to the first page, dated 1974. It was a simple double-entry system, meticulously kept and balanced each year to the very last cent, especially in those first few years. Then, the total budget for the home had been less than was now being pumped in as the result of just one contribution.

"It's usually locked away," Moxley said, "but I was working on it this morning, when you arrived."

Conroy did her best to show an interest in the early entries, commenting especially on how difficult those early days must have been. About the beginning of 1985, however, something had radically changed. Large donations, sometimes in excess of ten thousand dollars began to appear in the ledger.

"Are these all your records?" Conroy asked. *Need to see where the children ended up.*

"No, ma'am," Moxley replied. "Placement records are in another book, also stored in my safe. The information is strictly confidential."

"Of course. Has it been easy to place your children?"

"Not when we first started. But recently we're doing better."

"May I see that book, too, please?" Conroy said, trying to communicate as clearly as she could by tone of voice that she had a right to see it.

"Yes, ma'am, of course," Moxley replied. She walked over to the ancient but sturdy steel safe behind her desk and twisted its brass dial as Conroy watched over her shoulder: 21 right, left one full turn past 21 to 44, right 65. She had the combination memorized and was studying the financial ledger intently when Moxley next glanced her way.

Moxley carefully laid the placement book next to the other and opened it to the first page.

Conroy's pulse quickened in anticipation. *Time to meet some missing links*, she thought. But just as she leaned over the new book, Moxley's helper, Alicia, appeared in the office doorway.

"Excuse me, ma'am, but Erietta is ready," the girl said, "and the lady is waiting outside in her car. What shall I tell them?"

Moxley, suddenly flustered, reached over and closed the book. Then, apologetically, she said to Conroy, "Sorry. No one else even knows about this book."

"In that case," Conroy replied, picking up the book, "let's put it away until you come back." Casually she walked over to the still-open safe, placed the book inside, closed the door, and turned the dial. By twisting her hand, she made it appear to have turned at least one revolution, when in reality it had only moved slightly left.

"But while you're taking care of that," Conroy said, "I'll study the other journal, if you don't mind."

Visibly relieved, Moxley followed Alicia to the outer room as Conroy turned her attention to the financial journal, reaching for her camera-in-a-compact as she leaned over the desk. *Not enough*, she thought, frustrated. *I need them side by side.*

She looked at the safe, then at the open door leading into the small adjacent office, where Moxley was now talking to someone. *Is it worth risking? If Moxley comes back in here for something, I'll be caught red-handed. Just do it,* she decided.

Quickly and quietly, Conroy slipped behind the desk, knelt in front of the safe, and turned the dial clockwise to 64. Click, the tumbler fell in place, and the door opened. In a single motion, Conroy retrieved the ledger, opened it to the final page, and laid it out on the desk beside the other one.

Davidson was right, Conroy murmured as the pages confirmed what she suddenly realized she had been secretly wishing wasn't true. *Large sums of money . . . adolescent females . . . prostitution . . .* Davidson's words rang in her ears. In less than ten seconds, she had the evidence on microfilm. Then, startled, she looked again at the last entry in the placement journal: Erietta MacIlmore, 14; Guardian: Melissa Costellini; New York, NY, U.S.A.; 14 December, 1992.

Today! Right in front of my face, Conroy muttered angrily, *and I can't do anything to stop it.* In the financial ledger, $12,250 had been penciled in—as if the figure were promised but not yet delivered—from Eagle Corporation. *If I could just get a little picture of Costellini and this girl together. . . .*

Momentarily, Conroy became distracted as she tried to figure how to alert Davidson to tail Costellini and Erietta stateside. Suddenly, the sound of someone approaching the door snapped her back to Jamaica. *Now what? No time to return this to the safe.* Conroy kicked the safe door closed and sat down in the chair behind the desk, pulling the placement ledger into her lap. A split second later, Moxley appeared in the doorway to see Conroy looking casually into the mirror of the little compact she still held in her hand, the financial records lying on the desk between her elbows.

"Miss Conroy," Moxley said, "I would like you to meet one of our girls who is about to leave us for the U.S."

"I certainly would," Conroy replied, still gazing into her mirror, and now touching her eye as if trying to retrieve an errant lash. "May I join you in just a second?" *Much too close for comfort, Agent Conroy. Don't blow everything now.*

"Of course," Moxley said. "We still have some travel things to talk about. Erietta has never even been out of Mandeville."

Three minutes later, Conroy stepped into the outer reception room, where Moxley was talking to the girl. "Are you excited about moving to New York City?" the agent asked, struck with the young woman's delicate and fresh beauty, her light bronze skin accented by her long black hair.

The girl looked anxiously at Moxley, who nodded.

"Yes, ma'am," she answered.

"And a little worried, too?"

"Well, yes. I've lived here all my life. But I have studied about America, and Matron Moxley has helped me get ready," the girl replied, a tear forming in her right eye.

"Here, child," Conroy said, reaching out with a tissue. "Your mascara is running." *Somebody give the girl a crash course in makeup. She's wearing more than I am.* "See," Conroy said, holding her compact open about eighteen inches from the girl's face. She aimed the lens to capture not only Erietta's face, but also the vehicle sitting just outside, its female passenger framed nicely by the open window. Conroy coughed quietly to cover the sound of the camera's click. "There, you got it," she said. "But you are so pretty, you hardly need any makeup at all."

"Thank you, ma'am," MacIlmore said.

"Erietta is very lucky," Moxley commented. "A New York family has sponsored her. They will cover her education and all her other needs, and in return she will work as a maid in a resort in the mountains. The arrangement benefits everyone, you see."

I'll bet, Conroy thought. *Everyone but Erietta. She'll be lucky to reach eighteen without blowing her brains on crack.*

"Is that her sponsor, waiting?" Conroy asked. "Perhaps I could thank her for her generosity myself." *And see if I can get a photo to tie this up as tight as a drum.*

"Yes, ma'am, it is," Moxley said, "but. . . ."

"Not to worry," Conroy said over her shoulder as she stepped into the sunlight. "I'll introduce myself." She walked toward the car, where an impeccably dressed young woman sat in the back seat, the window rolled down. Conroy had only taken three steps toward the vehicle, however, when the driver's door opened. Out stepped an enormous bodyguard, who immediately placed himself directly between Conroy and the car.

"As Dr. Jenner's personal assistant, I just wanted to thank Miss Costellini for her generosity."

The bodyguard's gaze became only slightly more congenial. *Obviously not expecting North American company*, Conroy thought. The man glanced quickly back at Costellini, who nodded, an undisguised frown on her face.

Looks like a brief audience with her majesty. So, as the guard stepped aside to let her pass, Clare, still holding the compact in her right hand, pulled her shoulder bag around in front of her, as if to put the personal care item away. As she unzipped the bag and dropped the compact into it, Conroy managed to click one more shot.

"Excuse me," the driver said. "Let me see that bag."

Hoping her voice would not betray her alarm, Conroy joked, "What's the matter, forget your own purse today, big guy?" *Did he see that?*

"Left it home," he replied gruffly. "Nobody gets near Miss Costellini, 'cept I check for pieces . . . guns," he explained.

"Guns?" she laughed. "We fight our battles with other weapons, but go ahead and look if you insist."

Again the guard glanced at Costellini, who said, "It's okay, Frank. She looks harmless enough." As she spoke, the svelte, dark-haired, olive-skinned woman opened her door and stepped out to meet Conroy. She removed her sunglasses to reveal eyes as dark as her hair.

"Moxley didn't say anything about . . ." she began.

"She didn't know," Clare lied. "But since I was touring the facility, I thought I should at least thank you on behalf of ETR. Without your benevolence, this home might not exist."

"No thanks necessary," Costellini replied, briefly shaking Clare's outstretched hand as Moxley and Erietta approached the car. "Just helping a few poor kids make something useful of themselves," the woman added with a slightly twisted smile. Her guard visually devoured the young Jamaican as if she were a piece of tender meat.

22

Clare Conroy watched vacantly as the boys of the Good Shepherd Children's Home kicked a soccer ball around the field behind Moxley's office. Sitting on the embankment by herself, she was thinking about Erietta MacIlmore and hating herself for not preventing the violation of this innocent adolescent, who certainly had no idea what was about to happen to her. *But interfering might have blown my cover. I couldn't compromise the whole investigation to save one girl's innocence. Or was I more worried what might happen to me? Coward! And now it's too late.*

With tears in her eyes, Conroy leaned back on the grass and gazed skyward. The imminent assault on Erietta's innocence had become a very personal issue for the agent, as if her own virtue were on the line. *Do you see what's going on here, God? Do you care about one little Jamaican girl . . . or even one little American girl, 'cause that's what I feel like at this moment? If there really are guardian angels, would you assign one to Erietta . . . just for a while, until I can do something?*

Conroy's reflections were interrupted by the sound of a plane flying overhead, followed by the loud Creole conversation and laughter of two men who were working just beyond the hedgerow behind her. "Hey, mon," one of them called to the plane, "gange spraying up the valley . . . ha, ha, when it's all right here in the shed! Ha, ha."

"Yeah, mon," the other laughed "Bomb this barn, de whole town get high."

Gange . . . the Jamaican word for marijuana. Another piece to the puzzle. Clare decided it was time to be a little chummy with the locals. *No wonder we're invited to Colombia,* she thought as she rose to take a walk past the storehouse. There she engaged the men in a brief conversation while getting them and the building on film. *In one day, a whole album, Bruce. This place is a gold mine.*

Nanook I am not, Davidson muttered as he struggled to follow Wilkes on snowshoes along the back side of the ridge, through the timber and then out into the open area on the east slope. *Must be born with these things on their feet in Maine,* he thought, looking down at the webs. *Good thing he's breaking the trail. Never make it alone.*

Despite the hundred-pound pack of batteries on his back, Wilkes seemed to be enjoying himself immensely. As they broke into the clear, he started to run along, lifting one knee high as he pushed off with the other leg, dancing and laughing.

Not to be outdone, Davidson tried to imitate his friend. But he only made it about five steps before he lost his balance, tripped, and fell clumsily off the trail. Tumbling down the slope, he was suddenly swimming in powder instead of standing on it. When he finally came to rest, he was nearly upside down, the snowshoes the only thing that kept him from disappearing completely into the deeply drifted snow.

In the distance, muffled, Davidson could hear Wilkes laughing. He would have joined him if he hadn't been so afraid at that moment of suffocating in the drift. *Snowbanks and claustrophobia. Can't touch bottom. Which way is bottom?* he wondered as he started to panic. *Wilkes isn't here, I'm a snowball until May.*

He focused his thoughts until only one question needed answering: *How am I going to stand up?* He searched with his hands for something solid. *Nothing.* Slowly he worked the snowshoes down and underneath, pushing himself upward toward the surface, surprised to find it was really only a foot or two above his present level. "Here," he heard Wilkes saying, "grab this rope, and I'll pull ya out."

Once Davidson was rescued, Wilkes chuckled, "Guess you didn't use snowshoes much down Texas way! In Maine, you learn 'em soon as you kin walk, or you don't get around in winter."

"Thanks," Davidson said, trying to catch his breath as he brushed off the powdery snow. "Don't know what . . . I would have done . . . without you."

"Prob'bly been fine. Ain't never slept in a snowbank? Warm as toast, if you do it right. That's the way pa'tridges survive in the northwoods, y' know. Fly into a big snowdrift at night 'n' stay there 'til the sun comes up ag'in. Snow is good insulation!"

By the time they reached the mine entrance, Davidson was exhausted, although he hated to admit it. The homemade elk jerky Wilkes provided certainly tasted good, and fresh water dipped from the mountain stream along the way helped with his dehydration. *Forget the halizone; I'll take my chances.* As he munched, Davidson eyed the snowshoes, now sticking out of the snowbank next to the entrance. *Have to get a set of these babies and practice before I come up here again. This is embarrassing.*

This time through the tunnel, Davidson felt far more relaxed, though he still had moments in the darkness when he felt that unseen walls were closing in around him. *At least it's not crushing my chest*, he congratulated himself. As far as the sleeping bruin was concerned, Davidson hardly gave it a thought, though now the cave smelled more like the inside of a stable than it had before.

When they reached the observation point, Wilkes again excused himself. "Don't get in here often enough," he said. "Like to find some more'a them gemstones."

Davidson aimed the parabolic dish on the medical center this time, listening long enough to be sure he was focused on the right place. Someone was talking—a female voice that clicked on the voice-activated recorder at Davidson's feet.

"A wise decision, Winters. You're the ninth of twelve. By the time the team returns, we should be ready to get this underway."

"Will it hurt, Dr. Bradley?"

"You won't even know anything has happened," the doctor replied, "until, of course, the baby starts to grow. But you won't feel much until maybe twelve weeks have passed. Toward the end it might get uncomfortable. But when you're ready to deliver, we'll do a C-section to ensure nothing happens to the boy."

Davidson took off the earphones; he could listen later. Right now he wanted to get some more pictures. Looking through the camera lens, he noted that the building under construction earlier was now apparently finished. The compound seemed almost vacant, except for an occasional maintenance truck plowing and a couple of workers shoveling walkways.

The only other activity he could see involved two men wiring a large box on a utility pole immediately in front of the new building. Davidson watched for awhile, but even with binoculars he couldn't see what they were mounting there. He snapped a few pictures to analyze later. *Light fixture, maybe.*

About an hour after he took up his position, Davidson noticed through the camera lens that it was snowing. When he put the camera down for a moment, he realized the storm was intensifying quickly. *Starting to look serious,* he thought as he heard Wilkes behind him in the dark.

"Pretty good storm brewing," he said. "Think we should leave for the cabin with the weather setting in like this?"

"Don't worry," Wilkes said, "I kin find m'way home blindfolded in the dark. First just follow our own tracks till we can't see 'em anymore. Then follow my nose. There's already six feet'a snow out there—what's a little more?"

Noticing Davidson's concern, Wilkes chuckled, "Course, we could stay right here if ya like. Maybe snuggle up to that furry little bearskin rug inside. Be nice and warm, I wager, an' she'd never even know. You game? Or are ya thinkin' 'bout the guy that went out huntin' for a bearskin coat and the bear that was lookin' for a good meal—and they both got their wish? Ha! Ha!"

Wilkes was still chuckling when they reached the mouth of the cave and peered out to see that a blizzard was indeed setting in. "Trust me," he assured Davidson, "and don't let them negative thoughts convince ya anyways else." He handed Davidson one end of a twenty-five-foot length of quarter-inch nylon rope. "Tie this 'round yer waist, and I'll tie t'other end 'round mine, just in case."

"In case of what?" Davidson asked, as he tied on the snowshoes.

"Case it gets so bad you can't see yer own hand in front of yer face, and the wind's howlin' so bad ya can't hear yerself scream!" He smiled, but it was more the benevolent smile of a doctor giving a difficult diagnosis than of a jokester pulling Davidson's leg.

Davidson glanced back over his shoulder, considering for just a moment what a night in that cave might do to his psyche, whether or not Wilkes was in there with him. Then he looked at Wilkes and said, "If it gets that bad, my friend," he said, "you may end up pulling me out of another snowbank."

"No problem," Wilkes said. "Carry ya out if I have ta."

With that the shepherd led the way into the storm. The deadliest challenge was crossing the rock slide right outside the cave. The wind roared up the east slope as they slowly made their way across the unprotected area. Davidson fought not only to move forward a few inches at a time, but also to maintain his balance as the gale caught his parka, threatening to rip it off, and nearly lifting him into the air several times.

People die in blizzards, Nanook, he told himself after a half hour's struggle had taken them only halfway across the rocks. *Not a chance of a snowball in a holocaust we'll find that cabin.* But each time Davidson paused to ponder his fate, the tug of the rope kept him moving, inching his way toward the shelter of the pines ahead.

Sometimes it wasn't his doubts but his disorientation that made Davidson pause. The snow was coming so fast he thought he was back in that snowdrift upside down—or maybe in the middle of a very cold dream. He couldn't even see his hands in front of his face, although when he held them there the biting wind stopped and everything went black. But he couldn't feel the mittens against his skin. *My face is frozen.* He stuck his mitten in his mouth and bit down on his fingers to make sure he wasn't hallucinating. *And the rest of me will be frozen before long. I've heard it's not a bad way to die. Just go to sleep.*

Again he felt Wilkes tug, an unseen guide pulling him gently forward by a synthetic umbilical cord, his lifeline. He wanted to tug back, to let Wilkes know he was there, too, but he didn't want to risk making his friend lose his balance. Wilkes needed to reserve all his energy for breaking the trail.

For what was, undoubtedly, the longest hour of his life, the agent struggled to stay calm. Occasionally he checked the rope's knot, just to be sure. Without that cord, he was a dead man. *Even with it I'm a dead man—if Wilkes gets lost.*

But Wilkes proved himself right. After they reached the trees, the journey became much easier, though for Davidson it remained an exercise in absolute trust. It was a feeling he'd had occasionally as a kid, but not since his father's death had he been willing to risk it again. For the moment, though, he had no choice. It was trust or perish.

From time to time as they crossed the ridge and then descended the valley to the cabin, in the lee of the storm, Davidson chastised himself for the doubt that had nearly paralyzed him during the difficult trek. When they finally reached the cabin—Cyrus greeting them joyfully—he was sure that no place was more like heaven on earth.

Once inside, all Davidson wanted to do was curl up in his sleeping bag next to the stove and sleep for about a week. Wilkes, however, insisted they have some dinner first.

"You weren't nervous back there, were ya?" Wilkes asked between mouthfuls of beans, jerky, hot bread, and molasses. How he had the energy to create a meal, Davidson couldn't figure, but the food tasted so good he wasn't about to complain.

"Truthfully," he responded, after giving the question some thought, "*panic* would be a better word. But the rope kept me sane. Once when we stopped and the wind was howling and the snow was blowing and the rope went limp, I wondered if you were still there. Couldn't really tell from my end. Had to fight the temptation to yank on it till I could see you."

"Little like faith, maybe?" Wilkes remarked.

"Yeah," Davidson nodded thoughtfully. "But what if you do yank, maybe even real hard, and nobody's there?"

"Don't know. Felt that way m'self sometimes. Maybe just means he's closer than we think, and we didn't take up enough slack to find out."

Under cover of the blizzard, Adam Putnam snuck into the Data Center and flipped on his workstation. "Obewan," he typed, "I am a prisoner on the Imperial Starship commanded by Dr. J. R. Jenner and based at Walton's Creek, Colorado. The Rebel force is small here. I alone am left. I have the blueprints of the Death Star, which I will provide when you come. Attached are some samples. Save me, Obewan. You are my only hope. Yoda."

Putnam typed in the commands and fired the message via modem to the unlisted Pentagon telephone number he still remembered. *Connect! They didn't change it. Claude, hope you still get your mail at this address.*

23

"See ya again soon?" Wilkes asked as Davidson prepared to leave.

"Couple weeks too soon?"

"Okay by me, but every year Mr. Bryan has us down fer a few days in January to make plans for the new year. Comes up and gets us with one'a his ranchhands. Cyrus loves t'ride in a little wagon on the back of th' snowmobile."

"Well," Davidson hesitated, "I was hoping to check on the equipment about then."

"Fine. Use the cabin. You know yer way around it by now, and I'll feel better knowin' somebody's here instead of leavin' it empty fer three days. Won't hafta take the sourdough with me, either. You kin sleep with it while I'm gone! Ha, ha."

"How about if I arrive before you go and keep an eye on it until you come back?"

"January first, one o'clock in the afternoon, Bryan'll be sitting right there, rev'n' his engine. He's never late."

"I'll get here in the late morning, then," Davidson said as he punched the EXT's starter switch. Cyrus started bouncing all over the place and barking as if he wanted to go along. "See you in a couple of weeks," Davidson said. *At least I can meet Clare in a warm place*, Davidson thought as he headed for Hunter's Creek Pass.

But when he got back to Boulder, the report on his desk made Davidson wish he'd focused the dish on another building in that compound. *What is this?* He studied the sheets of paper that had just been delivered from XRAY, trying to decipher the meaning of the printout. He was still looking at it when the phone rang—his secure line. *Trouble.*

"Davidson?" the voice on the other end asked.

"Yes."

"Jeffers, Willie . . . Shadow. Remember?"

"No kidding, Willie. How's Pentagon life?" Davidson said, remembering that Jeffers had stayed with intelligence after their MI stint together in Vietnam.

"Kicked me upstairs, Ninja, to keep me out of trouble, I guess . . . upstairs as in three stars—the works." Jeffers paused, then got to the point, "Got a weird one here. Thought I'd take a shot in the dark and see what you know about it."

"The Bambi thing?" Davidson ventured, working from the raw data still in his hands.

"That's it. Then you do know about it?"

"Yeah," Davidson said. "Looking at it right now."

"This guy Putnam's a little wacko, don't you think?" Jeffers said.

Putnam? Must be Yoda's real name.

Jeffers was still talking: "*Bambi Meets Godzilla*? Shipping manifests for hydrochloric acid? File numbers involving large amounts of money? And he shoots this whole thing into our mainframe through a secret back door, addressed to his friend Claude—that's Obewan, who still works here. Putnam gone psycho or something? And what's he mean, 'Save me, Obewan; you're my only hope'?"

"Like you say, Putnam *is* a little wacko," Davidson said.

Can't let MI into this now, or Clare's at risk, he thought. *Have to get the scoop on Putnam from somebody else in Washington. But what in the world is he doing at the Institute?* "Maybe he's just fooling around, you know, the way hackers do sometimes. Who knows what looking at a computer monitor for days at a time will do to a guy?"

"You got that right. When he was with us, he was always goofing off, screwing around with codes and stuff. Got Ivan pretty worked up once by sending out data proving SDI would kill anything they had." Jeffers laughed, then added, "And that was after he showed us SDI would never work!"

Jeffers paused to let the comment sink in, then continued, "Putnam is good, very good. He's in trouble, we're very concerned."

"Hear you loud and clear, Shadow. But I wouldn't worry about Putnam too much. He's involved in one of our projects. Maybe just staying in touch with an old buddy. Have to put a muzzle on him. Sorry. And . . . if you don't mind, keep a lid on it at your end. Some people at risk here."

"Understood," Jeffers said. "And you know what to do with that telephone number. You need any help, a certain G3, Colonel Warren Zewolski, Fort Carson, will provide any support you need. We still think of Putnam as one of ours. Glad you found him something constructive to do with his talents. After he finished here he was one lost puppy. Didn't want to stay. Too much of a peacenik, religious variety. But if he falls into the wrong hands, we're talking national security risk. Am I making myself clear enough?"

"Of course. I'll give Zewolski a call if we run into trouble."

"Do that. Red line is 719-555-0222. He's ready."

Davidson hung up, looked again at the sheet and then at the topaz crystals sitting on the mantle behind his desk. *RADON leaking all over the place.* "Be careful, Clare," he muttered, as he dropped the gemstones into his pocket and headed out the door.

Monument Hall was crowded, overflowing into Sabina Park in Kingston, Jamaica. The public-address system normally flooding the street with reggae music, had been temporarily converted to a more pious purpose.

Clare Conroy's first impression as she followed Dr. Jenner to the platform was that very few inside the hall had bathed properly in some time. The overhead fans helped a little, but about all they accomplished was a thorough melding of a variety of body odors. *Open the windows, at least,* she thought. *They're already open? I think I'm going to die.*

The second thing Clare noticed, to her surprise, was that Joanna Jackson and her grandmother were sitting in the front row, not more than ten feet away from the podium.

". . . and I would like to introduce my new personal assistant, Miss Clare Conroy," Jenner was saying. "This is her first visit to your beautiful country. Perhaps she'll share some of her impressions."

At first, Clare spoke slowly, enunciating clearly in typical American English. "What a delight it has been to tour your country and even to make some new friends. Your people are so gentle, so gracious and kind. Even little babies are mild-mannered and well-behaved. How do you accomplish this?" she asked.

"More amazing is the way you drive. You just ride along like nothing remarkable is happening, with us terrified in the back seat wondering if we will live. . . ."

And then, to the crowd's amazement and delight, Clare switched in midsentence into Creole, describing her wild ride through the hills from Montego Bay to Treasure Beach. "How do you learn to drive this way?" she continued in the vernacular, laughing. "You act like it is *no problem*. First we think you are driving on the wrong side of the road, and then we think we must certainly crash into a donkey or goat or meet one of your buses coming from the other direction!"

Now the crowd was laughing and clapping. She knew they loved to think of Americans as timid and themselves as very brave. And they loved to hear about wild rides, because most of them never got to ride anywhere at all.

"This must be how you train your Olympic bobsledding team!" Again they applauded, even more loudly.

"But mostly," she continued in English, "I've learned some lessons about values and meaning. About life on a much simpler level than ours in America—always rushing but never really getting anywhere, always buying things we don't need, yet never really satisfied. But you know how to be satisfied," she said, looking directly at Winelda Storey, whose needs would now be taken care of by a benefactor she might never see again.

The old woman smiled as Clare continued, "You know the secret of contentment, which if it could be exported to the whole world like your bauxite, would give to every person everywhere the possibility of true happiness."

"Thank you, Miss Conroy," Dr. Jenner said as he walked back to the podium and stood beside her. "I wasn't aware that you were fluent in the native language of Jamaica. Perhaps you will assist me by repeating what I have to say in the patois. I'm sure the people will be grateful."

Again the crowd applauded, and those outside strained to see this young woman who cared enough about them to communicate directly to their hearts.

"You are no longer slaves," Jenner began, "but heirs, joint heirs of the kingdom." He paused and Clare repeated, "You are no longer slaves, but heirs, joint heirs of the kingdom." *Good place to start with people who were slaves until a few generations ago*, she thought. But after starting, she didn't really have time to interact with the message personally; she had to focus so intently on translating.

"Yet even though we live in an age of freedom, we all know that many things can enslave men, their families, and ultimately entire nations. All around the world, at this very minute, people are dying needlessly. There are wars and rumors of wars. Children are starving by the millions when, if only nations would beat their swords into plowshares and distribute the resources fairly, there would be enough for everyone. Enough food, enough money, enough of everything! And no one will kill or destroy on my holy mountain, neither will they learn war any more!"

The crowd applauded, politely at first, then building into a mixed crescendo of clapping and "yeah, mon."

He paused, scanning the crowd, many of whom probably hadn't had a good meal in weeks, then continued, "Did you know that even as we enter the third millennium, seven point six million children die every year on this planet. And just one day's military spending—two to three billion dollars—could save half of them. Half of them. Think of it! And think of what that same money could do for the Jamaican economy. What it would do for you personally. Three billion dollars . . . every day. You know how many dollars that is? Why, if you stacked one-dollar bills on top of each other, the stack would be higher than from here to the moon." He paused again to let the comparison sink in.

"But all that money is just being wasted, making the rich richer and the poor poorer. And in the name of what? Security? National Defense? Lies, all lies. Greed is the real cause. They build big bombs they will later throw away so they can build bigger bombs. My friends, the world is hurtling headlong toward chaos as great empires crumble and smaller nations are caught in the crossfire.

"And what will remain when the rich have killed each

other off in the great war that is coming? Jamaica! Jamaica will remain—with resources to feed itself and people to carry on. People who understand how to live in peace. And people to go from here to lead in the renewal that will follow . . . that must follow after all the shooting ends and the people have died everywhere else."

He stopped. The audience was transfixed. Clare was out of breath from trying to keep up with Jenner once he got rolling. She had heard most of this before via videotape, but it was quite different to hear it from her own mouth. *They want us to be right,* she thought. *They want to believe. In fact they do believe. But does that justify us, if all this is a delusion? Then again, is it so wrong to give them one delusion in exchange for another?*

"You may be asking yourself," Jenner began again, "how you can become part of our family. How you can become one with the End Times Renewal, the finger of God in today's world." Clare began to translate again.

"At this moment, moving among you are ushers to provide registration cards for any who wish to be part of our study groups. 'Study to show thyself approved. . . .' Knowledge is the key to fulfilling the will of God in our generation. And Jamaica is a key nation in the plan. For here, unhindered by the evil influences of the West and East, we will demonstrate what it truly means to fulfill your country's motto: Out of many, one people."

The people began to applaud and whistle, and some stood as they clapped. Eventually the whole group was standing. And as they stood, the ushers passed among them, handing out cards to just about everyone.

Clare watched, thinking, *They'll buy anything that promises stability—political or economic—or even a family identity. Beyond that, ETR offers status, even to peasant farmers like Winelda Storey.*

"But while you remain standing," Jenner continued, when the crowd quieted a bit, "let me ask you what it would be worth to turn this vision into reality? Would it be worth more than silver?" Clare wished she could back away from translating what was coming, but she couldn't think of a way.

"Yeah, mon," the group shouted.

"More than gold?"

"Yeah, mon."

"Ladies, would it be worth more than the cost of that dress you want to buy at the market?"

"Yeah, mon."

"Men, would it be worth more than that money you were going to spend on Red Stripe beer at the tavern tonight?"

"Yeah, mon."

"Then I ask you to give generously. Reach down a little deeper and give sacrificially, cheerfully and wholeheartedly, for the Lord loveth a cheerful giver."

Jenner looked at Clare, who was stumbling a bit with this last part as she tried to temper his solicitation. It was a futile attempt, since the people could understand both of them.

The ushers passed among the people again, taking the offering as Jenner continued to exhort the crowd: "And don't forget, people; you can never outgive God. If you give, he will give it back, pressed down and overflowing, sometimes tenfold, sometimes a hundredfold."

And just as she was repeating those very words after Jenner, regretting that she had shown off earlier, Clare happened to see Winelda Storey dropping Jamaican bills into the plate—the equivalent of thirty U.S. dollars. Clare's first impression was to try to prevent this woman from giving what must have been her life's savings. But when Conroy remembered the value of the check she had written to

Matron Moxley, her anger turned first to amazement and then to wry satisfaction.

A hundredfold! He is *a prophet!* she laughed to herself. *But if he's going to use me to empty poor people's pockets, he owes me some kind of warning, if not an explanation.*

The first time Conroy could bring up the subject, however, was the next afternoon as the ETR group climbed Duns River Falls near Ocho Rios. Jenner and Conroy were last in a thirty-foot string of people holding hands and snaking their way up the falls after an experienced guide. The roar of the water made it possible to have a private conversation even as they continued climbing the picturesque tourist attraction.

"Dr. Jenner?" she began.

"Yes, Rachel."

"How would you compare this Jamaican trip to others you've made?"

"Wonderful," he said, "highly successful. After years of labor, our ministry is really taking root. Soon we'll export the model to Mexico, South America, and other lands where the poor long for some hope."

"But, sir," she said, "doesn't it bother you to take away what little they have in a collection, like last night, when we can't possibly need their money as much as they do?"

She could see the shock in his eyes. *First time anybody's ever criticized the prophet?*

"Even Jesus allowed a woman to pour a vial of very expensive perfume over his feet," he replied. "But some objected, among them Judas, because the perfume could have been sold and the money given to the poor. 'The poor you have with you always,' said Jesus. If they want to give, we should encourage them, for who knows what blessing they may get in return?"

"But can we justify separating them from their very last cent?" she asked, ignoring the fact that she had just been compared to Judas.

"My friend," Jenner replied, rather sternly, "I used to worry about questions like that . . . until I realized I don't have to justify *anything* to *anyone*."

With that, Jenner turned back toward the falls and away from Clare, who decided for the moment not to press that issue—or any other issue. However, she was relieved to have registered her objection to fleecing the likes of Winelda Storey so that the ETR team could have a weekend in Ocho Rios. She was even more relieved to think that the anger of J. Reuben Jenner might result in an extension of her probation and keep the JACOB project on hold just that much longer.

Dinner was at The Waterworks, a four-star restaurant set up against a rock cliff where one of the eight rivers of Ocho Rios tumbled toward the sea. Expecting scorn, Conroy was surprised to find Jenner even more animated and talkative than usual.

"Miss Conroy," Jenner said quietly when she had finished half of her shrimp cocktail, "about this afternoon . . . perhaps you sensed I found your questions disturbing?"

"Yes, sir," Clare replied, not looking up. "That was pretty clear." *What now, public humiliation?*

"Well . . . I've been thinking it over," Jenner continued, "and I would like to apologize. . . ."

Clare almost choked. She had never heard Jenner apologize to anyone. Quite the contrary, he had a reputation for never even changing his mind.

"Are you all right?" he asked, noticing her distress. When she nodded, he smiled and added, "I really hope that our relationship will continue to improve with time. One thing I would ask, though, is that if you have a question like today's, please ask it in private. It is better for partners to learn from each other privately, while presenting a united front to others. I trust you understand. . . ."

"Yes, of course," Conroy said. And then she blushed as she recalled the last time she had heard an apology like this, though the similarity was more in tone than content. Henry Rodnik, age eleven, had tried to kiss her on the way home from a sixth-grade dance. Liking the idea more than she cared to consider, Clare had slapped him, though not hard enough to make his face any redder than it was already.

Clare diverted her attention to the illuminated falls for a moment, thankful that the room's darkness hid her blush. When she turned back to her meal, a messenger was standing behind Dr. Jenner.

"I'm very sorry to disturb your meal, sir. But this urgent telegram has just arrived, addressed to you, and it is my duty to deliver it to you, personally, as quickly as possible."

"Thank you," Jenner said, handing the young man a Jamaican fifty-dollar bill.

Clare watched Jenner's face pale, even in the darkness, as he read and reread the message, then handed it to her. By now everyone in the party was aware that something awful had happened. Quickly Clare scanned the brief telegram, then handed it back to Jenner, saying softly, "I'm sorry."

"Read it to *them*," he said, his voice quavering.

"But, sir," she started to protest, realizing as she did that he wanted her to do it because he couldn't read it to them himself.

She stood up and said, in a somber tone, loud enough for everyone at the table to hear, "We have received sad news from Colorado," she began, "and Dr. Jenner has asked me to read you this telegram:

Clare sat down. But after a hushed several minutes, Dr.

telegram

REGRET TO INFORM YOU OF THE ACCIDENTAL DEATH OF PAUL WOODMAN, FAITHFUL SERVANT AND MASTER BUILDER AND FRIEND OF THE KINGDOM. MEMORIAL SERVICE TOMORROW PER ADVANCE DIRECTIVES. FOLLOWING CREMATION ASHES WILL BE SPREAD TO THE WINDS FROM PINNACLE ROCK WHICH WAS HIS WISH. IN YOUR SERVICE. WINSTON. STOP.

Jenner stood to his feet and said, "Friends, I've known Paul Woodman since before the New World Institute was built. He oversaw the construction of every square inch of our facility as carefully as he would have built his own home. Yet somehow the end has been decreed for him, as it will be for all of us someday. So, we remember Paul with fondness and appreciation—for who he was and for how much of himself he gave toward something bigger than any one of us."

He took his glass, which was filled with a fine Chablis, and lifted it high. "We toast you, Paul. You gave yourself that others might live in the light of the kingdom of God. Ashes to ashes, dust to dust, glory to glory. Amen."

24

M*ugged in the airport, in the middle of the day?* Conroy wondered as an unkempt character wearing a leather jacket and dark glasses suddenly stepped in front of her and Jonathan Dexter, the director of children's homes for ETR. They had just deplaned in Miami with a connection to Cali, Colombia.

"Drop the bags on the floor and step back," an official-sounding voice commanded. The young man's hand displayed the badge of a U.S. customs officer. *Welcome to the U.S.A!* Clare fought back a mixture of embarrassment and outrage as the others from ETR turned to see what was going on.

Stanton started to intervene, but backed off when the customs agent said rather tersely, "Routine inspection, folks. Your friends will not be detained long. Of course, we take volunteers, too," he added with a smile as he gave the bags a rather cursory inspection and handed them back.

Clare was relieved at the thought of rejoining the others, even though she had nothing to hide. But to her surprise the officer said, "You will both kindly follow me. We are conducting random searches of travelers from certain countries in our effort to enforce the president's war on drugs. This will only take a moment. I trust you will understand," he added, smiling again.

"Men that way and women that way," he pointed, then turned perfunctorily and headed back to his post.

You make it sound patriotic, pal. Hope you get the same treatment someday yourself, Conroy thought as she was ushered through what appeared to be the main room and into a smaller, more secluded, cubicle.

"May I see your passport, please," a woman younger than herself said with a Puerto Rican accent, "as well as any other I.D. you may have with you."

"Of course," Conroy said, laying her wallet open for a moment.

"And please empty your handbag on the table, Miss . . . Conroy."

Thank God I'm traveling light, Clare thought, spilling the purse's contents out quickly before the agent, who lifted the bag and felt inside it, as if looking for hidden compartments. Next she examined each item on the table until she got to the compact, which she opened. "Very nice," she said, looking in the mirror for a moment.

Conroy watched, hoping the operational design of the micro-camera would not fail at this moment. Even knowing the unit only opened when its four pressure points were hit simultaneously seemed not to diminish her anxiety much.

"Miss Conroy," the agent said in a more hushed voice, "is this unit helpful in detecting radon?"

"Why yes, Miss . . . Guerrero," Clare replied, peering at the agent's name tag while trying to hide her total surprise at hearing the code word. As she changed her position to read the name, however, Conroy noticed that another agent behind Guerrero, but probably out of earshot, seemed to be taking a special interest in their conversation.

"Then I hope you'll enjoy using the replacement sent by

Mr. Davidson," Guerrero continued, placing an identical compact on the table as Conroy's disappeared into the inside pocket of Guerrero's jacket.

"He has also sent a message with two parts. First, there will be a meeting at the shepherd's cabin, Miner's Pass, on the second of January, at thirteen hundred hours. Second, stay out of the Bronx."

Conroy repeated the message as she repacked her handbag, intrigued by the second phrase. But before she could really focus on it, she again noticed the other woman watching.

"Guerrero, is there anything extraordinary about this interview?"

"Not really, except that I haven't conducted a full body search yet."

"Well, I suggest we do business as usual. Your supervisor seems quite interested in this exchange."

"Good idea," Guerrero said. "Let's get on with it, then."

"Come in," Florence Bradley said, as the recorder kicked on seven hundred feet away.

"Sheriff suspect anything?" Winston asked.

"If so, he didn't let on. Pretty good piece of work, if I say so myself. Slash hardly showed. Should have gone into plastic surgery. Papers are in order, and the body is cremated. Why do you sound so worried?"

"Can't be too careful," Winston said. "Don't want anything to gum up the works—you know what I mean."

"I certainly do. Every time I get the train started, somebody wants to derail it."

"But Linda's cooperating now."

"Not talking about Linda. I'm talking about Mary Jenner. We're going to have to do something about her, too."

What does the Bronx have to do with Colombia? Is it a

zoo down there, and I need to be careful? Everybody knows that. Not worth risking the op. Something else. Suddenly Conroy remembered following Stanton to the Blue Flamingo and her own difficulty in getting out clean. *How can Bruce know about that? Tail? The other taxi! Thought we had lost them. Wonder if he got more than I did.*

Jonathan Dexter had the seat next to Conroy on the flight to Cali, which would include a brief layover at Barranquilla. "Miss Conroy, did you know there are eight thousand street kids in Bogotá alone?" Dexter said when they were finally airborne.

"Really?" Clare replied, figuring she might as well use the air time to discover how much Dexter knew about the connection between Eagle Corporation, the Costellinis, and the ETR children's homes. "I suppose that with all the bombings there must be a lot of orphans."

"Yes, that's partly the reason. The bombings get a lot of press, but many more killings occur more quietly. The Cartel is powerful and very rich. And in a land of such poverty, money can buy most anything, including murder. Why work hard all day for a dollar fifty when by killing someone you can make a thousand dollars in a minute?" Dexter observed.

"How do the street kids survive?" she asked.

"As far as I can see," Dexter continued, "the gamines—that's what they're called—do whatever it takes. Most of them, even little five- and six-year-olds, pick the dumps and rummage through street trash just for another bite of food. The older ones, especially the boys, mostly hang around together, sniffing glue and smoking *basuco*, a mixture of crude cocaine paste and marijuana or tobacco. Poor man's crack."

"What about the girls?" Conroy asked.

Dexter looked around, checking to see if their conversation was being overheard. When he continued, he was clearly embarrassed. “Well, I hate to say it, but it’s a fact of life, and one reason we’re so interested in helping out here. If the girls survive to, say, ten or twelve, very often they get involved in what is sometimes called the oldest profession. . . . I’m sure you know what I mean.”

“Of course,” Clare replied, intrigued that Dexter saw his mission as rescuing young women from prostitution, when some of his colleagues were doing just the opposite.

“I’m sorry,” Dexter apologized. “I didn’t mean to offend you, but facts are facts, and you did ask.”

“No problem,” Clare said, smiling to think how Jamaican the words sounded. “Can anything be done to intervene?”

“We can try, certainly, and other U.S.-based groups are trying, but the task is nearly overwhelming. Besides, anyone coming into this country from the U.S. is pegged as CIA.”

“If the Cartel’s so powerful, it must have been difficult getting an invitation to visit Colombia,” Clare commented, hoping to discover who was really behind the trip.

“We never go anywhere until we’re invited. In this case the Mayor of Dagua, a small village near Cali, invited us to do a site visit. He’d like us to set up a children’s home there as soon as possible.”

“Why not Bogotá,” Clare asked, “if there are so many gamines?”

“Bogotá is a key city,” Dexter said, “being the capital and all. We may well establish a home there later. But it’s easier to provide a family atmosphere in a rural setting. The kids may come from the city, but there is something . . . therapeutic about living in the country. There’s more room for recreation, gardening, raising livestock—things that build cohesion and teach responsibility.”

Not to mention making surveillance by outsiders much more difficult, Conroy thought, wondering how Dexter would handle discovering that his years of sacrifice had been flushed down the toilet by the Costellinis. *How did they do it?* she wondered, gazing at the ocean passing beneath them at 550 miles per hour. *How did they get their hooks into ETR without its knowledge or consent? Dexter doesn't know about it. What about Jenner?*

As she mentally reviewed the list of ETR insiders, the face of Paul Woodman came into her mind and a certain chill into her heart. *Murdered*, she murmured, *obviously. But why? What did Woodman know? What did he do? And if he was killed, who else is at risk? Anyone and everyone who gets in the way!*

"Did you say something?" Dexter asked.

"Someone has to stop these murderers," Conroy said, chastising herself for letting the danger get the best of her. *Hogan's Alley this is not,* she mused, remembering her training site. *No actors teaching the G-woman how to do the job without getting blasted. No debriefing. No second chances. This is reality. So what next? Shall I jump up and shout "Freeze. This is the FBI!"?*

"On behalf of the people of Dagua and the nation of Colombia," Mayor Carlos Mendoza began, "we welcome our visitors from the United States." The speech, though not excessively long by Latin American standards, took forty-five minutes because each phrase the mayor pronounced in English was repeated in Spanish by the local radio announcer for whatever audience might be listening. Every few minutes, the announcer paused to adjust the unit's small antenna, which appeared to be a modified coat hanger.

Who could be listening? Conroy wondered. *The whole town must be here.*

The one-hour trip from Cali had been like a journey back in time and across social boundaries. From high-rise buildings and late-model cars to single-story block dwellings with thatched roofs, and donkeys with baskets hanging on both sides. From high-fashion clothes to kids in rags running around barefoot and rolling their ever-present metal barrel rim down the dirt road with a stick. *Dexter was right. This is better. More stable. Safer. Won't hurt the local economy, either.*

Finally the mayor was through taking credit for bringing ETR to Colombia. But then it was time for every other official on the platform to share the glory, a process that ate up another two hours because the announcer insisted on repeating everything verbatim. Neither the speeches nor the ninety-five-degree heat seemed to bother the locals much, but Clare could see the other ETR people wilting in the humidity. She figured she would rescue them when it came time to make a response.

"Mr. Mayor," she said in Spanish, "and good people of Bagua, you make it sound like it is your honor to have us come to visit your beautiful country." She stopped, automatically, after each phrase as the announcer did his job, talking to nobody in the middle of nowhere, which hindered his enthusiasm not in the least.

"But it is *our* honor, I promise you, to be invited here. To work side by side with such courageous heroes who are struggling so hard to try to bring healing in the midst of suffering . . . and especially for the little ones, the future of Colombia, a generation in need of nurture and comfort. We thank you for your kindness and hospitality, and we look forward to spending these few days in your region."

She sat down, hoping her brevity would not offend them, but willing to trade that possibility for a cold drink—anything would do—at the reception immediately following at the mayor's hacienda. The crowd applauded, rather tentatively at first, and then more earnestly as the mayor and then all the other dignitaries stood and clapped as well.

After lunch, Conroy, Jenner, Dexter, and Stanton piled into a new Mercedes 500SEL for a tour of Bagua and vicinity. Conroy, sitting next to Pedro, the driver, translated all his pertinent comments for the others. In between translations, she carried on a secondary conversation with Pedro about the area's lifestyle, culture, education . . . whatever he was willing to talk about.

At first Pedro seemed reluctant to give Conroy more than minimal responses to her questions, but gradually he warmed up to her. At one point he even produced a photograph of his family, which consisted of two daughters, aged five and eight, and his wife of ten years, Maria. Conroy exclaimed over their beauty and passed the photo to the others in the back seat.

Everything seemed to be going smoothly in the tour until, just on the outskirts of Yumbo, the Mercedes stalled. Nothing Pedro could do seemed to make any difference. With the air conditioning off, it was too hot to sit in the vehicle, so Stanton suggested, "Let's find the local market and buy a Coke."

Conroy got directions from Pedro and passed them along to the others.

"You're coming too, aren't you, Conroy?" Stanton said.

"Well, no, not just yet," she replied. "I'm pretty good with cars from tinkering with my MG in college, so I think I'd rather stay and help Pedro get this baby going again," Clare replied as she opened her door and joined Pedro at the front of the car.

The driver protested, "No, please, señorita, this is not a woman's work. Look at you, dressed so pretty. I cannot let you dirty your hands."

Stanton was equally insistent. "Conroy, leave repairs to the mechanics and come with us."

"You don't need an interpreter to purchase a Coke," she

laughed. "It's the same worldwide. Just ask for the real thing." She could almost taste the drink, just thinking about it. But she reached under the hood instead, jiggling wires and tapping the distributor. *Strange*, she thought, *Mercedes never break down. Something must be loose.*

"Señorita, please, *please*, do not do this," Pedro pleaded, with an urgency that compelled Conroy to stop and look at him. His face had become tense and very flushed, and he was sweating profusely. His right hand was trembling, even though it was resting on the automobile as he stood next to Conroy.

"I must live here, señorita, even after you go back to America. What must my friends think if they see a woman fixing my automobile?" He smiled, but much more weakly than before.

"Okay, Pedro, if you insist," she said. "I'll go with the others."

"Si, señorita," Pedro agreed, obviously relieved as he handed her a clean white towel to wipe her hands. "And maybe you could ask for another car just in case this one will not fix."

"But don't you think it will go again?"

"I'm sorry, but I do not think so," he said as she turned to join the three men walking slowly toward the town.

"Glad you changed your mind," Stanton said. "Dexter was just about ready to come back for you. How can we talk to the locals without you? Maybe we should even call Mendoza for another car—if we can find a car that works, that is. You never know in a place like this what kind of crazy thing will happen next. . . ."

25

The bomb's blast knocked Clare Conroy to the ground. She turned in the dust to see an inferno of twisted steel where the Mercedes had been only moments before. Something was screaming—a shrill, inhuman squealing that was part of the scene, yet somehow detached from it.

"Oh, my God," Jenner said. "If we were still in there . . ."

"But Pedro *was* in there!" Conroy cried, horrified, as a human figure stumbled away from the wreckage with clothing aflame. She jumped up and ran toward him, arriving at the same time as another vehicle, which appeared from nowhere and screeched to a stop next to her.

The driver yanked a blanket from the back seat, dashed over to Pedro, and threw the blanket over him, smothering the flames. "Lie down," he ordered in Spanish. "If you are very lucky, you will live. I'll call an ambulance," he shouted over his shoulder as he ran back to his car and grabbed a microphone through the window.

Conroy leaned over Pedro. His eyes were barely open and slightly glazed as he drifted into shock. "Twenty seconds," he murmured. "He promised. . . ." And then he lost consciousness.

"Who? Pedro . . . *who* promised? What do you mean? Come back," Conroy pleaded. She wanted to shake him or slap him to wake him up. But as she looked at what had been a handsome face and saw his eyebrows and moustache gone, his lips charred, and his eyes already puffed up from the burns, the only thing she could focus on, suddenly, was finding a place to vomit.

She lunged for the privacy of the bushes, and tripped over something soft, a disemboweled sow dragging itself away from the fire. Six frenzied piglets raced around the pitiful animal, squealing. "Oh, God. . . ." she gasped. Then the mayor's banquet became part of the landscape.

When she returned, the man with the radio was waiting. "I am sorry," he said in nearly perfect English. "You are American, no?" When Conroy nodded, the man produced a badge. "I am Felix, DAS—secret police. You must come with me."

Then he addressed the others, who had arrived at the officer's car, too. "You must *all* come with me."

"Are we being kidnapped?" Jenner feebly asked Stanton.

"No, sir. I am Felix, DAS." He showed them his badge. "I hear the bomb and come quickly. Someone wants to kill you. I must take you away from here. Now get in, please. The others will stay with him," he said, pointing toward numerous local residents who were now converging at the scene, some carrying buckets of water for the fire.

"Take care of him," Felix shouted to them as he got into the car with the others, "and watch the car for me. I will return." They sped away, the car careening crazily through steep gorges and trails hardly wide enough for one vehicle, let alone two. Conroy, fully expecting to die at any moment, listened as Felix talked excitedly to his contacts by radio, driving with one hand while holding the microphone with the other. He did not slow down until he was confident no one was following them.

"Why would anyone want to kill *us*, Felix?" Dr. Jenner asked, finally. "We only want to help."

"Yes, Dr. Jenner, we know. But they think you are CIA. They think all Americans are CIA. And they are not afraid to kill anyone. They would have killed your president, who was brave to come here."

"We aren't CIA," Jenner replied.

"We know that, also, señor, but these assassins respect no one and will stop at nothing."

"Perhaps we should reconsider, Dr. Jenner," Dexter commented, quietly. "Is it fair to ask our people to come into this kind of anarchy?"

"Good point. But our homes are run by nationals. Shall we abandon the children because some hooligans try to assassinate me? All the more reason to confront them. All the more reason to proceed exactly as planned!" Jenner said forcefully. "What do you think, Mr. Stanton?"

"You are brave," Stanton replied. "You do best when you follow your heart. Whatever you decide is fine with me. I'll try to protect you, whether we're here or in Colorado."

"Would they even pursue us there?" Jenner asked.

"Who can say, sir," Stanton replied, "but it's better to be safe than sorry."

"Miss Conroy?" Jenner asked, as they turned into Mayor Mendoza's driveway to find the hacienda suddenly bristling with arms.

"I think," Conroy said, "I need some distance from this place. I can't be objective until we get back to the U.S. of A."

"This will happen . . . tomorrow, señorita," Felix interrupted as the mayor walked toward the vehicle. "But tonight you are guests of the U.S. embassy in Bogotá, where you will be safe.

"You leave as soon as possible," he continued. "An armored vehicle will take you to Cali, and a government plane will fly you to Bogotá, accompanied by armed troops. You will be there by evening. And tomorrow you will return to America with our humblest apologies. Good-bye señorita, señors. I must return to the scene and learn about this bomb."

"Yes, Felix," Conroy said in Spanish, "and please see if there is anything left of my purse. It was on the front seat. So stupid of me! *No lie, babe. The wrong people get their hands on that camera. . . .* My passport, credit card, everything is in there. Can you help me?"

"Not to worry, señorita. If anything is left we will return it to you. The car is guarded until I am returned. The embassy can give you new papers. Everything will be all right. You will see."

"Miss Conroy, Mr. Clark will see you now." The embassy secretary ushered Clare into the office of Special Assistant William Clark, who stood with his back to them, flipping through some files in the file cabinet. The secretary motioned Conroy toward a comfortable leather chair in front of the large teak desk.

"Thank you, Abrams, you may go now. It's been a long enough day," Clark said without turning around.

Odd way to greet a special guest, Clare thought as she sat down, *but there's something very familiar about that voice.*

Abrams turned and left immediately. As soon as the door shut, Conroy heard the diplomat say, in Russian, "Well, Punkie, finally we meet again!"

Then Clark turned around, and Clare found herself face

to face with her own father. He was grinning as he walked toward her, tentatively, as if waiting to see how she would greet him after more than a decade of silence.

"Had me worried silly," he said in English, "especially when I saw the photos of the vehicle."

For a moment, Clare sat frozen in place, her mouth wide open in a half-gasp of astonishment. Then she leaped from her seat into the hug she had been missing for longer than she cared to remember.

"*This* is where you've been?" she asked tentatively as they sat sipping cold Perrier with a little lemon, trying to catch up on fifteen missing years in just a few minutes.

"Not the whole time," he replied, in a tone that meant he couldn't really tell her what he'd been doing. "But obviously your mother never told you I worked for the Company. And you weren't quite old enough to handle it when she decided she'd had enough of never knowing if or when I might come home again."

"She never told me you were CIA," Clare said. "I always thought you were a professor of linguistics."

"Good place to recruit spies, don't you think?" he said, with a wink she had seen before after some practical joke. "The plan was to stay in New Haven until you could finish at Miss Putnam's school and then take another international assignment. But you know what they say about the best-laid plans. . . ."

He stopped and looked at Clare, who was fighting back tears. "I expect Wilbur was good for Gladys," he continued, "providing the security I could never give her."

"But," Clare wanted to argue with him, but she knew her mother had been much happier with her stepfather. Until this moment, however, she had never known why. "But . . . what about *me*? *I* wasn't happier. Wilbur was good to me, too, but I needed *you*. You were my security . . . my best friend, and then you just . . . disappeared."

She wanted to punish him, but now that she had found him again, she discovered this was all the anger she could muster. She looked at her father's face, bronzed from years in the tropics and hardened a bit. There were more lines now—lines of concern, not joy—and there was more gray hair . . . a lot of gray hair.

"I know, Punkie. I'm sorry. I don't know how often I've had my hand on the telephone, just wanting to hear your voice. It was hard, very hard, to leave you. But there was no way Gladys would follow me to my next assignment, and it was no place for a teenaged girl. So I just had to keep up with you from a distance—you know, through channels."

"All this time you've been keeping tabs on me without my knowing?" Clare asked, impressed that he would care that much.

"It wasn't really that hard, with the friends I have in various places. Remember how the diplomatic corps tried to recruit you away from that banking position, once you started looking for different work?" he asked.

"That was *your idea*?" she asked, surprised as he nodded.

"But I chose the Bureau because I figured I needed to stay in the States and be available to Mom," she said.

"Totally understandable, since you're her only child." He paused, and Clare noticed that he, too, was struggling for control. When she saw a tear in his eye, she realized that although they had shared a lot of laughter, she had never seen her father cry.

"Have you enjoyed, uh, your assignment—whatever it is Davidson has you doing?" he asked softly.

"You know *him*?" she squeaked. "Does he know you?"

"Certainly he doesn't know me by the last name *Conroy*.

We've met several times, actually, though since you started with him I've been careful to keep my distance, for safety's sake."

He paused again as she pondered how close she had just come to being another Colombian statistic.

"By the way, how did you get linked up with this religious group?" he asked.

"Not sure how much is classified," she said. "But I've been spying on the far-flung kingdom of Dr. J. Reuben Jenner, checking out certain allegations made by former group members. Surely not too exciting by Company standards."

"Interesting, though, no doubt," Clark said. "And obviously not without risk. I'm not referring just to the car bomb. I assume you know that one of your traveling companions has been on the Bureau's most-wanted list?"

"Who?" she asked, answering her own question almost immediately. "Stanton?"

"Perelli is his real name," Clark said. "Funny Davidson didn't tell you, considering their history. Perelli was never nailed for anything, but without doubt he is a hit man who may have once had a contract on Davidson himself. Too bad about Davidson's wife, though. Ellen, I think her name was."

"Oh?" Clare said. "Bruce never said anything about her, either. Figured he was always single. What happened?"

"Car bomb with his name on it, but Ellen turned the key instead."

"Is it possible Stanton—Perelli—had something to do with today's bombing?" she asked.

"Fits his M.O., though it was arranged very cleverly. We're waiting for the driver to recover so we can see what he knows."

"Will he make it, do you think?" Clare asked, thinking about Pedro, and especially about his daughters.

"Doctors say yes. But the biggest question is not whether he'll survive the burns, but how he'll stay alive later if he was supposed to have been killed by it in the first place."

"He did say something . . . strange, as he was going into shock," Clare offered. "'Twenty seconds,' he said. And then, just before he passed out, he added, 'He promised.'"

"Helps," Clark said. "Somebody promised him a delayed explosion but then rigged it to go immediately when tripped. From the burns and the fact that he was thrown away from the car instead of dying inside it, it appears that he leaned inside with the door open and activated the timer, thinking he would have time to escape before it blew. Who the 'he' is in this instance will be interesting to find out. There are some pretty smart ones in Cali. We call it the 'white-collar' Cartel. Wonder if Perelli and Hernandez know each other?"

"Why do it this way?" Clare asked.

"There's a good question. Any hunches?" he probed, "especially hunches based on what you know about ETR?"

"Well. . . ." she hesitated. *How much should I tell him? How much would Davidson tell him? Everything? Nothing?*

"If the car was rigged with a timer," she continued, shuddering as she recalled fiddling with the wires, "and not really intended to kill us, then it must have had another purpose—maybe to remind us that Americans aren't welcome here?"

She looked at Clark, who simply nodded. "Or, maybe, that *ETR* is not welcome in Colombia?" she continued.

"Or," he interjected, "to make it *seem* that ETR is not welcome in Colombia."

"Why would Perelli be part of that, and why would they need to kill Pedro?"

"Money in large enough amounts makes anything worthwhile to the criminal mind," he replied.

"It does connect," Clare added, "with evidence I uncovered in Jamaica, where marijuana is being stored on the premises of one of our children's homes."

"Of course!" he said. "Who would think to search *there?* If they can make it seem like your group is on their hit list, but you build the facility, anyway . . . the Cartel will be able to use it at will and with less risk of the government snooping around. In fact, their goods would be safer there than in their own storehouses, because the government itself would undoubtedly guard the place. Exactly. Hmmm . . ."

Clark got up, walked over to his desk, and retrieved his pipe and tobacco, thoughtfully taking a few puffs. Clare had seen him do this many times, but now she knew it meant he had just unraveled some aspect of a difficult case.

"After this is over," he said as he sat down again, "how about joining the Company? We would make a good team, Clare. Very good."

"When this is over," she replied, "how will I *find* you?"

"Don't worry. You'll hear from me. By the way, there's lots of action in the Middle East—Iran, Iraq, especially Libya."

"Plenty of action in my own backyard, thank you," she replied. "I'll consider the idea, but I don't think Davidson will like it too much."

"Oh? You two have something going?" he winked again, just like when she told him about slapping Henry Rodnik. She blushed, surprising herself.

"Of course not," she replied, but suddenly Bruce's special interest in her took on a new dimension. "What I meant is he's invested a lot of time and energy in my training, and I doubt he would be very happy to see me transfer out."

"Anything can be arranged when you get your orders from the Oval Office," Clark said with another wink that told her she now knew more than she should.

"For now, you'll be needing these," he said, handing

her a pile of officially stamped papers. "To replace these," he added, smiling, as he held up a clear plastic evidence bag containing the remains of her purse and the compact-camera.

"Don't make cameras like they used to," he said, laughing, but when she reached for them he pulled back the bag. "What would you do with these? Less to explain if you go back clean. Besides, we need them for lab tests—see what the explosive was. I vote Semtex.

"Be careful, Punkie," he added, giving her another hug. "They'd just as soon kill you as Pedro—or anybody else, for that matter. Money is their god. If you stand between them and it, only one rule applies. Winning."

"No!" burst from Bruce Davidson's lips when he saw the photo just FAXed in from Colombia. "Not again. . . ." he murmured as he looked at the second photo of the same burning vehicle.

Images of another burning vehicle flooded his mind as he waited for the machine to produce its next sheet. Ellen's last words still rang in his ears, even after ten years, "Can I use your car, honey? Mine's in for repairs. Just a little errand. I'll be home before you know it."

Every time he saw a burned-out car, it all came back, like a bomb bursting in his own heart. "Perelli. Clare is hurt . . . you die."

In his mind, since Ellen's murder he'd already killed Perelli a hundred ways. Now it was only a matter of time. The third FAX showed Conroy kneeling next to a body. Davidson picked up a magnifying glass to see if she was hurt. *Safe. Thank God!* FAX number four showed three men running toward the scene. "Jenner . . . Perelli . . . Dexter," Davidson said. As the pain in his chest started to subside, he read the report on FAX number five:

18 DECEMBER 1992 14:25 YUMBO, COLOMBIA #5

CAR BOMB, DRIVER INJURED. OTHER ASSETS INTACT, RETURNING TO BASE. INVESTIGATION CONTINUES. END.

26

I'll handle these passengers, Guerrero," Jeanette Newhouse said, stepping into the U.S. customs booth. "Take a break."

Guerrero looked first at her supervisor, then quickly at Clare Conroy, now just three back in the long line in front of her. Each person in the ETR group had taken a different line thirty minutes earlier after arriving in Miami.

Conroy placed her passport on the counter as Newhouse asked for her identification. "Miss Conroy. You have a new passport."

"That's correct," Conroy replied. "While we were in Colombia, the original was destroyed. The embassy helped me out."

"How did it happen?" Newhouse asked as she paged through the document.

"Our car was bombed—an apparent assassination attempt on our leader, Dr. J. Reuben Jenner," Conroy said, nodding toward Jenner, who was near the front of the adjacent line.

"Oh, yes. We heard something about that. I hope no one was injured," the customs officer said in a concerned voice.

"Our team escaped unhurt, thank you," Conroy said. "But

the driver was badly burned. My purse was in the vehicle, and its contents were destroyed."

"Did you make any purchases or leave any other personal effects in Colombia?" Newhouse asked, examining the customs declaration.

"No, ma'am," Conroy said.

"We'll just take a quick look through your bags, anyway. We can't be too careful when it comes to people making quick trips to and from Colombia. I'm sure you understand."

Clare nodded, placing her two pieces of luggage on the thigh-high examination counter and unzipping both.

Newhouse looked inside the first, feeling the lining for any hidden pockets. "Everything seems to be in order here, but perhaps I should also inspect your purse."

"Certainly, Agent . . . Newhouse," Clare replied, having by now read the woman's name tag. Conroy watched closely as Newhouse felt through her purse, wondering if this agent, like the first, was looking for something specific. *Another exchange out here in the open?*

"Agent Newhouse," Conroy said firmly, "all the contents of my purse were destroyed. Everything."

The people behind Clare were becoming restless, and now her party had already cleared customs.

"I hope nothing irreplaceable was lost. And it does seem appropriate that there has been a change in plans."

Conroy looked at Newhouse, wondering if she might be trying to pass a message, all the while maintaining a neutral expression as she waited to hear the code word. She considered asking Newhouse to clarify her meaning. But just as she was about to risk pursuing the subject, Clare glanced down at the woman's left hand to see a REGENCY ring.

Conroy tried to conceal her shock as she said, "Yes. There was a change. We decided to skip the Mexico visit because it just seemed safer to come back to the good old U.S.A. You know, when something like this happens, you can't be too careful!"

Conroy looked directly at Newhouse. "Perhaps you've heard of the New World Institute in Colorado, our headquarters? A beautiful place this time of year, compared to this oppressive heat, don't you think?" She smiled, then adjusted her own ring for emphasis.

"The heat here is okay. It's my assignment, and I'm only glad to do my part. Like you say, you can't be too careful."

Should have known, idiot, Conroy scolded herself. *This is where a lot of our orphans come into the states. Why didn't I see it sooner? Guerrero is keeping an eye on Newhouse. Newhouse is keeping an eye on Guerrero. Cat and mouse, and this time I was almost a mouse.*

"Hello, Davidson? Juanita Guerrero, Miami. Something funny here. Newhouse just intercepted Conroy on her way through customs. No, sir, nothing too strange, as far as I could see. But she did put herself in my line just as Conroy was near the front. Only time she's ever done that. And she searched Conroy's bags very thoroughly. I think she was looking for the compact. Maybe saw it when we made the exchange before. I didn't see it this time, myself. No idea where it is. I did notice something else, sir. Something small, but important I think. Both women, Conroy and Newhouse, were wearing identical rings. Can't possibly be a coincidence. I've never seen rings quite so . . . unique."

"I see you met Miss Newhouse," J. R. Jenner ventured twenty minutes into the flight to Denver.

Clare nodded.

"She has helped us a great deal," he continued.

Conroy focused intently on his choice of words, still unsure how much he actually knew about what was happening. "I can imagine," she said, "she keeps an eye on our connections through Miami."

"True," he said, "and it's the reason we route all our flights that way. Never know when some new customs person will detain you for no good reason—like what happened to you on the way down. Make a big fuss about nothing. One time they gave us an apple to eat with lunch on the segment from Mexico City. I just stuck it in my carry-on until later. But would you believe it, they were going to fine me fifty dollars for importing produce until Jeanette told the agent to ignore it if I would eat the apple on the spot. . . ."

He chuckled nervously, then looked out the window with the phrase hanging as if he would continue in a moment. "I've been thinking," he said, turning back toward Conroy, "about what happened. That bomb. At first I wondered why someone would try to assassinate me."

Clare nodded without comment, encouraging him to go on.

"They want to frighten us away from helping those poor children."

Again Clare nodded, and he continued, "But now I have even greater resolve to do it. We can't let terrorists dictate what happens. Wouldn't you agree?"

"We can't let others run our lives," she ventured. "But we should be objective about it . . . base the decision on the need and our resources, regardless of other factors."

"I like that," he said. "Go on."

"For instance, based on what we saw in Dagua and its vicinity . . . if there were no drug Cartel, would we hesitate to help?"

"If there were no Cartel, there wouldn't be such a need," he said. "But, yes, I think we would go ahead. We *will* go ahead with it," he said more forcefully. "It will be our first location in South America. And you know our goals—every continent by the year 2000. Every nation by 2010."

Jenner turned back toward the window, then continued, "But who would hate *me* so much they would try to kill us all—even you?" Clare waited for him to answer his own question.

"That's kept me awake every night since the incident," he said. "And I have a theory."

"Love to hear it," she said, leaning toward him.

"The real question is who hates *truth* enough to silence me. To whom are we a threat, even long-range, to their own goals?"

"Good question," she said.

"You don't think this is crazy?" he asked.

"Prudent, I'd say. It's more crazy to disregard your real enemies in a case like this. Any specific ideas?"

"Well, yes. But this is confidential," he said as he spoke more softly. "First I wondered about the KGB or even the CIA. East-West politics what they are, they might even be working together.

"But what made more sense was Iran, or a radical Muslim group. Or maybe the Zionists. They want to restore the glory to Jerusalem in preparation for their coming Messiah. They're rebuilding the temple from underground as we speak."

"Really? I didn't know that," Conroy said.

"Not many people do," he replied. "But my real concern is the *Sionists*, otherwise known as the Knights Templar, whose goal has always been world dominion. Their king is waiting to reclaim his throne, their monetary system is in place, and the establishment of the European Economic Community could be the final piece in the puzzle of a new global economic system."

"Their *king* is waiting?" Clare exclaimed.

"*Kings* would be more accurate, I suppose," he replied, "since the heir apparent to the Merovingian throne is one of the Hapsburgs, probably on the Spanish side. The secret society behind the Knights Templar is the Priory of Sion, sometimes called the 'Guardians of the Grail'—but I don't suppose you've heard much about all this."

"Not much," she admitted.

"Of course not," he said, "since most historians act as unwitting accomplices of the conspiracy by either ignoring it or labeling it legend. But Hitler believed it—especially the power of the Spear of Longinus. And who can say how many have believed in the powers of the Holy Grail or died trying to defend it?"

"Sounds like *Indiana Jones and the Last Crusade.*"

"The form, without the substance—like most modern thought."

"Forgive my ignorance," Clare said softly. "Most of this is new to me." *Balderdash would be a better word.*

"I know, Rachel. But I have high expectations for you. Right now, however, it seems they have discovered our strategy."

"Every continent, every nation?"

"Yes, but more specifically our strategy of using the orphanages as a foothold in each place and the orphans as—what shall we call them?—the *worker bees* of the new order."

"I've never heard them referred to that way," Clare replied, surprised. "Is that the way you've always seen it?"

"No, though perhaps it was always in my mind, unconnected, until the rest of the vision came clear. You don't like the phrase? Worker bees are the backbone of the hive. Without them the whole society of bees would die. And without bees, *human* society would die. Obviously you've never kept bees," he said.

"True. But we're talking about human beings here, not insects."

"And what we're doing for these human beings is helping them make something of their otherwise worthless lives. Where would they be without us? In a gutter somewhere sniffing glue, or picking dumps . . . maybe worse. We're letting them be part of something bigger."

Can't risk an argument now, she warned herself. "But how is our movement a threat to the Sionists?"

"Any threat must be eliminated," he said. "It's always been their way. Which is why you need to know two things. First of all, they will succeed. They always do."

"You mean," she interrupted, "they will *kill* you?"

He nodded, solemnly, but with a faraway, transcendent look in his eye that Clare found both intriguing and frightening.

"They have people everywhere, as we do, and it's only a matter of time." He looked at her, pausing.

Everywhere? Maybe even your personal assistant?

"But you should also know that in succeeding they will fail," he continued.

"You're confusing me."

"I know. It *is* hard to understand. But this is true with all the prophets. The adversaries murder, thinking they have won, but then the prophet's heirs arise and claim their rightful place."

"But—" Clare had never heard anyone talk this way before. *Jenner needs a shrink. Bruce . . . how do we keep a paranoid prophet with delusions of grandeur from decompressing before we get what we need?*

"What about the End Times Renewal and REGENCY and the Institute?" she asked.

"I am torn between departing, which would be better for me, and remaining, which would be better for you."

She couldn't think of anything to say. But then she noticed a new look in his eyes. "Rachel," he said. "It is time for the JACOB project to commence. In light of these past few days, we must not delay."

D-Day. As in donation. "But sir," she replied, "isn't it rather obvious I'm not ready? There are so many things I don't understand, so many gaps to fill. How can I be worthy of this honor when I hardly know a thing about the Master Plan?"

"You need not understand perfectly, as long as you remain open to truth and obedient to the truth you already know. In the end, truth will triumph. It is the key to all things."

"But what is truth?" she asked, trying to divert his attention from reproduction to philosophy.

He just chuckled. "Pontius Pilate said that to the very man with whom his destiny would be intertwined forever."

She tried again: "But I am still uncomfortable with this. I thought we would have time to get to know each other." A tear was forming in her eye. *Nice touch, kid.*

"You have nothing to fear," he said gently, reaching over to dry the tear with the corner of his silk handkerchief. "Dr. Bradley assured me the procedure is virtually painless and takes only a few minutes. A few minutes that will change the face of human history—think of that."

"I know. It's an honor to be the chosen one," Conroy said quietly. "And perhaps the chaos of these past few days has influenced my judgment. I really need some time, some quiet time, to work this through."

"Certainly," he said. "We'll have almost six weeks at the Institute before the crusade in Brazil. I want you to spend the whole time in relaxation, recreation, and study until you know the time is right. As for myself, this brush with death tells me that *now* is the time—now, while there still *is* time.

Cryopreservation will keep the dream alive if something happens to me."

Conroy, relieved that she had managed to postpone the procedure again, was about to thank Jenner when he added, "But I want your contribution before we travel together again. Why risk failure, if they should kill us both, when our lineage can so easily be preserved?"

D-day, February 3, when I must snatch the world from the grasp of a nonexistent Jesuit conspiracy. "That will be plenty of time. Thank you for understanding."

"I do, Rachel, completely."

Instead of returning directly to Colorado, Milo Stanton took a flight to New York.

"How did it go?" he asked by telephone once he arrived.

"Exactly as planned," Winston replied. "Must have been running full speed when he hit the wire. Nearly cut off his head."

"Pretty messy?"

"Bled like a stuck pig. But that don't bother me."

"How'd you get rid of it—the blood, I mean?"

"Didn't have to. Already snowed once since then. No joggers in the winter, so who's gonna know?"

"I hope you like the layout," Jenner said with a smile as Clare emerged from the van in front of the VIP apartment that was now hers by virtue of her new position. She opened the door to a double "welcome"—her kitten, which ran over, purring, and a room-sized replica of the Edlin train layout at FAO Schwarz.

Conroy stood there in the doorway for a moment, her mouth open in surprise.

"Try it," Jenner, who had followed her up the stairs, said. "Let's see if it works."

Clare walked over to the control panel, where everything was clearly labeled. A few flipped switches turned on the lights in the little town at the center of the room. Water started flowing down from the mountains built up against the wall to the right, through the town, and back under the mountains, where it disappeared into a crevice to be pumped back up again. Three separate tracks, each with a complete train awaiting her commands, intersected at the switchyard directly in front of her.

"It's beautiful!" she breathed. "But you shouldn't have. This must have cost . . . well, it must have cost a lot of money." *Like twenty-thousand dollars—maybe more.*

"Leave that to me, my dear," Jenner said. "You've earned it, considering what we've just been through." He paused, watching her move the switches.

"Aren't you forgetting something?" he asked.

"What?" she replied blankly.

"Your engineer's hat, right over here on the wall. You didn't even notice." He took the hat off the wall and placed it tenderly on her head.

Clare, whose first impulse was to hug him, turned on the trains instead, showing Jenner how to control them. For a few minutes they ran the layout together, but then Jenner excused himself, saying he ought to be getting home to Mary. "Merry Christmas, early," he said.

"Thank you . . . Jacob," she said. "This is the nicest present I've ever had." Almost as an afterthought, Clare gave Jenner a little peck on the cheek.

J. R. Jenner wondered what Mary's greeting would be like this time. When he was on the road, he would often envision coming home like other weary travelers to a warm home and a welcoming hug. Someone to listen. Someone to hold him. Someone to love him. Ever since the bombing, that particular need had become much more intense.

But as he opened the door to his own quarters, Mary was not there to greet him. There was no hug, no warm embrace that promised things to come. Mary wasn't in the library, or the front room, or the kitchen, or even in the bedroom. She was in the master bathroom, with the door ajar.

He knocked. "Mary, I'm home."

"Come in," she said.

He opened the door to a scene he'd witnessed often before. There she stood, looking at herself in the mirror, without a stitch of clothing on, washing her hands.

"I'm sorry," she said. "I couldn't decide—help me decide . . . what to wear. It is so hard . . ."

Doesn't she have any idea what nakedness means to a husband returning from a long journey? Is she a little child, or is she punishing me? "It's okay, dear," he said, sadly. "Anything is fine." *Nothing is fine.* "Just put on your robe," he added, handing it to her from its hook on the door.

Jenner was sitting on the edge of their king-sized bed, the twin streams of hope and desire now effectively dammed again, when Mary finally emerged from the bathroom, clutching her wrinkled hands to her chest.

"I'm sorry," she said as she sat next to him, gazing at the lamp.

"Don't apologize . . . please," he said.

"I must," she insisted, still looking at the lamp. "Everything I do, I must undo, and when it's undone I feel guilty because it was better before, and now I've ruined it."

She started to cry, quietly. He reached out and put his arm around her, paternalistically, like always. Then he fixed his eyes on their wedding photo on the dresser. *How strange. Everything else I do prospers. Everywhere I go, women long to meet my needs. I don't know how much longer I can take this.*

He stood up, shaking his head, and walked to the door. "I'm sorry, Mary, I really am. I wish I could help you. Actually, I wish *you* could help me. But it's late, and it's been a very long day, so let me tuck you in now, and you can go to sleep. I'll come to bed later."

Instead, he fell asleep on the sofa in the den, before a warm fire he kindled himself. When he awoke at six in the morning, Jenner called Dr. Bradley on her private line.

"Florence," he said, "I'm ready to pursue the JACOB project, as soon as possible." He listened for a moment, then responded, "I'll be there in a half hour, but Rachel will make her own arrangements before we go to Brazil."

He put down the receiver. Fixing his eyes on the world map above the fireplace, its color-coded pins marking REGENCYs on all the major continents, he dialed another number. "Good morning, Rachel. Sounds like the trains are still running. All night? Really. Guess you do like them. Hope you're not too tired to do a little snowmobiling. No hurry . . . say eight-thirty, at the snowmobile shed."

As he turned toward the master bath to shower and shave, Jenner noticed Mary standing in the doorway. "Hello, dear," he said. "You're up bright and early today. I'll be gone for a little while, but let's have supper together tonight. I'll notify the chef, and the housekeeper will take care of everything else. All you have to do is get yourself dressed by six o'clock."

27

Either I'm totally wasted from playing engineer all night, or something has changed, Conroy mused as Dr. Jenner tore around the corral on the brand new Arctic Cat El Tigre snowmobile.

"Nice machine," Jenner yelled, stopping the snowmobile in front of Winston. "Hardly touch the throttle, and she just wants to take off! How fast will it go, anyway?"

"Pretty fast, sir," Winston replied. "Over a hundred on a fast track. But," he added quickly, "on our trails, you don't want to do more than fifteen to twenty miles per hour."

"In that case," Jenner replied, "we'll take it out on the Prairie. People ride there all winter, don't they?"

"True," Winston replied, "and there is a gate in our new fence, up where our timberline intersects the Prairie, but. . . ."

"But what?"

"But you go out there, how will I protect you?" Winston said. "Mr. Stanton wouldn't like it, after what happened in Colombia."

"Hang Stanton," Jenner chuckled. "He and Worthy are in

New York. Who's to tell them? Anyway, if the bad guys ambush us, will they be able to catch us?"

"Unlikely," Winston replied.

"Then hop on, Rachel. Let's see what this baby will do in the open."

Winston reluctantly handed Jenner the key to the gate. "Any extras?" Jenner asked.

"A few," Winston said, "but we're very careful about who has them. Why put up a fence if anybody who wants to can get through it?"

"You can trust us, or you can't trust anybody, so fetch a key for Miss Conroy, too. Then we won't bother you when we want to take two machines out for a ride," Jenner said, revving up the engine for emphasis.

Winston returned in a moment. Clare climbed aboard, and they zoomed away. *Picture postcard*, she thought as they made their way along the jogging trail. The evergreens lining the trail bent under six inches of new snow. Golden sparkles flashed from the sun's rays, contrasting with the blue shadows of the trees against the snow. *Sure beats the tropics*, Clare thought as they rode along, her arms around Jenner. *But a little bulky if you want to get intimate.*

Not that she wanted to, exactly. But in spite of her down vest and Damart thermals, the driver seemed close, very close, and Conroy felt a certain warmth she had never felt before. *Love? No, impossible. But it's hard to hate a guy who treats me this well.*

Suddenly Jenner stopped the snowmobile. "Look at that," he said, pointing to a large, reddish-brown stain that started in the trail and trickled off the edge toward the timber. The new snow almost covered the spot, but its peculiar intensity seemed to overwhelm the pristeen whiteness.

Wouldn't even notice this in New York, she thought, *since any snow that makes it through the smog is rust-colored when it lands.* She got off and kicked, the new snow away with her Hermann Survivors, but as she kicked she became increasingly aware she was trampling upon a fairly large pool of blood.

"What is it?" Jenner called.

"Can't tell for sure," she said, "but it looks like blood." She looked at Jenner and reached the same conclusion he expressed at that moment, "*Human* blood? Is this where Paul Woodman died? But what did he hit?"

There was nothing, not even a fresh stump where a tree might have been down across the trail. The closest obstacles were medium-sized spruce trees, ten feet from either edge of the trail.

"Doesn't figure," he said, shaking his head. "Paul was very good on a snowmobile. We'll have to ask Winston when we get back. But, for now, let's go. I can see the Prairie from here, and I want to air this beauty out a little!"

Clare climbed aboard again, cleaning her boots with a handkerchief that she folded carefully and put inside the vest. Her FBI mind was occupied more with the evidence than the thrill of speed as they passed sixty miles per hour.

Either Woodman flipped it and killed himself, or he had some help, she concluded as she clung to Jenner to keep from being blown off the vehicle. *If he flipped it, why so much blood? A broken neck or a crushed chest wouldn't bleed like that. Something opened him up pretty good.*

"What'd ya think?" Jenner asked. They had reached the other end of the Prairie already. Conroy hadn't even noticed.

"Awesome," she said. "All I could do to hang on. Didn't know you were such a speed demon!" She laughed. They both laughed.

"Want to drive?" he asked.

She hesitated, then realized it would be helpful to know how to run it, especially if she needed it to meet with Davidson in a few days. "Okay," she said, "but you're taking your life in your hands. Let's go back a different way," she shouted as he climbed on behind her.

"Anything your heart desires," he commented. As she set the snowmobile on a course that would take them within view of the entrance to Miner's Pass, she noticed Jenner seemed to be hugging her much more tightly than their speed required.

When they reached the corral, Jenner congratulated her on how well she had driven. "We should do this again soon, don't you think?" he said.

"Fine with me," she replied. "Great way to clear the mind—or freeze the face. But to tell you the truth, I prefer cross-country skiing. Quieter, more natural. Used to do that quite a lot when I was a kid. Bet it would be fantastic up here, especially along the edge of the Prairie."

"Isn't the snow too deep?" he asked as Winston appeared and walked toward them to put the machine away.

"The big places out East set tracks with a special sled, like a heavy toboggan with runners. You just break the trail after each snowfall. And skiing is good exercise . . . the best cardiovascular workout there is. That's probably one reason Scandinavians live so long."

"Sounds like you had a pretty good time," Winston said. "Machine work okay?"

"Great, thank you," Jenner replied. "And we'll probably go out every day. But we saw something strange on the trail, just before the gate."

"Oh?" Winston said. "What was that?"

"Well . . . it seemed to be blood. Possibly *human* blood." Jenner watched Winston intently. "Is that where Paul Woodman died?"

"Oh, no, sir," Winston replied immediately. "He ran into a fallen tree further up the trail, beyond the gate. Maybe some animal got killed there by a cougar. Never know when one of those guys will sneak through looking for something—or someone—to eat."

"I didn't know the cats were up here this time of year."

"It's rare," Winston said. "They'd rather hang around the herds down below. But sometimes a deer will follow a packed trail all the way up here. Cat picks up that scent, deer wouldn't have a chance. It jumps off the trail to get away; it's dead meat. Snow's too deep."

"Poor thing," Jenner replied, looking at Clare, who was suddenly feeling the combined effects of the change in altitude and temperature, as well as more than twenty-four hours without sleep. "Rachel, you look exhausted."

Turning to Winston, Jenner said, "Take me out and show me where Paul died. He and I were very good friends, you know. I want to spend some quiet moments out there alone with the memories. You lead the way."

"Yes, sir." Winston replied. "Give me a minute."

Conroy watched the two men ride away as she trudged slowly back to her apartment. The Jacuzzi was especially relaxing today. An hour later, clad only in the "Jamaica No Problem" nightshirt she'd picked up on the trip, Clare curled up in a down comforter with a cup of hot chocolate in front of the fireplace and reviewed her first itinerary with Dr. J. Reuben Jenner.

The more she recalled, the warmer she felt. Just as she finished the hot chocolate, she drifted off to sleep on the couch, thinking as she closed her eyes, *If I weren't FBI . . .*

The next thing she knew, there was Christmas music coming from the front room. *Is this a dream?* She focused on the clock on the mantle, then on her kitten, then on the fireplace where the coals had burned out. Then she heard the trains begin to run. Throwing on her robe, she peeked through the door to see J. R. Jenner, wearing her engineer's hat, at the controls.

The music came from a laser disk playing in the new Fischer entertainment center in one corner of the room. In the other corner stood a small blue spruce, fully decorated. The scent of Christmas was already filling the room. Under the tree, Clare could see several brightly wrapped presents, but the thing she noticed first was a set of cross-country skis leaning against the wall next to the tree.

Sometimes this is like a fairy tale, she thought as she stepped into the room.

"Welcome back from dreamland," Jenner said with a smile. "I hope everything fits, but if not, Ernie's in Walton's Creek will take care of it."

"You shouldn't have!" she exclaimed, as she walked over and examined the skis and poles and unboxed the boots.

"Why not?" he said. "Might as well make the most of our month in the mountains before we go back to summer . . . and who knows what else."

"But I didn't get you anything."

"Not true," he replied. "Maybe nothing in pretty wrapping, but more than money could buy. You've given me hope."

"What can I say?" she asked, walking over to his side. "Thank you . . . again. Nobody has ever treated me this nicely." Then, without even thinking, she kissed him lightly on the cheek.

"Just the beginning," he replied, putting his arm around her waist in a very brief embrace, which he immediately stopped, as if embarrassed. "Sorry. You haven't had time to get dressed."

Clare ignored the comment as she walked barefoot toward the kitchen. "Care for some supper?" she asked.

"Supper happened twelve hours ago," he laughed. "It's

six o'clock *in the morning*. Have you been asleep since yesterday?"

"Can't believe I was *that* tired! Only did that once before, after finals in college. Well, how about breakfast then?"

"Love to, but I just stopped in to make this delivery, like Santa Claus. People might talk, you know, if they see me leaving your apartment after the sun comes up."

"What people?" she asked. "Nobody's here, to speak of, until the new class arrives. And . . . by the way, how'd you get in? Your own key, I suppose?"

He nodded. "Hope you're not offended," he said, holding the key out to her. "Just wanted to bring you this little surprise, and even though I may be Santa Claus, I don't do chimneys!" He laughed.

Conroy reached out to take the key, then pulled her hand back. "Keep it." *Might as well make him feel welcome, since he can get the key from security anyway.* "Just let me know when you're coming by, please," she smiled, "so I'm not running around in my underwear!"

"Of course," he replied, pocketing the key and turning to go. With his hand on the knob, he said, "Think you can teach me how to ski this afternoon, or would you rather put it off . . . go snowmobiling, or just veg out for a couple more days?"

"You have skis, too?" she asked, surprised.

"Identical to yours, only longer. I had Ernie's set up twenty pairs that will be available to the staff, but the whole program will depend on you as instructor. You can give lessons to anyone who wants them, and then people can ski the jogging trail and stay as fit all winter as they are all summer. Thanks for the idea. Meet you at the stables at say, one o'clock this afternoon?"

"I'll be there," she said.

"Good. Oh, by the way, you can open the two larger boxes

today. Ski duds. Hope they fit. But the little one has to wait until Christmas morning," Jenner added as he stepped into the hallway. Then, with a little smile, he was gone.

"Stanton, you stud . . . right again," Johnny Winston said out loud as he watched the monitor in the surveillance control room under the new audiovisual building. So far only four cameras were operational, but one of them was trained on the VIP suites, which J. R. Jenner was just leaving. "No doubt about it; those two got something going on!"

Winston had just stopped in to check the recorders attached to all four units to see that they were running. At the end of the day, each tape was monitored at high speed to be sure nothing extraordinary had been missed earlier. It was really more than one person could manage, but Stanton didn't want anybody else to know about this facility yet. So until the rules changed, Winston was spending a lot more time underground than he was outside.

But this was also his morning to patrol the fence, which he much preferred. He grabbed his jacket and headed for the snowmobile shed, muttering about having to pull the tracksetter Dr. Jenner had purchased.

"Hello . . . Mom, is that you? It's me, Adam," Putnam began, and then all the emotion of the past few weeks let go like a ruptured dam. The young man started to blubber like a baby.

"I'm sorry, Mom. It's just been so long," he sniffed when he had achieved enough control to continue.

Since Thanksgiving, the computer expert had become increasingly depressed. Each day he had watched for evidence that his message to Obewan had gotten through. Now, with Christmas Day approaching, Putnam was desperate to make contact with somebody outside.

Every day he read his Bible and prayed, crying out to God for mercy, and asking especially for somebody to help him extricate himself from ETR. And every day he waited for just the right time to take what he expected might be his only shot at freedom. With Worthy and Stanton gone, and with Winston obviously away on the morning security check, Putnam was in the data control center, determined that this time he would talk to a real person—someone who would listen.

"Where are you?" she asked. "I've been so worried. Nobody knew where you were. Why didn't you call? Why didn't you write? Will you be home for Christmas?"

"Mom, slow down, please," he interrupted. "I don't have much time. Just listen . . . please," he pleaded. He was fighting emotion again—not only his present despair, but the memories of the domineering mother he had fled home to escape. At the moment, however, he would have traded a week-long harangue for another day in the New World Institute.

"Mom . . . write this down. Ready? I'm involved with a group called the End Times Renewal. No, Mom, it's not what everybody thinks. It's not what I thought when I went to their rally and then came here. I'm at the New World Institute near Walton's Creek, Colorado. Mom . . . this is a cult, and they're into some bad things—things that make me wonder what they'd do to me if I tried to leave.

"Just recently there was a murder here. I can't go into it now. And I was part of a secret initiation that involved drinking blood. . . ." He paused as what he had just said hit him again. On the other end, there was only stunned silence now.

"I'm afraid, Mom. Really afraid. They have their ways. But I want to get out. Please find somebody to get me out. Please. I don't care who it is or how they do it—just do it before something awful happens to me."

Putnam paused again, then added, "This is no joke, Mom, like before. This is real. I have to hang up. Somebody may be listening, and somebody may trace it, so don't wait. I love you, Mom. And, Mom, I love Jesus, too, and that's why I have to get out of here."

Putnam hung up and looked around the work space that had become his universe in the past few months. No one else, as far as he could determine, was in the building. He hoped—how he hoped—that no one would discover his disloyalty before help arrived, whatever form it might take.

He booted his workstation and began looking for more tracks, an electronic hunter intent on discovering just what James Worthy had done with those files. If he could find out how Worthy had disguised the data, who could say what other gems lay hidden along the same computer pathways. That data just might be his life insurance—if he ever needed it.

Eileen Putnam, meanwhile, was frantically pacing around her living room in Cleveland. "What shall I do? What shall I do?" she pleaded, each time she passed the photo of her deceased husband.

She knew what he would say. "Pray. Get down on your knees and pray."

Which is what she did. When she arose, she had the beginnings of a plan.

"Hello, pastor? This is Eileen Putnam. Sorry to bother you, with all the holiday programs going on, but . . . I just got the most disturbing call from Adam. I know, he's played a lot of tricks in the past, but this is real. He's in trouble, I'm sure of it. A mother knows. He's involved with a group called the End Times Renewal. I know; they do some good things. I've seen the ads, too. But he sounded so scared. And he talked about somebody being murdered, and a blood initiation, and he called it a cult and begged me to find somebody to rescue him."

After a momentary pause, Pastor Bob Fillmer replied, "I have a friend who rescues people from cults. I know you don't have any money. Don't worry about that; the church will help. And besides, Gunnar's work is underwritten by a foundation he started after his own sister died at Jonestown. Grew up in a Christian home and then followed Jimmy Jones all the way to hell. So now Gunnar will go anywhere and do anything he can to help. No better time than Christmas to liberate people, after all. Let me give him a call. I'll get back to you as soon as I know anything. Don't worry."

"Thank you, pastor. If I had a recording of what Adam said, you would know why I *am* worried. But I'll try not to let it get the best of me."

In the back room of the Walton's Creek Super Service station, special agent Willard Stevenson was worried, too. He listened to Adam Putnam's call again as he made a copy that would be in Bruce Davidson's hands in a few hours. *This op is coming unglued,* Stevenson muttered to himself. *Chalk off months of work and one nearly dead agent. Too bad. Davidson will need more than luck to head this one off at the pass.*

28

Conroy smelled the wood smoke even before the cabin came into view, set back among the trees and covered with two feet of snow. A thin white ribbon floated lazily upward from the chimney, drifting among the pines as it reached for the blue sky. Clare paused at the top of a little rise, savoring the scene's quiet beauty before skiing the last hundred meters to the front porch.

The door opened as she arrived, and Bruce Davidson emerged, wearing jeans and a green-and-black mackinaw shirt, a steaming cup in each hand. "Smooth," he smiled. "And quiet. Wondered how you were going to get here."

Taking one cup from his hands, she replied, "Me too, until Jenner decided to get me these. Figured I might have to come roaring up on a snowmobile. Some cabin," she continued, as she followed him inside. "How'd you arrange this?"

"Easy," he said. "Shepherd's gone below, so I just borrowed it for awhile. Good staging area, don't you think? A guy could fall in love with this place. Maybe I won't even go back to the office."

Clare looked around, taking in the handmade furniture and the cared-for appearance. Then she noticed, under the side window, the specialty radio. "Looks like you brought the office here," she said.

"Pays to stay in touch. Sometimes a guy just has to phone home," he laughed.

"Now and then, wish I could do that, myself."

"Like when your taxi gets blown up?" he asked in a serious tone, laying some photos of the burned-out Mercedes on the table between them. "Almost lost my lunch when that was FAXed in."

"I *did* lose mine," she replied. "Not used to the smell of fried flesh, I guess. How's the driver?"

"He'll make it, and he's cooperating. Probably knows his days are numbered if he doesn't find another place to live. I.D.ed the perpetrators, but the motive is in doubt."

"Fit's Perelli's M.O., don't you think?" she interjected, then stopped, recalling how she had learned Stanton's real identity.

"That's affirmative," he replied, "but how did you learn his real name?"

Clare pondered the implications of what she was about to say. "It came up in Colombia when I was discussing the bombing with one of the embassy people. Company rep named William Clark. Know him?" When he nodded noncommittally, she continued, "He knows you. And he knows me, too, since his real name is Charles William Conroy."

"Did you tell him anything? I mean about RADON?" Davidson asked, studying her face closely.

"Nothing," she replied. "At least nothing really important, like the code name." But then she paused, recalling how much she had actually discussed with her father.

"Continue, please," Davidson urged her. "I need to know everything. This investigation could catch some big fish, but if the net leaks, good people might get hurt."

Good people like me? "Well, we were talking about the

bomb, you know, just trying to figure who did it, when Daddy—sorry, that's what I always called him—told me about Perelli . . . and about Ellen."

Conroy stopped as she saw the look on Bruce's face. When he looked away, Clare reached across the table and took his hands in hers. "I'm sorry," was all she could think to say. "Then it's true."

Davidson turned to face Conroy without letting go of her hands. Tears started to form in his eyes, and it was obvious he couldn't speak. Conroy didn't know what to do for a moment. Then she slipped around the table, sat down next to Davidson, and put her arm around his waist.

"Thanks," he said quietly, after an eternity of moments. "I should have told you, I suppose. But now that you know this much, there's a lot more you need to know."

Conroy slid away to a discreet distance, then got up as if to refill her coffee cup. When she returned, more photographs lay on the table. She sat down across the table from Davidson and looked at the enlargements from Jamaica.

"Nice work," he commented. "How'd you get the ledgers on film, especially *both* ledgers?"

"Bought off the matron with ETR money," Clare said with a chuckle that died quickly as she picked up the photo of Erietta McIlmore, now probably a prisoner of drugs and prostitution somewhere in New York City. "Anybody notice Melissa Costellini in the car?" she asked.

"Course," he replied, "especially with the close-up you took right after that one. He paused, then continued, "What's in the sheds? Grass?" When she nodded, he said, "Figured. Jamaica is into marijuana exports big time. But we couldn't be sure just from the photo."

"Sorry," she said.

"No problem," he continued, picking up the next set of photos. "We don't expect captions!"

But when he noticed she didn't smile at the joke, he stopped.

"What I mean," she said, "is I'm sorry I also mentioned the drugs to Daddy."

"Not good procedure," he said, "but nothing big, either. He's probably part of WASHTUB. Special project, CIA and Interpol. President's orders. If we take this apart, we'll need Company help. Easier working with somebody already in the loop." He smiled. "Anything else?" he asked.

"Not much, but after we figured out Perelli was behind the bomb, we tried to figure out why."

"And?"

"We couldn't be sure, of course, but maybe they wanted it to look like ETR is not welcome in Colombia . . . with the hope that if we went ahead anyway, the government would never suspect the Cartel was using the orphanage for storage and transfer of cocaine."

"Interesting strategy," Davidson commented, obviously impressed. "Best theory so far."

"It worked, too, from what I can see," Conroy added, "at least in terms of Dr. Jenner. Initially, he seemed fearful, but then he became even more resolved to pursue the plans. Pigheaded, courageous—I'm not sure which. He's tough to figure. The way he was talking on the way back, you'd call him paranoid."

"Tell me about it," Davidson said.

"Well, Jenner believes the Knights Templar are out to get him because ETR is a potential threat to their goal of world dominion. He thinks he's a marked man, and that he's going to die a martyr no matter what, because their people are everywhere. I thought that conspiracy expired with Jacques Demolay. What do you think?"

"My opinion on that is irrelevant," Davidson said, "in terms of this investigation."

Which means there is some truth to it, Clare thought, intrigued.

"What is important, though," Davidson continued, "is how our Dr. Jenner decides to act on his convictions."

"Well one result, so far," Clare said, "is his decision to go ahead with JACOB. It's a high-tech reproductive project that will give him twelve sons, each born to a different REGENCY-level surrogate mother, but all full brothers . . ."

She paused, considering her next words carefully, ". . . because not only would the sperm come from him, but the eggs would all come from one hand-picked woman. Three guesses who the chosen one might be."

Davidson seemed stunned by the revelation, recoiling physically as he sat at the table. "Clare," he responded when he regained control, "have you? I mean, you don't have to submit to this kind of . . . violation. Nothing is worth that. We have enough data now to make several charges stick. I can't allow this. . . ."

"I managed to buy some time," she interrupted. *Daddy was right about Bruce.* "I can put it off until as late as February 3, the day before we leave for Brazil. But no later—not without bringing my loyalty under suspicion. He's worried that if we don't leave our offspring on ice, the Sionist conspiracy will put an end to the legacy of J. R. Jenner."

"In that case," Davidson said, "I will meet you here on February 2, and we'll close this one down."

"But what about Linda Landau?" Conroy replied. "Can we just abandon the person who drew us into this?"

"Maybe she'll be okay until we come back to make some arrests. Trying to rescue her alone might be too dangerous. Oh, by the way," he said, placing a snapshot on the table, "here's the only photo we could get of Landau and her husband. Neighbor shot it with an Instamatic. Best we could do."

Conroy held the photo close to be sure Landau was the woman she had seen on the video. "I've seen her," Conroy said, finally. "She's in the medical center." But as she studied the other face, she realized she had also seen John Williams.

"Winston!" she hissed. "I've seen him, too, with a beard and another name, probably his real one. He's Johnny Winston, second in command, of Institute security. Maybe his reward for turning in his own wife?" *But he's REGENCY, too. If only I had scanned the HANNAH files more completely, I would have known. But Jenner* did *know! Whaaa—?*

"Then he sent this telegram?" Davidson asked, laying the announcement of Paul Woodman's death on the table.

"Yes. But we've been wondering, Dr. Jenner and I, about that," Clare said, pulling out the bloody handkerchief. "Forensics might find this interesting. Big pool of it up on the trail. Winston claims it was a cougar kill."

"Unlikely," Davidson replied. "But we may not be able to make a case anyway, since the body was cremated. Unless . . ." he said, pulling another folder out of the briefcase, "unless this guy actually knows something."

"Putnam," Clare said, staring at the Pentagon photo I.D. "But why would the Pentagon have anything on him?"

"Let's say his skills have been useful in at least one big-time classified project."

"Putnam is working *for us*?" Clare said, flabbergasted by yet another crucial fact withheld by Davidson.

"Not exactly," Davidson said, "at least not officially. Best guess is he found a niche in this group, but once he figured out what was happening he wanted out. So . . ." he continued, handing her a sheet of paper, "so he sent these by modem to a hacker friend still at the Pentagon—that's Obewan. Had all I could do to convince the brass this was just a hacker's practical joke."

Conroy immediately recognized the first sheet as the numbers of bank accounts. "Big bucks," she commented.

"Maybe just the tip of the iceberg," Davidson replied. "But to confirm, we need more data."

He handed her another sheet containing shipping manifests and bills of lading. "Make anything of these?"

"Bambi? Means nothing for now, but I'll work on it," she said. "Hydrochloric acid? Why do we need that? Is this a misprint, or maybe to cover something else? Saw Stanton at the storage sheds once. Maybe I should find out what's in there."

"We may not have much time. Our Mr. Putnam is becoming desperate. Just recently he decided to reach out and touch someone. Listen," Davidson said, activating a palm-sized tape player he had just pulled from his pocket.

"Any response?" Conroy asked, fighting back her own emotions when the tape was finished. "I mean, has Putnam's mother done anything yet to try to rescue him?"

"Nothing we know for sure," Davidson said. "She hasn't called the FBI, though, or any other police agency, so far. So she may be making other arrangements. Certain people specialize in liberating cult members, and the church she attends would be more concerned with this than some others are. So we won't be surprised, and you shouldn't be either, if somebody comes nosing around. Which is why I want you to keep this guy sane for the next month and then bring him out with you. Use your imagination. See if you can get him to redirect some of that energy constructively."

"You want me to enlist *Putnam*?" she asked. "When he's that unstable?"

"This whole deal is getting unstable, which is why it's time to get what we can and get out. It would be nice to have more documents and data in our hands, though. Evidence has a way of vaporizing when the bad guys think we're on to them."

"Maybe that's what happened to Paul Woodman," Clare said. *And if Woodman, why not Putnam and Conroy?*

"Maybe. Like to find out. *Murder* would look pretty nice at the top of our list of indictments, especially if we can pin it on Perelli.

"What about Jenner?" Conroy asked. "What will happen to him?"

"Have to be a prophet to know that! But it depends how much he's involved. What do *you* think?"

"It's hard to believe," Conroy said, picking up the picture of Erietta McIlmore. "It's hard to believe that somebody who started out helping orphans could end up collaborating with organized crime."

"You like him, Clare?" Davidson asked. "He's treated you pretty well, after all," he commented when she didn't answer. Conroy placed the photo on the table, then followed Davidson's gaze to the fourth finger on her left hand. She was wearing the new ring she'd received for Christmas, an exquisite ruby surrounded by twelve small diamonds and bordered by sapphires all around.

"He has treated me well, yes," she replied, feeling more than a little bit defensive. "But he hasn't forced himself or his ideas on me or on anyone else, as far as I can see. The people who come to ETR all come of their own free will."

"But do they stay of their own free will?" Davidson asked. "More important, would *you* stay of your own free will if you were given the chance . . . and if you didn't know what you know about the rest of this web?"

"Hypothetical questions are always hard to answer, professor," she replied. "For instance, would you be so determined to nail Perelli if it weren't for what he did to Ellen?"

She paused, suddenly realizing the conversation was becoming too personal, and that Bruce was just trying to do his job. "I'm sorry," she said, "I guess I do like him—more than I realized. It's hard to hate someone who treats you respectfully and then showers you with gifts. But would I stay if I had the choice? Honestly, I don't know. ETR is doing some good things. I might be able to help, if there were just some way to get rid of the evil."

"Like the HANNAH project, for instance?" Davidson asked. When she nodded, he continued, "Or the JACOB project?" This time she took longer to agree. "Or the whole idea of a worldwide kingdom—what do you think of that?"

"I'm not so sure all of it is evil, once you take out the Perelli connections. Especially if all the participants are consenting adults, most of what Jenner is doing is legal."

"Maybe so," Davidson said. "But evil is like a certain gas that seeps in undetected . . . and before you know what's happening, everybody's dying of cancer . . ."

"Radon," Clare murmured. "I wondered where we got. . . ."

"As to the question of legality," Davidson continued, "there is often a big difference between what's legal and what's moral."

"Morality is culturally defined and therefore relative to its context," Conroy replied immediately, parroting her college ethics professor. But as soon as she heard her own words, she realized they were bankrupt, if not patently false.

"True enough," he replied, "in the classroom. But morality that consistently works, even as situations change, must be tied to something more durable than the way we feel at the moment."

"Makes sense," she said. "But how do you keep your feelings from influencing your better judgment in a case like this?"

"A good question, Spock," he said with a laugh. He rose from the table and walked over to the wall, where a snowmobile jacket hung on the hook by the door. "A question without a perfect answer until we find some Vulcans to work for the FBI. In the meantime," he continued, walking back toward Conroy, "we'll have to use people—real flesh and blood people like us, whose feelings *do* get in the way until they find ways to focus them on the task they're assigned."

He handed her what looked like a ballpoint pen, but was much heavier than an ordinary PaperMate. "Careful," he said with a smile. "It's loaded. Here, let me show you." Reclaiming the pen, he sat down next to Conroy, demonstrating how to arm and fire what was actually a single-shot .32-caliber self-protection device.

"If I were you," he said, "I would keep this on my person at all times. Snakes don't always rattle before they strike."

29

"Relax, Worthy. High time you enjoyed life a little," Stanton coaxed. "Erietta here—that your name, honey?—she's my maid for the weekend. We'll have a real nice time, won't we?" Stanton said as he draped his arm around the girl sitting next to him in the back seat of the limo.

"A little young, don't you think?" Worthy protested.

"Don't worry, pal. We got a nice one for you, too. You know what they usually get for these Fantasy Weekends?"

"Not really."

"Thousand, maybe more. Depends on the package. But you don't seem very appreciative."

"Figures on a page are one thing. This is more personal."

"Perks of the position. Don't go moral on me now—not when we're just arriving at Paradise Suites."

Stanton handed the driver a twenty and bestowed another twenty on the bellman who carried in their bags.

"Mr. Stanton, you have a message," the desk clerk said. "The caller said it was urgent."

Stanton ripped open the envelope.

MESSAGE:

For: Mr. Stanton

URGENT

Message: Return home immediately. Security problem requires immediate attention.

Winston

"Don't unpack yet, Worthy. And hold the limo. Look's like we're taking the midnight express to Denver. Sorry, honey," he said to Erietta. "We'll have to get acquainted some other time."

Turning to the clerk, Stanton said, "Here's your newest maid. Please see that she finds her quarters."

"Good morning, Dr. Jenner. Sorry to call you this early, but I thought you should know that some kook is in town making noise about the Institute. Guy named Tellefsen. Claims Adam Putnam's mother hired him to rescue her son from our "cult." Worthy and I were back east at the time, but we flew in late last night to find out what gives."

"Cult?" Jenner replied, surprised.

"Compared it to Jonestown—even claims somebody was murdered here."

"Murdered? What could he be talking about?"

Jenner noticed, as Stanton continued, that Mary was now standing in the doorway of the study. *Hope she didn't hear that.*

"Who knows?" Stanton replied. "Maybe it's about Woodman's accident. But all the papers are in order, as far as I can see. Sheriff signed the police report himself."

Stanton paused, then continued. "Probably just some crackpot trying to make a name for himself."

"What do you suggest?" Jenner asked.

"Well, I already told Sheriff Stone to let the guy out of jail. Had him in there overnight, just to be safe. But all we need is somebody crying about harassment. And get this: Instead of leaving town, Tellefsen phones the *Denver Post*. So now we got reporters on their way to Walton's Creek. . . ."

"Can't be ignored then," Jenner said after some thought.

"Too risky," Stanton agreed.

"But we'll meet them on *our* terms," Jenner stated. "How about the school lounge? And let's invite some of our Walton's Creek friends. Might as well make it a public forum. Miss Conroy should speak for us. And Putnam will have to come, too, of course."

"Are you sure?" Stanton said. "What if he says something?"

"What could he possibly say?" Jenner replied. "He's not a prisoner. We have to make that clear."

"I suppose," Stanton grumbled.

"But . . . is this Tellefsen person dangerous? I mean, is he out to get *me*?"

"You mean like in Colombia? No, sir, I doubt it. We can make sure he's not armed. But some people are dangerous in other ways."

As the ETR Suburban approached the school that afternoon, it pulled up behind a remote van from TV-38, its satellite dish readied to transmit immediately.

"Reporters making news, like always," Stanton commented. "But we'll give them their biggest nonstory of the year, won't we?" he said to Putnam, who hadn't said a single word all the way to town.

"Dr. Jenner," a reporter asked, sticking a microphone in the prophet's face as he stepped from the vehicle, "are people being held at your Institute compound by force?"

Jenner smiled and began walking toward the front door of the school. "Students have been coming and going for years," he said calmly. "They do so of their own free will."

"Including Adam Putnam? Why would his mother hire Tellefsen to rescue him?"

"I don't know his mother or anyone named Tellefsen," Jenner replied. "But you can ask Putnam for yourselves if you'll just be patient."

"People, people," the voice of Mayor Mindy Copperthwaite could be heard above the crowd noises, "a little restraint, and a little respect. This isn't the big city. Let the group in so we can get underway."

The interview began when Tellefsen, the mayor, Conroy, Putnam, and Jenner had all taken seats in a semicircle at the front of the room. The press, consisting of a TV crew with one reporter and a correspondent from the *Denver Post*, were in the front row, with thirty or forty townspeople behind them and Stanton prowling along the back wall.

"Dr. Jenner," the Mayor began, "thank you for coming today to answer a charge by Mr. Tellefsen that your personnel are kept at the Institute against their will."

"Excuse me," Tellefsen interrupted, "but what I said was that *Adam Putnam* is being held there against *his* will. He said so himself in a recent phone call to his mother."

Jenner turned toward Putnam, and asked, "Is this true, Adam? Aren't you free to leave?"

Putnam, who had been looking down at the floor, now looked directly at the camera. Haltingly and in a monotone, he began, "Yes, sir, I joined you freely, and I'm grateful to contribute to something more important than myself."

As Putnam talked, however, he seemed to be having a problem with his eyes. He was blinking rather rapidly.

Jenner reached for his handkerchief, and was about to hand it to Putnam when he noticed that the blinking had a certain pattern, one he himself had learned as a Boy Scout. Morse code. "P1439," Putnam was saying to the camera with his eyes. "P1439," he repeated. There was no way it could be happening by chance.

"Adam, did you call your mother recently?" Tellefsen asked Putnam.

"Yes," Putnam said, "to wish her a Merry Christmas."

"Tellefsen," the TV reporter asked, "what is your *real reason* for coming to Walton's Creek?"

"The purpose of Liberation Services is to rescue people from the more than five hundred cult groups active in the United States. And my reason for coming here is to rescue Adam Putnam and bring him home to Cleveland."

"But," the *Post* correspondent injected into the discussion, "Putnam doesn't need or want your help, as far as I can see. So what's the big deal, that we should drive all the way down here, with a crew and all, for nothing?"

"Why don't you ask *them* why I made that call from jail?"

"I can answer that," Copperthwaite replied. "According to Sheriff Stone, Mr. Tellefsen showed up late yesterday at Emma's—that's the only restaurant in town—asking a lot of questions about the Institute and Dr. Jenner and all. He even managed to get into a rather heated discussion with Mr. Gavin, president of our bank, who was in the diner having a cup of coffee. Now, in a town like ours, people disturbing the peace stick out like a sore thumb, and since you never know what's in a person's mind, the sheriff thought the safest place for Mr. Tellefsen was the local jail until we could check out his credentials."

The reporters glanced at each other as Tellefsen played his trump card. "Well, then, what about the *murder*? When Putnam called home, he said there was a murder recently at the Institute. Is it any wonder he might be frightened to speak his mind? Tell us, Adam, tell us about it."

This time Putnam didn't answer, but again Jenner could read Morse code in the blinking of his eyes: MD, MD, MD. When the young man failed to respond, Conroy produced the accident report furnished by Stanton.

"Perhaps you are referring to the recent accidental death of one of our most loyal staff members, Mr. Paul Woodman. Accidents do happen, Mr. Tellefsen, even in a place like the New World Institute. We think you'll find this police report in order, and we hope you will stop maligning our group. Or one might think that you had something to gain, such as free publicity."

Conroy smiled, then turned toward the reporters, continuing, "But we wouldn't want the press to go home with no story at all. So perhaps the mayor will show them around this new school, named in honor of Dr. Jenner."

Copperthwaite was quick to seize that moment, and she launched into a repeat of the dedication speech she had given a few weeks earlier, telling the reporters everything she could think of to demonstrate the positive impact Dr. Jenner had made on her town. And although the reporters seemed uninterested in touring the entire facility, they did take some shots indoors and then some photos outside, with Copperthwaite and Jenner standing next to the marker that bore his name.

Strange, Jenner thought as he stood next to the stone. *Seems more like a gravestone today. Maybe it's the weather. No, something else. Something about this whole thing isn't right.*

Agent Willard Stevenson tailed Gunnar Tellefsen for twenty miles before pulling him over. Davidson wanted a message delivered in no uncertain terms.

"Mr. Tellefsen," Stevenson said, holding his badge about ten inches from the rescuer's face, "you have involved yourself in a sensitive government investigation. I am not at liberty to discuss the case. But you are hereby notified that if you pursue this matter further, you will be charged with obstruction of justice."

"The only thing that matters to me," Tellefsen replied, "is getting Adam Putnam out of that cult. His soul is in danger, and maybe even his life. And that, to me, is more important than whatever the FBI or anybody else is doing here."

"If you persist, you will be arrested."

"On what charge? It's a free country. Don't threaten me. I have to answer to God before I answer to the FBI."

J. R. Jenner walked directly into his study upon his return to the compound. All the way back to the institute, he had been trying to figure out why Adam Putnam had sent two messages in code.

He picked an old Bible off his shelf and started paging through it. *Proverbs? Doesn't fit. Psalms has to be it, and Psalms 143:9 is the only verse it could be.* He flipped to the text, then sat stunned as he read, "Deliver me, O Lord, from mine enemies: I flee unto thee to hide me."

Enemies? Putnam is among friends, all intent on the same purpose. What's wrong with him, anyway?

But then another option came to mind, especially as he

pondered the second code message of Putnam, the one somehow related to Paul Woodman's death. *MD. MD. What could it mean? Maybe he knows what happened to Paul, but is afraid to talk. I'll talk to him myself as soon as possible,* Jenner thought as he got up to look for his wife.

"Mary," he called softly. "I'm home. It was just some guy trying to promote his business. A rescuer, of all things, coming to set our people free—as if they couldn't free themselves," he muttered, searching through the apartment room by room until the only room left unsearched was the bedroom.

"Mary," he said quietly, pushing the door open, "I'm home."

Mary, he could see, was lying on the bed, asleep. But she was fully dressed in a white dress with lots of lace. Strange. As he walked closer, expecting her to awake any moment, he could see that she was clutching something to her breast with both hands—their wedding photo. *She's wearing her wedding dress!*

At almost the same moment he saw the note and the empty pill bottle on the nightstand, realizing the truth in one part of his psyche while denying it in another. "Mary," he said louder, fighting back the horror. "I'm home!"

Still she didn't stir.

Now frantic, Jenner leaped on the bed next to her. He shook her, first gently, then more vigorously. Still there was no response.

He searched for a pulse.

Nothing.

"Mary," he started to cry, overwhelmed by the final failure of their twenty years of marriage. "Why?"

He reached for the note. "Dearest," the typed message said, "please don't be sad or blame yourself. I hid my pills until I had enough to set you free. And now you are, and so am I. Your wife, Mary."

Jenner reached for the medicine bottle, trying to read the prescription through his tears. But the only words he could makeout clearly were the last: "Florence Bradley, M.D."

As he read the name, something clicked—some fact he wanted to recall but could not because his conscious mind was engulfed in the pain of the moment. He picked up the telephone and quickly dialed Bradley's number.

After calmly describing the facts to the doctor, who said she would come immediately, Jenner began to shake. He collapsed into the overstuffed chair in the corner and looked again at Mary, vaguely thinking she might still wake up. For the first time in two decades, her face was serene. The storms had subsided, and in their place a quiet beauty had returned, the very thing that so charmed him once.

Overwhelmed by this obscenity, he bolted from the room, even as he heard the door of the apartment open and running footsteps in the hall. He passed Bradley without a word as he rushed toward the study. Locking the door, he threw himself down, fists clenched and face to the floor, and began to sob quietly. Whether it was for Mary or for himself, he could not tell.

He heard muffled voices and other sounds outside the door as he lay in that position for what seemed like hours. He knew, somewhere in the still rational part of himself, that eventually he would have to get up and face whoever was outside. But they could wait, he told himself, until he was ready, until he was in control again.

Even if it took all night.

30

Clare Conroy woke up quickly when Dr. Jenner emerged from his study, cursing herself for having fallen asleep on the couch. Bradley, Stanton, and Winston had taken care of Mary Jenner's body, but somebody, they all agreed, should stay with Dr. Jenner. Nobody should have to face a tragedy like this alone.

Jenner seemed momentarily startled to see Conroy in the room as she stood to greet him, but then he relaxed as she walked toward him. "I'm sorry," she said softly as they embraced. "If only someone could have known, maybe we could have stopped her."

Jenner seemed to nod, but as tightly as he was holding her, Conroy couldn't be sure. Any second, she expected Jenner to let go and back away, but for more than a minute he clung to her. "*I* should have known," he said, the words muffled because his face was partially buried in Conroy's collar.

"I should have known," he said again as he took a step back and looked into Conroy's eyes. The hurt she saw was enormous. Far beyond sadness, despair, guilt, or remorse, far beyond any words at all, his eyes held a brokenness she had never seen before in any man. Certainly not in this one.

She reached for him again, just as he began to weep, and she gently guided him toward the couch where she had been sleeping only moments before. Sitting down next to him, she put her arm around him and pulled his head to her shoulder. For a long time, neither one of them said a word.

Finally, however, Jenner broke the silence, sitting up straight on the couch without moving away from Clare's side. "I'm sorry," he began. "Not much of a man, I guess. Should be able to handle this without falling apart."

"No apologies necessary," Conroy answered. "The more you love, the more you hurt. It takes a real man to face it—somebody with heart."

"You think I loved her, then?" he asked.

"Can there be any doubt?" Conroy said immediately, surprised by the intensity of her own emotions. "And," she added, "she must have loved you, too."

"Then why . . ." He stopped.

"Sometimes we don't know why we do things ourselves," Conroy answered. "How can we hope to understand someone else's motives?"

"But it seems like such a waste," he said. "So sad. Mary was a good person. She deserved better than this."

Suddenly he stood up, turning as if to go toward the bedroom. "Is she . . . I mean, is her body . . . still in there?" he asked.

"No. When you didn't answer your door, we figured you wanted to be left alone, so we took care of everything, and then I volunteered to stay here and be with you."

"Will there be an inquest?" he asked, sitting down again, this time at the other end of the couch.

"Not likely," Clare replied. "But just to be sure, we asked the sheriff to come by and take a complete report. And since Dr. Bradley is the only M.D. for thirty miles . . . " She stopped midsentence when Jenner vaulted to his feet.

Conroy waited for him to say something, since he seemed quite agitated, but when he just stood there looking at her, she finished the thought, ". . . she sometimes functions as the medical examiner, so everything is already taken care of."

"I'll just bet it is," he said, an unmistakable bitterness coloring his voice.

Surprised by this outburst, Conroy said, "I'm sorry, sir, I don't understand."

Jenner looked around, then sat down again, this time in a chair facing Clare. He pulled it closer to the couch so that his face was no more than five feet from hers.

"Is anyone else here?" he asked in a whisper.

"We're alone. The others left hours ago."

"Good," he said. "Something you just said solved the mystery I was working on when I came home from that press thing yesterday. Putnam started it. Did you see him blink his eyes toward the camera?" Conroy nodded as Jenner continued, "Well, he wasn't just blinking. It was Morse code, I'm sure of it. Learned it by heart to make Eagle Scout. Anyway, he gave two messages. The first was P1439, and by the time I got back here I had figured out it was a Bible reference. I looked it up, and it said, 'Deliver me, O Lord, from mine enemies . . .' from Psalm 143:9. You think I'm crazy, right?"

"Not at all," Conroy replied immediately, recalling Putnam's strange eye movements and wondering how she had missed recognizing them, too. She also wondered if anyone else had noticed. "Go on, please," she said. "Sounds like there's more."

"There is," he said, his voice rising as he talked. "The second time Putnam was questioned, about the murder, he gave another Morse code message: MD, MD, MD. And I couldn't figure it out until just now when you said Dr. Bradley sometimes is the medical examiner. I wonder . . ."

He stood up again, this time pacing thoughtfully around the room. "I wonder if Putnam can connect Bradley with the death of Paul Woodman? Remember that pool of blood on the trail?" he asked, sitting down again in the chair.

"But Winston said it was from an animal. And didn't he take you out and show you the place where Woodman died, right after that?" she asked.

"He did, but I wasn't convinced, though I didn't let on. I knew Paul Woodman like my own brother, and there is no way he could kill himself riding a snowmobile. A tree had been down across the trail all right, but even so, I didn't believe it. I wonder what really happened. I bet Putnam knows."

"Then let's ask him," Clare replied.

Now the tone of secrecy returned to Jenner's voice, "Good idea, except the pieces of this puzzle fit together too neatly, don't you think?"

"I'm not sure I follow," she replied.

"Well, the first thing we should ask," he said, "is why people around J. R. Jenner are starting to die."

He looked into Conroy's eyes again, and it was clear that his hurt had turned into anger. "Why cars are being blown up . . . " he continued. "Something's going on, that's for sure. Some kind of conspiracy. I wonder . . . who can we trust? For instance, if Bradley's in on it, was she somehow involved in Mary's death? Come to think of it, Mary had an aversion to typewriters. Too dirty, I guess." He paused. "Am I going mad?"

"Pretty reasonable so far," Conroy answered, trying to keep him talking. "But why shouldn't we talk with Putnam?"

"Well, if Putnam actually did call home, and his mother

really did hire Tellefsen . . . who would want most to prevent Putnam from leaving?"

"Someone with something to hide?" she responded, trying to act as naïve as possible without appearing stupid.

"Of course. But who specifically?"

"Not you, surely," she answered.

"True. I had nothing to hide, nothing to be ashamed of . . . until today."

"You think Bradley's involved?" Clare asked.

"At least her, and maybe the sheriff, if he signed the report. Certainly Winston, since he tried to cover up the murder. I thought he was so trustworthy, especially when he came back to us after Linda's death."

So he doesn't know about Landau, she thought.

"But he works for Stanton," Jenner continued, "and Stanton and Worthy are like hand and glove. All the bad things have happened since those two joined us. So if we're going to find out what Putnam knows, we have to be very careful. I doubt he would trust me, but maybe you could . . ."

Again he paused, looking deeply into Conroy's eyes. This time she knew he wanted to discern which side *she* was on, and it felt like his blue eyes were looking right into her soul.

Conroy fought for composure with all she had. And then, when she realized her eyes might betray her, she reached toward him, taking his hands in hers as she walked into his arms. Jenner, his arms around her waist, seemed not to know how to respond to such an advance. But then, as she entwined her hands lightly behind his neck and leaned back just a bit playfully, he embraced her.

Their first kiss was tentative, though Conroy was sure Jenner was now convinced of her complete loyalty. But when the first gave way to another, and another, each more passionate than the one before it, Conroy began to understand how pain and pleasure are sometimes intertwined.

Jenner, who only minutes before had been nearly overwhelmed with grief, was now aroused by what she'd intended as a diversion.

To compound the situation, she felt herself slipping, too. She was liking this too much. But even as her sense of pleasure increased, at the same time she became more deeply afraid as the emotions so carefully restrained since early adolescence now surged. Frantically, Conroy freed herself from Jenner's embrace, stepped back quickly, and sat down on the couch. She felt quite flushed—whether from embarrassment or from excitement, she couldn't tell.

Jenner just stood there, hands limp at his side, looking confused.

"I'm sorry, sir," she said.

"'*Sir,*' you call me, after kissing me like that?" he said with a laugh as he walked to the couch, sat down, and put his arm around her shoulder. "And what is there to be sorry for?" he continued. "We are free now. We can become truly one. I know you want it as badly as I, and now there is nothing to keep us from being together forever."

"But this is so fast," she replied. "Too much, too soon. Yes, it is something I want, but we must remember who we are."

"In the mind of God, we are one. One flesh, already, in the mind of God. Stay with me tonight," he pleaded, reaching over and taking her hand. "Don't let me be alone. I've been alone so long, and I don't want to be alone again. I need you. I love you."

She looked into his eyes again, torn between her own desire to stay and her professional principles: *Honesty. Loyalty. Integrity. Discretion. Morality. Character.*

"Jacob," she said tenderly. "Remember . . . we have enemies. All the other prophets have had enemies. What if they find out? What if they discover I stayed with you the very night your own wife . . ."

She stopped cold, not wanting to hurt him. More significantly, she realized the others had framed her. *They told me to stay so they could say I spent this night—of all nights—in his apartment. Blackmail? Try "motive," if there's ever a question about foul play. This whole thing smells worse by the minute. But one thing's for sure: Mary Jenner's death was no suicide.*

Now Conroy wanted to run away somewhere, or at least to beam herself into her own apartment to show them all, to prove to them all . . . what? What difference did it make, really, whether or not she stayed with him all night? What difference did it make if she gave in, just this once, to the yearnings that felt so good, beyond anything she had ever imagined?

She turned back toward him, as willing to stay as, moments before, she had been anxious to leave. But it was clear from his face that her comment about Mary had iced his desire, at least temporarily.

"I'm sorry," she said.

"No, it's okay," he replied, now quite restrained, "you're right. We should wait. And not only out of respect for Mary, but because of who we are. People all over the world are looking to us as leaders. We will wait an appropriate period of time, maybe six months, and then we will be married . . . if . . ."

He stopped, looking deeply into Clare's eyes. *Interesting proposal,* she thought, *that didn't sound much like a question.* But as she returned his gaze, Conroy saw, for the first time since she had known this man, what looked like doubt. Or was it fear? She waited, wondering what he was thinking.

After what seemed like minutes, Jenner continued, ". . . if

we are both still alive. It is as I predicted on the plane. First Paul, now Mary. You could be next, or possibly they will assassinate us together."

Again he stopped, reflectively. "Do you think this Tellefsen fellow could be part of a plot . . . that maybe he was just testing us to see how easily we could be lured out into the open? Or perhaps distracting us so someone could get to Mary?"

"It's hard to believe that someone would go to all that trouble—make up a story and call in the press—to get us out in the open when we're out in public on a regular basis," she said, trying to inject a little rationality into his flight of paranoia.

"But think of the timing," he insisted. "I'm accused of running a cult that holds people against their will, and the same day my wife commits suicide. Could be incriminating if the word got out. If they can discredit me, they won't have to kill me. But in that case, I'd rather be dead anyway.

"On top of that, you spend the night with me. Think of what the press would do with that if they knew. They really set a trap for us; there's no doubt about it.

"We must be careful, Rachel," he said forcefully as he looked in her eyes. "We must be very, very careful."

31

During the first ten days after Mary's memorial service, J. R. Jenner spent most of his time in his office with the door locked. Sometimes he even slept there instead of returning to the apartment. His usually well-groomed appearance gradually gave way to shagginess. His hair, beard and fingernails grew much longer than he would ordinarily have tolerated. The room smelled of perspiration and rotting food from unfinished meals brought in from the kitchen.

Conroy visited him regularly during this period, but usually in the afternoon, when there were secretaries present in the outer office. As far as she knew, she was the only person with access to Jenner now. He had simply withdrawn into himself, or become lost in his research of the Knights Templar, or both.

Scattered all over the office floor were copies of book pages, many of them with ancient-looking inscriptions, charts, genealogies, and maps. Clare helped where she could, finding obscure references in Jenner's substantial library. Occasionally, he would try to show her how all of it connected to the present conflict between the Sionists and Dr. J. R. Jenner, as if all human history hung in the balance.

Clare was both saddened and frightened by the change she saw in this man. Day after day he seemed to slip farther into a very complicated world of his own creation. *If it's a grief reaction, how long do we wait before intervening?* she wondered. *And how would we intervene if we decided he needed it? Not medically—that's for sure. Neither one of us would trust Bradley enough to ask for help.*

God, she prayed, *this guy is falling into a black hole. I know he's one of the bad guys in this op . . . sorry, operation . . . but that doesn't mean he deserves insanity. Besides, if he goes over the edge, I may not be able to complete this investigation before Bruce comes back. If you have any control over what's happening in one man's mind, especially this one's, we could use a supernatural injection of rationality here. Thanks.*

"Rachel," she heard Jenner say. "I have finally traced the Merovengian genealogies as far back as I can. This year, this very year, it will happen. The United States of Europe is the key. Their currency displayed the bust of Charles V, the progenitor of the "Spanish" Hapsburgs. The only question remaining is which descendent will become the leader of the new Holy Roman Empire. Without doubt we stand in their way. Which explains why they have escalated their attempts to get rid of me, especially if any of their clairvoyants have computed the numerology of my name!"

He glanced at Conroy, who was torn between wanting to believe him and writing him off as deranged. "Have you finished the whole chart, then?" she asked, gently, taking the scroll of several dozen scotch-taped legal-pad sheets from his hand. She unrolled it as he explained.

"This is the line of Merovee. Some claim he was a descendant of Mary Magdalene after she fled to France from

Jerusalem when the Romans destroyed the Temple in 70 A.D. Her offspring married into the royal family, and Merovee was the first king of the Franks—from 447 to 458 A.D. The small birthmark over his heart, in the form of a cross, became the emblem of the Guardians of the Grail.

"Now, look over here . . . in 1188, Jean de Gisors became the first Grand Master of the Priory of Sion—the same year he founded the Rosicrucians. Through the years their membership has included: Leonardo da Vinci, Robert Boyle, Isaac Newton, Victor Hugo, Claude Debussy. Their current leader, Jean Jacques Sainte-Marie, has admitted that the Priory of Sion possesses the treasures of the ancient Jewish Temple and that they will be returned to Jerusalem *when the time is right*. Well, by my calculations, the time *is* right. The time is *now*."

"This is all very interesting," Clare admitted, "and anybody can see that you have invested a huge amount of energy in the research. But . . ." She hesitated, unsure how he would react to the expression of even the slightest doubt, "How can you be so *sure* that all this is coming true *now*? I mean, look at the number of centuries—millennia—represented on this chart. It's almost like saying that every major historical event—for instance, the assassination of John F. Kennedy—can be related to this endless conspiracy."

"Well, some have even speculated that JFK was killed because he dared to oppose the Sionists, who are sometimes called the Illuminati. But the conflict I'm describing is much bigger than that. It's our people against their people. And with victory so close, they cannot tolerate *any* resistance." He paused, looked at Conroy, and smiled benevolently. It was the first time in nearly two weeks she had seen anything but focused intensity in his face.

"Don't worry," he said. "I've been studying this for years. For now, all I ask is that you trust me."

"I do," she lied. "But if you get burned out poring over ancient documents to prove a worldwide conspiracy, how are we going to stop this local conspiracy?"

"They may be one and the same," he replied. "But you're right. Have you talked to Putnam yet?"

"Not yet. I'm waiting for the right opportunity. But I *have* been snooping around a little in relation to Stanton and Worthy, and I think I'm onto something. It's tricky, though. Once they get wind we suspect something, there's no telling what might happen. So I'm taking it very, very slow."

Actually, I'm taking it very, very fast, just in case you come unglued and this deal blows sky high. It's time for me and Bambi to thump our local thugs a bit. If I don't get access to those financial files pretty soon, I never will.

"It's open," Worthy called from inside as the door to his office swung open to Conroy's knock. Worthy and Stanton were sitting on the leather couch, each holding a cup of coffee, when Clare walked in, her purse under her arm.

"Morning, Conroy," Worthy said. "Right on time. You're looking quite energetic for the hour." He motioned for her to take the armchair across the glass table from the two men.

"Skiing will do that for you," she replied, smiling. "Did the whole trail before breakfast. Gets the blood flowing, and it's a great way to clear the mind. You should try it sometime."

"Us couch potatoes prefer snowmobiles," Stanton interjected, "but it's getting harder and harder to ride that trail without running over somebody on skis, thanks to you."

"And Dr. Jenner, don't forget," Conroy replied. "It was his idea, after all."

"Yeah, sure," Stanton said. "How's our leader doing these days, anyway? He didn't look too good at the funeral, and I haven't even seen him since, though I suppose you have."

Stanton was smirking a bit, as if amused by his own suggestive comment.

"I have, which I'm sure you know; your cameras are everywhere, like a prison camp. Dr. Jenner is recovering quite well, considering the shocks he's experienced—from the news of Woodman's death, to the bombing, to that rescuer showing up, and then to find his wife dead in her wedding dress! That's certainly more than most people could endure without going off the deep end."

"Is he . . . acting irrationally?" Worthy asked, leaning forward. "We need to know, for the good of the organization. If Jenner is having a nervous breakdown, we're all in trouble."

"He'll be reassured to hear of your concern," Conroy said, trying not to sound too sarcastic.

"Mine, too," Stanton said quickly. "After all," he added, "without Dr. Jenner, we're all back out on the street."

Or in prison for life—or, even better, an electric chair, she thought as she decided it was time to pursue her objective.

"He'll be relieved because for the past few days he's been wondering . . . *we've* been wondering why things are going bad around here when until very recently everything was so good."

Worthy looked at Stanton, who replied, "Stuff happens, Conroy. Sometimes it's just that way. Bad things come in threes, sometimes fours. And no matter how hard you try, you can't avoid it. It's no different here than anywhere else."

"Interesting perspective," she said, "for someone who is supposed to be in charge of security. And Dr. Jenner might be willing to accept that explanation, though I'm sorry to say he's also wondering whom he can trust. He's convinced there is a conspiracy—a worldwide conspiracy—to kill him. In fact, he seems rather resigned to the idea of becoming a martyr. I find it quite unnerving to hear him talk that way . . ."

She studied their facial reactions closely as she continued. ". . . and quite sad to see happen, close as we have become. It may take him awhile to regain his composure. All this is confidential, of course," she paused, "and maybe I've already said more than I should about it, since I don't know whom to trust, either."

"You can trust *us*, of course," Worthy protested. "We're part of the team. Somehow we'll have to help him get beyond this. We'll all have to work together." Stanton nodded, a little too solemnly, she thought.

"I do appreciate the sentiment," she replied dryly, "but let's consider the evidence for a moment."

"Evidence?" Stanton's voice rose in mock alarm. "Somebody on trial here?"

"Just putting two and two together about the recent incident with Tellefsen. He shows up out of nowhere with a story that could have been concocted out of thin air . . . except for one thing."

"What's that?" Stanton replied as Worthy stood, closed the office door, and returned to the couch, not bothering to refill his coffee cup.

"The part about a murder," she replied, returning his gaze without blinking. "Tellefsen needs to stay in business, so he crisscrosses the country looking for people to rescue. And maybe he runs into Putnam's mother and convinces her to send him here. But unless Putnam really made that call, and unless he really talked about a murder, who on the outside is going to know anything about it?"

Worthy glanced worriedly at Stanton as she continued, "It was easy enough to see, at that press conference and on the way into town and back, that Putnam was one very scared little rabbit."

"Speculation, Conroy. I thought you said evidence," Stanton said, leaning back on the couch.

"I don't recall seeing any bruises on Putnam," she replied, "so I asked myself what kind of intimidation might shut him up. And," she said, reaching into her purse, "I found this videotape. I believe you know what's on it. Of course you do, since there's a whole truckload about to be shipped out of here."

"Bambi?" Stanton said as he read the label of the shrink-wrapped cassette. "This isn't a very funny joke."

"No joke, Stanton, though you should think about acting. Let's see what's inside."

Stanton unwrapped the tape, then set it on the table, still in its brightly colored container decorated with a picture of a baby deer and all his little forest friends.

"Looks innocent enough," she remarked, "but we all know what is really inside." She picked up the tape container and ripped off the outside cover to expose another hidden cover underneath. This one portrayed an entirely different scene, graphically depicting various acts of torture and homosexual activity.

"Disgusting, don't you think?" she commented, placing the tape back on the table with the cover plainly in view. "And capable of instilling more than a little fear in the bones of Adam Putnam. But certainly not something we would want Dr. Jenner to know about."

The men looked at each other; then Stanton replied somewhat tentatively, "What, exactly, are you driving at, Conroy? Let's stop playing games and get to the point."

"Okay, if that's the way you want it. Point number one is that you made some kind of deal, with whoever produces filth like this, to duplicate and ship their tapes. Probably a lot of bucks changing hands. Paul Woodman figured out what was going on and threatened to blow the whistle, so you had him killed."

Conroy could see from Worthy's face that she was close

to the truth, so she continued. "But whoever did it—Winston gets my vote—botched the job enough for Putnam to get suspicious."

"Even if you're right, you can't prove anything," Stanton replied. "But something tells me you didn't come here to tell us what bad boys we are."

"Good guess," Conroy said. "I could expose you myself. But a scandal of that magnitude would undermine our effectiveness, specifically the financial effectiveness of the expanding worldwide program of Dr. J. Reuben Jenner. In that case, I would have to give up a position I'm just beginning to appreciate, especially since the untimely death of Mrs. Jenner."

She smiled a little crookedly, just to encourage their filthy speculation. "I propose we work together. You manage your side. I'll keep Jenner happy and the press off our tails. And we all go on our merry way."

"This was in your mind all along," Stanton said, "ever since you laid eyes on Jenner. I've known women like you before."

"Now, now, aren't we being just a bit self-righteous considering the tape on the table and who knows what else you've arranged under cover of this wholesome little ministry! For instance, I'd like to know what's in that storage shed. . . ."

"Why don't you just go check it out," Stanton offered.

"Maybe I will," she replied, enjoying the moment. Finally she had Stanton off guard. She could also see that he was impressed, so she continued, "Gentlemen, it's time to start sharing the wealth."

Worthy, who was squirming more than just a little, replied, "You've seen the reports. You know we run in the red."

"I've been in banking, I remind you," she replied flatly. International banking, the Pacific Rim, where you can learn a lot about managing money in a very short time if you pay attention. And I do pay attention," she added.

"To other people's business," Stanton snapped.

"Might seem that way when you're the one caught with a hand in the cookie jar. But you don't know how much Dr. Jenner and I have discussed the problems of managing this movement. Nor do you know how much of it he has already entrusted to me—which makes *your* business *my* business, too.

"But if we were partners, all my reports would keep our leader from worrying about anything except how to reach the masses with his message."

"In exchange for?" Stanton said.

"Twenty-five percent," she replied, "of everything you're skimming, put into an account only I can access. I'll help manage the rest, of course. Who knows, with my creativity and experience, you might end up with more than you would have had without me."

Stanton's mouth dropped open, as if he were stunned. *Male chauvinist crook*, she thought as she awaited their response. *Rub your face in it.*

"Too much," Stanton replied after a moment. Something in his voice told Conroy it was time to stop fooling around. "Ninety-ten; our ninety, your ten. Even that's too much, considering our investment as compared to yours."

"Agreed," she replied with as level a voice as she could muster, "for now. But you cheat me, I pull the plug."

"Partners don't threaten each other," Stanton replied calmly. "Or bad things happen."

"*That* sounds like a threat," Conroy countered.

"Take it any way you like," he said, "but it's a fact. We work together, we're family. We succeed, we all succeed. We fail, we all fail."

"Stanton," Worthy interrupted, "I'm not sure this is a good idea. We don't know we can trust her. Maybe she's setting us up, with Jenner, to get rid of us. What if she's wearing a wire or carrying a recorder?"

Stanton stared at Conroy, who returned his gaze without blinking. Very slowly his eyes traveled over her upper torso, clad in a thin turtleneck under an unbuttoned flannel shirt. He was obviously looking for more than the telltale wire. It was all she could do to sit there and take it.

Then he turned his attention to the purse, lying open on the table. Conroy nudged it in his direction, bluffing. *No recorder, but if they fool around with that pen long enough . . .*

"Go ahead, take a look," she said. "I'd rather work with someone who's careful, anyway, since now it's my neck, too."

Stanton reached toward the purse, then stopped. But then Worthy grabbed it, nervously, and turned it upside down over the table. The .32-caliber pen fell out onto the glass. Conroy caught it on the first bounce, but Stanton reached for it, saying, "Now *there's* something interesting. Mind if I have a look?"

"Not at all," she replied. "Just a special gift I didn't want destroyed by Worthy's clumsiness."

Stanton tried to take the pen apart. First he unscrewed the top, then the bottom, but when his efforts to further disassemble it failed, he put it back together and handed it to Conroy.

"Heavy little bugger for a pen, but it's certainly not a microphone. Worthy's skittish since the scene with Putnam and that rescuer."

"Can't be too careful," Conroy replied, stuffing the contents back into the purse. "And speaking of Putnam, I suggest we give him so much to do that he won't have enough energy to get homesick again."

"He knows what'll happen if he so much as picks up that

phone or uses the computer to send a message. We're monitoring everything," Stanton assured her.

"That reminds me," Worthy interjected. "What about that signal we've been picking up since you got that fancy Czech scanner? Signal's screwed up, maybe scrambled. But there's a transmitter somewhere up here. What if it's Putnam? For that matter, what if it's Conroy?"

"Unlikely," she replied. "If you just compare my recent itinerary with your records, I think you'll agree. But . . ."

She hesitated, weighing the value of the radio in question, which she knew she had seen, against the possibility that if she could prove her loyalty now, she might gain more immediate access to their most sensitive records. *Cabin's empty. It's just a piece of equipment—not a bad trade.*

"But," she offered, "I can imagine where a transmitter might be hidden, if indeed there is such a device up here. Just the other day, when I was out snowmobiling, I passed a log cabin—not far down Walton's Prairie and into Miner's Pass. Be a good place to look, I'd wager."

Stanton studied her face for just a moment, then picked up the phone. "Hello, Winston. Remember that signal mystery we been trying to solve? Yeah, just the other night again."

Clare caught herself midgasp. *How? Can't be Bruce. Shepherd's gone, he said. So who could be there now? Whoever it is is about to be visited, and none too gently.*

"Conroy thinks we should check out a log cabin just off the edge of Walton's Prairie. I know. I know. She's working with us now. I'll explain later. Take a couple of guys for backup and pay our local deejay a visit. We'll be waiting at the control center. Bring back what you find. But don't go shooting up the evidence, y'hear. Bring 'em back alive."

32

Jeremiah Wilkes stood by his kitchen window, kneading the gases out of a fresh batch of sourdough. *Don't pound it too hard*, he reminded himself.

Cyrus jumped up from his cedar-scented blanket near the stove at almost the same instant that Wilkes heard the snowmobiles coming. The dog was wagging and whining, searching frantically for a tennis ball.

The three machines were traveling much faster than the occasional recreational riders who, if they should happen to head down Miner's Pass by mistake, were usually slowing up at about the time they reached the cabin to ask directions.

Wilkes wiped his hands on the towel by the sink, then scraped a little circle in the frost to get a better look. This was not some family out for a little ride, he could see immediately. Each rider followed the other exactly, as if on some mission. This was trouble, his instincts told him. As they got closer, Wilkes could also see that each rider had a rifle slung over his back, its barrel just protruding above shoulder height. Not that this was so peculiar, either, out in the wilderness, except that all the hunting seasons were over as far as he knew.

The shepherd glanced at his own rifle, standing in the corner, but quickly decided there wasn't much point in provoking things by a show of force—if you could call a .30-.30 carbine a show of force.

"Down, Cyrus," Wilkes said sternly to the dog as the machines came to a stop outside the door. "Bad," he snarled, slapping the dog's behind to send him slinking to the safety of the back room. *Sorry. It's for your own good.*

Opening the front door halfway, Wilkes stood with one hand on the latch and the other on the doorjamb. "Hullo, fellas," he said. "Out huntin'?"

"Might say that," Johnny Winston replied, sliding his thumb up under the rifle sling over his right shoulder and in one motion bringing the firearm to rest on his lap with the muzzle aimed in the general direction of the cabin. The other riders did the same thing.

"Nothin' in season, middle of January," Wilkes commented.

"Never know what you'll run into up here," Winston said. "Best be prepared."

Wilkes looked carefully at the rifle, realizing it was a small-caliber military weapon of some kind. "Not much match for big game, I wager," he said with a laugh, just as Cyrus suddenly burst through the door between his master's legs, tennis ball in his mouth, bounding toward the snowmobiles at full speed.

Winston, seated not twenty feet away, started to cover his face protectively. But then, instead, he leveled the Uzi, firing three rounds at the dog in a split second.

The first two shots hit the cabin about a foot away from Wilkes's left knee. The third struck Cyrus, midair, in the chest. He was dead before he hit the ground with a thud at Winston's feet, the ball now stuck in his mouth forever.

"Nooooo!" Wilkes cried, too late, as he heard the bullet's thud and he saw the dog's body fall in a heap. For a moment, it seemed like time stood still, as the sound of his cry and then its echo filled the valley. Wilkes started toward the murderer, who seemed momentarily stunned himself.

But almost as quickly, the mountain man decided if he was going to have revenge, bare hands would not be the weapon of choice. Diving inside the cabin, he slammed the door and quickly shoved the table against it. Then he lunged for his rifle as the bandits began smashing their way in.

The door would never last, he knew, but if there was going to be a gunfight, it might just slow them down enough so he could take them out one at a time. And he knew which one he wanted first.

Wilkes inched his way backward, on his knees, into the darkness of the back room, where he would have a clear view of the door. The intruders, however, would not be able to see him, especially coming in from the bright, snow-reflected sunlight outside.

He chambered a 150-grain silver-tip and waited, hammer back, looking down the rifle barrel through the buckhorn sights as the door disintegrated. He considered killing them by shooting through the wood, but what kept him from doing so was an intense desire to see this bandit's face as he took a slug between the eyes.

But as Wilkes waited, the rage of the moment gave way to a certain rationality that crowded, uninvited, into his mind. *Who are they? What do they want? Why are they breaking down my door? Shall I kill them all for murdering my dog?*

Almost too late, he remembered the radio, out in the front room under the shelf, just below the window. "If you ever need help, hit this button," Davidson had promised.

Trading the known for the unknown, Wilkes laid aside the rifle and dove for the radio just as the boot of Johnny Winston kicked through the door. It was followed by the rest of Winston, who blinked several times trying to adjust to the relative darkness.

"Give it up, pal," Winston said, leveling the gun at Wilkes, who was now sitting on the floor below the window with his back against the radio, which was now his only hope. *Davidson, you better be listening.*

"Don't shoot," Wilkes said quietly. "I'm not armed. And I don't have any money. Nothing worth robbing. . . ."

"Quit babbling like an old woman," Winston ordered.

"You killed my dog," Wilkes said more strongly. The only thing keeping him from tearing this punk apart now was the other two men, rifles ready, standing just inside the doorway.

"Stupid mutt," Winston said, spitting tobacco juice on the floor. "Attacked me. What was I supposed to do?"

"Trigger-happy idiot," Wilkes replied. "He just wanted to play, that's all. Thought life was one long, happy game."

"Shut up," Winston ordered. "Now let's see what you're hiding there. Easy . . . no quick moves," he said as Wilkes slid away from the window. "Why look here, boys," Winston said, "a radio. And not just your basic AM/FM, either. Batteries, too," he said, "and some kind of tape player. We found our spy all right."

"Spy? I'm a shepherd. Lotsa people like short wave. Have t' keep in touch with the world somehow."

"Like I said, shut up, and get on over in that corner where we can keep an eye on you," Winston said, pointing to the corner of the room farthest from the door.

Meekly Wilkes rose to his feet. As Winston examined the electronic equipment, the shepherd edged his way around the stove in the middle of the room, his face toward the guards at the doorless exit. Just as Wilkes was even with their position, he placed his right foot against the cast-iron stove and launched himself toward the opening. His lowered shoulders caught both men simultaneously just below the ribcage, smashing them into the door frame as Wilkes rushed between them toward freedom.

Vaulting the dog's body, Wilkes reached the lead snowmobile and hit the start switch about the same time as he heard the sound of breaking glass and Winston's cursing. A chair crashed through the window, followed by the barrel of a rifle.

The engine coughed, caught for a moment, then stalled. Again he pushed the button, praying, a prayer interrupted by a burst of bullets from the semi-automatic that froze Wilkes's hands to the grips as he waited to die. About the time he realized the shots were hitting all around him, everything suddenly went quiet.

"I wouldn't," Winston's voice said from the darkened window. "Another move like that and you're history." Wilkes took his hands slowly away from the handlebars, noticing the subzero temperature now for the first time as he sat on the machine in his jeans and flannel shirt.

The guards, by now back on their feet, rushed Wilkes. The first to reach him swatted the offender across the face with the butt of his rifle. Wilkes ducked to avoid being hit in the face again, but as he brought his arms up to protect himself, he was suddenly knocked off the vehicle by a savage kick from the other direction that caught him just under the ribs on his left side. Fighting for air, he now lay on his side, curled up in the snow, totally helpless as his two assailants towered over him.

"Enough," Winston called out. "Bring him back in here and tie him up. Kill him now, and we'll never figure out what he's doing with this fancy equipment. Stanton said *alive*, remember?"

As the others tied him, none too gently, to the chair near the only window left intact, Wilkes watched Winston tear through all the cupboards and closets, overturning everything except the stove, until the usually immaculate floor was strewn with all his possessions.

"Whattaya know, a religious spy!" Winston commented as he came to the small library, including the Bible. With a smirk toward Wilkes, he pulled the entire shelf off the wall and it, too, fell to the floor with a crash.

When he finished ransacking the cabin, Winston began searching outside, pushing over the woodpiles where he could. For awhile he could be heard noisily tearing things apart in the shed. Then he came into view outside the window, following a cable he was yanking from under the snow and ice.

Wilkes watched, wondering how close this outlaw would get to the antenna before he recognized it for what it was.

"Hey," Winston yelled finally, "lookee here. A Christmas-tree antenna! Now who would have something like that," he was muttering as he came back into the cabin, "unless he was a spy?"

"Who you working for?" he demanded menacingly, grabbing Wilkes by the shirt with his left hand and pulling him upward until their faces were only about eighteen inches apart.

"Mr. Bryan. Keep an eye on his sheep," Wilkes replied.

Without warning, Winston punched Wilkes full force on the jaw. "I don't like to play games, pal, in case you haven't noticed. Here you are in the middle of nowhere with a mess of fancy recording and transmitting gear. You're spying on us."

"I don't even know . . . who you are," Wilkes replied, dazed, though he knew they must be from the compound.

"Oh, I'm sorry," Winston laughed derisively, "we forgot to properly introduce ourselves, boys." The others laughed, too. "Winston. Barry. Stimson. Security for a certain local group that doesn't appreciate people sticking their nose where it don't belong. Now, you got one more chance. Who you working for?"

"Mr. Bryan . . . like I said. You know Mr. Bryan, the rancher that sold you the prop'ty?" Wilkes asked, which he realized was a mistake as soon as he said it. Again Winston hit him, harder than before, this time knocking him unconscious.

"Wake up!" Wilkes heard a voice saying from far away as a strange coldness brought him back. Water, mixed with snow, was still dripping off his beard as he opened his eyes, groggily trying to recall, and then suddenly remembering clearly what was happening.

Winston grabbed him again. "Three strikes, you're out, pal. Let's try it one more time," Winston said. "Where did you get this equipment?"

Wilkes looked at Winston. Then he looked at the others. Then he looked through the door, where he could see Cyrus lying dead in the snow, and suddenly he couldn't fight it any longer. "Davidson."

"And who is that?"

"Perfesser. Boulder," Wilkes muttered, his mind drifting now as he finally gave in, his chin falling to his chest.

Winston relaxed his grip. "Why?" he asked.

"Study . . . group . . . research," Wilkes said slowly, the pain in his jaw becoming more intense.

Winston paused, walked over to the equipment assembled on the floor, then came back, positioning himself squarely in front of Wilkes again. "Is this everything?"

Wilkes fought back the pain, trying to resist and wanting, with every ounce of energy remaining, to lie. Instead, looking down at the floor, he slowly shook his head.

"Where's the rest?"

"Cave," Wilkes said finally.

"Cut him free," Winston said to the others, "and load up this equipment. We got one more stop to make."

"Snowshoes," Wilkes said softly, thinking of himself as much as the others. "Never make it on foot," he explained as he started to shiver.

"Three pairs here," Winston said. "We'll take them all. And get this man some clothes. Then we'll warm him up with a nice little fire."

From the way he said it, Wilkes knew what was going to happen, but he wouldn't allow himself to believe it until he saw Winston actually light the match and touch it to the kindling from the door, now arranged neatly in a little teepee on the front porch. Sadly he watched the flames lick up the dry pine, then burn their way into the floorboards, igniting the rocking chair, the porch, the drapes on the windows, and then the main cabin itself.

Winston was using his own radio as they turned to go. "We have the transmitter and a prisoner, and we're stopping at a cave on the way back to pick up some more equipment. Oh," he added, "don't worry about the smoke. Just roasting some marshmallows. Should burn itself out in a couple hours, with all the snow around. We'll be back by then."

"Ten-four," a voice replied. "Good work."

Following Wilkes's directions, the group got as close to the cave as they could by snowmobile. That left about a mile through the timber for Wilkes, Winston, and Barry. Stimson waited by the machines, guarding the equipment.

By the time they had reached their objective, even Wilkes was winded, mainly due to his cracked ribs. Winston looked at Wilkes as all three tried to catch their breath. "This better be worth it, pilgrim," he said. "You first, then me with the big flashlight."

He handed Wilkes a small penlight, the only other artificial light source they had been able to find, and motioned for him to lead the way. Wilkes inched his way inside the opening more gingerly than usual, due to his bruises. He was glad he knew the route so well that he could feel his way all the way to the other side, if necessary. His eyes were puffing up so badly now that the penlight was basically useless.

"No tricks," Winston said behind him when they finally entered the main shaft entrance. "Man, what's that smell?"

Wilkes decided to teach this cowboy a lesson. Turning to the right, Wilkes carefully began to step his way along the main shaft, keeping hard against the rock wall on his left. Winston, close behind him, kept the beam of his own flashlight aimed straight down the shaft. But after they had gone perhaps thirty feet, he stopped, saying quite loudly, "Where's the stuff man? This tunnel goes on forever."

"You hear that noise?" Wilkes asked, trying to sound alarmed, pointing his little penlight to the right as if looking for something.

"What noise? All I hear is us. Let's go, I'm not in the mood for g—" Winston replied as his own flashlight revealed a large black, furry object in the cavern to their right—a furry object that was beginning to stir.

"What the—" he gasped. The bear opened its eyes just as Winston brought the Uzi to hip level.

"Don't." Wilkes tried to whisper, noticing too late that Winston had brought the rifle into the cave. "All we have to do is quietly. . . ."

The first burst of gunfire, even from such a small-caliber firearm, was deafening in the cave. Dropping to the floor, Wilkes began to crawl to safety along the back wall, reaching the entrance to the air passage about the same time the bear charged Winston. Covering his ears as the gunfire started again, Wilkes counted fifteen, maybe twenty rounds, rapid fire, as in the staccato light from the muzzle flashes the two figures converged in slow motion.

Even with his ears covered, Wilkes heard Winston scream, a horrifying sound that tapered off slowly into a low gurgle as the rifle hit the floor, followed by a muffled sound that could only be his body falling as well. Wilkes, afraid to turn on his own light now, small though it was, tried to determine where the bear was. He had no desire to go anywhere near a wounded sow in the dark, and he knew that if she was now between him and the entrance, there would be hell to pay just for trying to get past.

Straining to hear any sound that would tell him either the animal's location or Winston's condition, Wilkes now became aware of Barry's frantic shouting outside, though deep in the cavern his voice could barely be heard.

Gradually Wilkes began to separate the other sounds inside the shaft. Winston was still breathing, lying on the floor somewhere in the middle of the room, his respirations becoming less regular and the gurgling more pronounced with each breath.

Wilkes could also hear another sound, a repetitious low grunt followed by a muffled, gravelly sound that could only be the bear slowly dragging herself back to her den. Wilkes waited as that sound diminished into the distance of the little hollow that would now be her tomb. He was afraid to move, almost afraid to breathe until he was absolutely sure she was dead.

But as he waited, he heard a totally different sound coming from that same place, the faint squeal of a newborn cub searching for, then finding a place to nurse. Then he heard a sigh, a low moan that drifted off into nothingness as the mother bear died.

Winston was quiet now, too. As Wilkes crawled slowly over to his body, he could clearly see there was no reason to take his pulse. Staring back at him in the small circle of illumination from the penlight, was only half a face. One eye, wide open, gazed unblinking upward. Whatever else had happened in those few seconds, the bear somehow had cleanly swiped the other half away. It now hung, open to the air like an abandoned surgical experiment, by a single flap of skin.

33

Cyrus hit the switch—just fooling around. For ten bone-chilling miles up Hunter's Creek Pass, Bruce Davidson had been trying to convince himself the S. O. S. was some kind of mistake. The replacement unit strapped behind him would take care of that, and they'd be back in business.

His machine broke into the open at the southeast end of Walton's Prairie. *Some hot coffee will hit the spot. Be good to see these guys again so soon.*

But as the bureau chief stopped the machine to clean his goggles, he glanced to the northeast and saw the smoke for the first time, much more smoke than any chimney would normally produce. There could be no doubt about its origin, either, he realized. Heartsick, he gunned the snowmobile toward Miner's Pass.

Fire! he murmured, *chimney fire. Too late, but maybe everyone's okay.*

Five minutes later he came over the last little rise and saw the cabin's smoldering ruins. Davidson stopped the machine again, stunned. What had once been such a beautiful homestead was just a large blackened crater among the snow-covered trees—it looked as if the cabin had taken a direct hit from a meteor. Snow, sliding off nearby branches, extinguished the steaming rubble.

Distraught, Davidson scanned the area for Wilkes. *Wilkes! Where are you, Wilkes?* He fought back the thought—*you weren't in there. You* can't *be in there!* And then, as he surveyed the scene again, he saw what looked like a rust-colored shag rug lying in a pool of grayish water just in front of where the front porch used to be.

Davidson covered the final few yards in seconds, the reality of the scene pounding into his mind more fully with every passing millisecond. *Cyrus. No!*

He jumped from the snowmobile at the dog's side, grabbing the animal's face in his hands. "Cyrus," he called, imagining for an instant that if he could just wrestle that yellow tennis ball from the dog's mouth, as he had done so many times, and toss it far out into the snow. . . .

"Why?" Davidson cried out loud. "How?" as he tried to reconstruct how the dog might have died from the smoke, then make it this far from the building. Kneeling in the water, Davidson gently picked up the dog to carry him away from the mess. As he did, he heard the faint yet distinctive sucking sound that he recognized immediately as air being forced through a bullet hole to the lung.

It was a sound unlike any other sound on earth. He hadn't heard it since Nam, but for that moment he was carrying not a dog but another human body toward a waiting copter.

"What?" he choked, horrified, as he saw a small red spot on the dog's chest. Setting Cyrus down in the snow, Davidson probed with his fingers until he found the entry wound, not much larger than .22 caliber. Carefully he examined the dog now, looking for an exit wound, but there was none. "Uzi," he muttered, and at exactly that moment a hideous but far more reasonable interpretation of the evidence thrust its way into his mind.

Perelli! he thought, grabbing for his own revolver, even as another, even more dreadful, possibility hit him. *Wilkes! Not Wilkes, too!* Suddenly, Davidson felt exposed, out in the open, and he dove behind the snowmobile for cover. For several minutes he lay sprawled in the snow, collecting his thoughts and sorting out the facts, all the while wondering if he was under observation.

When it became clear that no one was nearby, Davidson holstered the weapon and conducted a thorough investigation of the scene. Immediately he saw that the evergreen antenna had been ripped from its place, so there was no doubt their transmitter had been discovered, somehow. Working his way around to the other side of the foundation, he noticed several casings lying in the snow. *Uzi,* he mumbled. *I was right,* as he placed them in one of the small plastic evidence bags he always carried.

When he came back to the front, he noticed blood on the snow. Not much, but there was no doubt about it. Kneeling, he collected the bloodstained snow with mixed feelings. He knew the blood might be from Wilkes, but at least that meant he hadn't died in the cabin.

Then Davidson noticed the boot tracks, partially melted from the fire but still clearly visible. He followed them, chastising himself that he hadn't seen them right away. The further he got from the heat, the more obvious it became that there were four separate tracks, all leading away from the fire and ending at the snowmobile trail. Three tracks were similar—sharply contoured lug soles in different sizes. The fourth set Davidson had seen before: the almost worn-out chain design of Jeremiah Wilkes's ten-year-old L. L. Bean Maine hunting shoes.

They've taken Wilkes somewhere, Davidson thought as

he surveyed the devastation, overwhelmed with a mixture of remorse and a rage so intense that his entire body became rigid. Teeth and fist clenched until the spasm became too painful to sustain any longer. Davidson focused his eyes on the dog and his mind on Perelli, hatred grinding his soul.

If they interrogated him before they left here, they must know about the cave! Maybe they even know about me. I never should have dragged Jerry into this. Or you, either, Cyrus. Sorry!

Fighting back the tears, Davidson took one more quick look around the area to see if he had missed anything. Then he started his snowmobile and headed for the mine shaft. He was thankful he'd brought snowshoes along, just in case.

By late afternoon, Davidson reached the place where the snowmobiles had parked. From that icy spot, a snowshoe-packed trail led eastward into the timber and toward the cave. There was no doubt now in Davidson's mind that their secret had been discovered. But as he began to traverse the trail, after hiding his vehicle in the trees, there was also no doubt that something dreadful had taken place between there and the rockslide.

In the middle of the snowshoe trail was a strange set of drag marks, accented every few feet by a small pool of blood. After picking up a few samples, he sat back on his heels and looked at the trail as it snaked through the trees. *What would they drag down there?* he wondered. But when he turned it around and asked, *What might they be dragging back?* he recoiled at the obvious answer. *Not what, but who! These drag marks are from boots!* Now on his knees, Davidson tried to tell what kind of boots, but there was no way to be sure.

Jerry? No, it has to be somebody else. Lord, let it be somebody else!

His pace intensified, since Davidson was sure that whoever had gone to the cave had also left. But he needed to know what they had taken. More than that, he wanted to get another look inside that compound, regardless of the risk to himself, on the faint chance that he might discover something about the current status of Jeremiah Wilkes.

The closer he got to the cave, the more abundant the blood along the trailside became, confirming Davidson's suspicion that whatever happened had happened inside the shaft. He tried to imagine, but the harder he worked on it, the more unlikely it seemed that Perelli would follow his hostage to this remote place, then severely wound or kill him, only to then drag him back over the ridge to the snowmobiles.

There had to be another explanation, but his musings were interrupted by personal concern for his own safety as soon as Davidson slipped past the abandoned snowshoes of the person in question and into the shaft. *Bear,* he remembered immediately from the strong musty odor that filled the cavern. *How did I forget?*

Clutching his unlit flashlight, he worked his way along the wall to his left, careful not to make any noise. He didn't want any trouble; he only wanted to get to the air shaft. *Just get to that opening! Relax,* he told himself, *deep breaths, slow release,* as he battled the claustrophobic panic. Eyes closed, he tried to shut out everything but the objective. Somehow he had to make it through.

But in the dark, Davidson stumbled and dislodged a large rock with his left hand. It tumbled loudly down the incline and toward the center of the cave. He waited, holding his breath, until the sound stopped with a distinctly metallic thud.

"What?" Davidson said out loud, turning on his flashlight and shining it first toward the bear's den to be sure the animal had not wakened. Reassured as he noticed the black furry mound in roughly the same place as during his last visit, Davidson next aimed his light in the direction of the metallic sound. He found the rock, finally, but it took a moment to realize it was resting on a rifle. Around it were scattered empty casings—the same kind he had picked up at the cabin.

Carefully, Davidson crawled toward the firearm, wondering why anyone would leave it behind. The answer quickly became clear when he noticed the blood—an extremely large pool that began adjacent to the rifle and led off in two directions. One path, he could see, led back to and through the entrance to the outside. The other blood trail ended at the bear.

Davidson cringed to think what had happened here. He slowly counted the shells, wondering who would be fool enough to challenge such an animal in such a place as this. Whoever it was—and he was certain it wasn't Wilkes—had paid dearly for the decision; that much was obvious. *Perelli?* For a fleeting moment, Davidson relished that thought. *Too smart. I'll have to deal with him myself.*

The bear had paid too, Davidson could see now. He took a step toward the animal, shining the light into the den to be sure. One eye was open, and her tongue hung limp from the side of her mouth. "Too bad," he muttered, shaking his head. "I'm sorry," he said, louder as he stood with rifle in one hand and flashlight in the other. Even as he spoke he realized he was now standing in the pool of blood.

"I really am sorry," he said sadly, out loud, addressing nobody in particular, except perhaps himself and God. But as he spoke those words, his thoughts turned to Wilkes. The shepherd urgently needed his help, and no amount of self-flagellation was going to accomplish that.

Leaning the rifle against the wall, Davidson turned and headed for the airshaft, intent on taking one last look down into that compound before he returned to Boulder to set up the rescue.

So focused was he on the goal as he moved through the darkness toward the opening, it never occurred to him that the dish and recorder would still be perched in that crevice. The lethal confrontation in the cave had evidently prevented Perelli's group from finding the surveillance gear.

Probably think Wilkes led them into a trap. That'll only make Perelli madder. Hang in there, Jerry.

The good news was that with the gear still intact, Davidson could search the compound electronically. With renewed energy he put on the headphones and began to listen, slowly touring the facility like a blind man with supernatural hearing. The main administration building was deserted at this hour, so Davidson switched to the medical center, moving from section to section until finally he heard the voice of Clare Conroy.

"There's been another tragedy today, sir," she said.

"What now?" Dr. Jenner asked.

Davidson, amazed at the clarity, had the impression he was right there with them.

"Winston," she said. "He went into a cave searching for something, and a bear attacked and killed him in there."

"Oh!" Jenner said, obviously shocked. "What a terrible way to die."

"I agree," Conroy said, "but now we may never know how Winston was involved in Paul's death."

"And Putnam is the only other person who might be willing to talk," Jenner replied.

"Exactly. The last time we discussed this, you wanted me to approach him sometime, but as I recall we left it hanging. . . ."

"That's one way to put it," he chuckled. "But now we must find out what he knows, Rachel. I want you to try as soon as you can, but secretly. We're still not sure which side some of these people are on."

"I'll get right on it," she replied, and Davidson could even hear the rustle of clothing as she stood up.

"Do you have to go so soon?" he asked. "Why not stay awhile?"

"Love to," she said, "but security will be preoccupied with this Winston thing tonight. I thought maybe I'd pay Putnam a visit. He'll be working late, as usual. If anybody gets nosey, I can always say you sent me."

"True enough," Jenner replied. The two could be heard walking to the door. And then, as clearly as if he'd been in the room, Davidson heard a kiss. Just a little peck on the cheek, perhaps, but still a kiss. Then the door shut and she was gone.

Okay, Clare, he thought, *but let's not take it too far.*

Davidson sat there wishing the equipment worked both ways as he followed the sound of Conroy's footsteps outside, down the walkway, and into her apartment. Watching carefully, he waited for a light to come on.

Instead he noticed that in just the past few minutes it had begun to snow, and not just a light dusting, either. The way this one was beginning, it already promised to be one of those quick mountain blizzards that drops two feet of snow overnight and is gone twelve hours later.

Either I head for the snowmobile right now, or I'm stuck here overnight. Turning to leave, Davidson realized he still hadn't found Wilkes. *Got to know where he is, if we're going to rescue him.* He had to stay and take his chances on the storm.

For an hour, as darkness fell and the storm intensified, Davidson listened. He focused on every building he could still see through the snow, but he never heard the voices he was listening for. Perelli or Wilkes—either one would do.

Frustrated, he stood up to stretch in the darkness. And looking down, he saw a small building he'd never noticed before. The structure, perhaps twelve by sixteen feet, was built almost flush against the sheer rock face of the cliff behind the main Institute buildings, which placed it directly below his feet.

Reaching the lightweight dish out over the edge, Davidson finally heard the voice of George Perelli. "I'm pretty tired of this. You're a shepherd, but you got this fancy radio stuff from some professor? You take my best man into a trap where he gets killed. No doubt about it, you're a spy. You got one last chance to tell me who you work for, or you're cougar bait."

There was silence for a moment, and then Davidson heard Wilkes begin to mumble, obviously in pain and laboring for breath. As he listened, astonished, Davidson realized his friend was praying.

"My God," Wilkes whispered, "will shut the lions' mouths, for I am innocent before thee."

"That's it," Perelli roared, slapping Wilkes so hard that Davidson could almost feel it himself. He longed for wings, a rope—anything to transport himself below to intervene somehow.

"God," he cried, "don't let him do this. Please don't let him do this. Not again, Lord. Not again."

Now there were other voices as two or three people, including Perelli, discussed the fate of Jeremiah Wilkes. To Davidson's relief the concensus opinion was that whoever this guy was, he was no longer capable of giving them anything valuable tonight. Tomorrow he might, or the next day, *he would.* No matter. Sometime he would finally tell them who was spying on them, and after that he would pay for what he had done to Winston that afternoon.

As they dragged Wilkes into one of the rooms in what

was obviously a detention center, Davidson could hear his friend still praying, "My God, my God, why hast thou forsaken me? Why art thou so far from helping me, and from the words of my roaring? Be not far from me, for trouble is near, for there is none to help. I am poured out like water, and all my bones are out of joint . . . my strength is dried up like a potsherd, and thou hast brought me into the dust of death."

Overwhelmed, Davidson could listen no longer. He laid aside the surveillance equipment, turned, and began to crawl back toward the cave, surprised at how cold it had become. But as he crawled, more and more slowly, there came a moment when all he could manage was to cry, and then to pray.

I'm sorry, Jerry. I shouldn't have gotten you involved. Another innocent victim, paying for my mistakes. Now, in that cold darkness, Davidson was a little boy again, listening to his Sunday school teacher, Mrs. Smedke, explain about kinsman-redeemers. About how Jesus had already paid the price for all little Brucie's mistakes . . . past, present, and future. For the first time since then, it not only made sense; it made the most sense of anything that had happened in the past ten years.

"Thank you," he prayed out loud. It was all he could say, but as he did so, an awful weight seemed to lift from somewhere deep inside.

Davidson began crawling again toward the main shaft. After thirty minutes he reached the cavern, shivering uncontrollably—whether from the shock of the events or from the cold, he couldn't tell. Not that it mattered much at that point. What mattered most was getting warm, whatever it took.

Maybe there's some wood in here. I'll start a fire in the entryway and wait out the storm. He started to follow the shaft downward searching for anything combustible. But the darkness seemed to close in around him with every passing step until the choice before him was between freezing to death or asphyxiating from panic.

Stumbling back up the incline, he remembered the extra pair of snowshoes abandoned in the drift outside. Quickly he wormed his way out, grabbed the shoes, and dragged them back into the cave. Examining them in the rapidly fading flashlight beam, Davidson began to doubt his own rationality.

Hypothermia? he wondered, shivering even more severely. Mostly rawhide around a hardwood frame, the snowshoes might burn, but it would certainly take more than the ten matches he had in his possession to ignite them.

Kindling. Got to have kindling. Then he remembered the dry needles and branches scattered around the bear's den. Desperate, he crawled into that corner, stuffing whatever he could scratch from the floor into the pockets of his jacket, which despite its impressive guarantees was proving inadequate. It didn't help that he was still soaking wet from the waist down, all the way to the skin, from the scene of the fire.

The closer he crawled to the animal's carcass, the warmer the room became. *Body heat. Fat and fur keep it in. How long 'til she cools down? Maybe I should stay right here.*

Repugnant as the idea seemed to him at first, the more he thought about trying to start a fire from twigs and keeping it stoked all night, the more reasonable it seemed to nestle as close as possible to this source of warmth, at least until he could stop shivering.

Tentatively, Davidson crawled closer to the bear. At first he curled up against her foreleg, but whenever he shifted his weight, gurgling sounds would come from the multiple wounds in her chest, accompanied by the foul odors of death.

When he slid himself toward her hindquarters, he heard what sounded like squeaking and felt movement behind his back. Rattled, he turned toward the sow and flipped on the flashlight again, wondering what animal would dare to be in the same den with this beast. Only very slowly did it dawn on him that he was looking at a tiny cub. The orphan was still nursing, unaware that its source of life had passed away.

The cub kept sucking, oblivious to Davidson's presence. Davidson, more careful this time, leaned back against the sow, cradling the little one in his left arm as he fell asleep.

34

Clare Conroy sorted through her closet, looking for clothing suitable for her midnight mission. *Dark and quiet.* Plagued by the knowledge that she had unknowingly betrayed a comrade, Conroy had a plan and the determination to carry it out regardless of the risk to herself. *If I don't get to Putnam tonight, it may never happen.*

She opened her apartment's bathroom window, slipped through it silently, and jumped to the snowdrift six feet below, then clambered quickly into the darkness against the back of the building. *No going back now,* she reminded herself as she snuck along toward the data center, where she knew Adam Putnam would be working late into the night.

At the back corner of the administration building, Conroy paused for a moment, reviewing her mental map of the compound's surveillance configuration. Ten cameras operating nonstop fed into a control room in the basement of the new audiovisual center, where Stanton and Worthy had taken her that morning after Winston left for the cabin.

All the main building entrances were covered, plus the storage sheds, the main road in, and several remote sections of the fenceline. Obviously proud of the system, Stanton had boasted that by spring, when it was completed, a snake wouldn't be able to cross the quad without being seen.

But what about a spy in a January snowstorm? With a hundred feet remaining, Conroy's pulse pounded in her ears as she tried to pinpoint the exact location of the lens trained on the computer building. *No way around it. Last thirty feet I'm centerstage.*

Frustrated, she was just about ready to dash across the opening, hoping that no one was watching that particular monitor during the few seconds she would be in the camera's field of view. Then she noticed that the only illumination for that area was a halogen lamp mounted near the corner of the building she was hiding behind. *Ice ball time.*

The first toss missed. Packing the second ball harder, Conroy began to wonder how a snowball might look on the monitor. *Missed again. Concentrate.*

The third toss broke the bulb. As the lamp went dark, Conroy scampered across the opening and ducked in the back door. It opened easily to her master key.

No Cy Young award, but at least it worked, she chuckled. Then she stepped into the bathroom to peel off her outer garments, which stuffed neatly into the nylon bag she'd brought along. She stashed the bag inside the ventilation shaft behind one of the stalls, confident that no one would ever see it there by chance.

Stage one, piece of cake, she thought as she straightened her hair before the mirror. But even as Conroy stepped into the hallway leading to Putnam's workspace, she heard a truck pull up outside, followed by the metallic scraping noise of an aluminum ladder being extended. Someone had come to replace the bulb. *Careful, babe. Big brother is definitely watching.*

"Putnam," she whispered as she stepped into the main computer room. Putnam was typing away, so absorbed in his work that he gave no indication of having heard her come in. Conroy walked up behind him and whispered again, "You work too hard, you know that? You should put in for overtime!"

Putnam jumped as if startled, then looked at his watch. "Overtime . . . right," he said out loud. Then noting Conroy's forefinger touching her pursed lips, he continued more quietly, "Is it night or day? Look at this pile of stuff Worthy dropped off on his way out, just when I thought I might catch up."

"Is this room bugged?" she asked quietly.

"You know that better than me," he replied. "If so, it has to be over there." He pointed to the wall, fifteen feet away. "Since I never talk to anyone but myself, I think the only bug is on the corporate modem." He paused again, looking confused, as Conroy flipped on a nearby fan for background noise.

"Ever since that rescuer showed up, we've wanted to talk with you . . . but privately," she said. "And with all the attention you got from security, there was no way we could talk during the day."

Glancing around the room nervously, Putnam said, "*We*? I'm sorry, but I don't want to talk about that. A mistake, that's all—error in judgment. Burned-out hackers do strange things, irrational things. It's happened to me before. All I can say is, it won't happen again." As he talked, Putnam continued looking around, obviously uneasy.

"Oh, don't worry, there's no one else here," she said. "When I say we, I mean Dr. Jenner and me. We've discussed your performance—sorry, I don't know what else to call it—during the press conference and, well, we think you may know more than you actually said about the death of Paul Woodman."

As she said this, Conroy began to blink in Morse code—

MD, MD, MD. She followed with a smile, as warm as she could manage, because for a moment Putnam's face became so horror-stricken that she thought he might faint.

"But . . ." he stammered. "But I figured nobody noticed, especially nobody from the Institute." Then he became silent, as if in mortal fear. He turned away and looked at the computer screen for a full minute while Clare let him collect his thoughts. Turning back toward her with a puzzled look, he said, "How do you know Morse code?"

"We'll come back to that later," she replied. "For now, let's just say I've had specialized training. Dr. Jenner was an Eagle Scout. But the main thing I want you to believe is that I'm here as a friend—a friend who wants to help."

"But how can I believe that, when you . . . when you all . . ."

"The snuff videos were Stanton's idea," she said calmly.

"You know about *them, too?*"

"I do." Conroy replied. "For now, Dr. Jenner doesn't. And in his present emotional condition, I'm not about to tell him that two of his most trusted staff members have been collaborating with organized crime to reproduce such degenerate videos in the new audiovisual center. I imagine that was in their minds all along."

"Without a doubt," he said. "The work orders are almost as old as the proposal." Again Putnam stopped dead and studied Conroy quizzically.

"I suppose you're wondering," she said, "whose side I'm on."

He nodded, again looking around the room worriedly as if convinced he had just walked into a trap.

"I'm on the side of truth," she said, "and justice." *Holy cow, sounds like the intro to Superman.* "What I mean is, bad things are happening at the New World Institute—and bad things are done by bad people. And I—I mean, *we*—

want to discover, if we can, who is responsible so we can deal with them appropriately. Get rid of the evil so the good we're doing can continue."

Putnam was silent for a long time, fidgeting with the pencil in his hand. "I think I can help you," he said finally. "If what you're talking about is the recent accidental death of Mr. Woodman from a broken neck." As he said that, he broke the pencil loudly with his hands. The effect was so dramatic that Clare jumped in spite of herself.

"Tell me about it, please," she said.

Again, Putnam looked around. Then, almost whispering, he said, "All I know is what I saw—Johnny Winston pulling a maintenance sled behind a snowmobile late one night, way after dark. I was down by the stables, getting some fresh air and trying to clear my mind a little.

"Then I hear him coming, so I jump behind this little spruce right along the trail. He goes by real slow, and in the moonlight—I couldn't believe it—there's a body in that sled. I can see it under a blanket, with boots sticking out the back." He paused as if wondering if he should go on.

"Continue, please," Conroy said quietly.

"Well, I watch where he goes, which is down around the back of the stables. Then—it's funny—he parks the machine behind the building in the darkest spot and walks over to the guard shed—maybe three, four hundred yards. He goes in, and after awhile, one by one the guards leave and walk off toward the compound until he's the only one left."

Clare nodded, urging him on.

"Now, Miss Conroy, hackers may be strange birds. But one thing we all have is curiosity, and when it comes to mysteries, we can't put 'em down until they're solved. It gets us in a lot of trouble, but that doesn't matter. Addiction, I guess. So I couldn't just walk back to my room. I had to know what—or who—was on that sled. So, while Winston is clearing out the guard shack, I mosey on over behind the stable and peek under that blanket, and there is Paul Woodman, dead as a doornail, with his throat slashed like somebody had tried to cut off his head."

"His *throat* cut?" Clare repeated.

"Yup!" Putnam said, "and I'd bet on some kind of wire—maybe strung across the trail so he would run into it."

"What makes you say that?"

"Because lying right on top of the body, under the blanket, is this coil of wire."

"Explains all the blood," Conroy muttered.

"No," Putnam continued. "That's the funny thing. There was blood on his clothes and all, but his face was white as . . . as . . . a ghost."

"I meant on the trail," Conroy replied. "Dr. Jenner and I were riding the trail a couple weeks ago, and we found an old but very large bloodstain under the new snow. That made us wonder. But . . .," she paused, "what does MD have to do with this?"

"Oh yeah, sorry I didn't finish. What happens after Winston clears out the guard shack is that pretty soon here comes Dr. Bradley. And they drag Woodman's body into the guard shack, and just the way they did it looked like they were in it together. But I wasn't about to hang around and risk my neck, too, so I walked the other way as fast as I could. The next day we hear that Woodman *broke* his neck running into a tree while snowmobiling. And a couple days later I see this sheriff's report saying the same thing. I just put two and two together and figure that she sewed Woodman up so good nobody noticed—or maybe the sheriff is part of it, too. Either way, it's just another reason for me to get out of here, the sooner the better."

"So that's why you called your mother—because you were afraid something similar might happen to you?"

"I suppose so," he replied, suddenly cautious again. "But—you may find this surprising—that wasn't what I was most afraid of, especially since initiation, when I finally opened my eyes."

"I remember," she said. "You seemed upset. What could possibly have taken place there to frighten you more than being murdered in cold blood?"

"Do not fear those who can kill the body," Putnam replied, "but those who can kill both body and soul in hell."

"Did you make that up yourself?"

"No, though I believe it with all my heart," Putnam said. "Jesus said it first."

"But what does that have to do with you?"

"Truth is eternal. If you're really after truth, like you say, you must always turn away from the lie. They can't be mixed together. Evil and good cannot flow from the same spring. He said that, too."

"Must we talk in parables?" she asked.

"All right, you're an educated person," he said. "Remember Faust? Power, wealth, influence—all exchanged for one small thing, the only thing that counted. His eternal soul."

"Gripping tale," she said, "but how does that connect with this?"

"Dr. J. Reuben Jenner is a false prophet," Adam Putnam proclaimed, "and in exchange for power and glory, he has lost his own soul. Maybe it *was* good in the beginning—I don't know. But somehow he lost his way, and now he's leading his followers on a path to destruction."

He stopped and looked at her. "You want to get rid of the evil in ETR? Well, it can't be done. It's already permeated everything, including me and you."

"Isn't that a little judgmental?" Conroy asked.

"I'll leave that up to God," he said, "but I've known since

that night that if I didn't separate myself from this movement somehow, my soul was at risk."

Conroy's first impulse was to tell Putnam to lighten up. But, seeing the sincerity in his face and hearing the urgency in his voice, she wondered, *Is he right? We used to argue about eternal security until late at night in that study group, but I never expected it to become as personal as this. Has just being here, just being part of this, affected me as much as he says?* She shuddered to think of how much she had enjoyed the notoriety, the power, the attention . . . and especially the affection of such a celebrity as Dr. J. R. Jenner. *And what have I given in exchange for that? Not my body . . . yet. My soul? Oh, God, I hope not. One of the guys used to say it's never too late for the prodigal to return to the father. I hope he was right.*

Crucial as the question of her destiny was, Conroy snapped herself back to the most pressing matter for that moment—enlisting Putnam's help in nailing the bad guys of ETR. She took a deep breath.

"Is that why you called Obewan?" she asked.

"What did you say?" he gasped.

"I asked, Yoda, if that was why you contacted Obewan," she repeated with a smile, producing a copy of his message to the Pentagon.

"How did you get this?" he asked urgently, scanning the room as if expecting Stanton's henchmen to pounce on him. "I thought they didn't put the tap on until after."

"True enough," she said. "But I got this another way, the same way I know *exactly* what you said to your mother and the fact that your Pentagon I.D. number is 607849."

Putnam's mouth just dropped open.

"FBI," she said quietly. "My assignment, to penetrate ETR as far as possible. Now I need your help—specifically, your help in filling in the gaps in these accounts and in gathering any other evidence suitable for a court of law." She paused, laying the other files he had sent to Obewan on the table.

Putnam studied her face. Then, apparently convinced, he said, "Okay. But I deliver, and I'm out of here."

"Of course," she replied. "We're all out of here. Now, how much time do you need to give me enough data to put these guys away?"

"Not much," he replied. "Done most of the work already." Putnam reached for a book on the shelf to his right, a large Bible. He opened it to the Psalms, and a computer disk fell out. He slid the disk into the workstation, hit a couple of keys, and immediately a long list of transactions appeared on the screen—both account numbers and the amounts involved, with supporting dates and transmission data.

"Around eight million dollars so far," he said with a nervous smile. "Worthy's been socking it away and losing it from the ETR records at the same time. I'm sure there's more. I set some bait awhile back. Figured I might need it to save my skin."

"Any other copies?" Clare asked.

"No. Didn't want any loose ends."

"Only one's too risky," she said. "Have to get these files out safely, just in case."

"In case of what?" he asked.

"In case anything happens to the originals . . . or to *us*," she said gravely. "Hate to see our work go up in smoke." Then, looking at the screen as he scrolled through the entries, she said, "A couple of things would really solidify this case. Ever see the name Costellini?"

He nodded, punching into search mode. "There . . . there. It doesn't show up very often, but if you look hard you can find it."

"Can you connect that name to the shipping manifests?"

she asked. Again he hit a few keys, and there it was, side by side with shipments of BAMBI tapes and hydrochloric acid.

"Save it," she said. "We may not have time to make all the links tonight. How about this one? Can you connect Eagle Corporation and large donations to specific orphanages?"

"How large?"

"Ten thousand dollars and up."

"Look at that," he said after about a minute. "Two full pages, mostly Mexico and Jamaica."

"Great. Now one last batch. HANNAH's children."

"Now *you're* speaking in parables."

"HANNAH is one of Bradley's projects. Try it."

"Right. There it is, but pretty scrambled. It'll take an hour to sort these files."

"Do the best you can," she said, "but there's one piece I really need. Type in 106-90-4445. Yes. See that site number, 2045? Can you trace it?"

"Bradley's private files. If I break in, she'll know as soon as she looks at them again."

"We'll take our chances."

"Okay," he said, punching in Bradley's password and the doctor's I.D. number, 233-84-6666 with the extension-2045.

"Bingo! . . . William and Eileen Bentsen; True's Brook Road; Saskatoon, Saskatchewan. REGENCY 1987."

"Run that search on every site number you find," she said. And then do three things, as quickly as you can. First, make two copies of this data, one for you and one for me. Then scramble the files so Worthy won't be able to retrieve *anything*. Finally, can you crash the system so it won't function again without professional assistance?"

"Piece of cake," he said, "but it'll take a few minutes to write. . . ."

A door had just opened in the outer office, followed by the sound of materials being dropped on a desk. Conroy looked at her watch. "It's two o'clock in the morning," she whispered. "Security?"

Putnam shook his head. "Worthy. Maybe to move some more cash."

"Will he come in here?"

"Doesn't need to. Has his own workstation. But I wouldn't rule it out, either, if he sees the light on."

"Not good," she said, looking around for a place to hide and settling on the utility closet directly in front of them. "Let's go to Plan B. Pull out the financial files and anything to do with Eagle Corporation or Costellinis. Make me a copy and stick yours back in the Bible. Skip the rest for now."

"Good," she said when he handed her a 3.5-inch high-density disk. "Now, can we see what Worthy's doing without his knowing?"

"Yoda knows all," he chuckled, hitting a couple of keys. As they watched, Worthy retrieved and diverted more than three hundred thousand dollars from several numbered accounts to a numbered account elsewhere.

"New code," Putnam commented softly. "He's moving funds stashed earlier to another location."

Naturally. Now that he has a new partner. "I have an idea," she said. "Let him go for a few minutes while you write a program to make him think the computer crashed."

"No problem," he said. "I'll power down the file server."

"Then, just before you run it, print out the stuff you showed me earlier, and I'll pay our comptroller a little visit," Conroy said.

Ten minutes later, Conroy knocked on the door of James Worthy's office. "Who's that?" he called tensely.

"Your newest partner in crime," she said, pushing the door open.

"Why are you here at this hour?" he said, moving quickly away from his desk and fumbling with the coffeemaker in the far corner, as if to deflect her attention from the computer screen.

"Ditto to you," she replied, sitting down on the corner of his desk. "But I see you're working with our assets. Interesting," she paused, as if reading the screen, "since I was doing the same thing just now with Putnam. He's been very helpful, considering the abuse he's been taking."

"Conroy," Worthy said in a menacing tone. "You know Putnam is a major security risk. The only reason he's still alive . . ." He stopped, midsentence, as Putnam stepped through the door.

"Working late, Mr. Worthy?" Putnam said. "Any coffee?"

"Yes. Help yourself," Worthy said. "I was just saying how indispensable you are to our entire operation."

"Which is why I enlisted his help," Conroy said. "Don't know why you didn't do it earlier. In fact, Mr. Putnam has agreed to help us recover all the funds lost last summer—I'm sure you recall that incident—in return for a small finder's fee. Don't worry; he just needs enough to cover four years at MIT."

Again Conroy examined the screen carefully, pulling a sheet out of a file folder in her hand and holding it up next to the monitor. "Why, thank you, Worthy. Have you been setting up my account already? I didn't expect you to work all night for that, but I do appreciate it."

"Well," Worthy said, "I couldn't work on it during the day, after all. We wouldn't want the wrong people to know about. . . ."

Without warning, the screen had gone blank. "Oh, no!" Worthy gasped, rushing to the keyboard. After several minutes of hitting switches and keys, the accountant looked at Putnam with terror in his eyes. "But you said it couldn't happen again."

"I was positive," Putnam replied. "How could this happen? You made a backup, of course." From the look on Worthy's face, it was obvious that he hadn't.

Putnam shook his head slowly. "Let me go down and see if it's your unit or the mainframe. Let's hope it's yours, or it might take forever to find those files."

Fifteen minutes later, Putnam walked back into Worthy's office, looking as if his best friend had just died. "I'm sorry. I can't make it work. It's crashed, pure and simple. Somebody has to look inside. Could be minor, could be major, but only a trained technician with highly sophisticated equipment can figure it out now."

Putnam walked over, poured himself another cup of coffee, and sat down next to Conroy, waiting for Worthy's response. But the longer they waited, the more obvious it became that Worthy was now in no condition to make a decision.

Finally, Conroy suggested, "Why don't we call IBM, leave a message that we need somebody out here as soon as possible, and then grab some shut-eye. It's been a long night."

Worthy nodded, and Putnam produced a business card from somewhere. Conroy picked up the phone and dialed the number. After the tone of the answering machine on the other end, she said, "Hello, IBM, this is Clare Conroy at the New World Institute in Walton's Creek. Our technician Mr. Putnam believes our mainframe is in immediate need of repair. This problem cannot be fixed by our people inside, but requires a specially trained crew equipped with whatever tools are needed for heavy duty work. Please send help immediately. Certain assets are at risk and may be lost if we don't rescue them without delay."

35

Zewolski's sending an A-team from Carson," Bruce Davidson said to Fred Billings as he spread out the topographical map on his desk. "We'll use the back door." Next to the map he laid out his own photos of the Institute and the RF-4 recon shots from the spring, with each building clearly marked and the new detention center drawn in with magic marker.

"Front door is yours. Here's XRAY," he pointed. Pausing for a moment, Davidson reviewed the transcript of Conroy's phone call. "Can you get an IBM van from Federal Systems Division and be in place at twenty-two hundred hours?"

"No problem. I want a piece of Perelli in the worst way," Billings replied. He flexed his stiff right hand, only recently released from its cast.

"I want him, too," Davidson said, "but we can't let personal issues interfere with good judgment. Too many people at risk. If this goes according to plan, there may not be any shooting. I want radio silence until I use mine—may be a scanner up there. How else could they know about the transmitter?"

"One possible glitch," Billings said as Davidson glanced

at his watch and then reached for his parka, nodding for Billings to continue. "Tellefsen. Doesn't give up easy. We had a report this morning that he's hired six Nam vets who spend their weekends playing war games in the mountains. They're in a motel thirty miles from Walton's Creek with a van full of rifles."

"Detain them," Davidson said matter-of-factly, as he turned to go.

"Love to, boss. On what charge?" Billings asked.

Davidson, sometimes frustrated by the same system that he was willing to die defending, replied, "Tail them, then. And be creative if they try to interfere. He's been warned."

"Understood. Good luck," Billings said. "See you at the New World Institute."

"Maid service," the young girl said quietly when the middle-aged man opened the hotel room door. She carried a small basket of toiletry supplies, under which was hidden a bottle of fine wine. She went first to the refrigerator, set the bottle in a bucket of ice, then walked over and stood in front of the man who had taken a seat on the edge of the king-sized bed. Slowly she unbuttoned the top button of her uniform as he watched.

"That won't be necessary, Erietta," Agent Daniel Stillman said gently. "Guerrero," he called, louder, "would you join us now?"

Agent Juanita Guerrero stepped out of the bathroom and walked over to the girl, who now stood motionless in the middle of the room, looking very confused. "Miss MacIl-more," Guerrero began, exhibiting her badge, "we are agents of the Federal Bureau of Investigation. You don't need to be afraid anymore. We know what's been happening to you, and we've come to rescue you."

"Will I go to prison, ma'am?" MacIlmore mumbled, beginning to cry.

"No, dear, but we want to be sure the people behind this get locked up for a long time. To do that, we need your help. This is what you must do. . . ."

This time up Hunter's Creek Pass, Davidson was followed closely by six other snowmobilers. All were dressed like recreational riders out for a late-night outing, in case they met anyone returning from Walton's Prairie. Their weapons were discreetly concealed beneath their clothing and in their packs.

Davidson stopped in front of the rubble of Wilkes's cabin for a moment. "Beautiful cabin. Wilkes built it piece by piece," he said solemnly.

As the others nodded respectfully, Davidson remembered Cyrus, whose body he had simply left lying in the snow in his haste to discover what had become of Wilkes. Heartsick, he figured coyotes had already devoured the dog's remains, but then he noticed the small mound under the new snow. "I'll be back," he muttered, "and we'll give you a decent burial."

This time, the trek through the timber on the north side of the ridge seemed shorter to Davidson, even in the dark. Having six commandos to share the trailbreaking helped, but as he watched the others struggle through the drifted snow, Davidson remembered the first time Wilkes had taken him to the cave by this route.

"Eskimo, Davidson?" Sergeant Miller laughed, trying to catch his breath when the group reached the entrance to the shaft. "Have to add these skills to our program. You can instruct!" Again he laughed, but his respect for Davidson's skill was obvious.

"Forget it," Davidson replied, "but Wilkes would be perfect. Up in Maine, they come with these things installed." Then he paused, munching on the high energy MRE and wondering if Wilkes was still alive. "You guys'll have something to show *me* in a couple hours. Fifty stories straight down isn't my idea of a picnic!"

"No problem, Captain," Miller replied, recognizing Davidson's former rank. "Jonesie here used to climb Chicago skyscrapers, right up the front, just for fun. Or was it to get away from all the other outlaws tryin' to kill him?"

"A little of both, Sarge," Jones replied with a chuckle.

"Spiderman," Miller continued. "Drops down a nylon strand, like a spider from the ceiling, and strikes. Rumor is there's suction cups on his fingers."

"Could come in handy," Davidson said. "But let's get under cover. Out here, we could be spotted. Inside, nobody'll know we're around."

One by one, the team slid through the entry, dragging in their rope-filled packs. Inside, they stripped off their bulky and noisy snowmobile suits, down to the high-tech, triple force thermolactyl survival gear by Damart.

As they painted their faces black to match their clothes, the soldiers commented, nearly in unison, on the putrid smell in the cave. "Pardon us, Captain," Miller said. "Smells like something died in here."

"Actually," Davidson replied, "*several things* died in here. Yesterday." With that he played his light on the coagulated blood on the floor in the middle of the cavern. Then he slowly followed the bear's blood trail into its den until, just as the light hit the animal, he jumped a little to test their reflexes.

In less time than it took for the echoes of their expletives to die, all six Rangers had unholstered their handguns and were crouched in different parts of the cave behind Davidson.

Impressed, he said as calmly as he could, "Not to worry,

amigos. She's dead already, along with the fool that took her on."

Reaching inside his own parka, Davidson retrieved the special purchase he had made that morning and started walking over to the nook that was now the bruin's tomb.

"Pardon me, sir," Miller said, "but is that a baby bottle?"

"Very perceptive. Standard FBI survival gear," Davidson laughed. "Ever see a bear cub this little, Sergeant?"

Davidson gently reached under the bear's hind leg, now stiffened from rigor mortis, until he found the little one. Still warm, but obviously hungry, it immediately began to suck on his fingertip. "Here," he said, cradling the cub in his arm as he placed the bottle's nipple in its mouth, "you'll like this a lot better."

"Little critter's guardian angel," Miller said quietly.

"Maybe so," Davidson replied. "But I also helped make it an orphan. Sergeant, if anything happens to me tonight, will you be sure this little bugger finds a home?"

"Consider it done," Miller said. "But is there something you haven't told me?"

Instead of replying immediately, Davidson illuminated the Uzi, still leaning against the wall of the cave. "Rescue missions can go bad," he said finally. "Remember Jimmy Carter's commandos. Got all the way into Iran and then crashed their copters into *each other*."

"My men are the best," Miller said. "No hair triggers. No mistakes. But . . ." he paused, shining his own light on the rifle, "do they all have those? Lot of lead to dodge if they see us coming down that cliff."

"Billings should keep most of the guards occupied. But it's not them worries me. They're just hired guns. Perelli is another story." He wrapped the cub in his own down parka and set it down with the bottle propped against the sow's leg.

"Let's get over to the opening so you can get a look for yourselves."

"Yeah, and some fresh air."

Davidson glanced at his watch when they reached the observation point. *One hour. Billings, be there*, he thought. He picked up the headphones to listen again, immediately aiming the dish straight down.

"Gas?" Fred Billings asked as he talked to the driver of the forest-green Astro van, who nodded. "Lucky you the Super Service is open late tonight! Fast and friendly. What'll it be?"

"Fill 'er up. High test," Tellefsen ordered, sounding very frustrated. "Don't understand this. Had a full tank this morning."

Funny such a new van would have a little leak in the gas tank, Billings thought with a smile as he yelled, "Hey, Jimmy, git out here and pump this man's gas while I check 'is oil. Pop the hood, mister; might as well git yer money's worth!"

Tellefsen reached down to pull the hood lever. When he sat back upright, he was nose to nose with the 9mm in the hand of special agent Willard Stevenson. "Welcome back to Walton's Creek, Mr. Tellefsen. You are under arrest, as promised."

When the other men in the van began to scramble for weapons, Stevenson said calmly, "Not advisable, gentlemen. We're not talking splat ball tonight. If you look closely through the doorway there, you'll see several high-powered rifles aimed at your chests. Now just relax, and let me outline your options. One, you can go to jail with Mr. Tellefsen for interfering in an FBI investigation. Two, you can cooperate with us for a few hours. Three, you can die."

Quiet. Too quiet, Davidson thought, as his worst fears

gripped his mind. *Too late? Wilkes. Where are you? God, don't let it be too late.*

He heard a faint, rapid slapping sound. *Card game, but nobody's talking. Solitaire. Good news, though. If Wilkes is dead, they wouldn't need a guard. Maybe he's sleeping.*

Then he heard the murmuring, Wilkes talking to himself, still in the same room.

"Bobby," he whispered, "wanna go fishin'? Nice day for it, huh? Let's go overnight. Take the Old Town and canoe the Allagash. Always wanted to do that with you. You been gone too long, son. I been missin' you awful. But now we'll never be apart again."

"No!" Davidson shouted, forgetting for a moment where he was.

"Captain?" Miller said, putting his hand on Davidson's shoulder from the blackness behind him. "Captain," he said again softly, lifting one of the earphones. "Careful, Captain, sound carries up here. Five-hundred feet ain't much."

Davidson nodded, then continued listening, silently pleading with Wilkes. *Help is coming, friend. Here I am, almost right over your head, man. Sense it, feel it, know it. Don't give up now. You can't give up now!* But even though he trained that dish on the same spot for ten more minutes, until his wrist cramped from holding the same position, Davidson never heard another sound. *If only I were God,* he thought sadly, handing the equipment to Miller. *I could make him hear me.* Then, shaking his head, he thought again, *Or could I? God . . . I haven't asked much of you lately. But if you can, please do this one thing . . . let Wilkes know that help is on the way.*

At about 9:00 P.M. Davidson said, "Sergeant, you can see the whole compound from here. Mostly deserted. New students arrive in a couple weeks."

"Good timing," Miller said, sliding the earphones on.

"Not our timing, though," Davidson said. *A little more time, and we might have caught some really big fish.* "There," he pointed, "try the guard shack, down along the southwest fence line."

Miller was silent for several minutes, listening. Then he pulled the phones off. "Impressive little gadget. Poker game. Five, maybe six men."

"About half the group," Davidson said. "Let me listen. I'd know Perelli's voice anywhere."

After a minute he handed the gear back. "Not there, as far as I can tell."

"How about that one?" Miller said, pointing to a building where a second-floor light shone. "Lab-type noises, and a typewriter," he whispered after a couple minutes. "But no talk. Maybe just one person."

"Medical center," Davidson said. "Target two. Jenks and Barkley. Arrest the doctor and find a hostage named Landau. Or Williams. Important records there, too. Secure the place; it becomes command central. Wilkes, if he's still alive, needs help. And if there are any casualties . . .

"Target three, the data center," Davidson continued, pointing to that building, about three-hundred feet northwest of the medical center. "Mainframe is supposed to be down," Davidson said. "But if it's working, don't let anybody but Putnam near it. Electronic files vanish very fast."

"Somebody's working, top floor. See the light?" Miller said. "This one's for me and Spider. Putnam's one of ours, right? Looks like security, first floor. I'll keep an eye on him while Jones arrives airmail. Spider, can you climb that wall and pay our friend a visit?"

"No problem, Sarge," Jones said as he continued working in the darkness behind them. "And Captain, this elevator's ready anytime you are. The only button is down. Sorry."

Davidson looked at his watch again. *Five minutes. Clare,*

he thought, focusing the binoculars on her apparently unoccupied apartment. *Wherever you are when this thing blows, stay there. Stay as far from Perelli as you can.*

At exactly twenty-two hundred hours—ten o'clock—a loud explosion rocked the air south of the compound, perhaps a mile away. "Right on time," Davidson said, training his binoculars on the guard shack. "One, two, three . . . six," he counted. Six snowmobiles were heading through the compound fence into the Prairie. "See that spot, Langston. Lock it shut. Nobody comes back in except an IBM van. Let's go."

Davidson stuck the glasses inside his shirt, pulled the black wool hat over his ears, and checked the ropes around his waist as Langston went over the side, repeating instructions one more time: "Follow me, Captain. Sitting position. Just keep bouncing away from the ledge while you let the rope out three, maybe five feet each bounce. Don't look down. Look at the rock right in front of your face instead. Think of it this way—one hundred bounces and Wilkes is free. See you in the lobby."

Silently Langston was gone, with Davidson right behind. He stepped over the edge, bounced away twice, looked down once, and froze. What had seemed so close now seemed miles away and receding fast. *Optical illusion. Get a grip on it.* He looked up to see Miller's face peering over the edge. "Go for it, Captain. Loosen up a little. Bounce," he heard him whisper.

It was all Davidson could do to force his hands open on the rope, right hand behind his buttocks, left at his chest. *Four hundred ninety-two feet to go. Can't clog the drain now. Go! Go! Go!* For just a moment, but just long enough, Bruce Davidson was back in basic training, hanging out of a helicopter thirty feet up with the sergeant yelling "Go! Go! Go!" as he launched himself into space. Before his mind could again register how close he was to dying, he was on the ground.

"Okay, Captain?" Langston asked.

"Okay," Davidson whispered, silently unclipping the rappelling gear and rolling out of the way as his partner, Joe Stevens, hit the ground five seconds later. By the time the whole team was down, Langston was already gone, moving like a shadow through the timber on the southeast perimeter. Davidson watched the others move off in pairs before he began to inch his way around to the north side of the detention center.

When he reached the window, he peeked in cautiously to see that the guard was talking into a radio. "Nothing here," he said. "Prob'bly just another bunch of kids having a bash on the Prairie."

"Be careful," Perelli's voice replied. "I don't like this."

"That's a ten-four. We're ready. Over and out," the guard said, laying the radio on the table next to his cards. He picked up what looked to be an AK-47 and trained it on some imaginary target just above Davidson's head. Then he stopped as if paralyzed, his mouth dropping open and his eyes rolling back in his head just before he toppled face forward into the wall between them, the gun crashing to the floor.

Startled, Davidson ducked by instinct, but when he looked back through the window he could see Stevens crouched where the guard had been standing, motioning him around to the back.

Commandos, Davidson thought, *probably kill everybody*.

When he crept through the open back door and inside, Stevens was dragging the guard into one of the cells. "He'll live; don't worry," he said, tossing a set of keys to Davidson. "But he won't wake up for awhile. No defenses in the back. Must've figured the cliff was enough. Wonder what's out front?"

"Check it out," Davidson said, his mouth suddenly very dry and his heart pounding as he walked down the hall searching for Wilkes. The key was in the lock when the second explosion occurred, still outside the compound, but strong enough to shake the building. *Billings. Just keep them occupied!*

In the semi-darkness, Davidson saw a figure standing in the corner of the cell he had just opened. "Look, Silas, the Lord hath sent his angel to deliver us," Wilkes said to nobody Davidson could see. "Are you Michael?" the evangelist asked. He stepped toward Davidson, who was suddenly torn between his desire to laugh because his friend was alive or to cry because he was hallucinating.

"Jerry," he said softly. "I'm no angel. Just Bruce Davidson, your friend. And you are Jeremiah Wilkes. I'm sorry for the hurt, but I'm glad . . . so glad you're alive."

Wilkes stared at Davidson for a long moment, and Bruce could see the struggle in his friend's eyes. "But the earthquake . . ."

"Explosion outside. Diversion, to get the guards' attention."

"But I was talking with Silas. Others, too. Daniel. Jesus." He looked at Davidson with what seemed more sadness than joy. "Even Bobby. We were goin' fishin'. I want to go fishin' . . . oh, God . . ." and he started to cry as he fell into Davidson's outstretched arms.

"Is this real," Wilkes asked after a moment, "or a bad dream?"

"Not a dream," Davidson said softly.

"Cyrus?"

"Sorry. Such a good dog."

"The cabin?"

"Gone. But Jerry," Davidson said, pushing his friend out

to arm's length and trying to lock into something coherent, "Marcy's waiting."

"What?" Wilkes replied as if he had been slapped into reality.

"I wanted to tell you. There's so much I wanted to tell you, Jerry. I couldn't . . . just couldn't. We'll talk in just a little while. Trust me. I'll be back. But first I have some unfinished business with the guy that did this to you."

I did this to you, he chastised himself as he turned as if to exit the front door. But he stopped short at Stevens's terse warning: "Not recommended, Captain, 'less you want to be in the movies. Video cam, thirty meters, one o'clock. Something underneath, too. May be armed."

Stevens's words cut into Davidson's mind like a knife as he recalled a similar box mounted on the pole in front of the data center. "Spider!" he exclaimed at almost exactly the same time as he heard Perelli's voice again over the radio on the table, this time barking an order, "Smith, there's a guy climbing up the outside of your building. Take him out, but be careful; could be others. And Smith," Perelli added, "Putnam doesn't leave that building alive, understand?"

"Ten-four," Smith replied. Bruce Davidson grabbed the AK-47 from the floor, opened the front door, and dashed through it just as he heard, from the radio behind him, another voice, "Mr. Stanton, there's a van at the gate. IBM repair crew, here to fix the computer."

The next thing he heard was a barrage of gunfire—right in his face, it seemed—coming from the small box under the camera. The only reason he survived was that, when the gun let loose, he was already at a dead run for the data center. Spraying ice hit his face as bullets hit on either side of his feet. He dove to evade what was obviously a fixed field of fire.

Instantly he picked the radio off his own belt. "Mayday,

Spider. Mayday. Watch out below," he shouted into the receiver. "IBM, crash the gate. Yoda needs you . . . now!"

But Davidson had only reached the medical center, where Barkley was crouched just inside the darkened doorway giving a thumbs-up sign, when the shooting began three-hundred yards away.

First there was a short, rapid burst followed by three single shots and a barrage of automatic fire lasting nearly thirty seconds. Then everything went quiet . . . until Billings rammed the gate and tore into the compound quad with the van, slowing as he passed the bronze statue long enough for two agents wearing bulletproof vests to jump out.

"Incoming!" one of them shouted as the antitank missile came screaming at the van from the left.

Billings heard the shout and turned his head just in time to see the rocket demolish the statue, which had come between the van and the rocket at the very last second. Suddenly what had been a man and a boy was now just a boy holding an amputated brass hand.

The explosion briefly illuminated the whole yard, as Billings gunned it for the data center. He could see at least two men down. Shots were being exchanged behind him, and the van was also under fire; the only window left intact when he pulled up in front of the building was the windshield. Sergeant Miller, his leg wrapped with a bandage from his own first-aid kit, peeked around the end of the building; then he and Putnam quickly dragged Jones to the van.

"Good timing, sir," Miller said. "Jones took a couple in the gut. Needs a plug right away. That one's dead. Security. Didn't like him painting my man with lead. But then that thing let fly," he said, pointing to the Gatling gun fifty yards away.

"Caught me in the thigh 'fore I could find cover."

Billings picked up the microphone as he headed for the

medical center. "Gunmen, four, maybe more. One dead. XRAY in pursuit. We have two casualties, one serious but hanging on. ETA, medical center, sixty seconds. Over."

"Ten-four. We're ready," Davidson replied. "Barkley, inside. Get that doctor out here on the double. This is now the E.R., and you're a medic."

"Right, Captain," and Barkley was gone, returning in fifty-eight seconds with a stretcher, IVs, gauze, tape, and a doctor who kept talking about trading records for immunity.

"Dr. Bradley," Davidson said gruffly, "you have the right to remain silent. Anything you say here can and will be used against you in a court of law. But if you won't remain silent, we're going to use that tape on you first."

The van careened around the corner, slamming to a halt right in front of them with the back door open. Inside, Spider was lying on his back with several spots of blood showing on his shirt.

"Thanks," he muttered weakly as he saw Davidson's face. "I was almost history. Sarge took him out just in time."

"I'm not a surgeon," Bradley complained, examining the wounds.

"Did a nice job on Woodman, though," Adam Putnam said as he stepped around the corner, face to face with Bradley.

"Cut the chatter," Sergeant Miller shouted. "We need some holes plugged. Let's get it done."

They disappeared into the building just as the gunfire inside the compound stopped. Down on the Prairie, an occasional explosion could still be heard. "Billings," Davidson asked, "if you're in here, who's down there?"

"Funny thing, Boss. Tellefsen buys some gas at our filling station in Walton's Creek and finds himself dealing with the muzzle of Stevenson's gun. We explained their options and, being reasonable people, they decided to cooperate. Security guards never had a chance."

"Dead?"

"Not at all. They're sitting in a little circle surrounded by a couple vets glad to see a little action, while their buddies blast a few more snowdrifts down on Walton's Prairie to make it sound like there's a fight going on."

"Billings . . . XRAY," Stevenson's voice said over the radio. "Two gunmen in custody. Lost the third. Request further orders. Over."

"Ask them the other one's name," Billings replied.

"Stanton," the reply came a moment later. "Ducked inside the administration building. Shall we pursue?"

"Negative. Cover the shed. We have a personal appointment with Stanton."

36

I knew they would come," J. R. Jenner said as the sounds of gunfire filled the compound, punctuated by periodic explosions outside.

Me too, but not so quickly. Bruce, where are you? Where should we be? Conroy thought as she knelt next to Jenner behind the massive desk in his main office where they had been planning the crusade in Brazil.

"They must stop REGENCY. They must kill me," he mumbled.

"Not if I can help it," Conroy replied.

"What can you do?" he said, taking her hand.

"At the moment," she replied, "there's nothing *to* do, except try to keep us both out of harm's way . . . and hope the shooting stops before it gets too close."

"Good idea, Conroy," Milo Stanton said as he stood in the doorway, one hand still on the doorknob and the other holding a handgun. "But why not let your director of security help? Dr. Jenner," he said, more forcefully, "the compound is under attack. Come with me, sir, to a more secure place."

"But we can't leave Miss Conroy," Jenner replied. "It's too dangerous. They're really after me, you know."

"No, we *can't* leave Miss Conroy," Stanton replied, motioning with the gun to Conroy to get up, too, "but we'll discuss that as soon as we get a chance."

"Are you going to take us outside into who knows what?" Clare protested. *Br'er Bear, not the briar patch!*

"Not at all," Stanton said, his tone becoming more menacing. "But let's move it. Got to see what's going on."

"AV," Conroy scratched in the dust on the bottom of the desk drawer as she stood to her feet. Then she followed Jenner out the office door, with Stanton behind her, his gun now aimed at her.

"Down," Stanton commanded as they got into the elevator. "Basement level."

"Why didn't I know about this?" Jenner asked as the paneled wall opened to Stanton's touch, and he directed Jenner and Conroy into the tunnel behind it. Large enough for two people to pass abreast, and about seven feet from the gravel floor to the corrugated metal ceiling above them, the shaft was illuminated by twin fluorescent tubes spaced twenty feet apart.

"New security feature," Stanton said, sounding apologetic. "Somebody should have told you. Sorry. I told him that once it was finished you should have a tour."

"Told who?" Jenner demanded as they walked along briskly.

"Woodman," Stanton replied. They entered a similar but much larger passage intersecting the first at a right angle.

"When we built the new A.V. center," Stanton said, motioning for them to turn right, "we dug new sewer lines and connected all the main buildings underground."

Conroy glanced quickly to the left and saw similar connectors some distance away. Then she turned to follow Jenner to the right, falling as flat on her face as she could without hurting herself. Jenner turned quickly to help her up, and as she brushed the loose dirt from her clothing, she briefly dragged her right foot in the gravel as if she had hurt her knee. *Got to leave a trail.*

"A little clumsy for such a good athlete, Conroy," Stanton said, prodding her in the back with the handgun once Jenner had turned around again.

A golf cart was parked at the tunnel's end, backed up to a sliding door, which, at the impulse of Stanton's electronic controller, opened into a richly appointed room, its light blue carpeting perfectly matched by the other furnishings. The walls were paneled with solid, oil-rubbed butternut and decorated with opals in circles of sapphire.

"Where are we?" Jenner asked, admiring the decor.

"It was supposed to be a surprise," Stanton replied. "Our little secret gift to Dr. Jenner. We're in an underground studio in the A.V. center—a studio you could have used to produce your own programs. Now your grand tour will have to wait awhile."

"That way," Stanton continued, pointing to another door. "Let's see what's happening upstairs. By now the boys should be back."

To their left as they entered the room was a wall covered with monitors, most of them blank and others showing some activity, especially near the medical center.

Jenner stared at the screens, then turned to Stanton. "How many of these are there?"

"Sixteen so far. That way we can keep an eye on things with just a small number of guards," Stanton said.

"Problem is, cameras can't shoot back," Conroy said as she pointed to one of the screens.

Two commandos, standing in front of the medical center, were firing directly at the screen. It was all Conroy could do to keep from jumping as she waited for the screen to go blank, which it did. That explained why only four cameras were left operating. One showed the entrance of the data center. A second was a remote, out along the trail somewhere. The third was the upstairs entrance of the building they were in, and a fourth was trained on the storage sheds, where several gunmen could be seen crouching in front of the door. One of them fired at the lock, and suddenly the door disintegrated from within from the force of the spring-loaded stainless steel Punji stick. Fortunately for the two gunmen, the door absorbed the device's force, leaving them staring death in the face.

"No wonder you wanted me to go check that out," Clare said, "but now I guess we'll discover what you've been hiding in there."

"I wouldn't be so sure about that," Stanton said, fishing a red key on a long gold chain out from under his shirt. He bent over slightly, without taking the chain from around his neck, and inserted the key into a lock under that monitor.

When he turned it, the storage sheds exploded. One commando flew high into the air and landed face down in the snow, as the building erupted in flames. The other could be seen dragging himself away from the scene, shouting frantically into his radio. "Man down. Fire at the storage sheds. Send help!" his voice shouted over the scanner behind them.

"What's going on?" Jenner said, sounding very confused. "I don't understand. If they're after me, why are they trying to break into those sheds?"

"For the same reason that Stanton, your faithful director of security, needs to blow them up," Conroy replied. She noticed identical detonators below every monitor, at the same instant she saw two men entering the data center.

"And why it's time to do the same to the data center," Stanton replied, placing the key in another hole. Jenner tried to intervene, too late. "All our records," he cried, grabbing at Stanton's wrist.

"I'm trying to save your life, Dr. Jenner," Stanton said, pushing him away with such force that Jenner landed halfway across the room.

"But you're destroying everything we built," Jenner pleaded helplessly as Stanton turned the key. Again the blast registered on the screen, followed by a fire that broke out in the downstairs lobby of the building.

"Would you believe all that from just six ounces of Semtex?" Stanton said proudly.

Got to stop this madman, Conroy thought, horrified. The monitor trained on the entrance upstairs showed three men approaching. James Worthy, his arm held behind his back by Bruce Davidson, was leading the group at gunpoint through the front door.

Stanton leaned toward the monitor, examined it carefully, then stuck the key in the slot and started to turn it just as Conroy launched herself, feet first, in the killer's direction. Her heel caught the side of Stanton's head, knocking him off the chair. The chain broke, but the key remained in place.

Shaking his head, Stanton pulled himself up the table, glaring at Conroy, who had bounced back next to Jenner. She was amazed that Stanton was still conscious. As if to make a point, Stanton resolutely reached up and detonated the bomb overhead, its muffled explosion reaching them a split second later.

I hope they got inside before that went off, Conroy thought as she noticed that Stanton had pulled his gun and was aiming it at her again.

"Now, Conroy," Stanton said, "before I kill you, why don't you tell Dr. Jenner how you happen to know FBI Agent Billings, who until a moment ago was being led here by Worthy."

"I don't know what you're talking about," Conroy replied. "You're a madman; that's the only thing I know."

"Conroy made a call last night that explains all this, Dr. Jenner."

"I called IBM for repairs," she said as calmly as she could.

"Sure, and just by chance a bunch of commandos assault this compound," Stanton replied.

"And then you decide to blow it up," she said, "just like you blew up our car in Colombia."

"*You*?" Jenner said, looking at Stanton.

"All he knows how to do is blow things up and kill people," Conroy said. "And embezzle your money," she added. "And use your children's homes for drug smuggling and your orphans for prostitutes and. . . ."

Perelli fired, just as J. R. Jenner jumped between them, yelling, "Nooooo!"

Jenner, thrown backward by the force of the bullet striking his chest, landed on top of Conroy, who was now sitting on the floor. Jenner feebly raised his hand to his chest, then looked up into Conroy's eyes as she held him in her arms.

"Rachel," he whispered. "Take care of the children."

"I will," she replied as his eyes closed and his head fell back against her thigh. *HANNAH's.*

"Touching," Perelli said. "Might as well die together."

But as the gun came up again and Conroy waited for the bullet, the voice of Bruce Davidson said from behind her, "Freeze, Perelli. FBI. You are under arrest and completely surrounded. Surrender or die."

"Says who?" Perelli yelled, diving behind Conroy and grabbing her around the neck. "You wouldn't kill our little friend to get to me, now, would you?"

Conroy felt herself being pulled up to a standing position. The body of J. R. Jenner flopped unceremoniously to the floor, a trickle of blood now oozing from his mouth.

Billings dove behind the shoulder-high room divider to his left. Davidson remained standing behind the human shield of James Worthy, but only for a moment. Perelli fired two quick shots, and the comptroller also slumped to the floor.

Clare watched the third shot spin Davidson as he dove, too late, behind another divider to his right, clutching at his left shoulder.

"Bruce," she yelled, unable to help.

"You know *him*, too? Figures. How could I be so blind?" Perelli growled as he dragged Conroy backward by the neck toward the console. He opened a small red metal panel, stuck in the detonator key, set the timer to twenty minutes, and turned the key with a malevolent grin. Then he dropped the key into his shirt pocket and buttoned it closed.

"Just a little surplus nuclear weapon. Amazing what money can buy now that the Cold War is over." He laughed as he dragged Conroy toward the tunnel, his gun pressed hard behind her right ear.

"You can't kill all these people just to cover your tracks," she said.

"Shut up, scum," he growled in her ear. "I can do whatever I want. You'll discover that soon enough."

They had almost reached the sliding door in the conference room when Davidson and Billings caught up to them, their handguns appearing at opposite corners of the wall between the two rooms.

"Hold it right there," Davidson said.

"Hold it yourself," Perelli said, firing a quick shot at both positions.

"Heard a lot about George Perelli down through the years," Davidson called. "But something tells me he's just a coward at heart."

"Why's that?" Perelli replied.

"Cowards kill defenseless people, especially women."

"This one's not too defenseless."

"Maybe not, but what about the others?"

"Such as?"

"Nobody knows how many, I'm sure. But I know at least one, personally. My own wife. You had a contract on me, once. Davidson, Bruce. Ten years ago? Remember? We have a personal score to settle, and you want to hide behind a woman!"

Perelli was quiet for a few seconds, then responded, "It wasn't my job."

"Liar!" Davidson shouted. "I tracked you for six months myself. All the clues pointed to you. Everything."

"Yeah? Maybe you *wanted* them to. Ever think of that?"

"'Course," Davidson said, but not as confidently. "Then who did it?"

"What difference does it make, man? You think taking me out will bring her back?" Perelli laughed derisively, pushing the button on the wall and backing into the doorway.

"I'll tell you one thing that *will* make a difference. In about sixteen minutes and thirty-two seconds this whole place will be vaporized—you and all your commandos. And by the time somebody figures out what happened, me and my girlfriend here, we'll be in Mexico on our honeymoon.

"He's a madman, Bruce," she said. Disconnect the swi—"

"That's enough, dear." Perelli interrupted, tightening his grip. "He'll sweat real good before he fries."

As the door slid shut between them, Conroy saw Bruce Davidson step out from behind the wall holding his blood-stained shoulder, a picture of utter frustration mixed with concern as he turned back toward the control room.

Next thing she knew, Perelli threw Conroy behind the steering wheel of the golf cart and took the seat to her right. He shoved the Glock 17 into her ribs, none too gently.

"Drive," he said. "Fast . . . and no funny business. Hate to have my trigger finger slip."

Rushing through the tunnel in the semi-darkness, Conroy tried to calculate the distance they were putting between them and the compound. More important, she discovered, glancing at her watch, four minutes had elapsed by the time they reached the end of the tunnel, where a small helicopter pad was set back in a bunker and out of sight.

"Surprise!" Perelli said, hitting the switch that opened the bunker doors. The platform moved outward, extending itself over the edge of a cliff. He forced Conroy into the passenger side of the Hughes 500, shut and bolted the door, all the while holding the gun on her. Then Perelli walked around to get in the pilot's side.

It was the one chance she had. Pretending to fasten her seat belt, Conroy retrieved the .32-caliber pen from the inside pocket of her suit. Quickly she aimed the device and, when Perelli swung into the pilot's seat with a big grin, fired the weapon.

The hit man slumped face first onto the seat.

Dead? she wondered, searching for a jugular pulse even as she started to shake uncontrollably. *Still alive. Now what? Slit his throat? Blast him with his own piece?*

When Conroy moved her hand from Perelli's neck, she noticed a thin red welt near his collar. *From breaking that chain,* she thought, *wish I'd kicked even harder . . . the detonator key!*

Conroy dashed around behind Perelli. With her right hand she rolled his body upright just enough to reach in with her left hand and rip the shirt pocket open. For a moment, Perelli's head fell against her shoulder as she struggled against the weight of his upper body. He was bleeding from the shot that had evidently only grazed his left temple.

"Love to dance, pal, but I hate to lead," she grunted.

She grabbed the key and looked at her watch as Perelli flopped back to the seat, still unconscious. *Four minutes, fifty-eight seconds to detonation. Bruce, I can make it!*

She wheeled the golf cart around and headed full speed for the control room, her heartbeat and respiration out of control as the end of the tunnel came in sight. But as she saw the door, she remembered the electronic control, still on Perelli.

Less than a minute, she thought. *Can't go back. One chance.* She gunned the vehicle to its top speed and crashed it into the door, jumping off with only ten feet to spare.

Lying on the floor, covered with dirt, several things struck Conroy at exactly the same instant. *Doorway's open. I can get through. Leg is broken. How can I get through? Key . . . have to get the key to Bruce,* she muttered as she started to crawl, holding the key in her teeth to keep from losing it in the dust.

A figure appeared in the doorway. *Billings!*

"Conroy? Is that you, Conroy?" Dazed, she held the key out, muttering "Bruce needs this," as she passed out.

Next thing she knew, Bruce Davidson was kneeling next to her in the tunnel, trying to pick her up.

"Here, boss. You can't do that—shot up. Let me help," Fred Billings said. He lifted Conroy and carried her into the control center, setting her down gently on the couch inside.

"Clare," Bruce said, kneeling next to her. "I was frantic. The control was too complicated, or I was too dazed, but I couldn't disarm it. When you crashed the door, I had almost given up hope."

"The key must have worked," she whispered, "since we're still here."

"Well, yes . . . and no," Davidson replied. "Yes, it disarmed the mechanism with only seven seconds to go. But

. . . then we followed the lines and discovered it wasn't even hooked up. Perelli is . . . was? . . . a master of deceit."

"Is . . . was . . . is still an open question, I'm afraid," she said. "I only had one opening to use the pen, but I wish it came with two shots instead of one. Glanced off his left temple, but knocked him out. He was still alive when I left, but I thought the key was more important. You won't believe this, but when I shot him, we were getting ready to take off in a . . ."

"Captain," a voice came over the radio, interrupting her, "Langston, southwest quadrant. An aircraft, must be a small helicopter, just took off outside the fence line, flying due west."

"Blast it!" Davidson growled, struggling to his feet.

"Out of range already, Captain. We can scramble some folks from the Springs, but with the mountains, time we find that bird, whoever's in it will be long gone. Key player?"

"Affirmative," Davidson said, slowly settling to the floor, his back against the front of the couch.

"Sorry, Captain."

"Me, too," Davidson said quietly, to no one in particular, handing the radio to Billings, who turned to leave the room.

"I'll go see if the fires are out," Billings said quietly. "And check on Linda Landau's condition. Sergeant Jones reports she's alive but very confused."

A moment later, Billings came back into the room, with a quizzical look on his face.

"What's up?" Davidson asked.

"Strange," Billings said, shaking his head. "The prophet, Jenner. When I was walking past his body in the other room, I noticed something, doesn't make much sense. He's dead enough, all right, though you'd expect a guy like him might resurrect himself. But one of his fingers is missing, specifically, the end of his left pinky. Somebody else been in here since we came down?"

"The devil himself could have come in and we wouldn't have noticed!" Davidson replied with a laugh. "Maybe it got shot off when Perelli blasted him. Make a note of it for the coroner. We'll let somebody else find the missing parts, long's the body doesn't disappear, too." Again he chuckled.

"Whatever you say, boss," Billings replied over his shoulder as he turned to leave. "Probably not a big deal, either way, considering everything else that just happened. Don't even know why I noticed, except maybe I'm into fingers now that some of my own don't work exactly right."

"Clare," Bruce said, after several minutes of silence. "Before, when I thought you were gone . . . I mean, when it seemed like he might kill you . . ." His voice drifted off as Clare put her hand on his right shoulder.

Davidson took her hand in his as he continued, "What I'm trying to say is . . . I decided right then, if I ever saw you again, I had to ask you . . . ask you if you might consider another . . . career."

"Yes, now that you mention it," she replied. "I've been thinking about the CIA, maybe going to work with Daddy somewhere. This stateside stuff is too dull, if you ask me."

Davidson turned to see her smiling. He raised himself gingerly to one knee, still holding her hand, and reached into his pocket for the exquisite ring Norman Michaud had made from the topaz. With an exaggerated Southern drawl he said, "Frankly, my dear . . . I had something else in mind altogether."